*"Come to me."*

There was something beneath the command in his deep voice that had her rising to her feet. Her eyes locked with his as she walked to the edge of the dock. The dancing moonlight shimmered across the water, illuminating his serious expression. For some reason this was important to him. Maybe he needed to know she trusted him to take care of her, to protect her.

She looked into the murky depths. Oh God, she really didn't want to get in the water. But from day one, this man had pushed her out of her comfort zone. Why did she expect him to change now? Taking a deep breath, she loosened her towel, letting it drop to her feet.

"You are the most beautiful woman I have ever seen, Vivi Westfield," Chance said in a strangled voice, his eyes drinking her in. "I'll catch you."

Vivi didn't let herself think; she just closed her eyes and jumped.

"4 Stars! A quintessential romance with everything readers love: familiar and likable characters, clever dialogue, and a juicy plot."

—*RT Book Reviews*

## THE TROUBLE WITH CHRISTMAS

"A fun and festive tale, flush with small-town warmth and tongue-in-cheek charm. The main characters are well worth rooting for, their conflicts solid and riveting."

—*USA Today*'s Happy Ever After blog

"4 Stars! This is a wonderful story to read this holiday season, and the romance is timeless...This is one of those novels readers will enjoy each and every page of and tell friends about."

—*RT Book Reviews*

"The lovers are sympathetic and well drawn...Mason will please fans of zippy small-town stories."

—*Publishers Weekly*

"I'm very impressed by [Mason's] character development, sense of humor, and plotting...Ms. Mason wraps this book up as if it were a very prettily wrapped package. Why not open the pages and have a Christmas present early?"

—LongandShortReviews.com

"Debbie Mason has created a humorous, heartwarming tale that tugged at my heartstrings while tickling my funny bone...a community that I enjoyed visiting and hope to visit again."

—TheRomanceDish.com

# Wedding Bells
## *in* Christmas

# Debbie Mason

FOREVER

NEW YORK   BOSTON

Copyright © 2015 by Debbie Mazzuca
Excerpt from *Snowbound at Christmas* copyright © 2015 by Debbie Mazzuca

Forever
Hachette Book Group
1290 Avenue of the Americas
New York, NY 10104

www.HachetteBookGroup.com

Printed in the United States of America

First Edition: May 2015
10 9 8 7 6 5 4 3

OPM

Forever is an imprint of Grand Central Publishing.
The Forever name and logo are trademarks of Hachette Book Group, Inc.

The Hachette Speakers Bureau provides a wide range of authors for speaking events. To find out more, go to www.hachettespeakersbureau.com or call (866) 376-6591.

The publisher is not responsible for websites (or their content) that are not owned by the publisher.

**ATTENTION CORPORATIONS AND ORGANIZATIONS:**
Most HACHETTE BOOK GROUP books are available
at quantity discounts with bulk purchase for educational,
business, or sales promotional use. For information,
please call or write:

**Special Markets Department, Hachette Book Group**
**1290 Avenue of the Americas, New York, NY 10104**
**Telephone: 1-800-222-6747  Fax: 1-800-477-5925**

*To Perry, my one-and-only. I wouldn't want to be on this journey with anyone but you.*

# Acknowledgments

Thanks once again to my incredibly talented and dedicated editor, Alex Logan, who makes every book so much better and is such a pleasure to work with. Thanks also to my wonderful agent, Pamela Harty, for all her support and efforts on my behalf.

Many thanks to the sales, marketing, production, and art departments at Grand Central Publishing/Forever for all their support and efforts on behalf of my books. Especially my publicist Marissa Sangiacomo, production editor Jamie Snider, art director Christine Foltzer, copy editor Patricia Callahan, and editorial assistant Madeleine Colavita.

Thanks so much to my family and friends for always being there for me. Please know how grateful I am to have you in my life. And to my wonderful husband, amazing children, and adorable granddaughter, thank you for all your love and encouragement and for supporting me in doing what I love to do. Love you all so very much.

My heartfelt thanks to the wonderful readers, bloggers, and reviewers who take time out of their busy lives to spend time with me in Christmas, Colorado. Your lovely e-mails, tweets, Facebook posts, and reviews are much appreciated.

# Wedding Bells
## *in* Christmas

# Chapter One

*Dear Heartbroken in Hoboken: Two years? Seriously, it's time for you to move on. Stop with the what ifs. Stop trying to figure out what went wrong. This guy has taken up space in your head and heart for way longer than he deserves. You have a job you love, family and friends who love you. Focus on that, embrace that, and start enjoying your life again.*

Vivian Westfield stood in the long security line at LaGuardia airport rereading her responses to next week's letters from the lovelorn. Satisfied that they met her new criteria—the one where she no longer kicked butt but gently smacked it—she sent her Dear Vivi column off to her editor. At least Heartbroken had a job that she loved, Vivi thought as she shoved her iPad in her carry-on.

Vivi remembered the feeling. Oh, how she remembered it. Ten months ago, she'd landed her dream job as an investigative reporter for the *Daily Spectator*. All the long hours and hard work she'd put in at online newspapers had finally paid off. But she'd had only four lousy months to revel in the sweetness of her success.

While working on her biggest story to date—the story guaranteed to earn her editor's respect and, more importantly, protect her best friend Skylar O'Connor—Vivi's career imploded as spectacularly as a sinkhole opening up on Fifth Avenue in the middle of rush-hour traffic.

Looking back, and she'd done so every day since that bitterly cold November night, she realized where she'd gone wrong. She'd let Superman into her life. She should have known that someone who named himself after a comic book hero would turn into an overprotective wack job. In her defense, until that story, he'd fed her information she never would have gotten on her own. And over the months they'd spent texting each other on a daily basis, she'd found herself thinking about him all the time.

As embarrassing as it was to admit, she'd been crushing on Superman, fantasizing about becoming his Lois Lane. Which was ridiculous. She had no idea what he looked like. She hadn't even spoken to the man. The only thing she knew for certain was that in his misguided attempt to protect her, her sources had dried up overnight. And that's when her story went sideways. But Vivi was no quitter, and she'd tracked down the woman at the safe house to get the goods.

Lesson learned: bad guys don't quit, either.

The NYPD hadn't been happy…Okay, so that was an understatement. She was lucky they hadn't thrown her in jail and sued the newspaper for her interference in an ongoing criminal investigation. Actually, luck didn't have much to do with it. The credit went to the *Spectator*'s legal team. Too bad they hadn't been as successful when it came to her job. She was put on a six-month probation the same day ninety-year-old Hilda Branch, aka Dear Hilda, died in her sleep. Vivi'd sat across from the *Spectator*'s editor in chief, staring at him in stomach-dropping horror as he gave her her new assignment.

Everyone, other than the editor in chief obviously, knew that Vivi was the least qualified person for the job. And it wasn't because she'd never been dumped before. Of course she had, she was thirty for god's sake. What thirty-year-old hadn't been dumped, had a couple of those he's-just-not-into-you revelations that broke her heart? No, the reason Vivi wasn't suited for the job was because she was the most unsympathetic person north of Wall Street. And that was why, once she'd recovered, she didn't yell and she didn't argue. She smiled and graciously accepted the position. With her in-your-face attitude, she figured her stint as Dear Vivi would last...about a day.

But people obviously enjoyed having their butts kicked, because her column had been an overnight sensation. Which was why Dear Vivi's responses of late had gone from a butt kick to a light tap on the behind. She had no intention of being an advice columnist for forty years like Hilda Branch. One way or another, when Vivi's probation was up a few weeks from now, she was getting her old job back.

As the line in front of her moved forward as slowly as at Bagel Bagel on a Saturday morning, Skye's assigned ring-tone jingled from Vivi's carry-on. She'd been expecting her call. Their mutual best friend Maddie McBride had already checked in with Vivi on the cab ride to the airport. The three of them had been friends since their first day of college. As they were only children—technically that wasn't true in Vivi's case, but it's how she thought of herself—they'd become the sisters they never had.

In the past eighteen months, Vivi's "sisters" had abandoned her. They'd moved from New York City to Christmas, Colorado. Maddie and Skye said they fell in love with the small mountain town. Vivi knew better; they fell in love with the town's most eligible bachelors. Vivi no longer believed in a one-and-only, but even she had to admit, if there was such a thing, Skye and Maddie had found theirs.

She missed them. New York wasn't the same without them. But that didn't mean she'd cave to their pleading and cajoling and move to Christmas. Vivi didn't do the great outdoors. Give her concrete, skyscrapers, Bagel Bagel, and Roasters Coffee down the street any day.

"Where are you?" Skye asked the moment Vivi put the phone to her ear.

She sighed. Her best friends expected her to bail at the last minute. And Vivi knew why—Chance McBride. She did her best to avoid the small town of Christmas when there was a possibility he'd be around. Since his father was getting married next week, the probability that Chance would be there was high. Then again, he'd been home only once in the last five years. Vivi knew why he avoided his hometown, and that knowledge was probably the reason her voice came out more raspy than usual. "Security line at the airport."

"Vivi! Your flight leaves in twenty minutes."

Checking the time on her phone, Vivi glanced at the

ticket in her hand and grimaced. She was cutting it kind of close. "Relax, I'll make it."

"Don't tell me, you were working on your column and time got away from you. You're a workaholic, Vivi," Skye said in an exasperated tone of voice. "The week away will do you good. You can relax for a change."

Sometimes it was annoying how well Skye knew her. Only Vivi hadn't been working on her column before she left her apartment; she could dial those in. She'd been checking out a couple leads for a story. One that would knock her editor's socks off and get Vivi back her job.

She returned her attention to Skye. "Relaxing? I thought you guys said you needed me there to help with the wedding. 'Vivi, Maddie, and I will have nervous breakdowns if you don't come. We can't do this on our own. We're new mothers,'" she said, imitating Skye's angst-filled voice from three weeks ago.

"Hey, I did not sound whiny and hysterical."

"Yeah, you kinda did. But don't worry, I'm riding to the rescue in my big, white bird." Ten members of a seniors bowling team shuffled forward. "I have to take off my boots. See you soon."

"Okay, but don't, you know, tick off security. We really do need you here. Nell's driving us insane," Skye said, referring to Nell McBride, who looked like a sweet little old lady if you ignored the flaming red streak in her white hair. And no one should ignore that devil-red streak. The older woman was the biggest shit-disturber Vivi had ever met.

Vivi knew this because eighteen months earlier, she and Maddie got caught up in one of Nell's schemes. In the end, everything worked out well for Maddie. For

Vivi, not so much. She was still in recovery mode. Which was the reason why she'd agreed to go to Christmas in the first place. Like Heartbroken, Vivi had a man who'd taken up too much space in her heart and head: Chance McBride.

She opened her mouth to respond when Skye said in a voice tinged with nerves, "Um, speaking of Nell. This was all her idea, okay? So don't get mad at me and Maddie. We had nothing to do with it. N-O-T-H-I-N-G."

Vivi froze, balancing on one foot as she took off her rubber boot. "What was Nell's idea?"

"Gotta go. Evie's crying," Skye said, obviously using her five-month-old daughter as an excuse, because there was no noise in the background.

"Skye! Skye, don't you dare hang—" Vivi broke off at the sound of a beep. "Call Ended" flashed on her phone's screen. "Dammit, dammit, dammit," she muttered at the same time the bald, mustached man in uniform waved her over.

And since Vivi was now in a ticked-off, panicked mood, she managed to tick off the security agents. By the time they got through with her, she was late for her flight. Her carry-on banging against her hip as she raced to her gate, she accidently bumped into several people, ensuring she'd now ticked off half the airport.

Breathless by the time she reached the woman standing behind the desk in front of her gate, Vivi waved her boarding pass, panting, "That's my flight." It was while she watched the woman scan the nonrefundable one-way ticket Skye had sent her that Vivi realized what Nell was up to. The older woman had decided to help Maddie and Skye in their bid to keep her in Christmas. She almost laughed in relief. She'd been worried Nell's current scheme had something to do with...

"It's your lucky day," the woman said, handing Vivi back the boarding pass with a smile. "There was a problem closing the cargo bay door. The plane was delayed."

To a white-knuckled flier, a malfunctioning door didn't sound lucky at all. "Are they changing planes?" Vivi asked, because while she had no problem writing about aircraft falling from the sky and people getting sucked out of them, she had no intention of being one of them.

"No, everything's fine. Get going. They won't hold the plane much longer." The woman gestured to the narrow corridor.

"Okay. Thanks," Vivi said, even as near-miss, landing, and takeoff accident statistics popped into her head.

Replacing those thoughts with the more pleasant one of seeing her best friends, she ran down the blue-carpeted corridor. A few feet from the plane's open door, a blast of hot, muggy air slammed into her. The earlier thunderstorm hadn't cleared out the mid-May heat wave that had blanketed New York for the last three days. One more reason to head to Colorado: she'd be able to breathe.

But when the flight attendant showed Vivi to her first-class aisle seat, she stopped breathing all together. A long-legged, broad-shouldered man slouched in the window seat with a champagne-colored Stetson covering his face. Every time she saw a tall, exceptionally built man wearing a Stetson, she'd had the same reaction.

This was worse.

This was painful.

Because this man's scuffed, brown cowboy boots looked the same as the ones that had spent a week under her bed. So did the well-worn jeans that encased thighs that appeared to be as hard as the ones she'd run her bare foot along. She recognized the black T-shirt with the Rocky Mountain logo that hugged his wide chest. An extraordinary chest she'd kissed her way up and kissed her way down. Broad shoulders that she'd clung to. Muscular, tanned arms that had wrapped around her, and large hands that could easily crush a man but had caressed her gently, and at one time, she'd misguidedly thought, lovingly.

At the flight attendant's impatient sigh, Vivi dragged her gaze away. "Ah, is there another seat available? I'd rather not sit in first class. Too close to the front of the plane." The woman's black-penciled eyebrows snapped together when Vivi continued, her voice barely a whisper, "In the event of a crash, it's forty percent safer to be at the back." Safer for her. She needed time to prepare herself for the sight of his to-die-for face. She remembered that face, remembered kissing that face, falling head over heels in love with that face. And those amazing grass-green eyes of his wouldn't miss her reaction to seeing him for the first time in eighteen months. They'd never missed anything.

He'd know.

He'd know he'd broken her heart.

At least that was one positive thing that had come out of writing an advice column. Vivi had learned what she had to do to move on with her own life. She needed to prove to Chance as much as to herself that she was over him. That he hadn't ruined her for any other man. When Superman entered her life, she'd hoped that was the case. He'd been proof that all those soft, romantic feelings hadn't shriveled up and died. It didn't matter that he was no longer in her life. Everyone needed a rebound guy, and Superman had been hers.

Hopefully moving on from Chance would be as easy as moving on from Superman. Since the day Chance dumped her, she'd rehearsed her first face to face with him a million times. She knew exactly what she'd say and how she'd act. She'd even planned out what to wear. Which was so not Vivi. She was a jeans and T-shirt kind of girl. But she'd packed an outfit that oozed cool sophistication. It sure as hell wasn't the yellow rubber boots, black leggings, and seen-better-days, off-the-shoulder green T-shirt she currently had on. And a brief encounter with Chance on Main Street was not the same as being trapped beside him on the four-hour flight to Denver. Vivi's lungs constricted, and her face tingled. Good God, she was having a panic attack. And the flight attendant's tight smile and negative head shake was so not what she needed to see right now.

Maybe the woman at the gate was right and it was Vivi's lucky day. Maybe this guy who leaked testosterone from his pores wasn't Chance McBride after all. Her gaze went to the man's overlong, copper-streaked, dark-blond hair. No, it was not her lucky day. This was the second-worst day of her life. The worst day had been when she'd woken up to a note on her pillow. And the words "Take care, Slick" in Chance's bold, masculine handwriting.

\*     \*     \*

Chance McBride kept his body relaxed even though everything inside of him tightened in response to that raspy bedroom voice. He didn't need to see her to know who it was. That voice was imprinted on his brain. It had made him want things he couldn't have. Made him forget things he had no business forgetting. It's why he'd left her without saying good-bye. He'd known he was in trouble the first time he'd laid eyes on Vivi Westfield.

A hollow ache filled his chest at the memory of the days and nights they'd spent together. Of her gorgeous, toned legs wrapped around him, his mouth at her pink-tipped breast while his hands kneaded her amazing ass. Her long, dark hair spread across the pillow as soft, sexy sounds escaped from her parted lips. Full, sensuous lips he could spend a lifetime fantasizing about. But it was her eyes, incredible violet eyes, that did him in. And those eyes were the reason he'd left her. The emotion that had turned them from violet to black.

She'd fallen in love with him. A man who had no love left to give. The death of his wife, Kate, and their baby girl had seen to that. If he'd met Vivi before Kate, it would have taken an army to drag him away from her. But he wasn't that man, and he'd walked away from her without a backward glance. Didn't mean he didn't think about her, keep tabs on her. He might not be able to give her the love she wanted and deserved, but she'd damned well needed his protection.

Vivi Westfield was a hothead. She had no fear. She was driven, ambitious, going after a story with no regard for her personal safety. She'd nearly gotten herself killed six months back. He'd done what he could, but she'd shut him down as quickly as he'd cut off her sources. She'd given the slip to the tail he'd put on her that night in November. If he hadn't been on another job halfway across the country, he would have protected her himself. Done everything he could to keep her out of harm's way. At least he hadn't had to worry about her the last few months.

Thinking of her as Dear Vivi, his mouth twitched. He doubted she found the demotion amusing. And if she ever discovered who he was, she'd go ballistic. Her girls, Madison and Skye, they knew. Obviously they hadn't shared that he was Superman or Vivi would be straddling him right now, her hands at his throat. He shifted in the seat. He needed to get that particular visual out of his head.

Fucking Nell. He should have known his great-aunt was up to no good when she sent him the nonrefundable, one-way first-class ticket. She always had an agenda. Like the one that had put Vivi on his radar in the first place. He worked for an international security company and had been on assignment in New York when Nell tagged him to investigate Madison. A job that took him all of ten minutes. The rest of the time he'd spent with Vivi.

He'd assumed the plane ticket was Nell's way of ensuring he was there for his dad's wedding. If Chance didn't know it would break his father's heart if he was a no-show, Nell's nonrefundable ticket wouldn't have been enough to sway him. He'd been home only once since Kate and the baby's funeral. It had been tough being there. Tougher than he'd admit to anyone. Now with Vivi in town and his great-aunt apparently in matchmaking mode, it would be worse.

He took a moment to prepare himself, then pushed up the brim of his Stetson with a finger and forced a lazy, amused tone to his voice. "Hey, Slick. Long time no see."

# Chapter Two

*Long time no see.* Seriously? That's all he could come up with after he'd... Of course it was. For Vivi, her heart had been on the line, while for Chance, their week together had probably been nothing more than an extended one-night stand. And since that was something she didn't want him to know, she forced her face into what she hoped was a this-is-a-happy-coincidence expression and lifted her gaze.

Her knees went weak as she looked into his oh-so-green eyes for the first time in more than a year. She curled her fingers into the headrest of the leather seat. Any hope of forming a scintillating response fled at the sight of his beard-stubbled face. He was even more devastatingly handsome than she remembered. "Hey," she croaked, her greeting as lame as his.

The flight attendant played with her shiny, dark hair, flashing Chance a coy smile. With all of his attention focused on Vivi, he didn't return the woman's obvious flirtatious attempt. When the flight attendant realized she wasn't going to get the reaction she hoped for, she huffed, "Please take your seat."

*Right.* She had to sit beside him. Sit next to that prime example of male perfection with his hard muscles brushing up against her for the next four freaking hours and pretend he didn't affect her. That she didn't...

"Ma'am." The flight attendant raised her black-penciled eyebrows.

Vivi sat, then made a production of stowing her carry-on under the seat in front of her to buy herself some time. *Smile*, she ordered herself when she finally sat upright. What was she smiling for? She wasn't a smiley type of person. It would be a dead giveaway. Though she had smiled a lot with him. The reminder had her pressing her lips together as she hunted for her seat belt.

"You okay?"

Goose bumps raised on her arms in response to his deep, panty-dropping voice. She kept her head bent, digging between the seats as she tried not to touch his jean-clad thigh. "I'm good. But you're, ah, sitting on my seat belt."

She sensed him watching her as he raised his hip. He handed her the belt, his fingers brushing hers. A heated charge of memory and sensation rushed through at that simple, accidental touch. She suppressed a shiver. "Thanks," she said through clenched teeth while trying to fit the metal pieces together.

"You sure you're okay?" His big hand closed over hers as he clicked her seat belt into place.

"I'm good. Just a little frazzled because I was late

for the flight. I hate being late for anything, you know."
She was always late. "I was working on a story and time
got away from me." She rubbed her forehead when what
she really wanted to do was bury her face in her hands.
She was rambling, and Vivi never rambled.

"Big story?"

She heard what sounded like amusement in his voice
and glanced at him. Her overwrought nervous system must
be causing her to hear things because there was nothing
but a look of languid interest in his eyes. She nodded and
lied. "Huge story. Really big. Probably the biggest in my
career."

His perfectly sculpted lips tipped up at the corner, and
she was about to ask him what was so funny when the two
flight attendants at the front of the plane drew her attention. "Do they look nervous to you? Because they look
nervous to me. Must be that cargo door they were having
problems with earlier." All she could think was that God
worked in mysterious ways. She silently thanked Him and
started to unbuckle her seat belt.

Chance's hand closed over hers. She really wished
he'd stop doing that. "Better keep that on, Slick. We'll be
taking off in a couple of minutes."

"We can't take off. Not when there's a problem with the
cargo door. Do you want to get sucked out of the plane?"
she asked, her voice rising along with her panic.

"Mommy, I don't want to get sucked out of the plane,"
a little boy whined from behind her.

"Terry, there's something wrong with the cargo door,"
the older woman across the aisle from Vivi said to the
bespectacled octogenarian beside her.

"What's that, Ethel?"

"The cargo door, Terry. She says we're going to get sucked out of the plane," Ethel yelled, waving her hand at Vivi.

Penciled Eyebrows strode down the aisle. "What's going on here?"

Everyone pointed at Vivi, repeating her comments, while Chance sat back with a grin on his ridiculously handsome face, his arms crossed over his chest. It took a moment for the flight attendant to calm the passengers and to read Vivi the riot act. Vivi opened her mouth to refute the flight attendant's statement that flying was the safest mode of travel, then closed it. She didn't want to scare Ethel, Terry, and the little boy behind her any more than she already had.

"It's not funny. Everything I said was true," she muttered to the silently laughing man beside her. She tightened her grip on the armrests as they taxied down the runway. Closing her eyes, she chewed an imaginary piece of gum as the plane lifted off.

"Huh. And here I thought there was nothing the fearless Vivi Westfield was afraid of." He laced his fingers through hers, stroking his thumb over her knuckles.

At the confidence in his deep voice and his comforting touch, her heart beat double time in her chest, and her mouth went dry. Her reaction to Chance McBride was more terrifying than the thought of the 757 falling from the sky. "I'm not afraid. It's—" She jumped at the loud clunking noise coming from beneath the plane. "What's that?"

He gave her hand a light squeeze. "Relax, it's just the wheels retracting."

"How do you know that?"

"Because I've put in about twenty thousand miles in the last two months alone, and I have my pilot's license."

"Oh, right. I should have remembered that, seeing as it's how you kidnapped my best friend. My pregnant best friend who was wearing her pajamas at the time." Honestly, she didn't know why Skye liked the man after what he'd done, but she did.

"Worked out, didn't it? Sugar Plum is living happily ever after with her Prince Charming. And if you want to blame someone, blame Nell. She's the one who set…" His eyes narrowed, and he let go of her hand. "You buy your own ticket?"

"My plane ticket?"

He nodded.

"No, if I did, I wouldn't be sitting in first class." She didn't add "beside you." Her eyes widened as she realized why he'd ask. "Did you buy yours?"

"No," he clipped out.

She pressed her fingers to her temple. So this was what Skye had been talking about. Nell's plan had nothing to do with getting Vivi to move to Christmas. She was up to her matchmaking tricks again. Vivi drowned out the little voice in her head that cheered Nell on with a forced laugh. "Your aunt is deluded if she thinks she can get us together."

"I know that and you know that, but it won't matter what we say."

His answer wasn't a surprise. She knew how he felt about her, but to hear him so casually dismiss any chance…Good God, she really wasn't over him, was she?

Obviously the twinge of pain in the vicinity of her heart was reflected in her face, because he patted her thigh. "Don't worry about it. I'll figure something out."

"Good luck with that. She's three for three. The woman thinks she's…" She trailed off as the flight attendant began the safety briefing.

"Three for three? Who—"

She held up a hand and retrieved the illustrated card from the pouch in front of her. She caught the amused expression on Chance's face as he watched her. She ignored him, focusing instead on the flight attendant. When the woman turned to the person in the emergency exit seat, Vivi raised herself up as much as the seat belt allowed. "There is no way that guy will be able to throw the door." She cast a sidelong and slightly covetous glance at Chance's corded forearms and bulging biceps. "You should change seats with him."

"Slick, we're not going to crash. If you want to worry about something, worry about Nell and what she has planned for us."

Vivi dragged her gaze from his amazing biceps to… dammit, his equally amazing face. His eyebrows raised at what she belatedly realized had been her very thorough perusal of all his amazingness. Her face, along with a certain body part—one that had been piteously ignored for the last eighteen months—got warm and tingly. She fanned herself with the informational card, then realized what she was doing. She stuffed it back in the pouch. "Leave Nell to me. I'll talk to her and set her straight," she said with perhaps more feeling than was warranted.

"Trust me, I know my aunt better than you do, and trying to reason with her will do as much good as waving a red flag in front of a bull."

*Trust him?* Vivi didn't trust anyone. She hadn't since she was seventeen and found out that people you loved died and mothers who were supposed to love you didn't. Chance had made her forget those hard-learned life lessons. Only he hadn't been Chance then, he'd been James Harris. But he had more experience with Nell than she did. "So what do you suggest we do?"

"Simple. We'll tell her we're together, and she'll leave us alone."

Her and Chance…together. It was like her fantasy come true. Only it wasn't. She cleared what she imagined was a look of longing and hope from her face. "Are you crazy?"

"No. Think about it. If we don't cut her off at the pass, she'll drive us nuts. She won't let up, and she'll get her buddies in on the action. What's the big deal? It's only for a week. And it's not as if anyone will expect us to spend much time together. I'll be busy with my dad's wedding."

Vivi didn't think Nell and Christmas's matchmakers were that big a problem. Sure, they'd be annoying and no doubt drive them slightly insane. But pretending to be Chance's girlfriend? That would be a problem. All those soft, romantic feelings would come back to bite her in the butt. She opened her mouth to…What? If she didn't agree to his plan, he'd wonder why. He obviously had no qualms about pretending to be in love with her. She felt like bonking her head on the seat in front of her, but instead said, "Okay, fine. We'll pretend we're dating. But I'm telling Maddie and Skye the truth."

"Might as well forget about it, then. They'll blow it."

"No they won't. They—"

"Yeah, they will. Your girls have been under Nell's influence for what, over a year now? They'll cave. Guaranteed."

Okay, so he did have a point. She thought of a way

she could use their pretend relationship to her advantage. One that would take away the pitying looks from her best friends whenever they inadvertently mentioned his name. Sympathetic looks that made her feel as weak and as stupid as the women who wrote to her. Women who let their heartbreak define who they were for years to come. "All right, I won't tell them. But we end our fake relationship before we head out of town. Publicly. And this time, I'm the one who does the ending." Good God, did she just say that? It was exactly what she wanted to do, but she didn't mean to tell him! And she'd been doing so well playing it cool up until now.

He rubbed his jaw, then looked at her. And that's when she saw it—pity. He felt sorry for her. "Vivi, I never meant to hurt you. I—"

"Hurt me? Whatever gave you that idea? Come on, it's not like we had a relationship or anything. We had some laughs together, good times in bed, and—"

His brow lifted. "*Good* times in bed?"

*Typical.* Of course he'd hone in on that. Did he actually expect her to stroke his ego after he'd lied to her and left her without an explanation? As if she were going to tell him he was a sex god and had ruined her for mere mortal men. "Yeah, *good* times. It was fun while it lasted. But I knew what I was getting myself into. I might not have known your real name, but it was obvious you were a player."

"I am not a player."

"Right. And your name's James Harris."

"Look, I couldn't risk blowing my cover. My assignment was dangerous. I didn't want you to get—"

"It doesn't matter. No harm, no foul. I'll go along with your plan."

His eyes roamed her face, then he nodded. "If it'll make you feel better, you can break up with me in front of the whole damn town for all I care."

"Consider it a public service for the trail of broken hearts you've left in your wake."

"You saying I broke your heart, Slick?" His voice was low and gruff, an unreadable emotion in his eyes.

"Get over yourself, McBride. I already told you..." Vivi eyes widened as the 757 started to shake. She dug her fingernails into the armrest. *Oh, God, oh, God.* When the plane took a stomach-turning drop, she screamed, throwing herself into the arms of the man she wanted to smack only a few seconds ago. "Do something! You—"

He sighed, lowering his head to smother her panicked cries with a deep, soul-searing kiss.

\*       \*       \*

Hours later, Chance listened to Vivi's strangled cheeps as the 757 bounced along the runway. He smiled under his Stetson. She sounded like a chicken about to get its head cut off. Less panicked than she'd been a few hours ago though. He'd been worried once she started screaming that she wouldn't stop. It's why he kissed her. Might have been better if he found another way to calm her down. One that didn't involve his mouth on hers or that incredible body plastered over his, enveloping him in her familiar vanilla scent. She smelled amazing and kissed even better.

He'd forgotten how easy it was to lose himself in her sweet mouth. Within seconds, she took him from ten to two hundred on the heat meter. At least he didn't have to worry she'd get the wrong idea. She wasn't looking for a relationship, either. Seems he'd misread the emotion he'd seen in her eyes all those months ago. And why the thought triggered a tightening in his chest, he didn't know or want to think about. As long as she was on board with his plan to shut down Nell, he was good.

He straightened in his seat and pushed up his Stetson, fighting a grin when Vivi scowled at him. Honest to God, she was the prickliest woman he'd ever met. A regular hard-ass. He liked that about her. But she'd shown him another side, too—soft, sweet, and vulnerable. It was a side he could have done without seeing.

"You slept through the whole flight," she accused.

"Not the entire flight," he reminded her as he unsnapped his seat belt and stretched.

"What are you doing?" She reached for his seat belt, then snatched her hand back, flicking her fingers at him. "Put that back on. Can't you read the sign? We haven't come to a complete stop."

"You gotta do something about your fear of flying, Slick. Either have a couple of shots or get my dad to pre-scribe you some Ativan for the return flight."

"I don't need drugs. I'm not afraid of flying. I just have a healthy sense of self-preservation."

Thinking about her run-in with Jimmy "the Knife" Moriarty and several members of the East Coast mob last November, he snorted. "Sure you do."

She looked up as the passengers shuffled past, then unsnapped her seat belt and grabbed her carry-on. Taking her cell phone from her bag, she thumbed through her messages and heaved a sigh. "Skye says I'm hitching a ride to Christmas with you and your dad."

"Good. I was going to suggest that you do," he said as she moved into the aisle and he retrieved his duffle bag from the overhead compartment. He motioned for her to go ahead of him.

She walked down the aisle, stopping in front of the crew. "I have a question for you. Did the problem you had earlier with the cargo door have anything to do with the turbulence we experienced?"

"No, ma'am. It—" the pilot started to explain.

"Really? Because that was one of the roughest flights I've ever been on. A lot of the passengers were complaining, you know. How long have you been flying for—"

Chance placed his hand at the small of her back. "Thanks, folks." He gave the crew an apologetic smile and Vivi a gentle shove out the door.

"Hey, what do you think you're doing? I wasn't finished—"

"I was saving you from yourself. You'll end up on a watch list if you're not careful. Come on, we don't want to keep my dad waiting. Did you check any luggage?"

"They can't put you on a watch list for questioning the crew," she muttered, head bent as she worked her phone.

"Luggage, Slick, you got any?"

Still busy on her phone, she nodded and nearly walked into a man with a cane. Chance took her arm, guiding her to the airport shuttle. "You're a dangerous woman," he said as he retrieved his phone and texted his dad to meet them at baggage claim.

"No, that would be your aunt. I have five messages from her."

He sighed; so did he. "What did she say?"

She glanced at him as they stepped into the packed shuttle. "She's setting me up with every eligible man in Christmas. And just so you know, you're not one of them."

He frowned and opened his messages from Nell. "What's she up to now? She did the same to me."

She leaned into him, reading his e-mail. "Brandi. She's the waitress at the Penalty Box, isn't she?"

"I'm not dating Brandi. We have a plan, remember?" He snagged her phone. "Who's Dr. McSexy?"

"I don't know." She tugged her cell from his hand as they got off the shuttle and headed for the escalators. "But what I do know is we don't have to go through with the *plan* now. She's not trying to set us up."

"Yeah right. The two of us being on the same flight was no coincidence. Pretending that we're together is the only way to stop whatever she's up to now. Unless you're interested in dating Dr. McSexy? I wouldn't want to put a crimp in your love life."

"Of course I'm not interested. I'm not interested in dating anyone."

The muscles in his shoulders loosened at her response. Okay, that reaction had nothing to do with her not wanting to date, he assured himself. His relief was because he needed her to go along with the plan for his sake. "Good. We're on the same page. You tell Nell we're involved, and I'll do the same."

She gave her head a slight, worrisome shake. "The more I think about it, the less I like the idea. We'll get everyone's—"

Before he had an opportunity to address whatever excuses she'd come up with, he heard his father call his name. He looked up to see his dad making his way toward them with a relieved smile on his face. A twinge of guilt knotted Chance's gut. He'd disappointed his dad a lot over the last five years. The smile Chance offered in response faltered when he spotted the woman following behind his father.

An icy cold sensation flooded Chance's body, weakening his limbs.

Vivi touched his arm. "Are you all right?"

At least that's what he thought she said. He couldn't be sure with the sound of his heart pounding in his ears.

His father pulled him in for a hug. "It's good to see you, son. Welcome home."

He managed to return his father's greeting, then forced himself to look at the sun-streaked blonde hanging back with a nervous smile on her heart-shaped face. *Natalee. Kate's baby sister. Jesus.* His heart rate slowly returned to normal. He hadn't seen Natalee since the funeral. She'd been a mess that day. They all had been. But she'd been only sixteen at the time and had worshipped Kate. Natalee hadn't been able to look at him at the funeral. She'd blamed him for her sister's death as much as he blamed himself.

"Look who I've got with me." His dad stepped back, watching Chance closely as he waved Natalee over.

"Hey, Nat." Chance worked to keep the emotion from his voice as he walked past his father to draw the young girl into his arms. "You're all grown up, kiddo." Hardly a day had gone by that Nat hadn't been with him and Kate. He'd come to think of her as a little sister.

Wrapping her arms tightly around his waist, she buried her face in his chest as a sob shuddered through her delicate frame. "I know, kiddo," he said quietly, patting her back. "I know."

# Chapter Three

Vivi recognized the younger woman from the wedding photos that lined the mantel at Dr. McBride's. An unfamiliar burn stung her eyes as Chance drew his sister-in-law into his arms. Vivi prided herself on her ability to stay unmoved, unemotional in the face of human drama. As a journalist, that detachment served her well. Of course, there were editors who would disagree with her. Over the years, she'd been told that the one element her stories lacked was heart.

At that moment, Vivi's cool detachment seemed to have abandoned her, her throat tightening painfully at the shredded expression on Chance's face when his sister-in-law started sobbing in his arms. His deep voice quiet and gruff as he consoled her.

Vivi looked away. She couldn't do it. Couldn't watch as a man who'd been trained to use his powerful six-foot-four body as a lethal weapon and deal with life-and-death situations without blinking an eye, struggled to contain his grief. And maybe if she was honest, she'd admit the emotional punch came not only from watching him battle against his pain and heartache. It was due to the evidence of his deep, abiding love for his wife. After five years, Chance's feelings for Kate still had the power to shatter him.

Vivi stuck out her hand. "Hi, Dr. McBride. Thanks for offering to give me a lift to Christmas."

It took a moment for the dark-haired man with a touch of silver at his temples to acknowledge Vivi's greeting. He was obviously worried how Chance would deal with the unexpected reunion with his sister-in-law. Dr. McBride turned navy-blue eyes on Vivi. The sixty-something man was still as head-turningly gorgeous as his sons. And as Vivi knew from visiting Christmas, he was also a kind and loving father. Maddie adored him. But at that moment, Vivi wanted to shake her best friend's father-in-law because, along with the concern in his eyes, she saw the guilt. What had he been thinking forcing a public reunion on his son?

Every ounce of color had drained from Chance's face when he saw the younger woman in a pink sweater with matching leggings and wedge sandals, a large white bag over her shoulder, standing behind his father. Natalee with her delicate, winsome beauty looked so much like Kate McBride that Chance must have thought he'd seen a ghost. If he expected his family to pull crap like this when he came home, no wonder he stayed away.

Chance's father grimaced as he clasped Vivi's hand. No doubt her anger showed on her face. "That was unfair, you know. He deserved a heads-up." She didn't worry Chance would overhear her; he was focused on the small black-and-white dog Natalee had just removed from her bag.

Dr. McBride appeared taken aback by what she'd said, then he slowly nodded and squeezed her hand. "You're right. Nell thought..." He lifted a shoulder, glancing once again in Chance's direction.

She patted his arm. "Take my advice, Nell is the last person you should be listening to." Vivi nodded at the baggage claim. "I'll give you guys a few minutes alone and get my luggage."

As she began to walk away, Paul rubbed the back of his neck, something his son Gage also did when he was nervous. Vivi lifted her eyes to the airport ceiling, blowing out an aggravated breath. Obviously Chance had another unwelcome surprise in store for him courtesy of his great-aunt. Unwanted sympathy filled Vivi, and for all of a second, she reconsidered her decision not to go along with his plan. She'd started to tell him she'd had a change of heart, but his father's arrival interrupted her.

If Chance hadn't kissed her on the plane, maybe she'd feel more disposed to helping him out. But he did, and his mouth on hers felt as incredible as she remembered. With the familiar feel of his big hand cradling the back of her head, all that hard muscle beneath her, and his clean, manly scent, she'd lost herself in his kiss. So lost that she forgot he'd lied to her, that he'd kicked her to the curb without a backward glance. Until he eased her out of his arms and his perceptive gaze roamed her face.

There was no way he'd mistake her passionate response for anything other than what it was. He'd turned her, a woman who hated public displays of affection, into a quivering mass of desire...on a plane. Surrounded by people who no doubt heard those stupid needy sounds she'd made. It was then that she'd decided what he could do with his plan. But just as she'd opened her mouth to tell him, he'd put his damn Stetson over his face and fallen asleep.

As Vivi dug through the mound of luggage beside the carousel, she decided today ranked in the top ten of her life's most embarrassing moments. The neon floral suitcase near the bottom of the pile drew her attention. Like her yellow rubber boots, the suitcase was one of Skye's castoffs. Yep, walking around with a sparkly piece of luggage was the perfect way to cap off her craptastic day. Vivi tugged and shoved until she finally retrieved the suitcase. Pulling up the handle, she gave the hard frame a kick to get its wheels in motion as she contemplated the cost of taking a taxi to Christmas.

A large hand closed over hers. "Cute luggage, Slick. Never would have taken you for a girly girl," a familiar male voice said as he took the suitcase from her.

For a big man, Chance had an annoying ability to sneak up on her. She sighed and looked at him. His comment and his tone of voice had been lighthearted; the emotion carved into his face was anything but. "Are you okay?" she asked, unable to keep the sympathy from her voice.

"Fan-freaking-tastic," he muttered as he took her hand and headed toward his father and Natalee, who were waiting by the exit doors.

Vivi's gaze moved from Chance to his father, who was looking at her like she walked on water. Oh, good God, he'd told his dad they were dating. "Ah, Chance, I don't think—"

"Dad and Aunt Nell got my place ready for us, Slick. Isn't that great?"

She froze. "What?"

He let go of her hand and wrapped his arm around her, holding her tight against him. His arm felt like a band of steel. She couldn't move if she wanted to. And there was no doubt she wanted to. Because while pretending to be his girlfriend would be difficult, living under the same roof with him would be sheer torture. "No, no way, I'm not..." She trailed off as he looked down at her.

And in response to the pleading look in his grass-green eyes, the tension bracketing his beautiful mouth, Vivi, the most unsympathetic person north of Wall Street, did the unthinkable: she caved. But not without some attitude. "Fan-freaking-tastic," she muttered.

*      *      *

Chance sat in the passenger seat while his father regaled him with news from Christmas. For a small town, there was a hell of a lot of news. Paul had been talking nonstop since they dropped Nat off at a friend's place twenty minutes ago. It was a nervous habit of his father's. He knew he'd screwed up forcing a face to face with Nat.

Chance expected more from his father. Out of anyone, his dad should have known what today would cost him. Paul had lost his wife—Chance's mother—nine years ago to breast cancer. But maybe it was different when you did everything you could to save the woman you loved. When you weren't the one who put her in danger in the first place.

His father cast an anxious glance in the rearview mirror. "You're sure Vivi didn't hit her head when she fell? She was out cold fifteen minutes after we left the airport." Ever since his wife's death, Paul had turned into an overprotective worrywart. You couldn't get so much as a scratch or a headache without him jumping to the worst-case scenario.

Chance smiled at the memory of trying to hand Vivi the dog so he could load her luggage into his dad's SUV. In her panic to get away from an eight-pound Yorkie, she'd tripped over her suitcase. Leave it to her to make him laugh when he hadn't thought he'd get through the next ten minutes without losing his shit.

"She didn't hit her head, Dad. She landed on her ass. And believe me, she wouldn't feel a thing. That part of her body is well padded." He waited for a reaction from Vivi. Sure enough, his seat bounced with what he imagined was a kick from behind him. He knew she was faking it. She'd tried a couple of times to engage Nat in conversation. When she'd failed to draw anything more than monosyllabic answers from his sister-in-law, Vivi had yawned loudly and told the three of them she needed to catch some shut-eye.

"You're lucky she's asleep or you'd be paying for that comment, son." His father smiled. "You made me a happy man today. Vivi's a wonderful young woman. I couldn't have picked better for you myself."

From the backseat came a muffled groan. Chance didn't want to get his dad's hopes up any more than he already had. More importantly, he didn't want Vivi to bail on him. As she'd proved earlier, she was great at distracting him. And if he was going to survive this week, he'd need all the distraction he could get. "Dad, don't read more into it than there is. We're dating. That's all."

"Son, I may be getting up there, but even I know when you date someone it means you're thinking of a future with them."

"No, it means we enjoy spending time together. Leave it alone."

"I want you to be happy. I've been worried about you. We all have. You haven't had anyone in your life since—"

"Don't, okay? I'm not you, Dad. I..." He trailed off when Princess barked and scratched at the door. "What's wrong, girl?" Chance patted the dog, who'd been sleeping in his lap for most of the drive, and looked out the window to see what had caught her attention on the desolate mountain road. There was nothing, only the yellow guardrail running along the serpentine curve above the rocky gorge. He briefly closed his eyes. He hadn't realized where they were.

His father shot him a concerned glance. "Sorry, son. I should have taken—"

"I'm fine. Just drive, okay?" He was so far from fine it wasn't funny. His heart hammered against his rib cage, echoing in his ears. He needed... He shifted in his seat, stretched a hand out to Vivi, and patted her thigh. "Hey, Slick, time to wake up."

She sat up, rubbing her leg. "Geez, you're rough. It's not my butt you're patting, you know. My big butt with all the padding."

He stared into her grumpy, pissed-off face. He could kiss her right now. Instead he laughed.

Paul shot Chance an I-told-you-so look at the same time a smile spread across his face. Princess went crazy, growling and snapping at Vivi.

Eyes wide, she put up her hands. "Don't you dare let her go, McBride."

"Are you afraid of dogs, honey?" his father asked as they turned onto the long gravel road leading to the cabin.

At the sight of the copper roof peeking through the trees, the roaring in Chance's ears drowned out Vivi's response. He hadn't been back since the morning after the funeral. The cabin had been their dream home—his and Kate's. They'd spent more than a year planning everything, from the type of wiring to the hardware for the cabinetry. In his mind's eye, he could see her curled up on the couch knitting a small pink sweater by the fire, standing by the window with her hand on her rounded belly as she looked out over the frozen lake, waiting for him in their bed with a sweet smile on her face, laughing in the kitchen as she set off the smoke detector for the hundredth time.

She'd be there. He'd feel her presence everywhere he turned. And all that gut-wrenching longing, the fucking pain and guilt that he had been able to keep locked away, would escape once again.

# Chapter Four

"I'll see you later, Dad," Chance said, his face a hard, inscrutable mask. He didn't spare Vivi so much as a glance as he swung his duffle bag over his shoulder and strode toward the luxury log home's garage with the dog in his arms.

Dr. McBride set Vivi's suitcase on the gravel drive, his worried gaze following his son until he disappeared from view. Paul gave Vivi a weak smile. "I guess he doesn't want me to stick around."

She drew her gaze from the triple-car garage. "I wouldn't read too much into it. He knows you have a lot to do with the wedding."

"No, he's angry I made him come here." He looked around the heavily wooded, secluded property. Small patches of snow were still in evidence as the sun tried to shine through the leafy canopy where birds chirped overhead. Paul returned his attention to her. "I know I went about it the wrong way, but he can't go on like this. He hasn't dealt with Kate's death. He blames himself, you

know. It's time for him to let her go, and this is where he has
to do it. The two of them loved this place as much as they
loved each other. They were happier than—" He shoved his
hands in his jeans pockets. "I'm sorry. I wasn't thinking. It
must be tough on you to hear about Chance and Kate."

About as tough as lying to his father. Their fake relationship was a bad idea on so many levels. If they continued
the charade, Paul would be even more upset when the truth
eventually came out. And an upset Paul meant an upset
Maddie. Chance might not agree with Vivi, but it was time
to end the deception. "Dr. McBride, Chance and I aren't—"

"Paul. You're a member of the family now." He gave
her another one of his you-walk-on-water looks. "I'm glad
you're here to help him through this, Vivi. No one should
have to face this alone. He needs you. You make him happy.
And my son deserves to be happy. He's a good man."

Given her past experience with Chance, she could legiti-
mately challenge the "good man" part. Good men didn't
lie to women. But Paul was right about one thing: Chance
shouldn't have to deal with this alone. No one should. And
since he was as alpha as alpha gets, he wouldn't want anyone
to see his vulnerability. But Vivi had witnessed his suffer-
ing today and, she reminded herself, he'd asked for her help.
Though she was pretty sure this wasn't exactly the kind of
help he had in mind. "Don't worry, I'll take care of him,
Paul. You have enough on your plate with the wedding."

"Don't remind me. Liz has a list as long as my arm
of things that I have to accomplish today," he said with a
rueful grin. Liz O'Connor was his wife-to-be and Skye's
mother-in-law. "We'll see you both at Gage and Maddie's
tonight."

*Right.* Maddie and Skye had e-mailed her a schedule

of duties and events. Tonight they were making up the wedding favors. Vivi couldn't believe she'd let them rope her into doing this crap. Between that and babysitting Chance, she deserved a nomination for sainthood.

"Sure thing. See you there," she said as he got in his SUV. Watching him drive away, she debated whether she should give Chance a couple more minutes alone. An ominous rustling in a nearby bush made up her mind. She hightailed it up a stone walkway to the front door. Just as she raised her hand to knock, a door slammed. Moments later, a black truck kicked up gravel as it peeled out of the garage. "Wait, wait," she called to Chance, running down the walkway, waving her arms. He stopped, and the passenger-side window rolled down.

He looked beyond her, his face ravaged. "I've gotta get some food. There's nothing in the fridge. Don't let the dog out."

*Dog? No way.* "Chance, you can't just leave—" She began, but he didn't hear her. He gunned the engine, his tires spinning as he tore down the road without a backward glance.

Pressing her fingers to her temple, Vivi tried to remind herself that she felt sorry for the man. Instead, her grandma's words came back to her. Whenever Vivi couldn't hide her tears—like the time her grandma's Chihuahua Tinkerbell bit her and when the kids teased her for wearing clothes their mothers donated to charity and the day her father died—her grandma would say, "Sympathy is between *shit* and *syphilis* in the dictionary." Something Vivi needed to remember, she decided as she stomped up the walkway.

She tried the door. Locked. Clenching her jaw, she dragged the suitcase behind her and headed for the garage, which he'd left open. As soon as she stepped inside, she heard Cujo. She searched for something to protect herself and grabbed a broom off a hook on the wall.

The barking intensified as she inched open the door. She stuck her head into the bright and airy mudroom, searching for signs of the dog. From deep within the house, she heard scratching and the sound of something being thrown against a door. Chance must have locked her in a room. Vivi relaxed and rested the broom against the wall, then took off her boots. Her first impression as she walked farther into the house was that Chance didn't believe in roughing it. Everything was high-end: leather, wood, and stone. Masculine-looking with no sign of a woman's touch.

Dust motes floated on beams of sunlight that streamed through a wall of windows in a living room that overlooked a stone patio with a fire pit. Crocuses, tulips, and small green shoots poked through the dark earth lining a meandering pea-gravel path that led to a wooden dock jutting onto a pristine lake. Stunning view if someone enjoyed the great outdoors. She found it too isolated and, oddly enough, given the large, open space, claustrophobic. Maybe the heavy, disused smell in the cabin made it feel that way.

She moved toward the kitchen with its stainless steel appliances and dark oak cabinets. Skimming her hand along the cold granite countertops, she took note of the red ceramic container crammed full with every cooking utensil imaginable. No wonder Chance had teased her about her apartment's woefully inadequate kitchen when they'd cooked together.

Seeing his home made her wonder if everything he'd told her had been a lie. They'd had so much in common, they'd seemed the perfect match. They enjoyed the same books and the same movies. They liked to talk politics and read the newspaper together. She'd opened up to him, told him about her family, about her mother. She'd never told anyone about her mother, not even Maddie and Skye.

She'd told him everything, and he'd told her nothing.

What she'd had with him had been an illusion. What Kate had had with him had been real. They'd been in love for years. If Vivi's memories of their brief affair together caused a heavy weight in her chest, she could only imagine what Chance had dealt with for the last five years. No wonder he chose not to.

She kicked her suitcase to get the wheels in motion and headed toward the hall she suspected led to the bedrooms. The thumping and scratching got louder. She banged on the door. "Quiet, Cujo."

Moving on, she glanced into the adjacent room. Uh, no, she was not staying in here. It was obviously the master bedroom. A king-size bed with a rustic plank head and footboard took up the middle of the room. She walked farther down the hall, opening the door to a third bedroom. As her gaze cataloged the room's contents, she sagged against the doorjamb.

She now knew the reason why the cabin held no visible signs of Kate. She was here, in the boxes half-filled with feminine clothing and mementos that lay scattered across the white shag carpet. Framed photos of a smiling Kate and Chance were piled on a white dresser. And most heartbreaking of all, beneath a window dressed with pink eyelet curtains sat a white rocker and white wooden cradle overflowing with knitted blankets and stuffed animals.

Vivi briefly closed her eyes. This was to be the nursery for the child Chance had lost along with his wife. Feeling like an intruder on his life, his grief, she quickly shut the door. She leaned against it, waiting for her heart rate to return to normal, nearly jumping out of her skin when a pitiful whimpering filled the hallway. It took her a moment to realize the sound hadn't come from a ghost; it was Kate's dog. Vivi imagined it was as hard for Princess to be back here as it was for Chance.

Once again a pang of unwanted sympathy tightened her chest, and Vivi dropped her bags outside Chance's bedroom. "It's okay, Princess. Don't cry. I'll let you out." Edging the door open, she forced a smile for the dog with its pink-bowed topknot and sparkly pink collar. "There you..." Princess snarled, lunging at Vivi's stocking feet.

"No, let go!" She tried shaking off the vicious little beast. The dog whipped its head back and forth, pulling Vivi's sock off. While Cujo was busy tearing the gray wool to shreds, Vivi grabbed her carry-on and hightailed it down the hall.

*Yip. Yip. Yip.* Cujo chased her. Vivi ran into the kitchen and made a mad leap for the counter. She pulled up her feet, grabbing a wooden spoon from the ceramic container to brandish at the dog. "Get away. Shoo."

While the dog jumped up and down, barking, she dug in her carry-on for her phone. She tried to call Maddie. No service. Holding the phone at arm's length, Vivi waved it around the room to get reception. Nothing. Maybe there would be service down by the dock. Somehow, she had to get outside. All she had to do was distract Cujo.

She pulled off her other sock, preparing to book it as soon as she fired it into the living room. "Look Cujo, look." Vivi waved her arms. "Yum, a nice sweaty sock for you." When she got the dog's attention, its black, serial-killer eyes staring up at her, she flung the sock across the room and slid off the counter. At the sound of Cujo's frenzied attack, Vivi sprinted for the mudroom, grabbing her boots on the way. She got the door open...

"No," she cried as a ball of black-and-white fur shot past her.

*          *          *

Chance turned down Main Street, slowing outside the Penalty Box, the town's local sports bar. As he considered stopping in for a drink, an image of the panicked look on Vivi's face came to him, and he hit the gas instead. They hadn't been together long, but in that short time he'd learned a lot about her. She was a city girl through and through. She'd done him a favor. She didn't deserve to be left on her own while he drowned his sorrows.

He flexed his fingers on the steering wheel. At least he no longer had the shakes. The case of beer rattled in the backseat, reminding him of his plan for the night. He'd get shitfaced with Vivi. It was about the only way he figured he'd be able to deal with staying at the cabin. He knew it would be hard. He just hadn't expected it to be as hard as it was. If only he hadn't opened the door to the nursery.

He turned up the radio, drowning out the last conversation he'd had with Kate about the baby. Pushing the memories back to where they belonged. Locking them away. Emptying his mind. He opened the window, letting the cool mountain air rush over him. Breathing in the earthy scent of spring and pine trees. He'd missed that smell. There was nothing like it in the world.

The tension in his shoulders eased as he turned onto... Fuck. Mountain Road. He pressed the gas, taking the serpentine curves faster than he should, the wind whistling through the truck's cab. He flipped the radio's volume as high as it would go. He was nearly home free. Five minutes more and he'd be in the clear.

Four minutes.

Three minutes.

Two...Out of the corner of his eye, he caught movement. He eased off the gas and slammed on the brakes. The truck fishtailed, sending up a spray of gravel before coming to a jarring stop.

Princess, looking small and forlorn, sat beside the now-repaired guardrail.

His breathing a strangled rasp, Chance got out of the truck, focusing on his feet as he strode to Princess's side. No matter how hard he tried not to look, he did. He saw the rocks, the bark stripped clean from the blackened trees where Kate's car had ended up when she'd crashed through the guardrail in the snowstorm and rolled down the hill. A passerby had stopped, pulling her from the wreckage before the car burst into flames. Hours later, both she and their baby girl were dead. Only Princess had escaped unscathed that night.

The dog shivered and whined at his feet. Maybe she hadn't been unscathed after all. Maybe she was as messed up as Chance. He bent down to pick her up, and that's when he saw the white cross with Kate's and Emma's names etched into the wood. Timeworn pink plastic flowers lay half-buried in the gravel at the base of the cross. Chance slowly lowered himself to the ground, cradling the dog against his chest where the smothering ache continued to build.

Somewhere in the distance, he heard an animal's mournful howl. Over and over again, the animal wailed until

Chance's throat felt raw. He closed his eyes. The sound had been coming from him. Burying his face in Princess's fur, he rocked back and forth, silently railing at God for taking the two most precious things in the world from him. It should have been him. If not for his unrelenting pursuit of Jake Callahan, Kate and Emma would be alive. He should have killed Callahan when he had the chance.

It was the sound of cars whizzing by, Princess licking his wet face, that finally drew Chance back from the abyss. He didn't know how long he'd been there, but it was time to move on before someone called the sheriff. All he'd need was for Gage to find him here... like this. He stood and dusted off his jeans. Goddamn Vivi, it was her fault he'd had to relive that moment, that day, that month, that year. What the hell was she thinking letting the dog out? If anything had happened to Princess...

By the time Chance pulled into the garage, anger rolled off him in waves. No matter how hard he tried, he couldn't get a handle on it. He sat in his truck, waiting for the emotion to subside. When he finally regained a semblance of control, he opened the driver's-side door. In the distance, he heard Vivi and followed the sound of her raspy voice. She was in the woods west of the cabin.

"Cujo, come here. I've got a nice, sweaty sock for you. Yum. Yum. Come on, Cujo."

Chance rubbed his jaw. "She doesn't like you much, does she, Princess?" Through the trees he saw her yellow boots and headed toward her. "Slick, I've got—"

She was on her knees, digging in a snow-covered bush. "Be a good doggie. No biting, okay?" she said, as she started pulling something...

*Jesus.* "Vivi, don't—"

# Chapter Five

Vivi walked from the bathroom to the master bedroom wrapped in a towel. She stopped short at the sight of a clean-shaven Chance sitting on the side of the bed in jeans and a white shirt, drinking a beer. "Do not even think about laughing," she warned him.

He grinned, lowering the bottle from his mouth. "Come on, Slick. You have to admit it was funny."

"Easy for you to say, you weren't the one sprayed by a skunk." As she stepped into the room, she glanced at her fingers holding the towel in place. "Look at me, I'm shriveled up like a ten-year-old prune." She sighed as his eyes took a slow tour of every inch of damp skin the towel revealed. "I didn't mean that literally, you know. Go." She flicked her fingers. "I have to get dressed." And she had to stop remembering what had happened every time he'd looked at her that way. What he'd say. What he'd do.

He set the bottle on the nightstand and came to his

feet. "Dad called. Larry, the pharmacist, must have told him about your run-in with Pepé Le Pew. He wants me to check and make sure you weren't scratched."

"You're as bad as your aunt. Why didn't you just take out an ad in the paper?" she grumbled as she went to unzip her suitcase sitting on the oak floor. Realizing the view she'd provide, she straightened.

"I didn't say anything to Larry. He figured it out when I cleaned him out of baking soda and hydrogen peroxide. You have nothing to be embarrassed about, Slick." His mouth kicked up at the corner as he ambled toward her. "You can't help that you're farsighted and mistook a skunk for a Yorkie."

"I'm not farsighted, and you know it." She took a nervous step back. Her half-naked and Chance with a teasing look on his gorgeous face was a dangerous combination. She held up a hand. "No scratches or bites, see? Besides, I got a good look at Pepé before I threw him, and he wasn't foaming at the mouth. So you can go now."

"'Fraid not. Dad was adamant." He stood in front of her, sucking up all the oxygen from the room. Her heart pitter-pattered when he took her hand, stroking his long fingers up and down her arm. Then he turned her hand over to trace circles from her inner wrist all the way up her arm. Goose bumps raised on her skin when his knuckles brushed against her breast. She suppressed a shiver. "It's cold in here, don't you think?"

He lifted his hooded gaze, releasing her hand to feather his fingers over her collarbone. "I was thinking it was kind of hot."

The way his callused yet gentle fingers drifted to the edge of the towel was *hot*. The way his eyes caressed her face was really *hot*. The way his warm breath heated her cheek as he lowered his face to her hair was really, really *hot* and made her wonder if he wanted her right now as much as she wanted him. After what she'd witnessed today, she couldn't believe the thought had popped into her head. Was it possible that he still wanted her? Sure it was; he was a man. But she wanted a man who loved her. And Chance McBride couldn't give her what she wanted. Not now. Maybe not ever. She cleared her throat. "What are you doing?"

He rubbed his face in her hair. "Checking to make sure the solution worked."

She couldn't help herself, she leaned into all that hard muscle and warmth. *Maybe love is overrated*, her crazy side thought. *Don't you dare*, her sane side berated, *you deserve more than being a replacement for the woman he really wants*. She placed her palms on his wide chest and pushed. "It did." She sidestepped him. "I have to get dressed or we'll be late."

He gave his bowed head a slight shake before raising his gaze. "Late for what?"

"Everyone's going to Maddie and Gage's to help with the wedding favors. Your dad told you—"

He walked to the nightstand and picked up his beer. "Not happening."

"Ah, yeah, it is." She put her hands on her hips. "If I have to go, so do you."

"You don't have to go. We'll tell them the eau de Pepé hasn't worn off yet." She narrowed her eyes at him, and he laughed. "Come on, you don't really want to go. It's the perfect excuse. We'll hang out here, have a few beers, and pull a *Die Hard* marathon. I got you Rocky Road ice cream." He waggled his eyebrows at the mention of her once-favorite ice cream. She'd eaten so much of it during her he-just-wasn't-into-you funk that the sight of the flavor now made her sick.

And she'd probably end up feeling the same way if she agreed to share a night like he'd just described. It had been one of her favorite ways to spend time with him. Only the evening wouldn't have the same ending. "Good try. Your family's expecting you." She nodded at his beer. "How many have you had?"

"A couple."

Which probably explained his flirty behavior. "Fine, I'll drive."

"*You* are not driving *my* truck." He headed out of the room. "And I'm not going. Call your girls for a ride."

The last thing he needed was to be left on his own. "I am not calling *my girls*. You're going, and I'm driving." She put her hand on the door to close it behind him.

He backtracked, his stocking feet brushing up against her bare toes. "You're starting to piss me off, Slick. Careful or I'll let Princess out of her pen."

She had to tip her head back to meet his eyes. "You either go or our fake relationship is over. And, McBride, you don't want to test me. I have not had a great day."

"You're a pain in the ass, you know that?"

"So are you."

"Guess we're the perfect match, then."

\*     \*     \*

Chance scowled at her from the passenger side of his truck. "You're on a residential street, woman. Slow the hell down!"

"Stop yelling at me! You're making me nervous." Probably as nervous as he had been after he'd made his perfect match comment. He couldn't get out of the room fast enough. Which had been fine by her because, really, what was she supposed to say? *I thought we were, too.*

"Yeah, well, you're making me crazy. I'll have to take the truck into the garage tomorrow and have them check the . . . Jesus, you really do need to have your eyes checked. You just drove past Gage's street."

Vivi slammed on the brakes and put the truck in Reverse, ignoring Chance's pissed-off look as she turned onto his brother's street. He'd been in a mood ever since they'd left the cabin, and it had nothing to do with her driving. "You know pouting isn't attractive on a grown man, don't you?"

"I'm not pouting, smart-ass."

"Could've fooled me."

He stared out the window, the light from the streetlamps illuminating the hard angles of his face. "Cut me some slack, will you? Today hasn't exactly been a walk in the park."

She winced as she thought about what he'd dealt with over the last several hours and pulled in front of the McBrides' stone bungalow. Shutting off the engine, she shifted in the seat. She wanted to stroke the tension from his clenched jaw. Instead, she reached for his hand. "I know. I'm sorry, Chance. I'm so sorry you lost Kate and the baby. I can only imagine how difficult the past five years have been. How difficult today was for you." It was something she should have said earlier. But she'd been uncomfortable intruding on his grief. He'd never shared his real life or his loss with her. "If there's anything I can do to make this easier for you, I will."

He turned from the window, an unreadable emotion in his eyes as his gaze roamed her face. Then his mouth curved and he lifted his hand, threading his fingers through her hair. She let out a small, surprised gasp when he drew her closer. "You already have, Slick," he murmured.

His lips were tender against hers. No tongue or crazy passion, just a gentle touch. He kissed the side of her mouth, then nibbled lightly. Warmth flooded her body as his hand wandered over her before settling on her waist. He sifted the fingers of his other hand through her hair to caress the back of her neck. When he slanted his head and deepened the kiss, she pressed against him, unable to contain her breathy moan. Proof, she supposed, that she wanted him as much as she ever did. Maybe more because she now saw the man behind the mask.

She moved her hand from his thigh to his shoulder, her fingers curling in his crisp white shirt as the tips of their tongues touched and lingered. Was he trying to tell her that he wanted more from her than just sex? His words as much as his kiss seemed to imply that he did. A flutter of hope came to life inside her at the possibility. At the thought that, after finally having to face head-on the loss of his wife and baby, he could now move on with his life—with her.

*     *     *

Chance pulled back. It wasn't soon enough. One look into Vivi's beautiful violet eyes told him all he needed to know. He was an idiot. He shouldn't have kissed her. But she'd given him the soft and the sweet—her raspy voice heavy with sympathy. He couldn't take her pity. Not now.

He wanted his hard-ass Vivi back. The one with the biting, sarcastic sense of humor. The one who'd stood before him with all that smooth, olive skin on display, the skimpy towel wrapped around her incredible toned body. A body he'd buried himself in. A body that made him forget when he wanted to and when he didn't. He couldn't resist her siren call, even though he knew he should. If she hadn't pushed him away in his bedroom, reminded him about tonight, he wouldn't have stopped.

A mistake, just like the one he'd just made. He'd made too many with her today. Like telling her she was his perfect match. He'd been as surprised as she'd appeared to be when the words came out of his mouth.

Kate with her easy smile and easy laugh had been his perfect match. God, she'd been sweet. His beautiful, delicate wife who didn't have an aggressive bone in her body. She didn't care what was going on half a world away. All she cared about was creating a life and a family with him. She was happiest puttering around in her garden and making their house a home.

As the silence lengthened in the truck, a slow look of understanding came into Vivi's eyes. Her lips flattened. Good. And to ensure that pissed-off look remained, he shoved his fingers into her long, thick hair and messed it up.

Raising her hand to her head, she stared at him. "What the hell did you do that for?"

"We're dating, remember? They'll expect you to have bed head. And I guarantee that as soon as we pulled up, they all had their faces pressed against the window." With his desire for her not completely abated, he was pretty proud of himself for coming up with an excuse for that kiss. "Gotta put on a show."

She muttered something that sounded like "I'm such an idiot" before reaching in the backseat to grab the gift bags she'd brought with her.

"Don't tell me you've had a change of heart, Slick." If he screwed this up because he kissed her... "You offered to do anything to make this week easier, and this is it." He wasn't lying. He didn't want his family hovering over him, worrying about him. They wouldn't if they thought he and Vivi were together.

"Fine." She clutched the gift bags to her chest and opened the door. "But don't get handsy in there. My nieces are at impressionable ages."

"Handsy?" he said, fighting a grin.

"Yeah, no touching, kissing, or groping allowed."

"Come on. If I'm not groping you a little, they're going to think we're faking it." He patted her ass as they started up the driveway.

She nudged him with her elbow. "We *are* faking it."

"Keep your voice down. And remember what we talked about. We ran into each other when I was on a job in New York six months ago, and we've been seeing each other ever since."

She snorted as they reached the front steps. "Like Maddie and Skye are going to buy that. They know—"

As the door started to open, Chance hauled Vivi into his arms, shutting her up with a kiss. Madison and Skye stared at them with their jaws slack.

"Don't knee me," he whispered as he took his mouth from Vivi's. "We have an audience."

"Hey," she said to Madison and Skye, then shoved him. "McBride, I told you my nieces were at impressionable ages, so no more sticking your tongue down my throat."

"They're not even here. And they're my nieces, too." As she stalked into the house, he gave Madison and Skye a sheepish shrug. "She's not an easy woman."

"We know she isn't, but she's worth the effort. And you better be willing to put in the effort this time around or you'll answer to us," his sister-in-law informed him.

*Jesus.* Despite Vivi's decidedly unloving display, they actually believed they were together. And to prove it, Skye said, "I knew it was just a matter of time before you two got back together."

"I said the same thing to Gage. He didn't believe me until I explained about you being Super—"

Chance covered his sister-in-law's mouth with his hand. "Quiet. Vivi doesn't know, and she's not going to know, right?" She'd never go along with his plan if she found out he was indirectly responsible for her demotion at the *Spectator*.

His brother arrived at the door, his gaze moving from Chance to Madison. "Wanna tell me why you've got your hand over my wife's mouth?"

"She's a pain in the ass?"

Madison rolled her eyes and removed his hand. "He doesn't want Vivi to know he's her comic book hero," she informed her husband, thankfully in a quiet tone of voice.

"I don't know, Chance. Seems to me keeping a secret like that could ruin your relationship before it got started."

Madison patted Gage's arm. "While you try and talk some sense into your brother, we're going to get all the juicy details about their romance from Vivi, aren't we, Skye?"

"Oh, yes, we are. We want to hear how you won her over. Because knowing our best friend, you must have done some serious groveling." Skye pushed her long, curly, butterscotch-blonde hair from her face and grinned, giving him a hug. "I'm happy for you both. I knew you loved her."

"Thanks, sweet cheeks," he said, instead of denying his love for Vivi. It wasn't like he could argue the point when he was trying to convince them they were in a relationship. Sensing his brother wanted to have a word with him, Chance said, "Probably should get in there." He didn't feel up to a heart-to-heart with Gage, and he was nervous how Vivi would handle her best friend's questions. She wasn't exactly a woman who concealed her feelings.

He expelled a heavy sigh when Gage gave him an all-too-familiar look and stepped outside, closing the door behind him. "How are you doing? Dad told me he brought Natalee and Princess to the airport with him. If I had known, I would have given you a heads-up."

"Thanks, but I'm good. It was time anyway. Come on, we should get in there." He put his hand on the doorknob, anxious to end the conversation with his brother. Gage's sense of deduction was too finely honed.

"You okay staying at the cabin? You and Vivi are welcome here, you know."

"It's all good, Gage. Don't worry about me, okay?"

His brother looked out over the front yard. "Can't help worrying about you. You and Kate..." He shook his head and turned his sympathetic gaze on Chance. "I don't know how you do it. If anything happened to Madison..." He shoved his fingers through his dark hair, blowing out a breath. "Sorry, it's just that, until Madison came into my life, I don't think I truly understood the nightmare you've been living the last five years."

"Good thing you're not going to have to worry about that, then, isn't it?" Chance said tightly, looking up at the lavender-tinged Colorado sky.

His brother glanced at him, seemed to get that it was time to change the subject. "So, Dad's over the moon about you and Vivi. And Aunt Nell's grinning from ear to ear. I think she has you two in mind for her next book."

"Jesus. We're dating, that's all. No need to make a big deal out of it."

"But it is a big deal. You haven't..."

"Don't, okay? I'm hanging by a thread here, man. I can't keep..." It was the first time he'd been truly honest with his brother. He loved his family, but he'd shut them out and kept his distance for this very reason.

Gage slung an arm around his shoulders. "I've got your back, buddy. Come on, let's grab a beer. Tease Dad about the upcoming nuptials."

"You happy about the wedding?"

Gage frowned as he opened the front door. "Yeah, why, aren't you?"

He shrugged. "Not sure how I feel about it." The last Chance had heard, his dad had been dating Karen, a thirtysomething nurse, and Liz had been dating her son Ethan's campaign manager's father, Richard Stevens.

Annie and Lily, Gage's daughters, came running down the hall. "Hi, Uncle Chance," Lily said, wrapping her arms around his waist. "Thanks for our presents."

"Hey, Uncle Chance." Annie gave him a chin lift. "Thanks."

Vivi must have told the girls the presents were from him, too. He probably should have picked them up something. But he didn't really know the kids. He wasn't as

close to them as Vivi was. "No problem. Good to see..."
He broke off at the sound of raised feminine voices.

"You better get in there, Dad. Aunt Vivi said she's
going to throw Aunt Nell off the deck."

"I'm sure she was joking," Gage said to Annie as he
headed down the hall.

Chance doubted it and followed after him.

"No, she wasn't," Annie confirmed from behind him.
"Aunt Nell told Aunt Vivi she has to marry Uncle Chance
because they're doing the nasty and living in sin. She
wants them to have a double wedding with Grandpa and
Grandma Liz."

# Chapter Six

Sitting at the end of the dining room table, Maddie narrowed her blue eyes at Vivi. "Tell me again what he said when he saw you."

Vivi stifled a groan by popping one of the white chocolate hearts imprinted with Paul's and Liz's faces into her mouth. Honestly, between Maddie, Skye, and Nell wanting to know every last detail about Vivi's imaginary romance, she'd need copious amounts of chocolate to get through the next couple of hours. At least she got rid of Nell by threatening to throw her off the deck. Paul and Liz were out there with her now, laying down the law. Vivi snorted, as if that would work.

Maddie raised a brow, waiting for her response.

So she gave her one, just not the one she wanted. She held up a purple chocolate flower. "These things are orgasmic. Who needs a man when you have chocolate this good?"

Large hands settled on Vivi's shoulders, Chance's thumbs smoothing over the tense muscles along the sides of her neck. "Whoa, direct hit to the ego, Slick. I'm wounded."

Good, so was she. Her heart had taken a direct hit in the truck. She'd let her imagination run wild. Again. Which might have been the reason Nell's comment got to her. For a few fantasy-filled moments, Vivi had seen a future with Chance. She inwardly rolled her eyes. She had to stop letting him kiss her. It messed with her head. And she had to get him to stop touching her because right now his obvious attempt at relaxing her wasn't having the desired effect. She tipped her head back to look into his smiling face. "Your oversized ego can handle it, McBride."

Maddie laughed. "Don't worry, Chance, I said the same thing the first time I sampled one of Autumn's chocolates." Autumn Dane owned Christmas's candy shop, Sugar and Spice.

"Yeah, but that was before you were with me." Gage tugged on Maddie's shoulder-length blonde hair, then looked around the room. "Where's Nell?"

"On the deck with your dad and Liz. She..." Maddie trailed off when the French doors opened and the three of them came back inside.

Chance gave Vivi's shoulders a gentle squeeze. "Don't worry, I'll handle her."

"Good luck with that," she said, catching his great-aunt's gaze moving from her to Chance. Vivi popped another chocolate flower in her mouth and made a mental note to visit Sugar and Spice first thing tomorrow morning. She'd probably gain ten pounds before the week was out.

"Maddie ate sweets like you when she was pregnant

with Connor. Anything you want to share with us, girlie?" Nell asked, waggling her eyebrows.

Vivi choked on the chocolate.

"Aunt Nell," Chance gritted out at the same time as he patted Vivi's back.

"Nell, what did we just talk about?" Paul said.

"I'm just askin'. I don't understand what the…" she began, then looked at Chance and winced.

"I'm good," Vivi told Chance, whose patting was a little more forceful than necessary. She imagined Nell's comment was just one more reminder of what he'd lost. Looking repentant, Nell had obviously realized the same thing and took the seat across from Vivi.

Liz, with a smile on her pretty, tanned face, broke the strained silence. "Chance, it's so good to see you." She rounded the table to give him a hug. "Your father and I are so happy you could come home for the wedding. It wouldn't have been the same without you."

"Yeah, thanks. Good to see you, too."

Vivi shot him a surprised glance. She'd assumed he'd be as happy as Gage and Maddie were about the wedding, but from his less-than-enthusiastic response, he wasn't. Vivi shared a what's-going-on look with Maddie. Her best friend gave an almost imperceptible shrug.

Nell, who'd been watching Liz and Chance with a furrowed brow, turned to Vivi. "So, what the Sam Hill were you thinking picking up a skunk? Paul, you should probably start a round of those antirabies shots." She reached across the table and patted Vivi's hand. "Don't worry, I hear they don't hurt *much*."

Vivi knew what Nell was up to. And while she appreciated her attempt to take the focus off Chance and Liz,

Vivi wished she would have used something or someone else as a distraction. Which she conveyed to the older woman with a smackdown stare. Nell grinned.

Skye, who'd been walking back into the dining room, froze. Her caramel-colored eyes widened. "You have rabies?"

"No, I don't have—" Vivi began, only to be cut off by Paul.

His concerned gaze shifted from Vivi to his son. "Are you sure you—"

"Dad, she's fine. Not a scratch to be found. And I checked every inch of her very, very thoroughly, didn't I, honey?" His voiced dripped with sexual innuendo.

Vivi shoved another chocolate in her mouth. "Um-hm."

"Okay, ladies, let's get these wedding favors made up before Vivi eats all the chocolates," Maddie said.

Vivi swallowed and looked at the rows upon rows of white-lace-covered boxes they had to fill with the chocolates. "Wait a minute, how come they don't have to help?" She patted the chair next to her. "Sit right here, *honey*. I'll teach you how to tie the ribbons."

Chance snorted and rubbed her head, messing up her hair. Again. "Wouldn't want to show you up. Besides, it's women's work." His comment earned groans from everyone in the room. "What?" He looked at his father and brother. "Back me up here."

Eyebrows raised, Maddie and Liz waved boxes at Gage and Paul. His father and brother gave Chance way-to-go looks before sitting beside Liz and Maddie. Vivi fluttered her lashes and smiled at Chance as he pulled out the chair beside her. "You really are a pain in the ass," he muttered, picking up a box.

She held back a smart-ass response when she saw the way he looked at the chocolate heart imprinted with Paul and Liz's picture. She glanced down the table at Gage laughing with Maddie, Paul doing the same with Liz, and nudged Chance with her knee. He looked at her, his once clean-shaven jaw now beard-stubbled and tight. "What's going on?"

"Kind of weird seeing them together like this," he said in a voice that only she would hear.

She imagined it was. From what she'd heard, Chance's mother, Anna, had been a wonderful woman, beloved by her husband and sons. She bumped his arm with her shoulder. "He's happy."

As he watched his father tuck Liz's toffee-colored hair behind her ear, Chance lifted a shoulder. "You got me into this, so show me what I'm supposed to do."

An hour later, he said, "Slick, we're falling behind. Lily and Annie have doubled our output, and they sat down fifteen minutes ago."

Vivi looked across the table. He was right. "They're crafty kids with nimble fingers. You're not crafty and your fingers are too big."

"Never had any complaints before," he said, trailing his index finger down her arm with a suggestive grin.

She'd walked right into that one. The reason they were behind had nothing to do with his big fingers, which, as she well knew, were extremely agile and talented. No, the problem was that every time his father and Liz started talking about the wedding, Chance distracted himself by touching and flirting with Vivi. "Go have a beer. I'll be faster without you. You keep interrupting me to attach your flowers. This is an individual sport, you know. Not a team one."

"Okay, I want to hear you say it. Chance, you were right. Women"—he glanced at her boxes—"most women, are better at doing this shit than men."

"Your dad and Gage don't seem to have a problem. And just so you know, this bow is perfect." She held up the box, feeling quite proud of herself.

With an amused glint in his eyes, he said, "I did that one," and pointing to the box beside her elbow, "you did that one."

He was right. "Go have a beer." A sidelong glance revealed Skye and Maddie sharing an aw-they're-so-cute look. Vivi sighed and reached for another chocolate. The platter was empty. She did an internal happy dance and said, "Looks like we're done."

Paul and Gage got up from the table as fast as Chance did. "You kids did a great job. Thanks for helping out." Liz smiled at Paul. "You too, honey." Chance's dad leaned over and whispered in Liz's ear. Her cheeks pinked. "Yes, you have very skilled hands."

"Didn't need to hear that," Chance muttered, heading for the kitchen. His brother and father followed after him.

Liz bit her lip as she watched the three men walk away, then turned to Vivi and asked in a low voice, "Has Chance said anything about me and his dad getting married?"

Before Vivi could answer, Maddie said to the girls, "Lily and Annie, it's time to get in your pj's."

"Aw, Mom, it's Friday night. We..." Annie started to complain. Maddie shooed them off with the promise of a movie and popcorn.

"No, he hasn't—"

Skye interrupted Vivi. "It's been a tough day for him, Liz. Don't read anything into it. Everyone's happy you and Paul are getting married. I'm sure Chance is, too."

"It's just that he was so close to Anna. I don't want him to think I'm trying to take his mother's place. I loved her. She was my best friend." Liz twisted her diamond engagement ring. "It's no wonder he's having a hard time with us getting married." She shook her head when Maddie and Skye objected. "No, don't try and spare my feelings. It's obvious he's not happy. I don't know why I expected this to be easy. Look how long it took me to get over feeling guilty and admit my feelings for Paul. Do you think it would help if I talk to him, Vivi?"

"Umm, I, ah—" she began, only to be cut off by Nell this time.

"Leave Chance to Vivi. She'll talk to him and make things right, won't you, girlie?" the older woman said.

Vivi didn't get it. They'd picked up on Chance's feelings toward the wedding, so why hadn't they figured out that he and Vivi were faking it? And why the hell did they expect her to fix the man? Especially Maddie and Skye, who nodded in agreement with Nell. They knew Vivi wasn't one of those empathetic, maternal women who'd have a heart-to-heart with perfect strangers and do everything in her power to make them feel better. Unless they thought that now that she was an advice columnist, she'd turned into one. Obviously, they hadn't been reading her column.

Rubbing her forehead with the heel of her palm, Vivi reluctantly nodded. What else was she supposed to do?

Chance returned to the dining room with a beer in his hand. His brow furrowed, he sifted his cold fingers through her hair and rested them at the nape of her neck. "What's wrong? You have a headache?"

Because Skye and Maddie shared another one of their they're-so-cute looks and this time Nell got in on the act, humming what sounded like "Going to the Chapel" under her breath, Vivi said, "Yeah. Once you finish your beer, we probably should get going."

Chance looked like he wanted to high-five her. "We'll go now."

A phone rang in the kitchen. Moments later, Gage walked into the dining room with a grim expression on his face. He went to Maddie and kissed her cheek. "I've gotta take off."

"What's going on?" Maddie asked.

"Pharmacy was broken into. They tied Larry up and cleaned him out."

"They're getting bolder. You better find these guys before someone gets hurt, Gage."

"Doing my best, Dad."

"Larry has a good security system, cameras. You should be able to get something off them," Chance said.

Vivi glanced at the man beside her. Sometimes she forgot he'd once been Christmas's sheriff and now provided security for some very powerful clients.

"Haven't so far. They're smart. Security systems are disabled before they go in. This is the first time we've had a witness. Hopefully Larry will be able to give us something."

"How many drugstores have they hit?" Chance asked his brother.

"In the last six months, five, spread across two counties."

"Drug ring," Chance said, his expression hard as his eyes narrowed at his brother. "You looking at Callahan?"

Gage held up his hand. "Don't. Don't go there, Chance.

There's never been any proof to tie him to . . . You gotta let it go."

Their exchange was about more than a spate of robberies. This was personal. Vivi felt it in the dangerous, scary vibe Chance was giving off. There was a story here, and she wanted to know what it was. "Who's Callahan?"

Chance gave her an inscrutable look that reminded her exactly what he did for a living. "Stay out of it, Slick."

\*     \*     \*

No matter that he'd consumed more than his usual quota of beer, Chance knew he wouldn't be able to sleep in the bed he'd shared with his wife. It's why, despite Vivi's protests, he insisted she take the master bedroom. Now, lying in the bed in the guest bedroom, Chance decided the odds were still against him getting any sleep.

Vivi's voice came through the wall between the bedrooms. "There's a Darwin Callahan who lived in Logan County. Can't be him though. He's serving eight years for carrying chemicals for the purpose of making meth. Unless . . . You don't think he's running a drug ring from jail, do you?"

She hadn't let up on the drive home or during *A Good Day to Die Hard*. Since she liked that movie as much as he did, he figured the only way to shut her down was to go to bed. Obviously, his strategy hadn't worked. The woman was like a dog with a bone. She'd never give up. And he needed her to. He didn't want her anywhere near Callahan. He should have hidden her laptop and cell phone. "One more word out of you, and I'm letting Princess out." He patted the dog curled up at his side when Vivi didn't respond. He should have threatened her with Princess earlier.

Chance had just started to nod off when he heard, "Did you let Cujo out of your room?"

"No. Go to sleep or I will."

"Are you sure she's with you? Because I hear something scratching."

"Probably just the branches on the roof."

He heard the bed creak and the window sliding open. He pictured her sticking her head out the window to investigate. She didn't disappoint. "No, it's not the same sound. It's more like this." She scratched on the adjoining wall, and he started to laugh.

"Are you laughing at me?"

"No, I—" The sound of the window slamming shut cut him off.

"Chance. Chance, there's a bear."

"It's too dark for you to make out a bear. But so what if there is. You're in here, and it's out there."

"I don't find that a comforting thought, thank you very much."

A pack of coyotes howled.

"I'm living in the freaking Wild Kingdom."

"Go to sleep, Vivi," he said, unable to keep the laughter from his voice.

"Yeah, it's real hilarious, McBride." She sounded like she was punching her pillow.

Ears perked, Princess got up at the same time Chance heard the skittering of tiny feet in the ceiling over his head. Mice. A lot of mice. Looked like he'd be heading to the hardware store first thing in the morning. He patted the dog, listening for Vivi. When she didn't start yelling, he relaxed and closed his eyes.

They shot open when she screamed his name. He jumped

from the bed, grabbing the boxers he'd dropped on the floor. "I'm coming," he called out, hopping on one foot as he pulled them on. "Stay," he ordered the dog.

Chance flung open the door to the master bedroom and rushed inside, flipping the light switch. Vivi stood on the pillows in a black T-shirt and panties, pointing to the floor. "Mouse," she said in a strangled whimper. "It was . . . it was on the bed. A mouse."

"Okay, honey. Calm down." A tremor shuddered through her as he stroked her arm with one hand while shaking out the sheets with the other. "If there was a mouse, it's gone now."

"There was a mouse. I wasn't imagining things."

He didn't think she was. Not that he'd tell her that. "I'll be right back."

"Where are you going?"

"To get Princess."

"Right, like it's better to have my feet chewed off by a dog rather than a mouse."

"She'll sleep on the floor. Bed's too high for her to jump up on, and she's a mouser."

"Doesn't make me feel much better, McBride. The mouse is probably bigger than she is," Vivi called after him.

She was on her hands and knees when he returned, skimming her palms across the mattress. That was one view he didn't need to see and neither did Princess, who growled. Chance turned off the light and put Princess in her dog bed on the floor, then walked over to Vivi.

"Get under the covers."

She glanced from Princess, to him, to the bed. "Ah, maybe it's a good idea if you sleep here, too."

It wasn't, but in terms of either of them getting some sleep, he didn't think he had much choice. "Move over." He climbed in beside her.

She did as he asked. Then as soon as he stretched out, she moved in beside him with a full-body shiver. He sighed and wrapped an arm around her, tucking her close. She'd end up there anyway. Vivi was a snuggler, which seemed at odds with her personality. It had surprised him the first night he'd slept with her. Guess she hadn't changed.

"Jesus," he said when her ice-cold feet brushed against his leg. "I should have been prepared for that. Your feet were always freezing."

She lifted his arm, moving away from him to lie flat on her back and stare up at the ceiling. Part of him was glad she did, while the other part of him wanted her cuddled up next to him.

"Why did you leave without saying good-bye?" she asked in her raspy voice. If she was ever short of cash, she could make a fortune with that voice. It made a man think of hot sex and tangled sheets. He pushed the thought aside. She deserved an explanation.

He rolled to his side to face her. "I got a call at four in the morning with information I had to act on right away. I didn't want to wake you up." Her brow arched. "Saying good-bye, it's not something I'm good at, Vivi."

"I deserved at least that, Chance."

He was glad he couldn't make out the color of her eyes, see them change from violet to purple to black. She was the type of woman you want to make love to in broad daylight or with the lights on. And she was the one woman who'd gotten to him. "Yeah, you did. But I couldn't give you what you wanted or deserved. It was better to make a clean break."

"Maybe for you it was."

Turns out it wasn't. He hadn't been able to stay away from her. Not completely. And now, thanks to Nell, they were traveling down a road he had no intention of going. It was a dead end.

"I'm sorry." He leaned in and kissed her. He meant for it to be a brief, comforting touch, but her mouth softened, her lips parted, and that was all it took to make him forget the danger of succumbing to her siren call. With Vivi, he'd never had much control. He should have left after his first night with her. Just like he should make himself stop now.

Pulling back, he framed her face with his hands. "Nothing's going to change, Slick. I can't give you more than this."

"Maybe this is all I want."

He searched her eyes, wishing he could read the emotion lurking in their dark depths. Then nothing mattered but the way her body felt pressed against his. She ran her cold, bare foot along his leg, curling her hand behind his neck to draw his mouth to hers. "Life's short, Chance. We might as well take what we want while we can."

No one had to tell him that life was too short or that it changed in an instant. He'd seen too many good people cut down in the prime of life. As those memories threatened to overcome him once more, he did what he'd wanted to do since she got on that plane. He lost himself in Vivi. The one woman guaranteed to make him forget everything.

# Chapter Seven

Vivi woke up in the sun-filled room with a sense of everything being right in the world. The feeling warmed her from the top of her head to the tips of her toes. Weird, she thought, and kind of wonderful, too. There hadn't been much to smile about, let alone be happy about, these last few months. Now, thanks to the man taking up three quarters of the king-size bed, there was. She was exactly where she belonged. And if she weren't dying for a cup of coffee, she'd stay snuggled up to Chance's back, waiting for him to roll over with a lazy smile and take her in his arms.

Like he did every morning in New York. Only then she'd made an early morning run to Bagel Bagel and Roasters Coffee, sharing all that New York goodness with him in bed before he shared all his goodness with her. The man's ego was truly well deserved. And after the night they'd shared, she could now relive those memories without the tarnish of bitterness and recrimination. She smiled and planted a soft kiss on his warm, golden skin before carefully moving away in order not to wake him.

She froze at the sound of a low growl. Cujo. Vivi peeked over Chance's shoulder. The dog bared its razor-sharp teeth, snarling at her, the intruder in its master's bed. Kate and Chance's bed. The reminder cast a shadow over the glow of happiness that only moments ago had enveloped her. Vivi lay back down, staring up at the dust-covered ceiling fan.

Kate's presence may be boxed away in the other room, but she was here—in Cujo's heart and Chance's. Vivi'd gone into last night with her eyes wide open. This time she knew the risk, but she'd been willing to take it. He was worth it. He needed time to move on, that's all. Being with Liz and Paul had given her hope. A hope that had burned brighter with every kiss, every touch, every word Chance had whispered to her. If Paul and Liz, who'd been happily married to their one-and-onlys for decades, could move on, so could Chance. And last night, he'd taken what she believed to be a big step in that direction. He'd made love to her in his and Kate's home, in their bed.

"Quiet, Princess." Chance's gruff, sleep-laden voice startled her from her thoughts.

As he rolled onto his back, she waited expectantly for the smile she remembered, for him to wrap her in his strong arms. Instead, he looked around the room as if he didn't know where he was. She opened her mouth to say good morning, but as his gaze slid over her, he muttered a curse, covering his eyes with his forearm. Far from the reaction she'd hoped for. Lying tense and still under the covers, she wondered what to say. If she should say anything or leave him to deal with whatever he was dealing with on his own.

She decided to ignore his reaction and lighten the mood. The room and Chance were giving off a heavy-enough vibe. "If you keep Cujo from eating my feet, I'll put the coffee on."

As she threw back the covers and sat up, his fingers closed around her wrist. She glanced over her shoulder. "Don't worry, I know how you like…" She trailed off, her gaze unable to make the journey from his body to his face. And it wasn't his spectacular washboard abs and sculpted chest that caused her breath to catch in her throat; it was the ink on his pec. Kate and Emma's names with the words *Never Forget* burned into his skin over his heart. He'd hadn't had the tattoo when they were together in New York.

She raised her gaze and met his, forcing a smile to cover her reaction. "Black enough to curl the hair on your chest, right?"

"I'll take care of it." He let go of her wrist without returning her smile and swung his long legs over the side of the bed. Cujo barked and danced like a dog in a circus act, performing for her master, who sat on the edge of the bed with his broad shoulders bowed. Vivi's discomfort grew as the minutes ticked by.

He scrubbed his hands over his face, then picked up the dog and stood. She couldn't take her eyes off his powerfully built frame as he padded to the bedroom door. He stopped, half turning to focus on the window above her head. Self-consciously, she drew the sheet over her chest.

"I think it'd be best if you stay with Madison and Gage, Vivi."

She didn't know what she'd expected him to say, but it wasn't that. "You want me to leave?" She cringed when her voice came out sounding pathetic and sad.

His green eyes moved to her face, and he winced. "Vivi, I—"

"Don't." The last thing she wanted from him was another apology. At least this time he'd been honest with her. It was her fault for thinking anything had changed. For believing what she felt for him was enough until he got over Kate. That Vivi would be the one to heal his broken heart, the way Liz and Paul had healed each other's.

"I appreciate what you did for me. More than you know."

"I'm pretty sure I got as much out of last night as you did, Chance." She held the sheet to her chest, snagging her panties and T-shirt off the floor. "Now, if you don't mind, I'd like to get dressed."

When he didn't move, she got off the bed and yanked on her T-shirt. It wasn't as if he hadn't seen her naked before, and he didn't have any qualms about standing in front of her without his clothes on. She supposed if she looked like he did, she wouldn't have a problem with it, either.

He cleared his throat as she tugged on her panties. "I was talking about pretending to be in a relationship with me, not last night. Yesterday wasn't easy; having you here made it easier."

And yet he was kicking her to the curb. Again. She pushed the thought aside. She'd come to Christmas to get him out of her heart and her head. Instead, he was taking up more space than he had before. It was time for her to do what she'd set out to. To move on from him once and for all.

"I'm glad it did. If you'd let me, I'd help you move past losing Kate and the baby. But you're not ready. Maybe you never will be. Maybe you don't want to." She held his gaze. He'd been honest with her, and now she'd be honest with him. No matter what that honesty would cost her. "I fell in love with you, you know. So I wasn't really pretending yesterday. But it was hard. Probably harder on me than it was on you." A wary, pained expression deepened the fine lines at the corners of his eyes, the ones bracketing his beautiful mouth. "Don't worry, Chance. This was more for me than you. You were right last night when you told me I deserved more than you had to offer. I do."

\*       \*       \*

Princess barked, and Chance turned from where he stood staring out at the lake with a cup of coffee in hand.

Vivi's raspy voice came from down the hall. "Bye to you, too, Cujo. Can't say I'll miss you. You or the mice, skunks, wolves, bears, and whatever the hell else lurks in those woods."

At any other time, her comment would have made him smile. Only he didn't feel much like smiling this morning. He'd woken to the gut-wrenching realization that he'd made love to a woman in his wife's bed. In the morning light, with Kate's subtle citrus scent lingering in the room, he'd felt her presence as sharply as if she stood beside him—looking down on him and the woman he'd replaced her with. The woman who made him forget where he was. It had nothing to do with the beer he'd consumed last night. He'd been drunk on Vivi.

Vivi, who loved him. A woman who, if he said the word, would stick by him until he worked through his grief and his guilt. Accept whatever he had left to give her. But he hadn't said a word. And now he'd probably lost her for good. He didn't want to lose her. He liked being with her. She made him feel alive again, like there was something worth living for.

Dragging the sparkly floral suitcase behind her, she walked into the open space wearing a white shirt tied at her waist, a pair of frayed denim shorts, and flip-flops. Her white lacy bra and the curve of her breasts were visible through the water marks left by her long, damp hair. Another reminder of what he stood to lose if he let her walk out of his life. He'd never get to kiss her beautiful face again, touch her smooth skin, or bury himself in her gorgeous body.

A dull ache expanded in his chest. Just thinking of Vivi that way made him feel disloyal to Kate—his golden girl. His first and only love. No, he hadn't been a monk these past five years. Far from it. Only with Vivi, it wasn't just about sex, and that was the problem. He didn't know if he could fix it. Didn't know if he wanted to.

"Hey." Vivi lifted her chin. "Maddie's picking me up after she drops Lily at baseball practice."

"I would have dropped you off."

"I didn't want to put you out," she said, doing her best to avoid looking at him as she hefted her carry-on over her shoulder.

"You wouldn't be putting me out. I have to go into town anyway." He didn't add that he needed to pick up mousetraps. Though he guessed it didn't matter if he told her that now. She wouldn't be here.

"I'll see you around," she said, heading toward the mudroom. "Take care."

"Wait, don't go." He didn't want her to leave, not like this. She turned with an expectant look in her eyes. He tried to think of something to say to take away the sting of his rejection, to let her know how much he cared about her, how much she meant to him, but all that came out of his mouth was, "Madison won't be here for a while. I'll make you a cup of coffee. I've got bagels, too, if you want one."

She tilted her head. "You got me bagels?"

Uncomfortable with the soft look that came over her face, he nodded and walked to the kitchen. He didn't know what the big deal was. The woman loved her bagels. She hesitated, and for a minute, he didn't think she'd stay. The band of tension across his shoulders loosened when she set her carry-on beside her suitcase on the floor.

He poured her coffee. "Quarter cup of cream and four sugars, just the way you like it."

"Only when you make it, McBride. Thanks." She wrapped both hands around the mug as she rested her hip against the counter and looked across the living room. "Pretty view. Any giant eels or sea creatures hanging out in there?"

Okay, this was more like it. They could do the friends thing, he thought, smiling as he put a couple of bagels in the toaster. "You're a real city girl, aren't you?"

"I'm all about self-preservation. I'll take a mugger over a bear any day."

She probably could, and would, take on a mugger. Which wasn't the most comforting of thoughts. "So what's on the agenda today? You girls have stuff to do for the wedding?" he asked, pulling a tub of cream cheese and a jar of strawberry jam from the refrigerator to set on the counter.

"Thanks," she said when he handed her a bagel and a knife. "I have to check my list, but I think we're picking up stuff for the bachelorette party tonight. What about you?"

"I've got some things to take care of around here before Dad's bachelor party tonight."

She glanced at him as she slathered cream cheese on her bagel. "You should hang out with your dad today."

"He's probably busy with Liz. I'll see him at the Penalty Box tonight." He watched expectantly as she bit into the bagel. "Not bad, huh?" For some inexplicable reason, he wanted her to like them as much as Bagel Bagel.

"Not as good as Bagel Bagel, but close." She added another inch of cream cheese. "I'm sure Liz and your dad would love to hang out with you today. Why don't you give him a call?"

"Like I said, I've got stuff to do and so do they." He couldn't take his eyes from her mouth, swallowing a groan when she swiped the tip of her tongue over her upper lip.

"Liz is worried you're not happy about the wedding. Is she right?"

He dragged his gaze from her mouth. "My dad's old enough to know what he wants. If he wants to get married, that's his business."

"You didn't answer my question."

"Leave it alone, Slick." He snapped the lid on the cream cheese.

"If you can't be happy for them, the least you can do is fake it." She wiped her hands on her shorts and picked up her phone, sighing as she read a text.

"What's up?"

She pressed her lips together. "Nell."

"Don't worry about my aunt. I'll tell her we're on a break, and she'll leave you alone."

"It's taken care of."

An uneasy feeling came over him when she wouldn't look him in the eyes. "What do you mean?"

She shrugged. "We had an agreement, remember? I told Maddie and Skye that I broke it off. Obviously, Nell's already heard the news." She held up her phone as evidence.

"They won't believe you."

Her eyes narrowed. "Why wouldn't they?"

"Because they know you're in…" He stopped before he said "love with me." He didn't want to piss her off.

She flipped her hair over her shoulder and snorted. "Get over yourself. I have."

"Less than an hour ago you told me you're in love with me, and now you're not?" The thought that she didn't love him should make him happy. Oddly enough, it didn't.

She ignored him, typing, he assumed, a response to Nell. Then she lifted her head and gave him a thin smile. "There, that takes care of that. Now no one will think I'm pining after you, McBride."

"What did you do?"

A horn beeped. "There's my ride. Thanks for the bagel and coffee."

He followed behind her, flattening his palm on the door above her head. "Vivi, what did you do?"

She looked at him over her shoulder. "I let Nell fix me up with Dr. McSexy. We have a coffee date Monday at eleven. Now, if you don't mind, I have things to do."

# Chapter Eight

I like your answers, but this one's kind of mean, Auntie."
Lily looked up from Maddie's iPad to give Vivi a disappointed glance.

Annie leaned across Vivi to look at the screen her sister held up. "Which one are you talking about?"

Lying between the two girls in Maddie's bed, Vivi
thumbed to the letter Lily referred to on her own iPad. It
was one where she'd taken a kinder and gentler approach.
She'd told Dumped in Duluth to stop jumping through
hoops to make the men she dated happy and twirl one
around her waist instead. Not a man, a hoop. "What do you
think?" Vivi asked Annie. She trusted her opinion more
than Lily's. Lily was the more tenderhearted of the two.

"It's kinda harsh. Maybe if you hadn't listed all the
dumb things she did first in caps with all the question
marks, it would have been okay."

Vivi sighed. Sounded like she needed to work a little

harder on losing the kick-butt attitude. After her morning with Chance, that would take some effort. How many women had she advised over the last few months to never say the three words that were guaranteed to make a man run for the door? And Chance had already been halfway out of it when she'd said them. "Okay, from now on, I'm sending you guys my column to proofread first."

"If you lived here, we could come over to your house and help you. Uncle Chance—" Lily began before Vivi cut her off.

"I love you guys, but I can't move here. I have a good job in New York. And your uncle and I... we're not dating anymore." She'd known all along the charade with Chance would end up biting her in the butt. Only it had turned out worse than she'd imagined.

"He said you're on a break. That's not the same thing as being broken up forever."

Did he now? Maybe she should have stuck around when he'd arrived twenty minutes ago to pick up Gage for the bachelor party. She could have cleared up any misconceptions then, but she hadn't been ready for another up-close-and-personal so soon after her humiliating morning. Using work as an excuse, she'd taken off for Maddie's room before he'd made it through the front door. Annie and Lily hadn't left her alone for long. Probably a good thing. She hadn't had more than five minutes to wallow in self-pity.

"Lily—" Vivi began before Annie piped up beside her.

"Yes it does. Uncle Chance just said that so everyone would leave Aunt Vivi alone. I don't know why you want her to date him anyway. You heard Dad. He was worried Uncle Chance would hurt her again. He's still in love with—"

"Annie! That's private. You're going to make Auntie cry."

"It's okay, Lily. I—" Vivi began, giving Lily's hand a comforting squeeze.

"I am not." Annie shot Vivi a worried look. "I'm not, am I?"

"No, sweetie. Of course, you're not. I'm fine. I have a date on Monday, you know." She infused her voice with as much enthusiasm as she could muster while thinking she should probably thank Nell. Even though she was kind of worried what the older woman was up to. Because knowing Nell, she had to be up to something.

"Who with?" the girls asked in unison.

"Dr., um…" She racked her brain for his name. When she got nothing, she said, "McSexy."

"Auntie, he's got a name, you know," Annie said, her thirteen-year-old voice infused with disapproval. "How would you like it if someone called you Vivi McSexy?"

Actually, she wouldn't mind. Her ego could use a boost right about now. Having a man kick you out of his bed after one of the most incredible nights of your life was kind of demoralizing.

"I don't think you should date Dr. Trainer," Lily said.

She made a mental note of his last name. "Why? Don't you like him?"

"Yes, but Auntie Skye said Uncle Chance's eyes aren't sad when he's with you." Lily's chin quivered. "He lost his wife and his baby, and now he's going to lose you, too."

What was wrong with everyone? Couldn't they keep their thoughts to themselves when the kids were in hearing distance? Vivi planned to have a conversation with her best friends before the night was over. "Sweetie, he—"

"All right, you guys, the guests are starting to arrive. I could use a hand putting out the…" Maddie, wearing skinny black pants and a black-and-white knit top, came into the room, her gaze moving over their faces. "What's wrong?"

"Nothing. Lily and Annie were critiquing this week's column for me." Vivi wondered if she had time to make the necessary changes to her response to Dumped in Duluth. It was amazing how that simple thought shifted her focus from her being a dumpee herself. Work had always been her salvation. Given all the times she'd buried herself in her job, she should be editor in chief by now. Though she'd be more than satisfied just to get her old position back. Something she should be worrying about instead of whether or not Lily repeated their conversation to her mother.

Toward that end, she put her arms around the girls, giving them both a noisy kiss. "You guys were a big help. Thanks for saving your aunt Vivi's butt. What?" she said when the three of them stared at her.

"You sound a little manic. Are you okay?" Maddie asked.

Annie scowled at her sister. "Lily's making her feel bad for ending it with Uncle Chance."

"Am not."

"Are so. You should be happy she broke up with him. Uncle Chance doesn't care about anybody but himself. He's been home two times in five years." She shoved two fingers at her sister. "How do you think that made Grandpa and Dad feel? Now he's being mean to Grandma Liz."

"You're a poopie head, Annie. It's not his fault. His wife and baby died and broke his heart. He just needs someone to put it back together again. You could do it, Auntie. I know you could. You help people all the time." Lily pointed at the iPad, her big brown eyes pleading and tear-filled.

Vivi wrapped her arms around her sweet, tenderhearted niece. If she had as much faith in her ability to heal Chance as Lily did, she might be willing to take another shot. "I wish I could, sweetie. I really do."

Annie rubbed her sister's arm. "I didn't mean to make you sad."

"It's okay." Lily sniffed.

Maddie sat on the edge of the bed beside Lily. "Honey, we all feel bad about what happened to Kate and baby Emma, but we can't make Uncle Chance feel better. That's something he has to do for himself. We just have to be there for him if he needs us."

"Hey, girls, look who decided to join the party." Skye came into the room with her five-month-old daughter Evie in her arms. They had on matching outfits: white pants, pink sweaters and pink ballet slippers. Skye's wide smile faded. "Lily, what's wrong?"

"I'm just sad." Lily said, turning to give the baby a tremulous smile. She reached for Evie's hand. Which the blonde cherub promptly stuck in her mouth. Lily giggled. "I think she's hungry."

"She better not be. I just fed her ten minutes ago." Skye smiled. "Do you wanna come play with her in the living room?"

"That's a great idea, isn't it, Lily? Maybe Connor will wake up and they can play together," Annie said, apparently looking for a way to distract her sister.

Obviously it worked because Lily jumped off the bed.

"Hey, you two. No waking up your brother. I just got him to sleep," Maddie called after the girls.

Skye walked toward the door. "I'll make sure they don't. And I'll be expecting you guys to fill me in. Don't be long. Liz should be here any minute now."

"We'll be right out," Maddie promised, flopping down on the bed when Skye shut the door behind her. "What brought that on?"

"Chance saying we're on a break, I think. And you guys seem to forget there's little ears in the house. They've overheard stuff they shouldn't."

"Really?" Maddie grimaced. "We'll have to be more careful." She took Vivi's hand. "You did a good job of avoiding me today. I haven't had a chance to ask if you're all right. Are you sure you want to break up with him? He seems to want—"

She had to shut this down. "What you said to Lily is true, he's not ready to move on. Who knows if he ever will be. It was easy to pretend in New York. It's not so easy to do that here." She hesitated, realizing that she veered too close to the truth. "The longer we were together, I realized I didn't know him as well as I thought. He loves his cabin. And I don't. Besides being sprayed by a skunk, last night I saw a bear and heard a wolf, and I swear to God the place is infested with rats that are bigger than that dog he loves. I hate dogs, and I hate the woods. And he's moody and makes a horrible cup of coffee."

"Vivi Westfield, you've been my best friend for ten years. Do you honestly think I can't tell when you're lying?"

"What? You don't believe that's he's moody and makes horrible coffee?"

"No, I don't believe that you dated him for six months without telling me and Skye."

She rubbed her temple. "I told him you wouldn't buy it. But everything else I said is true. This was good for me. I can move on now."

"You sure about that?"

"Totally. And no more poor-Vivi looks from either you or Skye."

"You're going to tell her?"

"Yes, on the condition she doesn't tell Ethan or anyone else. Same goes for you. Chance doesn't want or need everyone fawning all over him, looking at him like he's a step away from falling over the edge."

"Is he?"

"Maybe. I don't know. He'll have to figure that out for himself."

"You're being a little harsh, don't you think?"

She shrugged. "I tried, Maddie. It didn't work."

"You're protecting yourself from being hurt, you know that, right?"

"Probably. And I'm fine with that."

"But what if it means that you're giving up on the one man who will make you truly happy?"

"I don't need a man to make me happy."

"No, that honor goes to your job, doesn't it?"

"So what if it does."

"I love you, Vivi, but sometimes you can be a real hard-ass."

Just like her grandmother. She would have been pleased as all get out to hear Vivi referred to as a hard-ass. As a young girl she may have wished that her grandmother had been less abrasive and more loving, but Vivi now appreciated the protective wall she'd taught her to build around her heart. "Let's hope some of that rubs off on my niece. We've got to do something about Lily, Maddie. Toughen her up or something. She's like this little empathetic sponge, soaking up everyone's emotions."

"Being sensitive and emotional doesn't make you weak, Vivi." Maddie angled her head, listening to the voices in the hall. "Nell's here. We better get out there before she comes looking for us."

*      *      *

An hour into Liz's shower, Vivi was cured of any secret wedding desires she may have harbored. She'd never thought of herself as the marrying kind until she'd met Chance. The man had a way of putting dreams in her head that had no business being there. As he'd proven this morning. So she supposed she should be grateful the newlywed game they'd played earlier had squashed any thoughts of white weddings that may have been lurking in her subconscious.

With a toilet-paper veil on her head from the last game, Vivi stood in the circle of laughing women, watching as the wedding bouquet moved from hand to hand. Since her goal was to be eliminated first, she angled her head to see the moment Annie raised her finger to shut off the music. She caught Liz's daughter Cat O'Connor doing the same thing. "No way," Vivi said to Cat, whose long, wispy bangs peeked out from beneath the voluminous toilet-paper veil covering her short dark hair.

"Way," Cat said, widening her stance as she narrowed her thick-lashed green eyes in Annie's direction.

"Your mother will be disappointed if you're out first," Vivi said, keeping a close eye on Annie's finger.

"Yeah, well, Nell will be—"

The music stopped. Vivi hip-checked Cat and grabbed the bouquet from Skye, who stood on the other side of her. "I'm out," Vivi made sure to sound disappointed while mentally giving herself a high five. Then she handed the bouquet back to Skye.

"You totally cheated," Cat said, crossing her arms.

"I did you a favor. Last woman standing gets a complete makeover from Holly and Hailey." The twins owned the Rocky Mountain Diner and were Christmas's self-appointed beauty experts. "Good luck." Vivi smirked and headed for the kitchen, laughing when she heard Cat mutter, "You suck."

She wasn't surprised when Cat joined her in the kitchen five minutes later. Vivi looked up from refilling the veggie tray. "So, who did you steal the bouquet from?"

Cat grinned, tugging off her toilet-paper veil. Vivi had gotten rid of hers as soon as she'd left the living room. "Grace." She wadded up the paper and tossed it in the garbage. "Need a hand?"

"Sure. We'll cut up some more veggies. We have to kill time or they'll make us take part in the next game."

"Bring on the veggies. They're playing Name That Romantic Movie next. I hate charades. My sister's the actress, not me."

"Where is Chloe?" Cat's identical twin sister, Chloe, was an actress on the soap *As the Sun Sets*. They lived in LA. Supposedly, Cat was her bodyguard-slash-manager. But from what Vivi had seen at Skye and Ethan's wedding, she was more of a babysitter-slash-lackey.

"She couldn't get away until the day before the wedding."

"Too bad. Do you like living in LA?" Vivi asked as she

opened the refrigerator to take out a head of cauliflower, a cucumber, and a bag of carrots.

"Hate it. But a job's a job, right?" Cat got a knife out of the drawer. "And Chloe needs me."

"You're a better person than me. I don't think I could give up a job that I loved for anyone."

"I didn't have much of a choice," Cat said, reaching for the carrots.

Even as a little girl, Vivi's curiosity had gotten her in trouble. By now she should have learned to control that burning need to discover what made people tick, to figure out why they did the things they did. She knew Cat had left the Denver PD under a cloud of suspicion. She'd been engaged to a man who, unbeknownst to Cat, had been running a Ponzi scheme. By all accounts, she'd been an amazing police officer. One of the youngest female detectives on the force. "Sorry, Cat, I shouldn't have brought it up."

The other woman waved off her apology. "No worries. That's the one thing about coming home. Someone's bound to bring it up."

"It wasn't your fault, you know. It could have happened to anyone. I'm sure you would have been exonerated."

"Probably, but it's better that I left. I didn't trust my judgment anymore." Cat looked up from chopping a carrot. "So, my mom tells me you're dating Chance."

Vivi wondered if there was a reason Cat segued from her own lack of judgment to Vivi's. "Was. I ended it this morning."

"You want to talk about it?"

Oddly enough, since Vivi didn't know her very well, it probably would be easier to talk about her relationship

with Chance to Cat than anyone else. She didn't strike
Vivi as the type to sugarcoat things. Not the way Skye
and Maddie had a tendency to do. More importantly, Vivi
could find out about Callahan. Because of the way Chance
had shut her down last night, she knew there was something more going on. Scraping the last of the dip from
the jar into the serving dish, she weighed out how best
to broach the question. She didn't want to give too much
away. "Not much to talk about, really. He's not ready to
be in a relationship, and I am. He's still got things to work
through. Did you know Kate?"

Cat slanted Vivi a sidelong glance and nodded. "They
were a few years ahead of us in school. Every girl wanted
to be Kate Porter and every guy wanted to be Chance
McBride. Chance called her his golden girl. She was one
of the sweetest women I've ever known. Everyone loved
Kate, especially Chance." Cat grimaced. "Sorry, that's
probably not what you wanted to hear."

"Actually, it is. The journalist in me, I guess."

"Or is it a woman trying to figure out the man she loves?"

"And to think I liked you."

Cat chuckled, then grew serious. "I like you, too. Maybe
that's why I want to save you from a lot of heartache."

It was a little late for that. Vivi knew she should leave
well enough alone, but she couldn't help herself and
asked, "You don't think he'll be able to move on, do you?"

"No. You're best friends with Maddie and Skye, so I
think you'll understand what I mean when I say Chance
had the same kind of relationship with Kate as they do
with Gage and Ethan. Seems to me the odds of finding
a love like that twice in a lifetime are about the same as
winning the lottery." Above the chatter in the living room,

they heard Liz laugh. Cat smiled. "Then again, maybe I'm wrong. Look at my mom and Paul."

Vivi tamped down a small flicker of hope, reminding herself why she'd begun the conversation in the first place. "Do you know anything about a man named Callahan?"

Cat gave her a wary look. "Yeah, why?"

"Because there's been several pharmacies robbed in the last couple of months and Chance asked Gage if he was looking at Callahan. Chance seemed, I don't know, tense, angry. It felt personal."

"Oh, it's personal all right. Chance blames Jake Callahan for Kate's death."

Her instincts had never steered her wrong in the past, so Vivi wasn't completely surprised. But that didn't stop a sour taste from filling her mouth. "I thought Kate went off the road in a snowstorm?"

"She did. But Chance didn't believe it was an accident. There'd been bad blood between him and the Callahans since he'd thrown the old man in jail. A couple of months before Kate's accident, Chance had been working with the local DEA trying to break up a meth ring. Jake was his primary suspect. When Chance raided Jake's garage, Jake threatened his family. Two days later, Kate was dead."

Vivi rubbed her temple. "What do you think? Could Jake Callahan be responsible?"

"I didn't know him well. Seemed like an all right guy. When I first heard about it, I didn't believe it. Something felt off. But Chance was very good at his job. He wouldn't let his personal feelings interfere with an investigation."

"So what happened?" From the way Cat averted her eyes, Vivi didn't think she was going to like her answer.

"After Kate's funeral, Chance went to Jake's garage. I

don't know if he was looking for answers or revenge, but he put Jake in the hospital. Chance left town right after."

Vivi swallowed past the lump in her throat. "How come none of this was in the paper?" She knew the incident hadn't been reported. When she'd first discovered who Chance was, she'd spent weeks investigating him. "Why wasn't he arrested?"

"The McBrides had the story buried. They're a powerful and well-respected family. They know the right people. Besides, no one blamed Chance. He was a decorated soldier and a good sheriff, and he'd lost his family."

"But he blamed himself."

"Yes, and I imagine he still does. It was tough to lose Kate and the baby the way that he did, but when you factor in the guilt, it's a nightmare. I'm sure it still haunts him to this day."

"I'm sure it does," Vivi murmured.

Maddie walked into the kitchen. "Hey, you two, we're splitting into teams for charades." She looked from Cat to Vivi and frowned. "What's going on?"

"Nothing. We were running out of veggies." Vivi forced a smile, arranging the carrots in the tray.

Skye stormed into the kitchen. "Maddie, why did you tell Sophia about Ethan doing a striptease for me? Poor Liz spilt punch all over her top."

Maddie made a face. "Sorry, it kind of slipped out when—"

"You're talking about my brother, right?" Cat asked.

"Gah." Skye threw up her arms. "Don't say anything to Ethan. He'll kill me. But right now we have another problem. Sophia says this is the most boring bachelorette party she's ever been to. She's threatening to hire a stripper."

"Good Lord," Maddie said, hurrying after Skye.

By the time Vivi and Cat refilled the veggie trays and returned to sit on the couch, Nell was staging a revolt. "Sophia's right. We should have gone to the Penalty Box with the men."

"We're not crashing Dad's bachelor party, Nell. I have karaoke. We can—" Maddie trailed off when Nell rolled her eyes. "What's wrong with karaoke?"

"Why don't we go check out the Garage?" Hailey suggested.

"Great idea, Hails," Hailey's twin sister, Holly, agreed. "We've been wanting to check it out since it opened last month."

"I don't think that's a good idea," Maddie said with a thick Southern drawl. When her best friend got nervous, she spoke Southern.

Which begged the question, why was Maddie nervous? Vivi's eyes narrowed when Maddie elbowed Skye, who sat on the floor beside her.

"Maddie's right. Ethan said the Garage is a biker bar." Skye made a concerted effort to avoid Vivi's suspicious stare.

"I'm in. I always wanted to check out a biker bar," Nell said. "And Liz deserves some excitement before she gets leg-shackled to my nephew. He's boring."

"Nell," Liz said with an exasperated head shake.

"The Garage is not a biker bar. My customers, they tell me the Callahan brothers spent *mucho dinero* on the place." Sophia, a former Playmate who owned the high-end clothing store Naughty and Nice, rubbed two fingers and her thumb together.

Vivi stared down Maddie and Skye. They'd known

about Chance's past with Jake and hadn't told her. "Okay, ladies. Let's get this show on the road. First round is on me," she said.

Maddie and Skye groaned when the other women cheered.

"Vivi, I don't think this is a good idea," Cat said under her breath, an apprehensive look on her face.

There was a part of Vivi that agreed with Cat. For a woman determined to get over a man, allowing herself to get sucked back into his life was a bad idea. But she couldn't help herself. And not only because the story intrigued her, which it did. She cared about him, and if there was a possibility she could help alleviate his guilt, she'd do it. And it didn't have anything to do with the thought that a guilt-free Chance might be able to move on with his life. Not at all. "It is, if we can find out the answers Chance needs."

"Okay, how did *I* get roped into this?"

"I'm a reporter and you're a cop. We're the perfect team."

"Ex-cop, and as I'm sure you know, cops and reporters tend to be on opposite sides."

"We'll be the exception. Come on, Cat. Chance is going to be your stepbrother. Surely you want to help him out."

"The last thing Chance McBride would want is you and me trying to get information on Jake Callahan. And Vivi, I've seen a ticked-off Chance, and he's freaking scary."

"He'll never know." Vivi's stomach dipped, and the nervous jitter had nothing to do with Chance's scary temper or facing down a supposed drug dealer and possible murderer. It was because Nell McBride was looking at Vivi like a spider who'd trapped a fly in its sticky web.

# Chapter Nine

Geezus, you've been in a mood since you picked me up. Do me a favor and lose the attitude. Dad's been looking forward to tonight," Gage said as Chance pulled into a parking spot on Main Street.

"I'm not in a mood."

"Yeah, you are." Gage gave him a knowing look as he got out of the truck. "It's because of Vivi, isn't it? Why don't you just call her and work things out?"

"Nothing to work out. We're done." He slammed the truck door, wincing as he realized the action supported his brother's theory. "If I'm in a 'mood' "—he made air quotes—"it has nothing to do with Vivi. It's the damn colony of mice that have taken up residence in the cabin." It had everything to do with Vivi. Learning about her date with Dr. McSexy had pissed him off. It shouldn't bother him, but it did.

Which his brother obviously knew because he said, "Right," and held open the door to the Penalty Box.

Tension knotted the muscles in Chance's neck as he walked into the bar. The place was packed with friends, neighbors, and his father's patients. The last time Chance had seen half the people in here was at Kate's funeral. He'd rather be in the middle of a shoot-out than deal with them now. Off to the side of the dance floor, his father stood surrounded by well-wishers.

Chance headed straight for the bar. "Tell Dad I'll be there in a minute."

"Come on, he—" Gage began, then searched Chance's face and nodded.

From where he stood mixing a drink behind the bar, Sawyer Anderson tipped up the brim of his baseball cap when Chance parked his ass on a leather stool. A couple years younger than Chance, the tall, athletically built Anderson had opened the bar after retiring from the Colorado Flurries, a professional hockey team. The rough-hewn walls were plastered with hockey memorabilia celebrating Sawyer's short-lived but lucrative career.

"Hey, Chance, good to see you, man. What can I get you?"

"Whatever's on tap," he said, relaxing when Sawyer didn't hit him with a bunch of questions. "Place looks good."

Sawyer slid a drink down the scarred dark-wood bar into another man's waiting hand. "Yeah, I'm happy with how it turned out," Sawyer said as he grabbed a tall glass from under the bar. "We're hopping tonight thanks to your dad. Good turnout."

"Yeah, he's a popular guy." Chance retrieved his wallet from the back pocket of his jeans. "Thanks," he said when Sawyer handed him the beer. He pulled out a twenty.

Sawyer waved him off. "On the house." His mouth crooked when Chance objected. "I owe you for letting me off with a warning when I took out the fire hydrant."

"Forgot about that." Chance laughed, returning his wallet to his back pocket. "You were a little shit." Sometimes he forgot not all his memories of his hometown were bad ones.

"Hey, not so little." Something caught Sawyer's attention by the door, and he rubbed his jaw before turning back to Chance. "Sorry, I took her off tonight, but I guess... Hey, Natalee, what are you doing here? Brandi was on the schedule."

Chance took a deep pull on his beer before swiveling on the stool. Nat walked toward him with a smile so like her sister's he felt like he'd been sucker punched. He probably should thank his dad. A reunion here would have been a lot tougher than at the airport surrounded by strangers.

"Her son had a baseball game. I offered to take her shift." She drew her attention away from her boss to give Chance a hug.

"How's it going, kiddo?" He closed his eyes at the warm citrus scent that clung to her black-and-white-striped uniform shirt. She even smelled like Kate.

Nat drew back, leaving her hand on his shoulder. "Good. How about you? Princess settle in okay?"

"Yeah, she's fine."

She glanced at him from under her long lashes. "Oh, I thought you'd have a hard time with her. She didn't like your friend."

His mouth curved as he thought about Vivi's interactions with Princess over the last twenty-four hours. Until he remembered watching her walk away this morning and his smile faded.

"Chance?"

He returned his attention to Nat. Might as well get it over with. She'd hear about it anyway. "Doesn't matter. Vivi's not staying at the cabin."

"I'm sorry." Her smile belied the sentiment. "But don't worry, I'll come by every day and help out with Princess. I can clean and cook for you, too."

There was something about the way she looked at him that made him uncomfortable. Which might've been the reason his response came out more curt than he intended. "Nat, I'm thirty-eight years old. I'm capable of taking care of myself."

She withdrew her hand from his shoulder, twisting her fingers in the strap of her purse. "I didn't mean . . . Sorry."

The wounded expression on her face made him feel like a jerk. No doubt he'd imagined the look he'd seen in her eyes. She was his wife's baby sister and almost seventeen years his junior. Kate would hate it that he'd upset her. "Don't mind me, kiddo. It's been a long day. You can come over anytime."

"You're sure you don't mind?"

"Of course I don't. Better get to work before your boss fires you." On second thought, maybe that wasn't a bad idea. He wasn't exactly thrilled to discover Nat worked in a bar. With her looks, she'd draw a lot of male attention. Though he trusted Sawyer to protect his waitresses. Still, Nat had been a brainiac in school. She should be in college. And it wasn't like she had to work while going to school. He'd made sure of that. It was something he needed to talk to her about.

When Nat left to get ready for her shift, Chance got up to go to his dad's table. Someone clapped him on the shoulder. "Hey, big guy, it's been a long time." He turned to see Ray, his brother's deputy who had once worked under Chance. He'd been with him the night of Kate's accident. He saw the memory lurking in the other man's eyes and prayed to God he didn't want to relive it now. "Good to see you, Ray. How's my little brother treating you?"

His former deputy took the hint, a toothy grin breaking over his smooth baby face. "He's a slave driver. No more poker parties or girls allowed to while away the hours."

"He never was any fun. Straight arrow through and through."

"I heard that," Gage said, walking toward them.

The three of them shared a couple laughs before they were inundated by a steady stream of guys Chance had gone to school with. Gage didn't leave his side. Anytime someone brought up Kate, his brother deftly changed the subject. But there was always one in the crowd who didn't take the hint. Chance had seen Earl Skully, Kate and Natalee's uncle and owner of the local body shop, eyeing him for the last twenty minutes.

Now that he had some liquid courage in his system, Earl ambled over. He hooked his thumbs in red suspenders, nodding to where his niece served a table of old-timers. "Pretty little thing, just like her sister. Must be tough on you, Chance, being reminded of Katie every time you see Natalee."

"Earl, we—" Gage began, but the older man kept talking.

"Never saw Katie without a smile on her face. Still can't believe she's gone. Lost a lot of sleep over the accident, you know. Felt bad, seeing as how I'm the one who sold her that car. If she'd been in a truck—"

"Why don't you just say what you really mean, Earl?" Chance got off the bar stool, pushing aside his brother's restraining hand. "You've always blamed me for the accident. And you're right, it was my fault. I should have been with her that night."

"Geezus, Chance. It was an accident. You—"

Earl interrupted Gage with a glower. "An accident that wouldn't have happened if he'd been at home, where he belonged. But instead he was off playing the big man in town. You're all the same, you McBrides, thinking you're better than the rest of us. One day, someone will teach—"

Chance deserved whatever the old man said to him, but he drew the line when it came to his family. He got into Earl's space. "That sounded like a threat to me. And I don't take kindly to threats."

The old man backed into a stool. "It wasn't a threat. I—"

Sawyer came around the bar. "Earl, it's time for you to leave."

Ray took the old man by the arm. "I'll see him home," he said to Gage, then held Chance's gaze. "Remember the O'Brien case?"

Chance knew what he was getting at, but it wasn't the same. Ray had done everything he could to save old man O'Brien. He just hadn't gotten there in time.

"It wasn't your fault, big guy. Stop blaming yourself," Ray said before leading Earl away.

"He's right," Gage said.

Before he had a chance to respond, Nat, with a stricken

expression on her face, rushed over. "What did Uncle Earl do?"

"Nothing. He's had too much to drink, that's all," Chance told her.

Her fingers whitened on the empty tray as she tracked her uncle's progress. "He blames himself...for the accident."

She looked like she was going to cry, and all Chance wanted to do was get the hell out of there.

"Natalee," Sawyer said, angling his head, "table four's drinks are up."

"Are you going to be here for a while?" she asked Chance as she retrieved the drinks from the bar.

"I'm heading—"

"Yeah, he is," Gage cut Chance off, giving him a light shove in the direction of Paul's table. "You are not letting that vindictive old man ruin Dad's night. I mean it, Chance."

"Sure. Whatever."

His father looked up as they approached the table. "What was that all about with Earl?"

"Nothing," he and Gage responded almost at the same time.

"Always could tell when you two were lying." Their father pushed out a chair with his foot. "Sit down. We'll discuss it later."

"Hey, Einstein, didn't see you come in," Chance said to Ethan, Liz O'Connor's son and his brother Gage's best friend. Chance had given him the nickname in high school.

"You were busy with your many admirers," he said to Chance.

Chance rolled his eyes and took his seat.

"Did you hear back from Jordan yet?" Gage asked Ethan. Jordan Reinhart was Denver's district attorney. Up until a few months ago, Ethan had worked for Jordan as ADA. But Ethan had recently been appointed district attorney, overseeing the thirteenth district, which included Christmas.

"Yeah, no connection to your case."

"Okay, you two, no shoptalk. We're here to celebrate my last days of bachelorhood." His father looked up, motioning at a brown-haired man with a military bearing. "Matt, over here."

Gage, who'd taken the seat across from Chance, rubbed the back of his neck. A nervous habit both his brother and father shared. Wondering what had brought it on, Chance scanned the bar.

"Good to see you, Matt," Ethan said with a smirk as the man approached the table. "I don't think you've met Paul's *oldest* son, Chance." *Jesus, he makes me sound decrepit.* "Chance, this is Matt Trainer. He works with your dad."

Yeah, so why was *Einstein* the one introducing them? And why did he seem to be taking such pleasure in doing so?

"Better known as Dr. McSexy," Ethan added, waggling his eyebrows at Chance.

He'd always been a pain in Chance's ass.

Trainer stuck out his hand. "Good to finally meet you. Paul talks about you all the time."

"Yeah, likewise," Chance said, sizing up Vivi's coffee date.

Trainer grimaced, shaking out his hand when Chance finally released it. "Powerful grip you have there."

Ethan chuckled into his beer while Paul frowned at Chance before saying, "Pull up a chair and join us, Matt."

Leaning back, Chance folded his arms across his chest. "So, Matt, how long have you been at Christmas General?"

"About two years now. I filled in for your dad when he took a cruise."

His father glanced at Ethan, looking uncomfortable. Chance had heard all about the cruise his aunt had orchestrated. His father's then girlfriend, Karen, had whisked him away on a romantic vacation only to discover that Liz was in the cabin next door. Courtesy of Nell, of course.

"Yes, and he did such a great job, I decided we couldn't let him go." His father smiled at the other man.

"Really? No family, kids, or wife waiting for you back home?" Chance asked.

Trainer shot Ethan, who was now laughing his ass off—*the little bastard*—a confused look before saying, "No, I'm single."

"I find that hard to believe. What are you...forty, forty-five?"

His father's jaw dropped. "Chance!"

Trainer didn't seem to be bothered by his line of questioning. He just laughed and scrubbed a hand over his face. "Guess I better knock off the all-nighters. I'm thirty-five."

"All-nighters? You into booze, drugs—"

His father pushed back his chair. "Son, I'd like a word with you. Now."

"Relax, Dad," Gage said, shooting Chance a don't-be-an-ass look before saying to the doc, "Don't mind my brother. He has a suspicious mind. Occupational hazard."

"Right, you're a security specialist, aren't you?"

"Yeah, when he's not masquerading as a comic book hero," Ethan said.

Chance opened his mouth to tell Einstein he also knew fifty ways to kill a man without leaving any evidence. But he thought better of it given his future stepbrother's position as district attorney.

"Oh, so you do like birthday parties for kids? Or do you work for a charitable organization that grants wishes?"

Before he could respond, his brother and Ethan's cell phones pinged. They shared a look after retrieving their messages and stood up. "We'll be back in half an hour," Gage said, rubbing the back of his neck.

Chance narrowed his eyes. "What's up?"

"Nothing, we just—"

Ted and Fred, his aunt Nell's best friends, sauntered over. They reminded Chance of the two old guys from the Muppets. The ones who sat up in the balcony giving everyone a hard time.

"You boys heading over to the Garage?" Ted asked.

His father gave the older man a confused look. "No, why would we?"

"Because that's where the girls are."

"No, they're at Maddie and Gage's place," his father informed Fred.

"Nope, they moved the party to the Garage." The old man held up his cell phone. "Me and Ted are heading over there. Someone's got to look out for them. It's a biker bar, you know."

Chance eyed Gage and Ethan. "Where exactly is this bar?" he asked Fred.

"Fred and Ted, why don't we—" Gage began, hustling the men away from the table.

"Logan County," Ted said over his shoulder. "Callahans opened it up about a month ago."

\*          \*          \*

"Do not fight me on this, Chance. You're staying in the truck. Despite what Ted and Fred said, the Garage isn't a biker bar. I'm sure everything's fine," Gage said from the truck's passenger seat.

Chance backed into a parking space in the packed strip mall. "Everything's not fine. Somehow Vivi found out about Callahan." He should have known she wouldn't give up and cut her off at the pass.

"So what? It's not like she's in there asking for trouble. She'll nose around and realize there's no story here." Ethan leaned forward to put a hand on Chance's shoulder. "He has nothing to hide. Gage and I have been keeping an eye on him. Let it go. No good can come out of you going in there."

Chance put the truck in Park and twisted in his seat. "You realize we're talking about Vivian Westfield, right? The same woman who, in trying to protect your wife, nearly got herself killed. She's a hothead, Ethan. She won't stop until she gets her story or gets hurt. And whether you and my brother believe me or not, Vivi getting close to Callahan can lead to only one thing—trouble with a capital *T*."

"Look, I get that you're worried about her, but you going in there will only make matters worse. You were lucky you didn't kill him that night, Chance."

"Luck didn't have anything to do with it. If I wanted him dead, he would be. I wanted answers." He still did, but he hadn't broken Jake that night, so he didn't fool himself into thinking that was about to change. All he could do was keep him on his radar and wait for him to screw up.

Gage shot Ethan a help-me-out-here look, but Chance was done talking. He got out of the truck at the same time his father pulled in beside them. When he saw Trainer in the passenger seat, Chance swore under his breath. Just what he needed to deal with on top of everything else. He headed across the parking lot. He made it ten feet before the four musketeers surrounded him.

"I'm going in there, and none of you"—he swept a finger around the circle—"can stop me."

"I think I might be able to." Ethan rolled up the sleeves of his white dress shirt to flex his muscles. For a guy who sat behind a desk all day, he had pretty impressive guns. Not that it would do him any good.

"You may be thirty-eight years old, but I'm still your father." His dad seemed to realize that wasn't going to cut it, and tried again. "Do you want me to have a heart attack? Because that's what will happen if you go in there and get hurt."

His father was as healthy as a horse. And playing the guilt card had never worked all that well on Chance.

"Took down a guy bigger than you last month. I've got this." His brother cracked his knuckles.

With his height, weight, and training, Gage would get in a couple of good hits, but Chance could take him if he wanted to. Only he had no intention of laying a finger on any of them. He'd been edging them closer to the entrance doors and himself to the outer fringe of their posse.

Like Chance had done earlier, Trainer sized him up.

"Haven't had a good workout in a while. Wouldn't mind a shot." The doc flexed his admittedly impressive biceps, then shot Chance a grin. "Delta Force, in case you were wondering."

So maybe he could give him a bit of trouble, but Chance was done wasting time. He was about to distract them when he heard a familiar voice behind him and felt something poking him in the back.

"Don't worry, boys. I can take him. I have a gun."

Chance sighed. "Fred, it's your finger."

"How did you know that?" Fred asked as he and Ted joined the other men, blocking Chance's intended escape route.

"Because this"—he reached in the back of his jeans and pulled the Glock from under his leather jacket—"is a tad bigger than what you were poking in my back."

"For chrissakes, Chance, put that thing away. I should arrest you," his brother said.

"You can't arrest me. I have a permit to carry concealed. Now if you boys don't mind, I need to track down my . . . a woman." He hoped none of them caught the slip. But of course they did. His father, Ethan, and Gage grinned.

His hands in his front jeans pockets, Trainer rocked on his heels. "You wouldn't be talking about Vivi Westfield, would you? Because I have a date with her on Monday, so I kinda think that makes her *my* woman. Not yours."

The guy was yanking his chain, but Chance stared him down anyway while returning the gun to the back of his jeans. And instead of telling the idiot she was his like he wanted to, he said, "You haven't met her, Trainer. So it's a little premature to be staking your claim, don't you think?"

"Just wanted to be clear on where things stand, that's all."

Forget it, he'd already wasted enough time as it was. He pushed past them, ignoring Gage and Ethan's warnings. "Don't worry," he heard his father say to his brother as they hurried after him. "Vivi will keep him in line."

They were worried about the wrong person. Chance had no intention of confronting Callahan tonight. There were too many witnesses. All he wanted to do was get Vivi out of there and shut down her hunting expedition.

It took a moment for his eyes to adjust to the bar's dim lighting. The place was all chrome and steel. A heavy pulsing beat pounded from the speakers near the crowded dance floor at the far end of the bar.

"There they are." His father pointed out the women jammed into two metallic booths about twenty feet away. Nell spotted them and said something to the women in her booth that sent them into peals of laughter.

Gage groaned. "They're looped."

Sophia Dane got out of her seat and did a sexy bump and grind. "Ethan, come dance for us. Skye says you are better than Channing Tatum." She waved a fistful of bills as the other women sang "It's Raining Men."

"Got something you want to share with us, buddy?" Gage asked his best friend.

Ethan, his face a dull red, set off in his wife's direction, muttering, "I can't believe she told them that."

"Keep your brother in line," his father said to Gage before heading for Liz.

"Come on, Fred." Ted tugged on the other man's arm. "There's a guy checking out Nell."

While all this was going on, Chance scanned the room for Vivi and the Callahans. He spotted Jake Callahan's brother Mike standing behind the stainless steel bar, chatting up a woman wearing a low-cut top, painted-on jeans, and mile-high shoes to match her out-to-there dark hair. "Thought you said there was nothing illegal going on?" Chance jerked his thumb at the bar. "Looks to me like the Callahans are making their money pimping out women."

Gage rubbed the back of his neck. "Ah, Chance, I think you might want to get your eyes checked. That woman isn't a prostitute. It's Vivi."

"What are you smoking? There's no way..." Chance began, when the woman in question laughed and swiveled on the chrome stool to face them. *Jesus, God.* She mouthed, *Oh, shit,* and slid off the stool, pulling a woman with short dark hair along with her.

Chance regained his power of speech when, beside him, Trainer said, "*That's* Vivi Westfield?"

"Don't even think about it, Doc," Chance warned him.

Trainer grinned. "Remind me to thank your aunt."

"Yeah, you go and do that." Chance wanted to talk to Vivi on his own. "Gage, your wife looks like she's headed for the dance floor with Big and Burly."

"Forget about it. I'm not falling for...Well, hell." His brother took off when he realized Madison was indeed being dragged toward the dance floor by a guy dressed in chains and leather.

Mike Callahan's eyes followed Vivi. Chance crossed his arms, staring at him over her head. It took a minute for Mike to sense he was being watched. Once he did, he took a startled step back, a look of panic on his face. He waved two linebackers over to the bar and took off. No doubt to call his brother and tell him Chance was in town.

"Chance?" Vivi said, a nervous hitch in her bedroom voice.

He raised a brow as he let his gaze drift down her body then back to her face. She shifted on her heels, her hand going to her hair. "I know, I know, you don't have to say anything. I look like a hooker. I should have listened to Maddie. But you wouldn't believe how stubborn Hailey and Holly are. And Nell didn't help because for some reason—"

Oh yeah, she was nervous. She always rambled when she was.

The woman beside Vivi cut her off with a you're-screwed look. "Hey, Chance. Good to see you. I'll just go—"

He frowned, taking in the woman's heavily made-up features. "Cat?"

"Yeah, Holly and Hailey got to me, too." She backed away. "I'll leave you guys alone."

"Cat," Vivi called after her. "Maybe she's sick or something. I'll just go—"

He grabbed her hand and pulled her against him, ducking his head to look into her eyes. "Am I making you nervous, Slick?"

She put her hand on his chest, her incredible violet eyes drinking him in. "Why would I be nervous?" she asked, her voice husky and low.

"Because you know that I know what you're doing here. And Slick, you're going to stop doing it right now."

"I don't know what you're talking about. Now if you'd let me go—"

He moved her away from the entrance, putting his back to the wall, making sure he had a clear view of all entry and exit points. Mike was back behind the bar talking to the two muscle-bound guys from earlier. Chance looked down at Vivi, sifting his fingers through her hair to curve his hand around her neck.

Leaning against him, she searched his face. "We broke up, remember?"

"Yeah, I do." He placed his hand on her hip to hold her close, lifting his gaze to the bar to make sure Mike was watching before looking down at Vivi. "But for your own good and my piece of mind, I'm going to make sure you're persona non grata at the Garage." He lowered his head to capture her mouth. And like always, as soon as his lips touched hers, any thought of keeping it to a simple kiss evaporated. He slanted his head, deepening the connection, exploring her warm mouth with his tongue. She bit it. He jerked back, touching his mouth. "What the hell was that?"

With fire in her eyes, she jabbed a finger in his chest. "You do not get to kiss me anymore, McBride. We're done." She shook her head. "You are such a jerk."

The muscle-bound guys, their hair buzzed, approached. Bouncers, he assumed from their matching black T-shirts. The older of the two asked, "Is there a problem here?"

They moved closer, too close to Vivi for Chance's liking. He positioned himself in front of her. "There will be if you don't back off."

She elbowed him aside. "No, there's no problem. Thanks."

The older guy looked back at Mike, who gave a jerky nod. "It's time for you to leave," he said to Chance.

Gage walked over with his dad, Ethan, and Trainer following behind. "What's going on?"

Chance opened his mouth to tell his brother it was fine, then bowed his head when the rest of their party joined them to loudly protest his being thrown out of the bar. Chance calmed them down and took Vivi by the hand. "Don't worry about it. We were leaving anyway."

And he would have, but the women didn't want to let it go. They got noisy and possibly a few elbows were thrown. But all hell didn't break loose until Fred poked his finger in bouncer number two's back and the guy put him in a headlock. Ted jumped on the bouncer's back to rescue his best friend, which pulled in bouncer number one. Sophia jumped on *his* back, and then that was it. Chance had no choice but to get involved.

Ten minutes later, Walker, the sheriff from Logan County, arrived. But no matter how hard Callahan pressed for charges to be brought, none were. There was no damage to the bar, and no one had been badly hurt—other than the bouncers and a couple of bikers who'd taken a hit to their egos.

"I told you, you should've stayed in the truck," Gage muttered, pressing his fingers to his fat lip.

Chance ignored him and called out, "Slick, I'll give you a ride."

She flipped him off and got in the car with his father, Nell, Liz, and . . . Trainer.

# Chapter Ten

Since Vivi shut him down two nights ago, Chance had decided to make a slight detour on the way to see his brother this morning. Doing his best to remain inconspicuous, he stood under the purple-and-white-striped awning of the Sugar Plum Bakery, pretending to check out the wedding cake displayed in the window while trying to catch a glimpse of Vivi. The six-tier cake with a bride chasing a groom on top made it difficult to see much of anything...except the attractive blonde owner, Grace Flaherty, waving him inside.

So much for being inconspicuous. But on a positive note, Vivi couldn't accuse him of spying on her if she happened to be inside. A waft of warm, sugar-scented air greeted him when he walked into the bakery. He pushed his aviators on top of his head, sweeping the shop with a furtive glance.

Fifteen customers sat at five of the ten black bistro

tables, none of whom were Vivi or Trainer. Maybe the kiss Saturday night had taken care of more than Vivi's ability to nose around the Garage. His mood lightened at the thought. After another night of haunted dreams, he'd woken up feeling like crap. His morning had gone from bad to worse. And it wasn't because the mice had eaten through the cable—they had—it was because he'd remembered Vivi's date with the doc today.

"Hi, Chance," Grace said from where she stood behind the glass display case with a knowing smile.

No doubt she thought he was here to check up on Vivi. Which of course he was, but he didn't want that getting around town, so he pulled a crumpled receipt from his jeans pocket and held it up. "Guys at the station are hungry this morning."

Her lips twitched. "They must be. Ray was here an hour ago to pick up their order."

Well, hell. "You got me. I ate half of it. I'll take whatever they bought the first time around."

"You want to replace their entire order?"

"Sure." To play it safe, because he had no idea what they'd bought, he changed the subject. Plus, he wanted to know how Grace's husband, Jack, was making out. He'd been a POW in Afghanistan for seventeen months before escaping his captors last year. Now he worked for SAR— search and rescue. "How's Jack doing?"

"Great. He would have been at your dad's bachelor party, but they had training exercises. He was disappointed he didn't get to see you."

"Probably disappointed he didn't get to take part in the brawl. How's your cheek?"

"Yes, he was." She touched her face and grinned.

"Cheek's fine. Don't tell him I said so, but it was kind of exciting."

Chance laughed. "I won't tell him. I'll give him a call. I'm in town until Sunday." He leaned on the counter, angling his body so he had a clear view of the door.

"You're leaving the day after the wedding?" Grace asked, filling a bakery box with chocolate cupcakes.

"Yeah, I..." He trailed off when he spotted Vivi jogging across the road, the sun glinting off her long, dark hair. He glanced at the clock on the purple wall behind the coffee machines—10:50. The woman was never early. She must be anxious for her date. At least she hadn't dressed up for the guy. He took that as a good sign. Then again, she'd never dressed up for him, either. Today she had on those same low-riding jeans with the rip in the knee and the long-sleeve purple thermal tee she'd worn when they'd gone for a walk in Central Park after their first night together.

He turned around, casually resting his elbows on the counter. Taping the top of the cake box, Grace gave him an expectant look. Right. He picked up where he left off. "I've got a job next Monday or I'd stick around."

He doubt she bought it. No one else did. But his family seemed to be slowly coming to the realization that this is the way it would be. After the events of the last few days, he figured he was past the worst of it now and could see himself coming home for the holidays at least. Should be enough to keep them happy. Christmastime was as big a deal for his family as it was for the rest of the folks in town.

The bells on the door chimed. He braced himself. "I'll take four coffees, too, Grace. Thanks."

From behind him came a pissed-off raspy voice. "I

don't believe this. You're stalking me now, McBride?"
Vivi nudged him over with her elbow.

He looked down at her, unable to hold back a smile
at the irritated look on her gorgeous, makeup-free face.
"Now, why would you think that? I'm here to pick up an
order for Gage."

"Sure you are." She hefted her black messenger bag
up her shoulder. The woman never went anywhere without her trusty laptop. "Hey, Grace. I'll take a latte grande
when you have a minute."

"They don't make your fancy-ass coffees here, Slick."

Grace smiled. "For Vivi I do. I'll be finished with
Chance's order in a sec."

His eyes widened as Grace began filling a second box
with cupcakes. He should have remembered Ray had
a hollow leg. He was about to tell Grace one box was
enough, but Vivi's smug smile and vanilla perfume distracted him. "You got stuff to do for the wedding today?"
he asked her.

"No, I have a date. Remember?"

So much for his hope that she'd canceled after the kiss
they'd shared. "Looks like he stood you up."

"He's running late," she said and headed for a table.

Chance paid for Vivi's coffee and his order. "Thanks,
Grace. Place looks great, by the way." Balancing the two
boxes and a coffee tray in his arms, he stopped at Vivi's
table. She was already on her computer. "What are you
working on?"

"Nothing." She closed her screen and nodded at the
coffees. "You better get going before they get cold."

"I'll nuke them." He narrowed his eyes at her. "I wasn't
joking the other night. Stay away from the Callahans."

"It has nothing to do with the Callahans."

"What do you mean *it*? What are you working on?"

She shrugged. "Mrs. Tate saw a black Mustang tear down Main Street around the time of the break-in at the pharmacy. Thought I'd check if anyone reported seeing one at the earlier break-ins. Not a big deal, okay?"

No, it wasn't okay. He'd shut her down Saturday night because his gut told him Jake Callahan was somehow involved. After seeing the bar, that feeling had only increased. They'd invested some serious coin in the Garage. And Vivi's piece of news was one more reason for his brother to take a hard look at Jake. His father, Darwin Callahan, used to drive a souped-up '76 black Mustang, and Jake specialized in refurbishing the model. "How did you hear about Mrs. Tate's witness statement?"

"I'm staying with your brother. I hear lots of things."

"Yeah, things you have no business hearing." Gage was doing his best to keep Chance out of the loop. He should be doing the same with Vivi. He planned to talk to his brother about watching what he said around her and to give him a heads-up. Gage would be as unhappy about her digging around in his case as Chance was. Hopefully his brother would have better luck shutting her down. But Chance had to give it another shot. "I'm sure you have better things to do than waste your time following a lead that's going nowhere."

It was too bad she didn't have a story back in New York to keep her occupied. No doubt she was bored to tears answering letters from the lovelorn. And a bored Vivi Westfield was a dangerous thing.

"Really, so you don't think there's anything interesting about the fact a *Mustang* was used as the getaway car?"

They'd done this before—puzzled out the leads on a story together. Only he'd been Superman then. He'd missed their e-mail exchanges these past few months. Missed working with her on a story and making sure she was safe. But this one hit too close to home. He caught the calculating glint in her eyes. She knew more than she was letting on. "You have no proof it was the getaway car. Probably a bunch of kids out for a joyride."

"Right. So—" She broke off when Grace approached with her coffee. "Thanks," she said, offering Grace one of her infrequent smiles. "How much do I owe you?"

"Chance took care of it for you." Grace smiled and began to walk away, then pivoted. "I almost forgot." Retrieving a set of keys from the pocket of her purple-and-white-striped apron, she handed them to Vivi. "Better give you these now. I'm heading out shortly."

"You're sure you don't mind, Grace?"

"Not at all. We don't have anyone renting the apartment until the end of June."

*Apartment?* He hoped he'd misunderstood and Vivi wasn't thinking about staying in the Flahertys' apartment above the bakery.

Vivi held up her coffee. "Thanks, McBride."

"What do you think you're doing?"

A dark brow arched. "Thanking you for my coffee." She took a sip. "Drinking my coffee."

"Don't be cute. You know what I'm talking about. Why are you staying at Grace and Jack's place?"

"Because while I love Annie, Lily, and Connor, I'm used to having my own space. What's the big deal?"

The big deal was there'd be no one to keep an eye on her. He never should have asked her to leave his place. At least he'd know what she was up to. "You'll hurt Madison and the kids' feelings."

She laughed into her coffee. "I can't believe you're worried..." Something caught her attention and she straightened, setting down the cup to wipe the foam from her upper lip. "Okay, it's time for you to leave," she said from between clenched teeth while offering a smile in the direction of the door.

"Hey, Vivi, sorry I'm late." Trainer pulled out a chair and nodded at Chance. "McBride." As he sat down, the other man glanced at the boxes in Chance's arms. "Now, I'd be derelict in my duties if I didn't advise you to go easy on the sweets, McBride. A man of your age has to start watching his cholesterol levels."

Chance gave him an intimidating stare. The jerk grinned. Vivi pressed her lips together. "We're not done with this conversation, Slick," he warned her and headed for the door.

\*          \*          \*

Chance was on a mission. From the bakery, he dropped off the coffee and cupcakes at the station, then drove straight to the O'Connor ranch. His brother didn't know where his wife was and she had yet to respond to the three messages Chance had left on her voice mail. So he had no choice but to talk Liz into helping him out. He needed her to keep Vivi busy with the wedding. It was the only thing he could come up with to keep her out of trouble.

And if that included no time to hang out with Trainer, so much the better. Now that she had her own private space, no time to entertain the doc had just moved to the top of his list. It wasn't as if Chance was jealous. He was doing her a favor. Long-distance relationships didn't work. Besides that, the doc was a bit of wuss. Vivi'd roll right over him.

By the time Chance drove through the wrought iron gates and up the long, circular drive, his mood from earlier that morning had returned. He didn't need to be dealing with this shit. All he wanted was for the damn wedding to be over and Vivi on a plane back to New York, where the only trouble she'd get into was pissing off readers with her unromantic, straight-shooting advice. New York, where he wouldn't have to worry about running into her on a date with a guy who looked at her like she hung the moon.

As he pulled in front of the elegant ranch house, he spotted Liz working in the front flower bed. She looked up, wiped a gloved hand across her brow, and gave him a wide smile. He could see why his dad was attracted to her. She was a beautiful woman. And he also knew: a good woman.

Liz had been his mother's best friend. Her biggest cheerleader throughout her battle with cancer. Near the end, she'd been the only one who could get his mother to eat. If it wasn't for Liz and her husband, Deacon, Chance didn't know how his dad would have gotten through those first few months.

He'd been a jerk the other night. Liz didn't deserve that. Vivi was right. She made his dad happy, and that was all that mattered.

"Hey, Liz," he said as he got out of the truck.

"Hi, honey. I'm so glad you dropped by." She stood up, brushing the dirt from her jeans.

"Can I give you a hand?" He gestured to the bags of topsoil.

She peeled off her gardening gloves. "No, I'm good. Come and have a cup of coffee with me. I need a break."

She looked like she could use one. Her face was pale, a damp sheen on her forehead. "You go on ahead. I'll take care of this for you first." She opened her mouth. No doubt to argue with him. "It'll take me a couple minutes, tops."

"Okay. But just those bags there. I'll get to the rest later."

He followed her gaze to three mounds of topsoil and at least thirty trays of white and pink tulips. "What are you doing, starting your own nursery?"

"You sound like your father." She gave him a self-conscious smile. "I want the beds to look good for the wedding photos. We had a heavy frost a week ago, and I lost most of my flowers."

"You can't do this on your own."

"I don't have much choice. The kids are busy, and Raul and Rosa went to visit relatives. They won't be back until a couple days before the wedding. I can't put it off any longer."

It would be easy enough for Chance to take care of it for her, but he had a better idea. He pulled out his phone. "I'll call Vivi. She'll give you a hand."

"I don't know, Chance. She doesn't seem like the gardening type."

"Are you kidding me? She has a green thumb." He smiled as he put the phone to his ear. The woman could kill a cactus. "You go on inside. Make a list of everything you need done. Vivi was just telling me how bored she is. You'd be doing her a favor."

"All right, if you're sure she won't mind. I could use a hand. Thanks, honey."

"No problem." His call went straight to voice mail. He tried again once he'd emptied a couple of bags into the bed. "Hey, Slick," he said when she finally picked up.

"What do you want, McBride?"

"Testy, aren't we?"

"I'm kind of busy here."

"Yeah, well, you'll have to tell Trainer to wrap it up. Liz needs your help out at the ranch. I'll pick you up in twenty minutes." Before she could object, he added, "You did tell me you were here to help with the wedding, didn't you?"

She sighed. "All right, give me half an hour."

That was more like it. He was feeling pretty pleased with himself when he walked into the house. Now he just had to make sure that Liz's list was long enough to keep Vivi busy for the next five days.

He walked through the slate foyer to the kitchen. "Hey, Liz. I'm going to pick up...Liz. Jesus. Liz!"

\*        \*        \*

Vivi put down her phone. Honest to good God, the man was a pain in the butt. After his performance at the Garage, she should've known he wouldn't let her enjoy her date in peace. She didn't believe for a minute that Liz needed her help. Not with all the family and friends she had willing to lend a hand. For a man who didn't want her, he gave a good impression of one who did. Which begged the question: Why was she letting him get away with it? Might be best if she pleaded the Fifth on that one. Because if she answered herself honestly, she'd feel like a bigger fool than she already did.

Matt glanced at his watch. "He held out longer than I expected."

"He was calling for Liz. She needs help with wedding stuff, I guess."

He angled his head. "And you believed him?"

She moved her coffee cup back and forth in front of her. "It's not what you think. He... We're not. Well, you know."

"Yeah, I do." He reached across the table, covering her hand with his. "I like you, Vivi. And if I thought I had a shot, I'd like to see where this takes us. But I don't think I do, do I?"

Her eyes dropped to the hand covering hers. He had great hands. He healed people with those hands. And the nickname, he came by it honestly. With his light-brown wavy hair and strong, angular features, he oozed sex appeal. He was also sweet. She hesitated, waiting for... something. Anything. That crazy electrical zing she got when Chance's hand so much as brushed hers. She got nothing—dammit.

"You're a nice guy, Matt." She slowly withdrew her hand from under his. "I'm just not interested in dating right now. I'm focusing on my career. And it's not like I'm in Christmas all that often."

He smiled. He had a great smile. Only it didn't cause the butterflies to take flight in her stomach the way Chance's did. Didn't make her dizzy or her heart pick up speed, either. Maybe that wasn't such a bad thing. Because really, how could all those "love" chemicals, cascading through your body day in and day out, be good for you? If she described her symptoms to Matt, he'd probably diagnose her with a life-threatening illness.

Huh, that wasn't a bad idea for a story. She picked up her iPhone and made a note to follow up on the idea— love/lust can be as deadly as a life-threatening disease.

She thought about how she reacted to Chance—love/lust is as addictive as crack. Now that was an even better angle.

"Where'd you go?" Matt chuckled.

She grimaced and put down her phone. "Sorry, occupational hazard. I thought of an idea for a story. If I decide to write it, I might give you a call if you don't mind, ask you a couple of questions."

"Anytime. And I mean that." He rubbed his jaw, a self-deprecating smile on his handsome face. "I haven't dated in a while. I think I'm supposed to be playing it cool. Pretty much blew that, didn't I?"

"No, you didn't." She eyed him curiously. They'd spent the last hour talking, and she hadn't been able to get him to open up about his past or his personal life. Now that she had an opening, she wasn't about to let it go. Everyone had a story, and she had a feeling Matt's was an interesting one. "And I don't believe you've been out of the dating game for that long. What's it been . . . a couple of months?"

He studied his empty coffee mug. "A while."

Okay, so the genial doctor could be as closemouthed as Chance. "I'll get it out of Nell, you know. You might as well tell me."

"No story here, Vivi. I'm an open—" He broke off when his beeper went off.

Vivi's cell rang at the same time. "Hey, Maddie, what's . . . Oh no, is she . . . I'll be right there."

# Chapter Eleven.

Chance stared out the hospital waiting room window, the landscape's vibrant hues of green and blue fading to static white as the memories overtook him.

*"Son, I'm sorry. They did everything they could to save Emma. She's with Katie now. She's with your mother."*

*He didn't want her with Kate or his mother; he wanted her with him. They told him she had a fifty-fifty chance of making it. Told him to hang on to hope. He'd clung to it like a lifeline in a storm-tossed sea. It was the only thing that had kept his heart beating, kept him from completely falling apart four hours ago when he'd learned Kate hadn't survived. The baby was part of her. A reason for him to go on. Without them both . . .*

"Chance, son, are you all right?"

It was this fucking room with the antiseptic smell. It brought everything back. Chance shook off the remnants of the memory as he worked to get the words out of his mouth. "How's Liz?"

His father took the seat beside him. "She'll be fine. With everything going on, she forgot to take her beta-blockers. It wouldn't have been a problem if she hadn't overexerted herself." Resting his elbows on this thighs, he scrubbed his face with his hands.

"I'm glad she's okay," Chance said, noting the slight tremor in his father's hands. He'd aged ten years in the last twenty minutes. It was all too familiar. "Why are you doing it, Dad? Why are you putting yourself through this again?"

His father lifted his head. "What are you talking about?"

"You and Liz. The wedding. It's going to happen all over again. You'll have to stand by and watch her slowly fade away, and there won't be a goddamn thing you can do to stop it. One day you'll wake up and she'll be gone. And then what? How long will it take you to recover this time? I'll tell you. You won't. Nothing will take away the pain."

"Liz doesn't have cancer, son. It's not the same."

"You weren't there. You didn't see her lying unconscious in a puddle of coffee." He'd thought she was dead. She'd looked like his mom the night she'd slipped away. Like Kate lying in the hospital bed with the baby swaddled in a pink blanket beside her. "Please, for me, just think about it. What's the rush? You don't have to get married right away."

"I love her. I want to marry her." His father rubbed his palms on his chinos. "Does this have something to do with your mother? Because, Chance, my love for Liz doesn't take away from what I had with Anna. I loved your mother. I always will. Same as Liz will always love Deacon."

"You know what, do what you want. But you and I both know there's only one way this will play out. Either you or Liz will have to live that nightmare all over again. And from what I saw today, it's going to be you."

Someone cleared their throat. Chance looked up to see Trainer at the door of the waiting room. "Paul, you can see Liz now. She's in room 217."

"You admitted her?" Chase then turned to his father, who stood and headed for the door. "I thought you said she was okay."

Trainer's brow furrowed as he looked from Chance to Paul. "She is. We're keeping her overnight as a precaution."

"A precaution, right." There was nothing left for him to say. His dad was a big boy. If he wanted to open himself up to a shitload of pain, there was nothing Chance could do to stop him.

\*       \*       \*

Chance pretended to be absorbed in an article about summer fashion trends, tossing the magazine on the empty chair beside him when his dad returned to the now-crowded waiting room. If possible, he looked worse than when he'd left the waiting room thirty minutes ago. Gage and Ethan broke off the conversation they were having by the window. Madison, Skye, Cat, and Nell looked up from where they sat against the opposite wall. They'd arrived a couple of minutes after his father had gone in to see Liz.

"Dad." Madison went to Paul and wrapped her arms around his waist. "How are you holding up? Chance said Liz is okay."

Paul patted Madison's back, looking over her head to meet Chance's gaze. Something was wrong.

"Can we see her?" Cat asked, her eyes red-rimmed. She'd been emotional when she'd first arrived. Chance supposed he hadn't helped matters when he tore into the lot of them for being too busy to give Liz a hand. But it needed to be said.

His father drew back from Madison and rubbed the back of his neck. "You might want to give her a few minutes, honey."

Ethan put his arm around his sister. "What's wrong?"

"She's..." His father cleared his throat. "Liz canceled the wedding."

Chance relaxed in the plastic chair. That was the best goddamn news he'd heard in months.

"Why? What happened?" everyone asked at once. Everyone except Chance.

"I suggested we postpone the wedding until she felt better. Chance and I were talking about it earlier, and he got me thinking. All the—"

A redhead in green scrubs poked her head into the room. "Dr. McBride, your patient is here." She looked around the room. "Do you want me to cancel?"

"No, that's fine, Karen. I'll be right there." He turned back to them. "When you go in to see Liz, don't pressure her about the wedding. She doesn't need the added stress right now. Nell, that goes double for you."

*       *       *

Vivi had a crying Evie on one hip, a crying Connor on the other. "Did you find their binkies, girls?" she yelled, bouncing the babies faster when they cried louder.

"Not yet," Lily and Annie shouted back.

"Let's sing a song. Do you want Auntie to sing you a song?" She started singing "Let it Go" from *Frozen*. She'd watched the movie three times with Lily and had the words down pat. Connor threw back his head and wailed. Oh, good God. "Okay, no singing. We'll dance. Let's dance." She shook her hips, dipping the babies up and down. "Isn't this fun?" she said breathlessly, wiping her sweaty forehead on Connor's head.

At the sound of feminine laughter, she spun around. "Thank God," she said when Skye and Maddie walked into the nursery. They retrieved their children, who instantly stopped crying.

Vivi sagged against the crib. "They hate me."

Skye laughed. "No, I think you may have scared them with your dance moves."

Maddie grinned, cuddling Connor to her chest. "No, I think it was her singing that did it. She sounds like a man. It probably confused them."

"You're both a riot. We lost their stupid sucky-things. You need to tie them around their necks." She eyed her two friends. "So, tell me, how's Liz?" Maddie and Skye shared a look. "Spill."

"Liz is okay, but Liz and Paul are not. She called off the wedding," Skye said, laying a giggling Evie down on the change table.

"Are you kidding me? What happened?"

"Your boyfriend," Maddie said, sitting in the rocking chair with a cooing Connor.

"Chance?" She gave a frustrated shake of her head when Maddie grinned. "He's not my boyfriend. Would you just tell me what happened?"

"Chance doesn't want them to get married, and he must have shared that with Dad. When he went in to see Liz, Dad suggested they postpone the wedding until she's feeling better. Liz got it into her head that he was looking for an excuse to get out of marrying her and called him on it." Maddie sighed. "It's a mess."

"It is," Skye agreed. "Ethan and Cat are steamed at Chance."

"Gage isn't happy with him, either. It's a good thing Chance left the hospital when he did."

"Now, wait a minute. How did Chance end up being the bad guy in this? Liz is the one who decided to cancel the wedding. You know how she reacts when Paul worries about her health. It's always been a hot-button issue with them."

"You're right. And I feel sorry for Chance. I think it was hard for him being there when Liz passed out. He laid into all of us." Skye picked up Evie, who chewed happily on the string of her mother's pink hoodie. "For a guy who everyone thinks isn't fond of Liz, he was pretty protective of her."

Maddie rose from the rocker with a sleeping Connor in her arms. "I feel bad for him, too. Gage thinks being at the hospital brought back memories of the night Kate and the baby died, and it had something to do with what he said to Dad. They'll sort it out. They're calling a family meeting when Liz gets out of the hospital tomorrow."

Chance didn't seem to be able to go anywhere in Christmas without being blindsided by memories of Kate and the baby. Vivi didn't like to think of him being alone. "Did he go back to the cabin?"

"No, Ted and Fred texted Nell just before we left the

hospital. They said he's at the Penalty Box. Gage'll stop by and check on him on his way home."

"I'll go," Vivi said, keeping her voice casually indifferent. "It's just down the road from the apartment anyway."

Skye's eyebrows drew inward. "What are you talking about?"

"She ditched us and moved into Grace's apartment."

"I didn't ditch you guys, Maddie. Tell the truth, it's easier without me here. Besides, now that the wedding is off, I'll probably catch an earlier flight home."

"No way. You promised to stay the week," Maddie protested.

"Yeah, we need more time to…ah…" Skye widened her eyes at Maddie, nudging her head in Vivi's direction.

"Give it up. I'm not moving to Christmas."

"Aw, come on. You miss us as much as we miss you. And it's not as though you love your job," Skye said.

"Of course I miss you guys. But while I may not love my current job, I don't plan on being Dear Vivi for much longer. I'm getting my old job back."

"What about Matt?" Maddie asked as she tucked Connor into his crib. "You didn't tell us how your date went. He'd be a good reason for you to move to town."

"He's a nice guy."

"No sparks, huh?" Skye said as they left the nursery.

"Nope, not a one." She held up the car keys, anxious to get to the Penalty Box. "I'm going to take off. You sure you're okay with me using your car, Maddie?"

"No problem. If Chance is in a bad way, you'll call, right?"

"What's wrong with Uncle Chance?" Lily asked, looking up from where she lay in front of the TV with her sister.

"Nothing. He just—"

Vivi cut off Maddie. She didn't want little Miss Tenderheart worrying about her uncle. "Hey, what gives? You two were supposed to be looking for the binkies. A lot of help you were." They grinned, and she kissed them goodbye. "See you tomorrow."

As Vivi headed for the door, she heard Maddie and Skye strategizing on ways to keep her in Christmas. They were getting as bad as Nell. Vivi wondered if she should be worried.

*       *       *

Vivi spotted Chance as soon as she walked into the Penalty Box. He sat at the bar with his back to her, talking to Natalee. An uneasy feeling came over her at the expression on Natalee's face. It was one Vivi suspected she'd worn herself when looking at the man. No, couldn't be. Natalee was too young, and more importantly, the man she was looking at with her heart in her eyes was her late sister's husband.

Laughing at something Chance said, Natalee lifted her head and caught sight of Vivi. The light immediately left her golden-brown eyes, and her fingers curled possessively around Chance's impressive bicep. Natalee didn't look so young and sisterly now. She looked like a woman staking her claim. And her hand dropped dejectedly to her side when Chance swiveled on the bar stool with a relieved smile spreading across his face when he saw Vivi. As soon as she got close enough, he hauled her between his legs. "Wondered when you'd show up," he said, resting his hand on her hip while his heavy-lidded gaze focused on her mouth.

*Good God. Not again.* "Hey, Natalee," she said, reminding him he had an audience. Shifting on her wedge sandals, Natalee played with the silver locket at her neck and gave Vivi a thin-lipped smile. From their previous encounters, Vivi imagined any further attempts at conversation would be a waste of time and returned her attention to Chance. "How much have you had to drink?" she asked as he twirled a strand of her hair around his finger.

"A couple." Behind him, Sawyer held up five fingers. Wonderful.

His gaze still on her mouth, Chance said, "Figured I'd crash at your place tonight."

Before Vivi could tell him that was not going to happen, Natalee said, "I can drive you home after my shift. You can't leave Princess alone all night."

Unraveling Vivi's hair from his finger, he gave the strands a gentle tug before glancing at Natalee. "She's with the neighbors. Pest control came today. I didn't want her to get sick. You better get back to work, kiddo."

He turned to Vivi with a grin when she muttered, "I knew you had rats."

Natalee stared at them with an unhappy look on her face, only moving when her boss called out, "Nat, drinks are up." Sawyer lifted his gaze to Vivi while loading Natalee's tray. "What can I get you?"

"I'll take a Coke, thanks." She went to step from between Chance's thighs, sighing when he tightened all that warm, hard muscle around her.

He leaned into her and sniffed. "Hate to tell you this, Slick, but you smell like puke."

She glanced down at the mark on her T-shirt; she should've changed before coming. "It is puke. Connor's puke, and possibly Evie's, too." She grabbed a napkin, wiping futilely at the stain.

"Let me do that for you," he offered in a lazy voice. But there was nothing lazy in the way his eyes tracked her hand or the way he brushed his beer bottle over her chest. Despite the cold from the frosted glass seeping into her skin, her body heated when he raised his gaze to hers.

"Got it covered," she said, wriggling from between his legs. She took the stool beside him, her body humming from his touch and the promise in his grass-green eyes.

Sawyer slid a tall glass in front of her. "Thanks." She took a long swallow, sagging against the high back of the leather bar stool.

Chance's mouth tipped up at the corner. "Kids wear you out?"

She nodded. "I got a better workout than going to the gym. I didn't know babies could cry that long or that loud. They're in love with those sucky-things. Next time, I'm taping them to their faces."

He smoothed his hand down her hair. "You're cute."

"You're drunk."

"Nah, it'll take another dozen to accomplish that." He took a pull on his beer, his gaze intent on the mirrored shelves behind the bar, taking in everything going on behind him. She'd seen him do that before. His easy, laid-back demeanor was an act. He was always on alert, hyperaware. *His* occupational hazard, she supposed. It was a much sexier occupational hazard than hers. With Chance, she'd always felt safe and protected.

His mouth on the bottle, he gave her a sidelong glance. "Madison and Skye send you to check up on me?"

She drew her gaze from the heavily corded muscles

of his tanned arm and nodded. "They're worried about you."

His brow lifted. "Thought they'd be more pissed than worried."

She watched him watching her in the mirror and held his gaze. "No, but I can't say the same for your brother and Ethan. Did you really convince your dad to back out of the wedding?"

"Liz canceled the wedding, not my dad."

"You don't seem too broken up about it."

He clanked the amber bottle against her glass. "I'm not." Something caught his attention, and he glanced toward the door. He muttered under his breath and set his beer on the bar, sliding off the stool to stand behind her. Resting his hands on her shoulders, he lowered his mouth to her ear. "Let's get out of here."

She turned to see Matt walking toward them. She should have known. Tipping her head back, she said, "You're as bad as Connor and Evie. Only *I'm* your pacifier."

He laughed, trailing his lips down her neck. "You're right. And I can think of several parts of your body I want to suck on right now."

She nudged him with her elbow. "That's not what I meant." She swiveled on the stool to face him. "Anytime you get uncomfortable or want to distract yourself, you use me to do it." She poked him in the chest with the glass. "I'm tired of it."

"We'll talk about it at your place. Come on." He took the glass from her hand and reached over her to place it on the bar, which put her nose in direct contact with his chest. His amazing hard, wide chest. Despite being ticked at his presumptuous manner, she couldn't help herself and sniffed. He didn't smell like baby puke. He smelled woodsy and warm and all male.

"McBride, Vivi," Matt said, coming to stand at the bar. "Twisted Pine Stout, Sawyer, thanks."

Chance slowly straightened. "Hey, Doc. Take Vivi's seat. We're heading home." He hauled her off the stool.

"Home?" Matt said, then slowly nodded. "Can't say I'm surprised." He smiled at Vivi, looking up when Dr. McBride's ex-girlfriend Karen called his name and waved him over to her table by the dance floor.

Vivi didn't know whether to be happy for him or offended that he had another date so soon after theirs. She was veering toward happy until she spotted the self-satisfied grin on Chance's face. Great, now not only had he dumped her, he thought Matt wasn't interested in her, either.

They said so long to Matt and headed out of the bar. The old-fashioned streetlamps cast a circle of light on the fragrant white flowers in the hanging baskets, while a full moon illuminated the pastel-painted storefronts on Main Street. It was the perfect night for a romantic walk. Only the man she would have chosen to go on that walk with her was silently laughing his ass off.

He wouldn't be for much longer. She knew exactly how to wipe that smirk off his face. "I'm glad Matt wasn't too broken up when I told him I couldn't date him. He seemed okay to you, didn't he?"

"Didn't seem broken up at all, Slick," Chance said with a hint of amusement in his voice. "So, you told him you couldn't date him, did you?"

"I had to. My boyfriend and I are getting back together. I didn't want to lead Matt on. He's a nice guy."

Chance stopped short, putting his hand on her arm. "Hold it, what boyfriend are you talking about?"

"The man I'm seeing in New York. We were on a break, and now we're not."

"You slept with me three days ago, and you're telling me you're involved with someone." He crossed his arms over his chest, the look on his face probably the one Cat had referred to. She was right. He looked pretty freaking scary.

"Like I said, we were on a break." She flicked her hair over her shoulder, going for coolly unperturbed instead of freaked out.

"What's his name? Where did you meet him?"

She forced a laugh while trying to think of a response to his rapid-fire questions. "Geez, McBride, you've been spending too much time with me." He stared her down, and without thinking, she blurted, "Clark Kent." She inwardly groaned when she realized what she'd said. Since she couldn't take the words back, she might as well go with it. "He's a reporter with the *Daily News*."

Chance rubbed his hand over his mouth, his eyes glinting with an emotion she couldn't read, but dammit, it looked like laughter. "Clark Kent as in Superman Clark Kent?"

"I know," she said as they began walking again. "He gets teased about it all the time. They call him Superman at his office. It kind of fits, if you know what I mean." She gave him an exaggerated wink. "He is pretty super."

Okay, now she didn't even have to guess at the emotion. He was trying to hold back a laugh, but it came out in his voice when he asked, "So, it's the real deal? He's the one?"

"He's the one." And since he looked like he didn't

believe her..."Actually, he texted me earlier, I should probably get back to him." She took out her phone. She could always tell Superman that she'd drunk-dialed him. But at least she'd prove to Chance she had other options, that, unlike him, there were guys out there who wanted her.

Superman's ringtone jangled on the cool, floral-scented breeze. She jerked her gaze to Chance. He came to an abrupt stop on the sidewalk, lifting his gaze to the starry night sky before turning to her. "Vivi, I can..."

No! There was no way he...Her fingers trembling as her pulse pounded in her ears, she redialed. He took his phone from his back pocket, the theme song louder and clearer.

Chance McBride was her comic book hero.

"Vivi, let me explain," he called after her as she took off down the sidewalk.

She turned, walking backward with her face burning, her vision blurred. "You ruined my career, you bastard. Don't ever contact me again."

# Chapter Twelve

With the sound of twittering birds and neighbors calling out to one another drifting through the bedroom window on a warm, cake-scented breeze, it took a moment for the memory of last night to hit Vivi. When it did, images of a laughing Chance walloped her with the force of a sledgehammer, obliterating the idyllic small-town morning smells and sounds.

She groaned, burying her head under the pillow. She didn't know which was worse: the fact that she'd waxed poetic about Superman, declaring him to be the *One*, to the man who was and didn't want to be, or that she'd fallen for Chance, not once, but twice. Twice! It must have something to do with those "love" chemicals short-circuiting her brain, because she wasn't stupid. She wasn't one of those women who needed a man in her life.

Other than being somewhat dissatisfied with the direction of her career at the time she first met Chance—and really, Vivi wouldn't be satisfied until she hit the big leagues—she'd been happy and content. And then he'd walked into her life and blown that happy contentment to smithereens.

It was embarrassing and pathetic. And it ended now. She probably should be thanking him. In the space of two minutes, he'd done what she'd been trying to do for the last eighteen months. She was over him. She no longer saw him through rose-colored glasses. The soft romantic feelings were gone. The butterflies in her stomach had shriveled up and died.

And now that she had her personal life sorted out, she had to do the same for her professional life. It was past time. She'd go after what she wanted, and if her editor didn't see that they were wasting Vivi's journalistic talents, she would…quit. Of course it wouldn't come to that. How often in the past had her editor remarked on Vivi's uncanny knack for sniffing out a story? Before the fiasco created by Chance, at least five times.

Vivi tossed the pillow aside and reached for her iPhone. E-mailing her editor, she requested a meeting for nine tomorrow morning. She'd bought her return ticket last night. She was flying out this afternoon. Someone, more like two someones, knocked on the apartment door. She hit "send" and tossed her iPhone on the bed. She knew exactly who the two someones were—her ex–best friends. She'd called them last night to vent. Only to discover that they'd known for months that Chance was Superman.

She marched to the front door and flung it open. Maddie's and Skye's eyes widened, and they took a couple of nervous steps back. Maddie held up a defensive hand.

"Okay, we know you're mad, but we didn't tell you because he was protecting you."

Vivi cocked her head and crossed her arms.

"Can we come in?" Skye wiggled a to-go bag and cup. "We brought you chocolate mousse cupcakes and your favorite coffee. We even had Grace put whipped cream and chocolate sprinkles on it."

"Fine." Vivi took the coffee from her. "But you'll have to talk fast. Cab's coming to pick me up in an hour."

"No way. You can't leave because of this. Just give us a chance to explain." Maddie said as she and Skye followed Vivi down the hall.

"You can't leave without saying good-bye to the kids. They'll be upset."

Vivi sat on the bed, brought the coffee cup to her mouth—inhaling the rejuvenating scent of chicory and cocoa—and arched a brow at Skye, who'd made the comment.

"Okay, so maybe not Connor and Evie, but Lily and Annie definitely will be. Especially Lily, you know how sensitive she is."

That was hitting below the belt, but Vivi couldn't let herself get sidetracked. "I'll call them tonight. I have to get back to work."

"Why? You keep telling us you can dial in your columns. Surely you can—" Maddie began.

"I'm not talking about my advice column."

Maddie shared a look with Skye, then sat beside her on the bed. "You got your old job back?"

"More like I'm giving my editor an ultimatum. I'm done wasting my time. I need to get back out there before I lose my street cred." She gave them a pointed look. "But enough with trying to distract me. Why didn't you tell me Chance was Superman?"

"Don't blame Maddie. It's my fault." Skye took a cupcake from the bag and handed it to Vivi. "They're off-the-charts delicious," she said with a hopeful smile.

"I don't care how off the charts they are. They're not getting you off the hook," she said, even as she took a bite. She closed her eyes. "Oh, God, they're as orgasmic as Autumn's chocolates." Since that was as close to an orgasm as Vivi'd probably get in the near future, she'd check and see if Grace would ship to New York. If she would, she'd place a standing order. She licked the icing off her fingers. "When did you figure out Chance was Superman?"

"Remember when I asked you for his e-mail address? I think it was the day after I married Ethan. Anyway, Superman knew too much about me, about you, and it made me suspicious."

"Would've been nice if you shared those suspicions with me," she said, remembering how she felt last night. He'd been laughing at her all along. The stupid woman who'd been crushing on a man she'd never met or spoken to.

"He cares about you, Vivi. He was trying to protect you." When Vivi responded with a snort, Skye's caramel eyes narrowed. "Yes, he was, and you needed protection and don't try and deny it. Jimmy broke into your apartment, and you wouldn't back off. Chance knows you. He knew you wouldn't leave it alone. He just didn't realize you'd outsmart the guys he had tailing you. Which, by the way, you promised me you wouldn't do. Honestly, Vivi, you're lucky all you lost was your job."

"I didn't lose my job. I was demot...put on probation."

"Demoted, probation, who cares. This is your life we're talking about. And not only yours. You led a known murderer and rapist to a woman in protective custody. If it wasn't for her uncle and his pals, who, I might add, you led there as well, she could have died. The same goes for the men responsible for protecting her," Maddie said.

"If McBride hadn't—"

"What? Shut you down? How many times do we have to tell you he was protecting you?" Maddie held up her hand. "And no, I don't agree with how he went about it. He should have told you who he was. But you might want to think about why he did that, Vivi. Whether you believe it or not, you matter to him. Yes, he screwed up. But it doesn't negate the fact he wanted to be a part of your life."

"She's right, sweetie. He's a good guy."

Some of her anger and embarrassment faded at the thought that Maddie and Skye might have a point. He hadn't walked away without a backward glance after all. Why else would he reach out to her, try to protect her, if he didn't care? She thought back to all their text conversations and warmth filled the previously hollow place in her chest. She closed her eyes at her reaction, reminding herself how she'd felt the morning after they'd made love at the cabin. The memory took care of the warm and fuzzies. She would never open herself up to him again. He might care about her, but he didn't love her.

"You know what, I'm done rehashing this to death." Vivi brushed the crumbs off her T-shirt and swung her legs off the bed. "And you two might have thought you had a good reason to keep his identity from me, but you didn't. I deserved to know. Thanks for letting me look like an idiot."

"You're right. We should have told you. I guess we thought you'd get your happily-ever-after with Chance and it wouldn't matter in the end." Skye offered her another cupcake.

"No thanks." It would take more than a chocolate-induced endorphin rush to fill the once-again empty space in her chest. And she'd been doing so well up until then. But Skye's words sent her tumbling down from the adrenaline high she'd gotten at the thought of taking back control of her career.

"You know, it always looks darkest before the dawn," Skye said with an encouraging smile.

Oh, God, she'd found her rose-colored glasses again. Skye had misplaced them last year when she'd lost her trust fund and ended up on Jimmy "the Knife" Moriarty's radar. Vivi'd been hoping they'd stay lost for good.

"Everything for a reason, remember?" Maddie shrugged at Vivi's you've-got-to-be-kidding-me look.

Vivi headed for the bathroom. "Okay, while you two have your platitude party, I'll grab a shower."

"Vivi, don't stay mad at us for long, okay? We'll do whatever we have to to make this up to you," Skye called after her.

She whipped her head around. Something in Skye's voice made her nervous. "No, no making anything up to me. I don't need your help or Nell McBride's. I've got it covered. By this time tomorrow morning, my career will be back on track."

"What if—" Maddie began.

"Don't go there." Vivi's cell chimed with her "boss is calling" ringtone. She rushed to the nightstand, giving her friends a zip-it look. "Hey, Meredith, how are you? Great news? Okay, I'm all ears." She gave Maddie and Skye a thumbs-up. They returned the gesture with an obvious lack of enthusiasm. Meredith continued speaking, and Vivi's knees went weak. She sank onto the bed.

"Going to a daily advice column from a weekly one wasn't exactly the news I was hoping for, Meredith. I have only a few weeks left on my probation, and I thought, well, I thought I'd be reassigned to my old position... Who? Okay, let me get this straight, you gave my job to *Darlene*? Would this be the same blonde bimbo who writes for the society page? The Darlene who got that position only because she's bonking the editor in chief... You think that's a little harsh, do you?"

Skye and Maddie lunged for the phone, trying to pry it from her hand. Vivi crawled to the other side of the bed, pushing them away to continue, "And I thought I was being diplomatic, considering this is nepotism at the very least, sexual exploitation if Darlene is as young as she acts." She paused, listening as Meredith took umbrage with her comments before trying to convince Vivi that a daily advice column was a wonderful opportunity and to please think about it for a couple of days. "Actually, Meredith, I don't need a couple of days. I quit."

\*       \*       \*

Chance woke up on a narrow cot that smelled like stale booze and puke. He turned his head and opened one eye. Through the bars, Ray sat reading a paper with his cowboy boots up on the desk. Chance was a little foggy on how he'd wound up in jail. About the only thing he remembered clearly was the humiliated expression on Vivi's face when she realized he was Superman. He sat up and groaned, as much from the memory as from the pain behind his eyes.

He heard a clunk and the wheels of a chair moving across the floor. "Keep it down, will ya," he muttered.

The door to the cell squeaked open. "Rough night, huh, big guy?" Ray held a mug of what smelled like coffee in his hand.

"Yeah." Chance stood up, twisting from side to side to get the kink out of his back. "Any idea how rough it was?"

Ray handed him the mug. "Not rough enough that you were arrested, but rough enough that we got called. Four yahoos wanted to see if you were as tough as you looked. Don't worry, you didn't put any of them in the hospital." He tugged on his ear. "Now that I think about it, if your brother had been on duty, you would have been arrested. The rest of us have your back though."

"Thanks for that." He took a mouthful of coffee, checking out his knuckles as he did.

Ray gave him one of his good-old-boy grins. "Not a mark on you. Kinda wish I'd been there to see you in action again."

Chance didn't remember much, but he thought there may have been a table or two involved. "Any damage to Sawyer's place?"

"A couple of broken chairs and a table. Sawyer says you can settle up with him today." Ray caught Chance's grimace and reassured him. "Don't worry about it. They've been giving him trouble every other week. You did him a favor."

"Guess I better clear out of here before Gage gets in." He walked out of the cell, setting the mug on the desk.

"You mentioned you were headin' out of town. That true?"

He wondered what else he'd mentioned. "Yeah, I'm booked on the red-eye out of Denver tonight." He'd reserved his ticket at the same time he switched from beer to Rye. Probably the reason he still remembered doing so. Everything after that was a blur. Everything but Vivi's face and the words she'd yelled at him.

Ray shoved his hands in his tan uniform pants pockets, rocking on his heels. "Too bad. I was hoping you'd come over for dinner. Meet Lauren."

"Lauren? Sounds familiar. You've been dating her for a while, haven't you?"

"Yeah, 'bout five years now. Finally got up the nerve to pop the question." He pulled a wallet from his back pocket, opening it to show Chance a picture of a petite brunette.

"Pretty lady. About time you made an honest woman out of her." Chance smiled, giving him the expected pat on the back.

A hank of dark hair fell over Ray's left eye, making him look about sixteen. So did the relieved smile he gave Chance. "Glad you think so. I was kinda worried about telling you, you know, on account of how you feel about marriage. You breaking up your dad and Liz like you did."

"I didn't break them up. Liz called off the wedding. Besides, it's not the same thing." Ray took Chance's proffered hand. "All the best to you and Lauren. We'll get together next time I'm in town."

Ray's face pinked as he shuffled his feet. "I don't want to put you on the spot, but I was hoping you'd be my best man."

"Oh, I…" Chance paused, a little surprised by his former deputy's request. He supposed he shouldn't be. Ray'd been a rookie when Chance had been sheriff, following him around like an eager puppy. "Sure, Ray, sure, I'd be honored—"

Ray drew him in for a man hug, patting him enthusiastically on the back. "That's great. That's just great. We haven't settled on a date, but as soon as we do, I'll send you the deets." He pulled back with a grin. "Oh, man, Lauren is going to be as happy as all get out. Told her all about you, you know."

"Jesus, you're worrying me now." He smiled and handed him his card. They usually kept their exchanges to e-mail, but with the possibility Callahan was linked to the drugstore break-ins, Chance wanted Ray to be able to reach him anytime, anyplace. "You can contact me at those numbers. Keep an eye on Callahan for me. Let me know when you find the black Mustang."

Ray tugged his ear.

"Something you're not telling me?"

He moved his head back and forth before answering, "Well, it's just that Gage warned us the case was off-limits to you. How did you hear about the Mustang?"

"Overheard Mrs. Tate talking about it." He didn't want to get Vivi involved, although it wouldn't matter now. After last night, he figured she'd be leaving town. About the only good thing that had come from her finding out he'd played her.

"Callahan's kept his nose clean. Took real good care of his brothers. He's made a name for himself. Don't think he's behind the break-ins. Might be time to let it go, big guy."

"Someone made that call to Kate, Ray." The last call on their landline had come from a pay phone in the strip mall where Callahan had his automotive business. It had come in twenty minutes before Kate's accident. Whoever made that call was the reason his wife and daughter were dead. They couldn't get any clear prints off the phone. But after the threats Callahan had made against Chance and his family two days prior to the accident, that was all the evidence he needed. Only it hadn't been enough. "All I'm asking is that you keep him on your radar. Follow the money, Ray. There's something there." Chance planned on doing the same.

"Okay, you leave it to me. I've got your back, big guy," Ray said as they made their way to the front of the station. "You take care of yourself now. No more drinking the hard stuff. Always did make you a little crazy."

"Thanks, Ray. I'll keep that in mind. Take it easy." As Chance left the station, he pulled his phone from his pocket. Ray was right. Chance and hard liquor had never been a good combination. He checked to make sure he hadn't texted or called Vivi. There was no telling what he'd say to her in the state he'd been in. He relaxed when he thumbed through his call history.

He hadn't tried to contact her, and she hadn't tried to reach him. A part of him wished she had—if only to give him hell. The muscles in his chest contracted painfully at the thought that she was out of his life for good. It felt like someone had ripped out his heart. Maybe she was right. Maybe he'd fooled himself into believing that she needed his protection when all along he'd been the one who needed her.

*    *    *

Chance stood on his brother's front step with Princess tucked under one arm, her food and treats under the other arm, her pink doggie bed in his hand, and a bag of her clothes and toys slung over his shoulder.

His brother opened the door. "Geezus, you've got as much stuff for the dog as we do for Connor when..." Gage's eyes narrowed. "Hold it. This is just for a visit, right? You're not planning on leaving her with us."

He shouldered past his brother. "Come on, the kids will love her. And it's only until tomorrow. Natalee will pick her up in the morning." At least he hoped she would. After how she'd acted at the bar last night, he'd put off calling her. He'd been hit on before and knew the signs. And if his sister-in-law hadn't been hitting on him, she'd been doing a good impression of someone who was. Then again, maybe she'd simply wanted to practice her flirting techniques on someone who was safe. Whatever it was, it had been damn uncomfortable. Still, he'd have to call her to say good-bye.

"Why? You planning on spending another night in jail?"

"I wasn't *in* jail. I was hanging out with Ray." He put Princess down and unloaded her crap by the door. She sat in front of him, whining. He sighed and picked her up, following Gage into the kitchen. "Job came up. I'm catching a red-eye tonight."

His brother rounded on him. "No, you're not. We have a family meeting scheduled to straighten out the mess *you* made. Have you told Dad you're leaving?"

"Just came from his place. Unlike you, he understands why I have to go." Possibly because his dad had spent the entire time Chance was there staring into space. The band across his shoulders tightened at the image of his dad moping around the house on his own. Then he reminded himself what his dad was feeling now was nothing compared to what he'd deal with when he lost Liz for good. Besides, in the end, it had nothing to do with Chance. He hadn't said anything to Liz, and she was the one who called off the wedding. Chance pulled out a stool and took a seat.

Gage leaned his hip against the island with his arms crossed. "Maybe if you told me what you told him, I'd understand why the wedding is off and why you're running away again."

"What am I, sixteen? I don't owe you an explanation, little brother." Gage opened his mouth, then closed it when Annie and Lily joined them in the kitchen. "Hey, girls," Chance said.

"Hey." Annie gave him a chin lift. She reminded him of Vivi—all attitude and pretty eyes. Only Annie's were pale green like his brother's.

"Hi, Uncle Chance," Lily said, coming to give him a hug.

"Shouldn't you two be in school?" he asked his nieces.

"We were supposed to go for our fittings today, so Mommy said we can take a mental health day."

How did he respond to that? "Uh...that's nice." His brother looked at him with a raised brow. At least Lily didn't seem to hold it against him. She snuggled up to his side. "Are you and your doggie coming to stay with us?"

"No, kiddo. I have to leave town. But Princess can spend the night." The dog whined, nudging her nose into his shirt.

"It's okay, puppy." Lily leaned in to cuddle Princess, then looked at him. "She doesn't want you to leave."

Chance laughed. "She tell you that?"

From her expression, his niece didn't think he was funny. "You shouldn't joke. Animals have feelings, you know." She fixed the pink bow in Princess's topknot. "Auntie Vivi's going to be sad, too."

He scratched his forehead. "I think your auntie—"

"No, she won't," Vivi Junior interrupted him with a sneer. "Why do you think Mom and Auntie Skye have been at her place all morning? She's leaving, too, and it's all his fault."

"Annie, that's enough," her father said.

"Superman, yeah right. More like Superjerk." Annie stomped from the kitchen.

"Really? That's something you felt the need to share with a thirteen-year-old?" Chance asked his brother.

Gage rubbed the back of his neck. "No, she must—"

"It's not Mommy and Daddy's fault. We listened at the door." Lily propped her face in her hands, those big eyes of hers zeroing in on his. "You shouldn't leave Christmas. You need your family and Auntie Vivi to make you better. And Princess needs you."

He shot a help-me-out look at his brother, who shrugged in response. Jesus, he'd rather deal with Annie than Lily any day. She was killing him. He touched the tip of his finger to her nose. "Thanks for worrying about me, honey. But I'm fine. And you know what"—he glanced at his watch—"I'd better get going." He'd hang out at the airport until his flight. "You take good care of Princess for me, okay?"

He handed her the dog and stood up. Princess whimpered, squirming in Lily's arms to get back in his. "See, she's sad," Lily said, her brown eyes filling with tears. "She doesn't want you to go, and neither do I. And Daddy and Grandpa want you to stay, too. Right, Daddy? Tell him to stay."

"Come here, sweet pea." Gage wrapped Lily and the now-barking dog in his arms. Chance met his brother's eyes. Yeah, he got it. He'd upset pretty much everyone he knew in Christmas. Gage was still comforting his daughter and the dog when Chance took off. Deciding he couldn't deal with any more drama, he texted Natalee instead of calling.

He shut off thoughts of Vivi and his family as he left the small town in his rearview mirror. An hour later, the tightness in his chest finally released. So when his brother's call came in, he let it go to voice mail. Gage didn't give up. He called again…and again. Chance sighed and answered. "If Princess is giving you trouble, ask Nat to pick her up after work. I'll give you her—"

"It's not Princess."

He didn't like the barely-holding-it-together tone in Gage's voice. "What is it?"

"Ray. He…Geezus, Chance, they don't know if he's going to make it."

# Chapter Thirteen

Chance shoved his hands in his jeans pockets as he stared out the hospital waiting room's window. Below, the midday sun sparkled on the water tumbling over the rocks in the fast-moving stream. A couple of old-timers fished off the wooden bridge while people biked and walked along the tree-lined boardwalk. Folks enjoying the unseasonably warm afternoon while a few feet away a man lay fighting for his life. Shit happened on idyllic spring days the same as it did in the middle of a blizzard.

He turned away from the window. The room had steadily filled up since he'd arrived ten minutes ago. Ray had more friends and family than Chance realized. He wondered if his former deputy knew how many people cared about him. *Doubtful*, Chance thought, having known the man as long as he had. He imagined they'd bring some solace to Ray's fiancée, who stood in the hall being comforted by Gage. Then again, no one had had as much support as Chance, and it hadn't done him much good. Maybe if he'd stuck around, it would have.

Gage caught his eye, raising a finger to indicate he'd be with him in a minute. He could take all the time he wanted, because Chance didn't plan on leaving. Not until he found out Ray's prognosis and how he'd wound up here in the first place. Looked like he was about to find out.

As his dad joined Gage and Lauren in the hall, his brother said something to the petite brunette, gave her a one-arm hug, then walked to the waiting room. If anyone could answer Lauren's questions and alleviate her fears, it would be his dad. Paul McBride was one hell of a doctor and one of the most empathetic, caring men Chance knew. He admired what his dad had done at Christmas General. Late last year, he'd been made chief of staff of the small, well-respected trauma center.

From the door of the waiting room, Gage waved Chance over. He silently followed his brother down the hall. When they were well out of earshot, Chance asked, "How's it look?"

Gage bowed his head and gave it a slight negative shake. "They nearly lost him twice. He's stable, for now. Both legs, his right arm, and ribs are broken, and there's some damage to his spleen. But they're more concerned about TBI—traumatic brain injury," his brother said, giving it to him in layman terms. Gage had been a paramedic before realizing he wanted to go into law enforcement. "He has a cerebral edema. Right now they're treating him with oxygen and IV fluids, but it's possible they'll have to do a craniotomy."

"What the hell happened to him?"

"From what we pieced together, he was on his regular

patrol route when he saw a black Mustang and decided to give chase. He radioed in for backup. Dispatch heard gunshots. They'd fired on him, took out his tires. He lost control of the car and hit a tree." Gage scrubbed a hand over his face. "It should have been me out there, not him. He was..."

"Say it. He was covering for you so you could be there for the girls while Maddie was with Vivi. If anyone has reason to feel guilty, it's me, not you. If it weren't for me, there'd be no need for Maddie to be at Vivi's, and if it weren't for me, Ray wouldn't have been so hot and heavy to chase down the Mustang. I'm the one who told him to be on the lookout for the car."

"Knock it off. You're not doing this again. I won't let you take this on, too. Did you not hear what I said? He was on his *regular* patrol route. He called for backup. I'm the sheriff, and whether you believe it or not, I'm damn good at my job. The whole department has been told to be on the lookout for the Mustang. If you want to blame anyone, blame the bastards who did this."

"Might want to take your own advice, then, little brother."

"Yeah, you're right. And do me a favor and knock off the 'little brother' shit. I'm only a year and a half younger than you." He looked past Chance. "Here comes Lauren."

Chance turned. The woman gave him a watery smile, her dark eyes puffy and red-rimmed. She stuck out her hand. "I'm Ray's fiancée."

Chance clasped her hand between both of his. "I know who you are, Lauren. Ray was showing off your picture this morning. Congratulations, he's a great guy. You've made him a happy man."

Her eyes filled, and she squeezed his hand. "He called me as soon as you left. He was over the moon that you agreed to be his best man. You're his hero." She pressed her lips together and shook her head. "I can't believe this is happening. A couple of hours ago, we were planning our wedding..."

Chance knew only too well how she felt. The shock, the numbness, the disbelief. Kate had changed her mind about how she wanted the nursery decorated the morning of the accident. Throughout the day and evening, she'd sent him pictures accompanied by sweet, cajoling notes to get him on board with putting a princess canopy over the crib, changing the paint color from lilac to pink and white stripes. He'd opened her last text two minutes before they told him she was dead. He still had the message on his phone.

He pushed the thought from his head and gave Lauren's hand a comforting squeeze in return. "He's tougher than he looks, you know. He's going to pull through this."

"Chance is right. There are a lot of people praying for him." When an older version of Lauren called out to her from the waiting room, Gage said, "Go be with your family."

She nodded, then looked up at Chance. "Ray said you were leaving town. Are you—"

"I'm not going anywhere, Lauren. I'm going to find whoever's responsible for this."

She hugged him. "Thank you. It would mean a lot to Ray knowing that you're here. That you're looking into this."

Gage turned on him as soon as she walked away. "Do not even think about getting involved in my case."

"Sorry, little brother, I'm already involved."

"Damn it, Chance." Gage speared his fingers through his short, dark hair. "Fine. You wanna be involved, I'll deputize you. But you work for me, remember that."

Chance weighed out the pros and cons. He'd have access to everything Gage had. On the other hand, all he had to do was pick up the phone and call his baby brother. Easton was staying at Chance's apartment in Virginia, recovering from the injury he'd sustained in combat three months ago. He'd recently been recruited by the CIA. Neither their father nor Gage knew about the posting or injury. Like Chance, Easton didn't like to be coddled or worried over. He'd been putting off coming home for the wedding until the last minute. His baby brother would be glad of the reprieve.

So when Chance factored Gage looking over his shoulder and second-guessing him into the equation, he decided he was better off going it on his own. Until he remembered Callahan's threat against his family that frigid morning five years ago and changed his mind. He nodded. "I'll pick up Princess. Take her home. I'll see you back here in an hour. Call if there's any change in Ray's condition."

"That's it? No arguments? No telling me you don't play well with others in the sandbox and you like to color outside the lines?"

Instead of answering, he headed for the elevators. Nothing Gage hated more than silence. It made him nervous. Chance could tell he was plenty nervous when he called. "Chance, this might not be a good idea after all. Chance!"

Probably wasn't. They'd drive each other nuts. And admittedly, Chance had a small problem with authority—

he didn't follow orders well. But he'd make it work. In his gut, he knew Callahan was the reason Ray was fighting for his life. And he'd be damned if he let Jake Callahan endanger any more of his family and friends. This was five years in the making, and Chance planned to end it once and for all.

*     *     *

As soon as he reached the flower-lined walkway at his brother's place, Chance heard Princess's excited bark. She knew it was him. She'd always been able to tell if it was friend or stranger the moment they pulled up to the cabin. She'd traumatized any number of deliverymen. They'd always walked away red-faced when they discovered they'd been terrified by an eight-pound dog with a pink bow in its hair.

He let himself in. Princess mauled his leg, trying to leap into his arms. She had on one of those pink ballerina thingies and two topknots instead of one on her head. No wonder she wanted to get out of there.

He picked her up, inspecting her nails for polish as he called out to Madison.

"In here," she responded, sounding like she had a cold.

But he knew as soon as he saw her leaning against the island in the kitchen that it wasn't a cold. She'd been crying. As he went to deposit Princess on the floor, the dog let loose a pathetic howl. Chance sighed and tucked her under his arm. Lily gave him a weak smile from where she sat beside her sister. Annie didn't look up, too busy pushing around the macaroni and cheese on her plate with a fork.

It didn't take much for Chance to figure out what was

going on. It wasn't easy being a sheriff's wife. After what had happened to Ray, the worries Madison was able to keep at bay would now be front and center in her mind. The kids', too.

He rubbed his sister-in-law's shoulder. "How are you guys doing?"

Madison leaned into him. "Been better." She lifted her gaze to his. "How's Ray?"

"No change, but he's in good hands. He'll pull through."

"Did they find the men who hurt him?" Lily asked, chewing on her bottom lip.

"Not yet, but we will."

"We? Does that mean you're staying?" Madison asked.

"Yeah, I'm sticking around. Figure my little brother could use a hand."

"I'm glad. But you might not want to call him 'little brother.' He hates it, you know."

He grinned. "I know."

Annie's pale green eyes took his measure. "It's your job, right, to protect people from really bad guys with guns and stuff? 'Cause we don't have people like that here. My dad hasn't shot anyone before, have you?"

"Yeah, I have. And none of the people I protected have ever been hurt, Annie. I'm not going to let anything happen to your dad." It was the truth. The only ones he'd failed to protect were his wife and child. And the weight of the promise he'd just made to Annie fell heavily on his shoulders. He couldn't fail again.

"Sweetie, your daddy may not have to use his gun very often, but he knows what he's doing. He's smart and well trained. You don't have to worry about him."

He couldn't help but note the defensive tone in his

sister-in-law's voice. "Madison's right. Your dad's good at his job."

Annie bent her head over her plate, hair as dark as her father's falling across her cheek. "But she was worried about him, too."

Madison closed her eyes and pressed her fingers to her mouth, then moved away from Chance to stand behind the girls and draw them in for a hug, kissing the tops of their heads. "I'm sorry if I upset you guys. I was worried about your auntie Vivi, and then when we heard about Ray..."

Chance stiffened, tightening his hold on Princess, whose low growl rumbled through her small body. "What's wrong with Vivi?"

"She quit her job and—"

"Princess bit her," Lily interrupted Madison, adding in a whisper, "She doesn't like Auntie Vivi. I think she knows she's scared of her."

There was no reason for Lily to whisper unless... "Vivi's here? I thought she was leaving town." Now more than ever, he hoped to God he was wrong and she was on a plane back to New York. Because Vivi quitting her job wasn't a positive development. There'd be nothing to stop her from sticking around.

"As upset as she was, we weren't about to let her leave town, Chance." Madison's tight expression made it clear she held him responsible for Vivi's unhappy state of mind. "She's on the deck."

Okay, other than Princess, there was only one reason Vivi wouldn't be in here comforting Madison and the kids. "She doesn't know about Ray, does she?"

When Madison shook her head, he released a relieved

breath. Things were looking up. "Good. And you three aren't going to tell her."

"Chance, there's no way we can—"

"You know what went down with Jimmy. Do you really want her out there trying to figure out who did this?"

"That was different. She wouldn't..." She sighed when he raised a brow. "Okay, you're right, you're right. But I hate the thought of her alone in New York with no one looking out for her."

"You can look after her, Uncle Chance. I know you can. She's sad. Please don't make her go away," Lily pleaded.

"I'm not your aunt Vivi's favorite person at the moment, honey. So she wouldn't make it easy for me to look out for her. And I'll be busy. When this is over, she can come back and stay as long as she likes." It wasn't a bad idea. Once this was taken care of, she'd be safer here than in New York. And he'd be long gone.

When Lily went to object, her sister intervened. On his behalf, which was a surprise. She didn't like him much, but she loved Vivi and obviously was smart enough to realize the consequences of her aunt staying in town. "Uncle Chance is right. He needs to help Dad, and Aunt Vivi will distract him."

Understatement if he ever heard one. Before his sister-in-law or niece came up with another reason to stop him, he handed Princess across the island to Lily and headed out of the kitchen.

"Chance, she's had a tough day. Don't upset her," Madison called after him.

He didn't care if he upset her or not. In fact, it'd be better if he did. Because one way or another, he was getting her out of town. Given how she felt about him, all he'd probably have to tell her was that he was sticking around. But any thought to what he'd say abandoned him when he stepped onto the deck and caught sight of her lying on a lounge chair in an itsy, bitsy red-and-white-striped bikini.

\*     \*     \*

"Please tell me you got hold of Superjerk and that Demon Dog has had her rabies shot," Vivi said upon hearing the glass doors slide open.

She frowned when Maddie didn't respond. That couldn't be good. Preparing for the worst, she slowly turned her head. Chance stood there looking as ruggedly impressive as the mountains behind him. She growled inwardly when the thought popped into her head, reminding herself he'd made a fool of her. She didn't want to deal with him on top of everything else. And she certainly didn't need to see her scantily clad body reflected in his mirrored shades.

She turned back to her iPad, wondering what the hell she'd been thinking donning the barely there bikini.

"Superjerk? Thought I was your one-and-only."

An amused cockiness tinged his deep voice—the bastard. How dare he make fun of her feelings. Her fingers tightened around her iPad; she was tempted to throw it at him when he moved closer. "Come on, Slick. You know I was just trying to protect you. You need a keeper."

"I do not need a keeper. Especially if that keeper's *you*. You can leave now." Of course he didn't listen and kept walking toward her. His ego was as overinflated as his muscles. Maybe if she ignored him, he'd go away.

*I should have known better*, she thought, when a shadow fell over her. She kept her eyes firmly on the screen. "Do you mind? You're blocking the sun."

He leaned over and hooked his finger under the narrow strap of the bikini top, sliding the red-and-white tie off her shoulder. "Looks like you've had more than enough. You're burnt."

"I'm not…" She sucked in a breath when he continued to lower the strap, unable to contain a shiver as her body reacted to the deep rumble of his voice, the way his knuckles caressed her heated flesh. She had to get rid of him before he noticed her nipples' reaction through the thin fabric. "Stop it." She pushed his hand away.

A warm breeze rustled the trees that stood sentry by the deck, filling the air with the smell of Chance's clean, sandalwood scent. She stifled a groan when he crouched beside the lounge chair and took her hand. He gently rubbed his thumb over her knuckles as he examined her fingers. "Where did she bite you?"

"On my toe," she said, because there was no way she'd tell him Cujo bit her on the butt. She'd been on her hands and knees, searching under the couch for Connor's binkie when the demon dog escaped from Lily's bedroom.

Vivi's sigh of relief morphed into an exasperated huff when Chance lowered his large frame onto the end of the lounge chair, draping her legs over his thighs. She nudged him with her foot. "Off."

"Not until I check you out." He smoothed his palm over one foot, then the other, inspecting them closely.

"She's had her rabies shot, right?" she asked nervously. Cujo had drawn blood, and Vivi could still feel the imprint of those dagger-sharp teeth.

He was too busy playing with her toes to respond. "No, don't," she gasped through an unintentional laugh.

"Still ticklish," he murmured, his mouth quirking at

the corner. His smile widened with a flash of strong white teeth. "She didn't bite your toe, did she?" Wrapping his hands around her ankles, he tugged her closer and went to flip her over.

"Don't you dare, McBride." She kicked her feet to loosen his grip, but he firmed his hold.

Her iPad hit the deck. They both reached for it at the same time. He got there first. The amusement left his face as he scanned the articles about her successful photojournalist half brother and broadcast journalist half sister. In their midtwenties, they were leaps and bounds ahead of Vivi career-wise.

He raised his mirrored gaze to hers. She waited for the lecture, waited for him to tell her to stop comparing herself to them. She'd heard it from him before. He knew her dirty little secret. He'd tell her to stop using them as a measure of her success. He'd tell her it didn't matter. They'd had a billionaire father who opened doors for them, whereas she'd opened hers for herself.

Only she'd done a good job slamming the last one shut. She fought down the wedge of panic in her throat and returned her gaze to Chance, to his overlong hair shielding his face from her as he studied the screen, the sun's rays turning his silky, copper streaks a fiery red.

"You shouldn't have quit your job." He switched off the iPad, tossing it on the chair by her hip.

Tell her something she didn't know—her job search so far had turned up empty. But still, his lack of support and encouragement surprised her. She covered her reaction with a snippy "Maddie's got a big mouth."

He lifted his head. Despite being unable to see his eyes, she could feel his gaze travel the length of her body. She pulled her knees to her chest to conceal her nipples' traitorous reaction to his attention. "What are you doing here, anyway? I heard you'd left town."

He looked out over the valley before responding. "Caved to family pressure. Nell guilted me in to sticking around." He turned back to her. "Too bad you're not staying in town, Slick. We could hang out."

He was so full of it. The light teasing voice was an act. She saw the way his beard-stubbled jaw tightened, the deepening of the lines bracketing his mouth. He wasn't happy to be staying in town. And hanging out with her? Yeah right. Been there, done that, got the T-shirt. And it sucked. Before she could call bullshit, he added, "I've got some time. I can drop you off at the airport if you need a lift."

"Sorry to disappoint you, McBride, but Maddie and Skye got me to cancel my ticket."

"Take mine. I'll transfer it to you, and you're good to go. I was booked on the red-eye with a connection in New York."

Wow, could he be any more obvious that he wanted to get rid of her? She ignored the dull ache in her chest. "Thanks for the offer, but I promised Maddie and Skye I'd stick around for a couple of days." She kept her tone light. She didn't want him to know he still had the power to hurt her. To that end, she probably shouldn't have added, "And *I* don't break my promises," but she couldn't help herself.

"Way I see it, Slick, you don't have much of a choice. You gotta get a job, and you're not going to get one sitting on your ass soaking up the Colorado sunshine. 'Bout time you put your needs before everyone else's. Lay it out there for your girls. They'll understand."

Vivi curled her fingers into her palms before she gave in to the urge to slug his chiseled, arrogant jaw. Instead she was about to tell him where he could shove his advice when Maddie opened the sliding glass doors and Chance's cell rang. Vivi frowned when she caught the anxious glance Maddie shared with her brother-in-law. Her frown deepened when she got a better look at her best friend. She'd been crying.

"Hey, what's wrong, sweetie?" Vivi said, getting up from the lounge chair to go to her.

Maddie didn't respond right away. She looked beyond Vivi. "She's going to find out, Chance. I can't keep it from her."

# Chapter Fourteen

Vivi pulled Maddie in for a hug when she finished telling her what happened to Ray. "You should have come and gotten me as soon as Gage called you."

"I know. I wasn't thinking straight, and then the girls..." She closed her eyes, giving her head a slight shake before saying, "I didn't handle it well, Vivi. I didn't hide my reaction. I should have—"

"Stop it. They're smart kids. They would have known you were keeping something from them. Tell me what I can do."

"You can head back to New York so she doesn't have to worry about you, too," Chance said from behind her.

She glanced over her shoulder, meeting his mirrored gaze as he shoved his cell phone in his back pocket.

Before Vivi could respond, Maddie said, "It's too dangerous to transport Ray to Denver, isn't it? They're going to have to do the surgery here."

His shoulders rose and fell on a heavy breath, then he nodded. "Yeah. Gage says they've got a neurosurgeon on the way." He lifted his chin at Vivi. "Get your stuff. I'll take you to the airport."

Ignoring him, she took Maddie's hand. "I can stay with the kids if you want to go to the hospital. We'll do something fun. Take their minds off everything."

"I'm not fooling around here, Slick. You're not staying in town."

Maddie's gaze shifted from Vivi to Chance. "Why don't I leave you two alone to work this out?"

"There's nothing to work out. He doesn't... You can't be serious. Maddie!" she called after her best friend, who ducked into the house. She whirled on Chance. "Dammit, McBride. I'm not going anywhere. She needs me right now. That's what friends do, you know. They—" She broke off, realizing that as hard as this was for Maddie, it was just as hard on Chance. Ray used to work for him. He was the reason Chance hadn't left Christmas.

"Look, I get that you're worried about your friend. But I'm not leaving town. And McBride, you don't get a say in my life. Not anymore." She walked to the lounge chair to pick up her iPad and towel.

"What if I told you I want one. That I need one." His voice was low and rough as he moved in behind her.

"Don't use my feelings for you against me." She grimaced when she realized what she'd revealed—as much to herself as to him. If it weren't for Maddie, she'd be on the first flight out of there.

"I'm not." He put his hands on her shoulders, lowering his mouth to her ear. "I care about you, Vivi. I need to know you're safe. If anything happened to you..."

She believed he cared about her. But it wasn't enough. "Give me some credit. I've been looking out for myself since I was seventeen. And I've done a good job of it." She moved her head and bent to pick up her iPad. Which was incredibly stupid because it put her bottom in direct contact with... She raised her eyebrows and glanced over her shoulder. "Really?"

"What can I say?" He gave a seemingly embarrassed shrug. Taking a step back, his gaze once again slid down her body. His brow furrowed and he reached out, the pads of his fingers grazing the cheek Cujo had latched on to.

"Hey, back off." She went to move away from him, but his hands clamped onto her waist, holding her in place. "McBride."

He crouched. "Jesus, she took a chunk out of your ass."

"Which is why I needed to know if she had her rabies shot." She bit the inside of her lip, holding back a moan when he gently traced the bruise. "Has she?" Her voice came out a breathy whisper. She inwardly rolled her eyes. Could she be more obvious?

A slow smile curved his lips. "Not sure. But knowing Nat, you're probably in the clear." His warm breath heated her skin as his mouth...

"McBride," she yelped when he planted a kiss on her butt cheek.

"There, all better now." He lightly patted her bottom as he stood up. "I've gotta take off. You need a ride to get your things from the apartment?"

"What are you talking about?" Again with the breathy voice. In her defense, she was still recovering from the erotic feel of his lips pressed to her naked flesh. She nudged him out of the way and headed for the patio doors.

"You're moving back in with Maddie and Gage. You'll have to clear out your stuff from Grace and Jack's—"

"Ah, no I'm not. I—"

He stopped her with a hand on her arm. "Don't test me, Slick. I'm not in the mood. You're staying here, and that's the end of it."

She jerked her arm free. "Bite me."

\*        \*        \*

Chance didn't bite her. Though, if his wolfish grin had been any indication, he would have been more than happy to. But Gage had called, and Chance had taken off for the hospital. Without his damn dog.

That had been more than two hours ago. Maddie had finally gotten tired of Vivi complaining and called Natalee. She was due to arrive any minute now to pick up Demon Dog. "Lily, Natalee's here," Vivi yelled when she heard the front door open.

"Ignore her, girls," Maddie called out and got up from the couch. "Natalee doesn't know us that well. She wouldn't just—" She broke off when Gage walked into the living room. Covering her mouth to contain a sob, Maddie ran to her husband.

Gage wrapped his arms around her. "Hey, what's all this about?" he asked when she buried her face in his neck. He stroked her hair.

"I'll go see what Lily and..." Vivi remembered that the girls were playing with Cujo in Lily's room. "If Connor's still sleeping," she amended.

Lost in each other, the couple didn't acknowledge her as she walked out of the room. It was difficult to see her best friend upset and vulnerable. Maddie had once been like Vivi, a tough, unemotional workaholic. Maybe there was something to be said for staying single after all.

Twenty minutes later, when Skye and Ethan arrived, Vivi was ready to swear off men and relationships all together. Skye had once been one of the most easygoing, fun-loving, self-confident women she'd ever known. Now she flounced into the house wearing a face of thunder with Evie in her arms.

"Sweetheart, how many times do I have to tell you. I wasn't *practically engaged* to Claudia." Ethan followed his wife into the house carrying a playpen with a pink diaper bag slung over his shoulder.

Maddie arched a brow at Vivi. Gage had worked his magic on his wife, and Maddie was back to herself. Well, not her old self, her married-Maddie self. The one who wore pink. In response to Maddie's raised brow, Vivi shrugged, and they followed Skye and Ethan into the living room.

"Hey, guys, everything okay?" Maddie asked.

Vivi gave her an are-you-kidding-me look. That was not a question to be asked right now.

"Everything's just peachy. Ethan's ex-fiancée and her father were so worried about Liz, they arrived today."

Oh, oh, this was not good. Not good at all.

Gage, who'd walked into the living room while on the phone, disconnected and said, "Geezus, Eth, they're staying with Liz? My dad's going to have a coronary."

Skye gave her husband an I-told-you-so look. Ethan dumped the playpen and the diaper bag on the floor, throwing up his hands. "What was I supposed to do?"

"Oh, I don't know, *darling*," which came out sounding more like *jackass*, "maybe you could have told them your wife and sister have everything under control and now wasn't a good time to visit," Skye drawled. "But that's not something you would say, is it?"

"Of course it is. You've been amazing with Mom, Cupcake. I—"

"Do not try to pacify me, Ethan O'Connor. I overheard you talking to Richard and Claudia when they arrived. You . . . you said they couldn't have come at a better time." She blinked her eyes while bouncing Evie on her hip. "You don't think I can look after Liz, do you?"

"It has nothing to do with you, sweetheart. I thought the distraction would be good for Mom."

"Hey, hope you don't mind that I let myself in. I knocked a couple of times but no one answered," Ethan's sister Cat said, her gaze flitting around the room. "Everything okay here?"

What was wrong with these people? Couldn't they see that everything wasn't okay, and by asking if it was, they were going to be subjected to another litany of what was wrong?

"Your brother hurt Skye's feelings by insinuating she can't take care of your mother. Skye's jealous because Claudia is in love with Ethan and now she's back in town staying with Liz, who made no secret that she would have preferred Claudia as a daughter-in-law. And Gage is mad at Ethan for encouraging the man who asked your mother to marry him to come and stay with her. That about sum it up?" Vivi asked. They stared at her, then started talking at once.

"All righty, I'll go and wait for Natalee." Vivi speed-walked to the front door before anyone could stop her. Stepping outside, she breathed in the scent of freshly mowed grass. She sat on the step, the muscles in her shoulders and neck relaxing as she watched the sun set behind the mountains. *The O'Connor and McBride siblings should hold their family meeting outdoors*, she thought. It might help to keep the tension at bay. Although that may be difficult with Easton and Chloe joining in via Skype.

Vivi drew her attention from the fiery orange–tinted sky as a white four-by-four pulled up to the front of the house. She recognized Natalee in the passenger seat and retrieved her cell, texting Annie to bring out Cujo. She frowned when Natalee didn't immediately get out. Chance's sister-in-law appeared to be arguing with the driver. He looked to be about Natalee's age with curly dark-brown hair.

Natalee got out of the Jeep, said something over her shoulder, then smoothed down her short black uniform skirt before coming up the walkway.

"Hey, Natalee. Thanks for coming to pick up Cu… Princess. The girls will bring her out in a minute."

Natalee nodded, fiddling with the strap on her purse. She avoided looking at Vivi by focusing on the wedge sandal she drew back and forth over the pavers.

"So, good day at work?" Vivi asked in an attempt to break the uncomfortable silence.

She shrugged, then lifted her gaze from her feet, biting her bottom lip. "I heard about—" She broke off when the Jeep door slammed, casting a nervous glance over her shoulder.

Tall and lanky, the Jeep's driver bounded up the lawn. He stuck out his hand as soon as he reached Natalee's side. "Hi, I'm Zach."

"Hey, Zach. Vivi." She shook his hand. *Friendly guy*, she thought, taking in his wide, genial smile.

Natalee's gaze flicked from Zach to Vivi. "We gotta get going. Could you get Princess now?"

"Sure." She sent another text to Annie. "Sorry to keep you waiting. They'll be out in a minute."

"Hey, no problem," Zach said, lacing his fingers through Natalee's. "Guess everyone's upset about the accident and all. Shame about Ray. He was a nice guy."

Natalee gasped, looking like she might cry. "Did... did Ray die?"

"No. In fact there's been some improvement in his condition in the last hour."

"Is that right? Well, that's good to hear, isn't it, Nat?" Zach said.

The younger woman jerked her hand from his and practically ran up the steps when Lily and Annie opened the front door. Natalee took the dog from Lily.

Vivi sighed when Princess snarled, then realized the dog wasn't growling at her, but at Zach. She chuckled. "Nice to know I'm not the only one she doesn't like."

Zach's peach-fuzzed upper lip curled. Natalee's boy-friend didn't look so friendly now.

Then he shrugged with an easy smile that made her wonder if she'd imagined the sneer. "She doesn't like to share Nat's attention with me, do you, you spoiled mutt?" He retrieved the dog's belongings from Annie, who narrowed her eyes at him.

"Bye, Princess," Lily said, reaching out to pat the dog. But Natalee was already moving down the steps.

"Natalee, is Princess up-to-date on her shots?" Chance's sister-in-law turned and nodded. "Great. Thanks again for picking her up. Nice to meet you, Zach."

"Same." He waved, then went to put an arm around

Natalee. She pulled away from him when Princess growled. "Shut up, mutt," Zach grumbled.

"I don't like him," Lily said.

Annie crossed her arms. "Neither do I."

"Yeah, I'm not getting the warm and fuzzies, either." Vivi stood up and started down the steps. "Natalee," she called out as the younger woman opened the passenger-side door, "if you and Zach have plans, the girls don't mind taking care of Princess till Chance picks her up."

"No, it's okay. We don't have plans," she said and got into the truck.

Vivi shoved her hands in her jean shorts' pockets as she watched them drive away. Zach waved, Natalee gave her a tight smile, and Princess growled at Vivi through the passenger-side window. It was possible, Vivi decided, that she'd overacted.

\*  \*  \*

Chance sat beside Ethan at Gage's dining room table. "Can't you shut her up?" Chance angled his coffee mug at the computer screen. He'd arrived half an hour late for the family meeting, and Chloe O'Connor had been talking the entire time. The dark-haired beauty with pouty red lips hadn't changed. She was still a drama queen. Even her sister thought so. Cat had deserted them ten minutes earlier to hang out with Vivi, Madison, and Skye.

"Would someone just unplug the computer or shoot the damn thing," his baby brother Easton said through the phone. He was on speaker.

"I can hear you two, you know. And need I remind you, Chance, you're the reason we're having this meeting in the first place."

"I don't know, Chloe. From what I hear, your mother's in love with another man. Looks like I saved my dad a whole lot of heartache and embarrassment."

Ethan slumped in his chair. "Did you have to bring that up again?"

Chance waggled his eyebrows at Ethan. Finding out Richard Stevens was in town was the third-best piece of news he'd had all day. Vivi staying put came in at a close second. But nothing beat hearing, barring any unforeseen complications, that Ray would more than likely pull through. "Sure did, Einstein. Appreciate you taking the heat off me." Feminine laughter filtered through the screen door off the deck. "Sweet Cheeks forgive you yet?"

"Gage, does he really have to stay? There has to be someone else you can deputize."

More laughter wafted into the dining room. His brother ignored Ethan, obviously more interested in what was going on outside. "You know," Gage said, "if we wrap this meeting up before midnight, we could join the girls in the hot tub."

At the thought of getting in the hot tub with Vivi, Chance shifted in his chair. That would be more temptation than he could resist. Despite his worry about Ray, he hadn't been able to get the image of Vivi in that bikini out of his head. Touching her warm, soft skin hadn't helped. Pressing his mouth to her gorgeous ass? Yeah, that had probably been the stupidest thing he'd done in a long time. Then again, she seemed to have the ability to make him say and do things that were stupid. But he couldn't help himself. Just like he couldn't get rid of the uncontrollable need to keep her safe. To that end, he had to get back out there. He pushed away from the table and stood up.

Gage frowned. "Where do you think you're going?"

"Break time's over, little brother. Gotta get back on the job."

A snort of laughter came from the phone. "You two won't last a week working together," Easton predicted.

"We're not working *together*. He's working for me."

Chance narrowed one eye at his brother. "You might be right, E. Are you—"

"This is not a McBride family meeting, you know. And Chance is not the only one with somewhere to be. I have to get back to work, so here's what I suggest you all do." Chloe stood up, shrugging out of a black satin robe to reveal...

"What the hell, Chloe? Put your clothes back on," Ethan yelled, reaching across the table to hide her from view.

"Are you telling me she just stripped in front of you guys?" Easton didn't wait for them to respond, not that they could after getting an eyeful of a woman they all thought of as a little sister. "She always was an exhibitionist," his baby brother muttered over the line.

"Ethan, calm down. You're such a prude. It's a bodysuit. I'm filming a love scene." Chloe's disembodied voice came from the computer. "And I didn't hear you complaining last time you saw me naked, Easton McBride."

"Wait, what? You saw my sister naked?" Ethan stared down at the phone.

Easton groaned, and Chance picked up the phone, taking his brother off speaker. "Saved you again, baby brother. Take it easy. And next time we talk, I wanna hear all about you and Chloe."

Ethan motioned for the phone. "I want to hear about it right now. Give me the—"

"Never say I don't have your back," Chance told his brother and disconnected. When Chloe started spouting through the computer, he reached over and unplugged her. "My work here is done."

Gage raked his fingers through his hair. "We're no further ahead than when we started."

Chance cocked his head. "And that surprises you because..."

His brother rolled his eyes. "I don't know why I even bother. You know what, you and Ethan figure it out. You two are the reason—"

"Hey, don't lump me in with him. My mother called off the wedding because he—"

"Okay, listen up. Dad and Liz have already dealt with losing the two people they loved most in this world. It nearly destroyed them. Do you really want to see them go through that again?"

"They're not going—" Ethan began before Gage cut him off.

"Eth, let me. Chance, Liz and Dad aren't—"

Jesus, why didn't they get it? "You two don't have a clue what it's like to go through what they did, but I do. It's like someone ripped out your heart. Nothing matters anymore, not without that one person by your side. That one person you shared everything with. The one person who knew you better than you knew yourself. Who made it worth getting up in the morning."

"And you don't think it's worth finding out if you can have that again, if my mother and your dad can?" Ethan asked quietly.

"I can't, and neither can they."

"If you'd give yourself a chance, I think you could," Gage said.

"No, there will never be another Kate." He put up his hand when his brother went to cut him off. He needed them to understand once and for all. "She was my first love and my last. I don't have anything left to give."

"Vivi, what's the holdup? I need..." Skye trailed off.

Gage rubbed the back of his neck, looking beyond Chance with a pained expression on his face. Chance turned. Vivi stood frozen in the open doorway with Cat, Madison, and Skye crowded in behind her.

# Chapter Fifteen

Chance's night hadn't improved after leaving his brother's place. It had been long and frustrating, and he couldn't get Vivi's face out of his mind. Bracing a hand on the shower wall, he shoved his head under the ice-cold spray. He'd arrived home at eight this morning and crashed. That was four hours ago. He had a feeling today wouldn't be much better. Chance wanted to stop by the hospital before heading out to question Darwin Callahan, and he had a meeting with the task force at five. Walker, the sheriff from Logan County, as well as agents from the DEA and FBI, were part of Operation Takedown.

Gage had already warned Chance to keep his thoughts on the Callahans to himself. A little late for the warning, since Chance had voiced his suspicions to Walker after the brawl Saturday night and at the latest crime scene. The Drugstore Bandits had struck again. This time in the district bordering Christmas and Logan County.

The call had saved Chance's ass—sort of. His radio had gone off as he'd locked eyes with Vivi across the room. He hadn't had time to apologize or give an explanation that would banish the pain from her violet eyes. But he'd spoken the truth, and not a truth she was unfamiliar with. If he could change one thing, it would be that she hadn't heard how he felt with everyone looking on. He regretted that the most.

There was nothing Vivi hated more than people feeling sorry for her. And it had been obvious that everyone in the room did—including him. He turned off the shower. If he had time between stopping by the hospital and the meeting, he'd pick her up one of those fancy-ass coffees she liked and drop it off at the house. He'd check up on her while he was at it. Make sure she stayed put.

Chance grabbed a towel off the rack and headed for his bedroom. He froze mid-stride at the sight of his sister-in-law coming down the hall and quickly covered himself. "Jesus, Nat, what are you doing here?"

Her cheeks flushed. "Sorry, I called out but you must not have heard me." Eyes averted, she held up a mug. "I made you coffee. Your omelet will be ready in a minute."

Princess darted past her, panting at Chance's feet, reminding him why Nat was here. She'd texted him last night to say she'd drop off the dog in the morning. He'd forgotten she had a key. Probably time to get it back. Then again, he didn't want to hurt her feelings. He cleared the frustration and discomfort from his face. "Thanks." He reached for the mug. "I'll be out in a minute," he said and backed into his room.

By the time he'd dressed, Nat had his breakfast laid out on the island. He leaned over to pat Princess, in part to cover his unease. She'd gone to a lot of trouble. The spread looked like something out of a magazine, complete with two white tulips in a small yellow bud vase. It was something Kate would have done.

He straightened and forced a smile, pulling out a stool. "Thanks, kiddo. Looks great. You not eating?"

Her face lit up at the compliment, and she shook her head with a smile. "I already ate. Do you want more coffee?"

"I'm good, thanks," he said and picked up the knife and fork.

"I can make you—"

"Nat, honey, I'm good. You don't have to do this, you know. I'm capable of looking after myself."

"I know. I just thought…" She shrugged. "I wanted to help out, that's all."

Again, a flicker of disquiet flared to life inside him. "You've been a big help. Thanks for picking up Princess yesterday."

With her gaze focused on the counter, she brushed off some crumbs. "Did Vivi mention anything about me dropping by?"

He stopped with a forkful of omelet halfway to his mouth. She was nervous, which made him nervous. "No, why?"

"Nothing, really. It's just that she asked if Princess had her shots, and I thought it was kind of odd."

Chance held back a grin. "Princess bit her. Vivi was worried she might have rabies."

"You really don't like her, do you, girl?" Nat laughed, rewarding the dog sitting at her feet with a piece of toast. Obviously, Princess wasn't the only one who didn't like

Vivi. Nat's cell pinged. She straightened, reaching in the back pocket of her white denim shorts. She glanced at the screen and her amusement left her face. She shoved her phone in her pocket without responding.

"Everything okay?"

"Yeah, everything's great. I, ah, better take off though. I have to get ready for my shift."

Chance put down his fork. "Not sure I approve of you working there, kiddo. How does your mom feel about it?" Knowing Mary as he did, he had no doubt she felt the same. Her husband had taken off when the girls were young. Mary had done a good job raising them on her own. She took her job seriously. Chance may have wished a little less seriously when he and Kate were dating. But as an adult, he understood why she'd been so strict and overprotective.

"She doesn't care."

"Doesn't sound like the Mary I remember."

"She's changed." Nat raised a negligent shoulder, adding defensively, "Doesn't matter anyway, I'm old enough to do what I want."

He didn't like to hear that Mary had changed. That because of Kate and the baby's deaths, Nat had in some way lost the mother her sister had growing up. Sending money may have gone a ways in assuaging his guilt, but he now realized it hadn't been enough. He should have been here for Mary and Nat.

"You're still living with her, aren't you?" She gave him a reluctant nod. She knew what he was getting at. She should. "You live under my roof, you live by my rules" was something he heard pretty much every time he visited the Porter household. The refrain was directed at Nat.

Mary never had to say it to Kate. She was as much the perfect daughter as she had been the perfect wife.

"What happened to college?" Nat had been a straight 4.0 student. She'd had big dreams. No one had doubted she'd accomplish them, least of all her mother and sister.

"Mom..." She crossed her arms, looking past him. "It doesn't matter. It was just a stupid dream."

His chest tightened. Too many dreams had ended that night. He wanted to give Nat's back to her somehow. "No, it wasn't. Your sister wanted that for you. We all did. I..." He hesitated, unsure how to ask, not sure he should, but he needed to know. "Nat, the money was there for you to go to college. I've been sending checks to your mom monthly since...since I left town." Money had always been tight for them. He'd made sure it was the one thing they didn't have to worry about. He had more than he'd ever need.

Nat stared at him. Then her face crumpled, and she bowed her head.

"Hey, it's okay. Don't cry." He got up from the stool, walking around the island to her side. He folded her in his arms.

She lifted her face from his chest, looking at him through tear-filled eyes. "I thought you didn't care about us anymore. But...but you did."

"Of course I did. I always will. I gave your mom my contact information. Told her to give it to you." He'd told Ray to keep an eye on them, too. He didn't have to ask his family. It's something they'd automatically do. He'd assumed Nat didn't want to talk to him. He hadn't blamed her. But now it looked like that wasn't the case.

"She didn't. I don't understand why she'd..." Her brow

pleated, then she briefly closed her eyes. "Uncle Earl. He's over all the time talking trash about..." She winced.

Chance didn't give a shit what Earl said about him, but if he'd conned Mary out of one red cent of the money he'd sent her, then he did have a problem with him. "Earl still gambling?" He worked to keep the angry suspicion from his voice.

*Obviously not hard enough*, he thought, when Nat's shoulders sagged. "Mom gave him the money." She moved away from him, retrieving her cell once again. Her delicate jaw tight, she stabbed at the keys.

He took the phone from her. "I'll handle it."

"But..."

"Nat, leave it to me." He nudged her chin up. "I'm going to look into this. And you, you're going to start looking at schools. Okay?"

He saw the hope flare to life in her eyes before she extinguished it. "I missed a lot of time my final year. My marks...I've been out of school too long. I don't think I—"

"No excuses. Do you want to go to college or not?" No matter how much he wanted her to go, in the end, the decision had to be hers.

"Yes, yes I do. I really do, but I don't think Mom will—"

"Let's take this one step at a time. You look into schools. Pick the one you want to go to. Then we'll figure out the rest from there."

"Okay." She wrapped her arms around his waist. "I'm so glad you're home. Everything's better with you here."

He tensed under the weight of her expectations. He was in town long enough to put the Drugstore Bandits behind bars and to make sure Ray was all right. That was all.

He didn't want someone else depending on him, some-one else to take care of, someone else to fail. Patting her shoulder, he stepped away. "You better get going or you'll be late for work. With tourist season around the corner, you might want to give Sawyer a heads-up."

"What if I don't get into school? I need my job. I make good tips."

Jesus, if she only knew how much he'd given her mother. She didn't need to work. "All right, wait until you decide what you're doing and go from there. Now get out of here. I have to get to work, too."

With a hug for him and Princess, she headed for the door, then stopped and turned. "Chance, maybe I should talk to Mom and Uncle Earl. I don't want him to make trouble for you, and he will."

No doubt he'd try. But Chance had enough on Earl Skully to bury him. "This is between me and your mom, kiddo. You let me worry about it." For someone who liked his life uncomplicated and without ties, it wasn't lost on Chance that his life had become increasingly more com-plicated the moment he set foot in Christmas.

*       *       *

Vivi left the gray stone correctional facility no further ahead than when she went in. Darwin Callahan was a silver-tongued devil and a good-looking one to boot. But as her dad used to say, "A con is a con is a con." And he would know, because he'd been one. She supposed she had him to thank for her ability to spot Darwin Callahan's tell within five minutes of sitting across the table from him. The man knew more about the Drugstore Bandits than he let on.

Which meant Chance was probably right and the Callahans were somehow involved. Then again, from the brief glimpse she'd managed to get of the visitor's log, Darwin didn't have a shortage of company. And other than a gut feeling he was hiding something, Vivi had nothing concrete to base her suspicions on.

As she headed for the parking lot, she caught a glimpse of two tall, broad-shouldered men in tan uniforms coming her way. They walked with the swagger of men confident in their ability to take down anyone standing in their way. The type of men who'd make a woman swoon if a woman was into big, bad, and dangerous.

Vivi wasn't, but she was a woman who valued her freedom. And if the deputy wearing the champagne-colored Stetson saw her, he'd probably lock her up and throw away the key. She ducked behind the nearest car. She didn't want to deal with him today.

And it had nothing to do with him stomping on her foolish dreams again. They'd shriveled up and died two days earlier. Nor was it because of the pitying looks she was once again on the receiving end of, thanks to him. No, it was because she didn't want him to know what she was up to. He'd shut her down. Again.

She had as much right to keep her best friend safe as he did. And as far as Vivi was concerned, the only way to keep Maddie and her family safe was to know exactly who and what they were up against. Vivi might not have the muscle or firepower behind her—or the law—but she could find out things he couldn't. Given their past history, the last person a Callahan would open up to was a McBride.

Crouched beside the black Impala's driver's-side door,

she held on to the handle and slowly raised herself up to look out the windshield. At the sight of two very fine uniform-covered backsides, she let out the breath she'd been holding. When Chance opened the correction facility's doors, Vivi used the handle to pull herself upright. The ear-piercing shriek of a siren rent the air. Dammit! She'd set off the freaking car alarm!

She ducked, punching the door on her way to the ground in hopes of turning off the alarm. No such luck. She turned, duckwalking to the back of the vehicle. She was about to make a run for her car, only to be cut off by a tan wall. A tan wall that had on brown, scuffed cowboy boots. She tipped her head back, way back, and looked into the beard-stubbled, pissed-off face of Deputy Chance McBride.

*Relax*, she told herself. Best defense was an offense. She plastered an innocent smile on her face. "Hey, how's it going? Did you happen to see a set of keys? I seemed to have dropped them." She patted the asphalt.

Crickets. Not a sound, not even a manly grunt. Not even a quirk of his oh-so-perfect lips. He crossed his arms over his chest and stared down at her. She was screwed.

"I don't know about you, McBride, but if I had a dollar for every time I heard that line, I'd be rich." The auburn-haired sheriff looked down at her through his mirrored shades. "Come on, gorgeous, you can do better than that."

"So could you. Those are the worst lines I've ever heard." Vivi stood and hefted her messenger bag over her shoulder.

"Feisty for a woman who got caught red-handed trying to steal a car," the sheriff said to Chance.

A uniformed guard came out and aimed a key fob at the Impala, turning off the alarm.

Vivi rolled her eyes at the sheriff's smirk. "I wasn't trying to steal a car. The alarm went off when I bumped into it while looking for my keys. Once Silent and Annoying recovers his voice, he'll tell you he knows me." She went to walk past them. "Have a good day, boys."

Chance's hand shot out, stopping her midstride. "I've got this, Walker. I'll meet you inside."

"He speaks," Vivi said, at the same time trying to free her arm. She glared at him when he tightened his grip. "If you don't let me go, I'll have you charged with harassment."

Walker laughed as he strolled off. "Sounds like I'll be starting without you, McBride."

"You have two minutes to tell me what you're doing here. You better make it good, Slick, because I'm this close"—he held his thumb and forefinger in front of her face—"to throwing you in jail."

"For what? It's a free country, McBride. I can come and go as I please."

"You went to see Callahan, didn't you?"

"So what if I did?"

He leaned into her, closing his hands over her shoulders. "I told you to stay out of it. And what do you do? You put yourself on his goddamn radar. And that puts your girls and their kids on there, too."

In her gut, she knew he was just trying to scare her. Callahan was not a murderer—he was a drug dealer with no history of violence. But that didn't stop the shiver of unease from creeping up her spine. "He doesn't know who I am. I told him I'm a reporter from New York and that I'm writing a book about the East Coast Mobs' connections to the Colorado drug trade."

She couldn't tell because of his shades, but she was pretty sure he rolled his eyes. "You think he's stupid enough to buy that?" His sarcasm-laced voice seemed to validate her suspicion about the eye rolling.

"Yes, I do. And if you weren't being such a jerk, I'd tell you what I found out. But you are. So I won't."

"What are you, fifteen? If you learned anything that pertains to this case, you have an obligation to report it."

"A little thing called the shield law says I don't. And if you don't back off, McBride, I'm calling my lawyer, who also happens to be the district attorney."

"Jesus, you're a pain in the ass." He took her chin in his hand. Her reaction to the feel of his strong fingers on her face was reflected back to her in his mirrored shades. She hoped to God it was just the smoky lenses that made her look all flushed and starry-eyed. Had to be, because she was not feeling the least bit starry-eyed. Flushed with temper? Definitely. "When are you going to get it through your beautiful head that I'm not trying to mess up your career? I'm just trying to keep you safe."

Okay, so maybe he still had the power to put stars in her eyes. Not good. She put her hand over his to remove it from her face and noticed his scraped knuckles. She frowned. "You didn't beat up Callahan again, did you?"

He flexed his hand. "No."

When he didn't elaborate, she'd had enough. "We're done here." She put her hands on his chest to push him away. The movement caused her to back into the car, her messenger bag sliding off her shoulder and hitting the trunk. The Impala's alarm went off.

*        *        *

After her run-in with Chance, Vivi had no intention of continuing her investigation into the Callahans. She figured she'd pushed her luck enough for one day. But when the needle on the gas gauge veered too close to Empty, and the sun's rays glinted off the gas tanks at Callahan Automotive, she took it as a sign from God and pulled into the strip mall.

She drove to the tank closest to the open bay doors where several men worked on high-end sports cars. A couple looked her way when she got out of the car. As she removed the gas cap, she lifted her chin and smiled, earning her a wolf whistle.

"What's a gorgeous gal like you doing driving a heap of junk like that?" a friendly giant with red hair and beard asked from where he stood under a blue Mustang up on the hoist.

"Stop flirting with the customers, Pat," a gravelly masculine voice ordered.

Pat winked at Vivi. "You'd flirt with this one, too, boss."

She followed his gaze. Just the man she was looking for. She would have known him without Pat giving his identity away. He looked like what she imagined Darwin Callahan did thirty years ago. Six-feet-plus with a leanly muscled body, Jake Callahan had black, wavy hair and a square jaw. His blue short-sleeve uniform shirt accentuated his dark-inked tattoo sleeves and gray eyes that roamed her face and body without seeming to do so. He approached, wiping the grease from his hands with a rag.

"Pat's right. What are you doing driving this piece of

crap?" His knowledgeable gaze ran over the red, rusted-out compact. "You're leaking steering fluid and oil. And your muffler's about to fall off."

She fit the nozzle into the tank. "It can't be that bad."

"Probably worse once I take a look under the hood. How long have you had her?"

"About four hours." Vivi didn't want Maddie to know what she was up to and decided to rent a car while she was in town. It had ended up being cheaper to buy one.

His lips curved slowly in an amused smile. "You piss off whoever you bought her from?"

"I don't think so. I bought the car from Earl . . ."

"Enough said." He extended his hand. "Jake Callahan. I'm booked solid for the next couple of days, but I'll try to fit you in and see what I can do for you."

"Vivi Westfield. And that'd be great. I really appreciate it." She felt like rubbing her hands together. She'd just been given the perfect opportunity to get the answers she was looking for. But he was being so nice that she felt kind of bad for the subterfuge. And while physically he was his father's son, she had the feeling the similarities ended there.

A white four-by-four pulled up to the garage. She recognized the driver—Natalee's boyfriend, Zach.

"Might be best if you park it until I can get you in. What's your number?"

She bent her head, letting her hair fall forward to shield her face as she pulled out the nozzle and gave him her number. She took her time fitting the hose on the gas tank, briefly closing her eyes when she heard a familiar voice call out, "Hey, Jake. Hey, Vivi." Zach bounded over to them. "Whoa, what are you doing driving that piece of shit?"

"Language, little brother," Jake said, his gaze moving from Zach to Vivi. "You two know each other?"

Vivi was too stunned to respond. Zach was a Callahan? And he was dating the sister of a woman Chance believed his brother Jake had killed. There was something wrong here.

"Yeah, met her the other day. She's Chance McBride's girlfriend," Zach said. His fingers curling into fists at his sides were at odds with his laid-back smile. Probably nervous she'd reveal his secret. He wouldn't want his brother to know he was dating Natalee.

"Is that right?" Jake said with a dangerous expression on his face.

"No, it's not. Chance and I aren't dating anymore."

"But you are the woman who was asking my brother Mike a bunch of questions the other night. The night of the brawl."

"It's not what you think. I'm a reporter. I'm writing—"

"Not interested."

"Guess our car date is off?"

"Smart lady. Now if you—"

Vivi spotted a white Suburban with a Christmas Sheriff's decal on the passenger-side door coming down the road. *Please let it be Gage*, she prayed. But Gage would tell Chance. She dug two twenties from her back jeans pocket, practically flinging them at Jake. "Thanks, gotta go."

She jumped in the car, patting the dashboard when she turned the key. "Come on, baby. Don't fail me now." Vivi gunned the engine and tore out of the parking lot at the same time the Suburban pulled into the strip mall. She was about to release a gratified breath when the Suburban pulled a U-ie. The vehicle's reversal didn't necessarily have anything to do with her, she reassured herself. Any number of things...

She heard the siren and glanced in the rearview mirror. Nope, not any number of things. It definitely had to do with her. Chance glared at her from behind the wheel of the white Suburban, gesturing for her to pull over. She thought about ignoring him, pretending she didn't see him, but then white smoke began billowing from underneath the hood of her car. A loud bang followed, and the hood popped open. She slammed on the brakes. Chance slammed on his.

Not fast enough.

# Chapter Sixteen

McBride, this isn't funny. Let me out of here now," Vivi yelled, rattling the cell door.

Who was she trying to kid? He wasn't letting her out. Even though, as she'd repeatedly pointed out, he had no legal grounds to throw her in jail. He hadn't responded—incensed glares didn't count. She'd seen him angry before, but nothing like he'd been thirty minutes ago.

Maddie and Skye were angry, too. So angry that they refused to post Vivi's bail. The trumped-up charges? Failure to stop, resisting arrest, driving without Colorado plates. She walked to the narrow cot and lay down, looking up at the grotty ceiling. She angled her head and sniffed...It smelled like...She jumped off the mattress. If she stayed in here much longer, she'd catch something. She tapped her fingers on her forehead, trying to think of someone who'd bail her out.

Cat O'Connor. As a former police officer, she'd totally

get that Chance had overstepped his authority. But Vivi'd used her one phone call. She eyed her messenger bag that held her cell phone, propped up against the side of the desk. She calculated the distance—about four feet if she could somehow get the bag to fall forward.

She took off her tennis shoe, stuck her hand through the bars, and let it fly. Her tennie bounced off the desk. Her bag didn't move, but the container of pens fell on the floor. She waited for someone to come and investigate the crash. They didn't. Probably because the task force meeting was under way. What she wouldn't give to be a fly on the wall.

Vivi took off her other shoe, said a silent prayer, and flung it as hard as she could. The desk shifted, and her bag fell on the floor. "Yes," she cheered, pumping her fist in the air. Once she ended her mini-victory dance, she lay on the floor, hoping it had been cleaned recently, and stuck her leg through the bars. She stretched out her foot. After what felt like an hour, but was probably only ten minutes, she got the strap between her toes and carefully edged the bag toward her. Retrieving her phone, she called Cat.

Vivi had just about given up when Cat answered. "Hey, it's Vivi. I need your help."

"I bet you do. I heard all about your adventures today from Skye. Your best friends aren't happy with you, you know."

"That's actually why I'm calling. They won't bail me out, so I was hoping you would." When Cat didn't respond right away, Vivi said, "Pretty please, I'll owe you big-time."

She heard a door close, then Cat came back on the line.

"Sorry, I didn't want Mom to hear me. I wish I could help you out, Vivi. But she's got me packing up anything that Paul's ever given her or that remotely reminds her of him. She's on a tear, and if I leave, she'll just start packing on her own."

"Don't worry about it. How did her follow-up go?" Vivi'd asked Cat to go with her to see Darwin Callahan, but she had needed to take Liz to the hospital.

Cat sighed. "Not good."

"Oh, Cat, I'm sorry. Is there anything—"

"No, physically she's fine. Mentally . . ."

"What happened?"

"You know how Dr. Trainer agreed to let Paul do the follow-up so Mom would at least have to speak to him?"

She'd heard all about Nell's latest plan last night. "Yeah, I take it Liz didn't go along with it."

"Oh, no, she did. I think she wants to see him, or I should say, wanted to, but was too proud to give him a call. Anyway, his receptionist seemed nervous when we arrived at his office. She tried to send us away, but Mom wasn't having any of it. She ended up walking in on Paul and his ex-girlfriend Karen."

"They weren't . . ."

"No, thank God. I think it looked worse than it was. Paul had lipstick on his collar and his cheek. He tried to explain, but Mom didn't give him a chance."

"I hate to say I told you so, but I did. You guys have to stop listening to Nell."

"Pot to kettle. You're no better. I told you interviewing Darwin was a bad idea." A frustrated breath huffed over the line. "I better go. I can hear her moving stuff around.

Sorry I can't help you out. Too bad you don't know how to pick a lock. I don't think they've changed them since the jail was built in the late eighteen hundreds."

Vivi straightened and glanced at the cell door. "Really?"

"Uh, Vivi, I was joking. You can't break out of jail. Chance would—"

"Come on, I wouldn't have a clue how to pick a lock." But her father had known how, and like any good father, had passed the tricks of his trade onto his daughter. "Besides, even if I did, I wouldn't break out. That'd be illegal, right?" She was so going to break out. She just didn't want Cat to inadvertently spill the beans. And since Chance had thrown Vivi in jail based on trumped-up charges, she had no compunction about using her get-out-of-jail-free card. "Go help your mom. I'll talk to you tomorrow."

As soon as Cat disconnected, Vivi got to work. All it took was some concentration and patience, the wire from her now-destroyed bra, and a pen. She smiled as the door clanged open. Free at last.

Once she put on her tennis shoes and cleaned up the broken pen holder, she shoved her bra in her messenger bag and headed for the door. Suze, the forty-something receptionist, and the dark-haired deputy, Jill Flaherty, were deep in conversation at the front desk. Vivi couldn't avoid them. She pasted a smile on her face and casually sauntered toward the front doors. Their jaws dropped.

Jill recovered first. "What…How…" She looked beyond Vivi as if expecting someone to be behind her. When no one followed, she put her hands on her hips. "Who let you out?"

"Ah…John. Now if you don't mind, I gotta get going."

Jill frowned at Suze. "Who's John?"

When the woman shrugged, Jill narrowed her eyes at Vivi. "You are not leaving until I speak to Chance."

"Come on, Jill. He…" Vivi trailed off at the sound of raised male voices coming from Gage's office. "That doesn't sound good."

"No, it doesn't." Jill gestured at one of the desks. "Sit."

"Maddie's right, you are a hard-ass." Jill and Maddie got along now, but it hadn't always been the case.

Jill smirked. "Takes one to know one."

"Ha-ha, but seriously, Jill, Chance—" She winced when a loud bang came from the office at the opposite side of the room.

"Has had a shit day thanks to you. And it's only gotten worse." She pulled out a chair from behind the desk.

She was about to take offense at Jill blaming her for Chance's crappy day, but focused instead on the latter comment. "How so?" she asked, taking a seat.

"You have to ask?" Jill sat behind the desk in front of Vivi. "Look, we've never been able to find a link between Jake Callahan and Kate's death, but Chance, he believes beyond a shadow of a doubt that he was responsible. So when you, a woman he's involved with—"

"We're not involved, and that's not—"

"You're involved. A man like Chance doesn't react the way he did unless he's in—"

"Don't, do not say it," she warned the other woman. "And you obviously don't know Chance if you think his reaction was unusual. The man's an overprotective control freak. Do you know what his handle is? Superman.

Yeah, that's right, Superman. Are you getting the picture now?"

"Yep, clear as crystal." Jill grinned. "You're his Lois Lane."

Vivi dropped her head on the desk, then lifted her eyes. "You're all nuts. There must have been a lot of cousins marrying cousins in the good old days." She angled her head and took out her iPhone. Not a bad idea. She typed, "Prevalence of quirky/weird/nosy/annoying people in small towns due to inbreeding."

"So, you going to tell me how you got out of your cell?"

"Your locks are crap."

"You're the shit. You two are the perfect match." She laughed, pointing at Vivi when she gave her the evil eye. "See, you even got his shut-up-or-die look down pat."

"Probably because he's used it on me every day since we arrived in town." It hadn't always been that way.

"He was going to let you out as soon as they wrapped it up in there." She nodded at Gage's office.

"Yeah right."

"No, he was. He told me so himself." At another loud bang from Gage's office, Jill winced. "That really doesn't sound good."

They looked at each other when they heard the Callahans' name shouted from behind the closed doors. "Oh boy, Gage is going to be ticked. He didn't want Chance bringing them up at the meeting."

"Why not? They should be looking into them. Darwin Callahan said a couple things . . . What?" Vivi asked when Jill gave her a startled look.

"Darwin Callahan? Don't tell me you talked to the old man, too."

"I thought you knew that."

"Nope, just heard about Jake. No wonder Chance lost his shit. Not cool, Vivi. Not cool at all."

Maybe Jill was right and Vivi had taken it too far this time. Yes, she had the right to talk to whomever she wanted. But knowing Chance's history with the Callahans, she could have been more considerate of his feelings. She might not believe the Callahans would hurt her, but he did. There were times when her curiosity, her need to be right and get the story, came back to bite her in the butt. Today appeared to be a case in point. She slumped in the chair, unsure how to fix this.

They both turned at the sound of the door opening. "Yeah, and I know what I know. So you either put the Callahans back on that board or I walk and go it on my own." Chance stormed from Gage's office.

"Chance, calm down, don't go off half-cocked." Walker followed him out of the office, while Gage, Ethan, and three other men stared after them.

Chance didn't respond to Walker. He came to a dead stop in front of the desk.

Scowling at Jill, he jerked his thumb at Vivi. "Did you let her out?"

"No, John did," Jill said at the same time Vivi said, "No, Joe did."

Jill stared at her, widening her eyes. "You said John did, remember?"

"Right, I forgot. It was Joe . . . I mean John."

Chance's narrowed gaze moved from Vivi to the door leading to the cells. He swore under his breath and stalked to the door.

Gage, Ethan, and the three men filed out of the office

while Walker stood looking down at Vivi. "So, Ms. West-field, what have you done now?"

"She broke out of the cell," Chance muttered as he came back into the room. "Jill, call the locksmith and have him change all the locks."

"Hey," Gage said, "you're not sheriff anymore. You don't get to call the shots. In fact, if I'm not mistaken, you just quit."

"No, he didn't quit," Vivi jumped in. Chance wasn't thinking straight. And that was on her. She'd pushed him too far. He needed these men at his back, if only to keep him in line. To keep him safe. "You need him."

The men stared at her while Jill, with the phone to her ear, gave her a knowing grin.

"Hold it, let me get this straight. She actually broke out of the cell... with no help?" Walker said.

Vivi wished he'd let it go. She didn't like the way the men wearing the DEA and FBI Windbreakers were look-ing at her. Ethan pinched the bridge of his nose, then moved to her side. "Don't say anything," he murmured, resting a hand on her shoulder.

"But I wasn't really under arrest. Chance just made those charges up so..." She trailed off when she noticed the FBI and DEA guys' attention had switched from her to Chance.

\*     \*     \*

Vivi was right. He didn't have a legitimate reason to arrest her and throw her in jail. But he hadn't trusted himself not to shake her until her teeth rattled. He hadn't recov-ered from the thought she'd put herself on Darwin's radar when he spotted her standing within a couple feet of Jake Callahan, chatting him up. It had been more than Chance's already-frayed temper could handle. And then the damn woman had driven that piece-of-shit car like the hounds of hell were after her. If she hadn't blown the engine, he figured she wouldn't have stopped.

She wouldn't be using her getaway car anytime soon. It was toast. Which wasn't entirely her fault. He should have slowed down as soon as he saw the puff of smoke. He flexed his hand. Earl Skully had just earned himself another visit. Chance didn't foresee this one going any better than the last.

He drew his gaze from his scraped knuckles to the room at large. His brother, Ethan, and the FBI and DEA agents waited for an explanation.

Walker parked his ass on the side of Jill's desk, looking from Vivi to Chance. "Can you loan her to me for a few hours? I could use her to test out my cells."

Chance couldn't believe she'd picked the frigging lock. And while she frustrated the hell out of him and caused him to lose his temper faster than anyone he knew, he couldn't help the surge of admiration he felt for her. Vivi Westfield was one of the most amazing women he'd ever met, and she'd probably be the death of him.

He rubbed his jaw, hiding his grin at the incredulous look she shot Walker, who was having way too much fun at her expense. "Did you just ask him to *loan* me to you?"

Lucky for Walker, Jill put down the phone, saving him from answering. "Locksmith is on his way." Her gaze moved from his brother to Chance. She cleared her throat. "You can take your dinner break. I've already had mine. I'll hold down the fort."

He knew what Jill was up to. So did his brother. Chance sent him a challenging stare. He wasn't about to back down.

Vivi huffed out a breath, stood up, and slung her bag over her shoulder. "Don't be stubborn. You're not quitting the task force, and neither your brother nor these guys want you to, right?" She dared the men to argue with a combative stare of her own.

As the tension-filled silence dragged on, she said, "Chance is right, Gage. I talked to Darwin Callahan. He knows something about the break-ins."

Gage swore and rubbed the back of his neck. "Fine, he goes on the board along with Jake. But you two need to straighten out whatever's going on between you. I don't want it interfering with this case. And Vivi, if I hear you've been within a hundred feet of the Callahans, I'll throw you in jail myself."

When she looked like she was gearing up to tell his brother what he could do with his warning, Chance took her by the shoulders and steered her toward the exit. "I'll be back within the hour, Jill. Go home and spend some time with your wife and kids, little brother. We've got tonight covered."

"You had to get in one last jab, didn't you?" Vivi said as they stepped outside.

"You weren't in there. He's a pain in the ass."

"Obviously it runs in the family."

"I want to hear you say it."

"You're a pain in the ass."

He laughed. "Not that. I want to hear you say 'Chance is right' again."

"You would glom onto that." She blew a lock of hair off her face. "Look, McBride, I get it, okay. I didn't interview

Darwin or talk to Jake to upset you. I'm a reporter. I'm curious. Plus, I figured they'd talk to me easier than they'd talk to you. And maybe I'd find out something you could use." She wet her lips before saying, "Like I told Gage, I think you're right. Somehow the Callahans are involved. But I'll back off. I don't want you worrying about me. Focus on your case."

His chest tightened, as much from what she said as the way she looked saying it. She was gut-wrenchingly beautiful. "Don't give me the sweet, Slick. Can't handle the sweet."

"You think I'm being sweet?"

"Yeah, and I don't like it. I like kick-ass Westfield better."

"Me too." She gave him one of her rare smiles. Wide and radiant, it was as hard to handle as her soft side.

He cleared his throat. "Come on. I'll buy you a burger, and you can tell me all about your conversation with Darwin."

She filled him in on the short drive to the Rocky Mountain Diner. He pulled into the space beside the log building. "Not really getting how you think he's involved from what you've just told me, Slick."

"That's because you weren't there. He does this"—she rubbed her forefinger back and forth under her straight, elegant nose—"when he gets nervous."

"Ever think he just had an itchy nose?" he asked as he got out of his truck. Other than attitude, he and Walker didn't get anything out of Darwin.

She shut the door and came around the back of the truck. "I know what I saw, McBride. He did it four times: when I asked him about his kids, the Garage, the break-ins at the drugstores, and the black Mustang. Then he'd start flirting and change the subject. And he had no problem talking about—"

"He flirted with you?" He reached for her hand.

She turned on the top step, looking down at their entwined fingers. "Yeah, kind of like you do."

He released her hand and opened the door to the diner. "I don't flirt with you, Slick," he said, placing his fingers at the small of her back to nudge her inside. "I'm just a touchy-feely kind of guy."

"Save the touchy-feely for someone else. We're friends and—" She broke off, narrowing her eyes at him.

He probably should have been happy she thought of him as a friend. It's what he wanted, wasn't it? To have her in his life without the worry of hurting her when he couldn't commit to more.

"Uh no, not the friends-with-benefits kind, McBride."

"I didn't say any…" He didn't, but the thought had crossed his mind. Maybe she'd nailed Darwin's tell after all. "You sure I can't change your mind?" he asked, only half teasing.

She pursed her lips, then nodded at Hailey, one of the twin sisters who owned the diner, approaching with menus in hand. "Hey, me and Holly were just talking about you. Figured you must be bored with no wedding stuff going on"—Hailey gave Chance a way-to-go look before continuing—"and wondered if you were up for a night out? Thought we'd check out the Garage again."

"No," Chance said as he followed them to a booth in the corner.

Both women turned to look at him, then Hailey arched a brow at Vivi. "Did he just say you can't go out with us?"

"Yeah, he did." He nudged Vivi into the red vinyl booth and sat beside her.

She scowled at him, sliding to the opposite end. "Sounds great, Hailey. But why don't we go to the Penalty Box instead?"

Chance reached over and patted her hand. "Good girl."

Hailey swatted him upside the head with the menus, then handed one to Vivi. "Sure. I'll let Autumn and Sophia know. You can ask Skye and Maddie, but they're probably busy with the kids." She gave Vivi a once-over. "We can pop by the apartment and do your hair and makeup. Holly saw a cute cut that would look great on you."

An image of Vivi from the Garage popped into his head. "She doesn't need you to do her makeup, and you're not cutting her hair." She had amazing hair. He loved the soft, silky feel of it, the way those long, dark locks felt wrapped around his fist.

"What is with you? You'd think she was your wife or..." She looked over her shoulder when someone called her name. "I'll be back in a minute to take your order."

Vivi whacked his arm with her menu. "Stop telling me what I can and can't do."

"You're beautiful. You don't need that crap on your face." He reached over and wrapped a strand of her hair around his finger. "And I like your hair the way it is."

"There you go again with the touchy-feely crap. Stop it." Cheeks flushed, she tugged her hair from his hand and opened her menu. "What's..." She looked past him and winced. "Ah, there's something I think you should know. Yesterday, when Natalee dropped by, she wasn't..." She sighed when he looked over his shoulder.

"What the fu...hell is she doing with him?" he asked at

the sight of Natalee with Zach Callahan. Chance stood up at the same time his sister-in-law glanced his way. She bit her lip, said something to Callahan, and tugged on his arm. The kid looked at Chance, but instead of turning tail to run, he took Nat by the hand and headed toward the booth.

Vivi slid along the bench, her thigh pressing against his. She nudged him. "Be nice." He glanced at her. She sighed. "He's just a kid."

Yeah, a tall, scrawny kid with curly brown hair and freckles. He looked about fifteen to Nat's twenty-one. Callahan thrust out his hand with a confident smile. "Hey, good to meet you, man. Nat talks about you all the time."

*Balls of steel*, Chance thought, accepting the kid's hand when Vivi poked him in the back. "Haven't heard a word about you." He raised a brow at Nat.

Vivi poked him again, then leaned around him. "Hey, how are you guys doing? Why don't you join us?" She shrugged when Chance shot her a look.

"No, we have a table…" Nat began, giving Chance an apologetic smile when Callahan took a seat.

"Probably a good idea to clear the air, you know, on account of you beating the crap out of my brother," the kid said.

Chance wasn't buying the conciliatory tone in Zach Callahan's voice. He decided to rattle him to see what shook out. "Put your old man away, too."

Something hard flashed in the kid's close-set brown eyes before he pasted that genial look back on his face. "I don't hold any grudges, man. Like I told Nat, it had nothing to do with us. That shit went down a long time ago."

"Watch your mouth," Chance growled and sat back on the bench, crossing his arms over his chest. He didn't buy the kid's "forgive and forget" act. "And you might not hold a grudge, *man*, but I do."

"Chance, please," Nat pleaded.

Vivi kicked him under the table. "I'm starved. Hailey." Vivi waved her over. "Okay, you guys must know what's good here. What should I order?"

Nat's gaze moved from him to Vivi. She chewed on her bottom lip and shrugged, twisting to watch Hailey weave her way through the tables.

"Thanks for trying, Vivi," Callahan said, his cheeks flushed. "Probably best if me and Nat get another table."

Nat jumped off the bench. Callahan came to his feet, wrapping an arm around her shoulders. She held herself stiff, her nervous glance darting from Chance to Callahan.

"Me and Nat love each other, and there's nothing you can do to change that."

"Zach, don't. People are looking at us. Let's just go—"

Callahan put up a silencing finger, and Nat wrapped her arms around her stomach, shifting on her sandals. "She told me about the checks and stuff. What Earl and her momma did was not cool, but I can take care of her." The kid puffed out his scrawny chest.

"What exactly do you do, Callahan? Work for your brothers?"

"Stop it, Chance. It doesn't matter. Come on, Zach." Nat tugged on her boyfriend's arm.

"You think you're a big shot, don't you, McBride? Think you can come back here and stir up all that shit again. Well, you can't. We're doing good now. We got money. You can't—"

Chance went to stand up. Vivi hooked her finger in his belt and pulled him down. "Problem here?" Hailey asked.

"Nah, just leaving. Lost my appetite," Zach said.

"Nat, stay. We need to talk," Chance called out as the kid dragged her after him.

"Let her go, Chance. She's embarrassed. Give her a call once you've calmed down and Zach's not around. She'll listen to you."

"I don't like the way the little bastard's manhandling her." He shifted in his seat. "There's something off with that kid."

"Yeah, I . . ." She pressed her lips together. "You didn't exactly make it easy on him, you know." She glanced at Hailey. "What's your take on Zach?"

Hailey slid into the booth. "I didn't catch all of it, but you're right. You gotta lighten up, Chance." When he opened his mouth to defend himself, she held up a hand. "I get it. But he's only twenty-one. He didn't have anything to do with what went on back then. I know you don't want to hear this, but Jake's done a good job with him. Kept him on the straight and narrow. Zach's a smart kid, just like Natalee. They've been hanging out together for years. If it makes you feel any better, I've never seen any sign of trouble."

"It doesn't." There was something in the kid's eyes. A look Chance had seen before, and one he didn't like. "But thanks for trying. We should order, Slick. I have to get back to the station in thirty."

Once they'd placed their orders and Hailey headed for the kitchen, Vivi asked, "What was that about checks and Earl and Natalee's mom?"

"Nothing."

"Fine, don't tell me," she said in an irritated tone of voice and reached into her bag, pulling out her phone and . . . a lacy black bra.

Chance grabbed the bra from her, letting the strap dangle from his finger. "What's this?"

"McBride!" She grabbed it from him, shooting a flustered glance around the restaurant as she shoved the bra back in her bag. She lifted her gaze to his, and her cheeks pinked. "Seriously, can you be any more obvious? Stop looking at my boobs."

"Little hard, honey. Now that I know you've got nothing under your top. Are you cold?"

"That's it, I'm outta here."

He held back a laugh, snagging her hand. "Don't go."

"Are you going to tell me about Earl and your mother-in-law?"

"You going to tell me why you have a bra in your bag?"

"I used the wire to pick the lock." She rested a hand on her crossed leg and placed one under her chin, effectively ruining his view. "Now it's your turn."

"You're not going to give up, are you?"

"No, and I want to know how you banged up your knuckles, too."

"Demanding, aren't you?" he said, raising his hand to inspect it. He might as well tell her. She'd just start nosing around if he didn't.

"You're a good man, Chance McBride," she said once he'd told her what happened. "And Earl Skully is lucky he dealt with you and not me. What a lowlife. I think I'm going to sue him for selling me that death trap. Have you talked to your mother-in-law?"

"No, there was this gorgeous brunette who kept me preoccupied."

She opened her mouth, then shut it when their order arrived. "Thanks, Hailey. Do you have any mayo?"

Hailey frowned. "I'm sure they put some on your burger."

"No, for the fries." Vivi plucked one off Chance's plate.

He grabbed one of her onion rings. "Yeah, and some vinegar when you get a chance."

"Why are you guys eating each other's food? And mayo on fries? That's..."

"Amazing. You should give it a try," Chance said. "Give me your pickle, Slick."

Vivi lifted her bun and handed over the slice of dill.

"Broken up, my butt. You two are totally still dating."

"No, we're just—"

Hailey cut Vivi off with a wave of her hand. "Don't bother denying it. I'll get your mayo and vinegar."

As she walked away, Vivi rubbed her temple. "So, Nat and school. That's a good idea. It'll broaden her horizons, give her a little distance from Zach."

Chance aimed a fry at her. "I knew it. You think something's off with the guy, too."

She lifted a shoulder. "Maybe. I can look into him if you want. Quietly, of course. No one has to know."

"We talked about this. You promised to back off."

"I just thought..." She sighed at his pointed look. "Fine."

He didn't trust her *fine*. She'd promised to stay away from Jake and Darwin, but sooner or later she'd be sticking her pretty nose into his investigation. The only way to keep her safe was to keep her busy. And the one person he trusted to do that was his aunt Nell.

# Chapter Seventeen

Vivi woke up from her nightmare in a cold sweat. She rubbed her hands over her eyes in an attempt to erase the image of her sitting chained to a desk, writing an obituary—her own. There'd been one line on the screen. A shadow blotted out the early morning light as she sat up, turning to see a huge crow sitting on the ledge of the bedroom window. She'd never seen one that large before. Maybe it wasn't a crow. Maybe it was a raven. And wouldn't that be the perfect way to start another day in Christmas.

Not only had she dreamed of her imminent demise, she now had the harbinger of death staring in at her. The bird gave the familiar caw of a crow and flew off. At least it wasn't a raven. Now all she had to do was stop eating before bed to take care of the nightmares.

But as she pondered the symbolism of the dream—one line on an otherwise blank screen equaled no accomplish-

ments, no significant other, no family, while being chained
to a desk represented a dead-end job she hated—she realized the quart of chocolate ice cream she'd eaten before
bed hadn't triggered the nightmare. No, it had been her
late-night stalking of her brother's and sister's Facebook
pages.

Her brother, Finn, had just been awarded an assignment with *Time* magazine in Iraq, and her sister, Brooke,
had announced her engagement to the VP of her father's
prestigious law firm. Unlike Vivi's, their obituaries would
be filled with their many accomplishments. She berated
herself for the thought. She had to stop her nightly forays
onto their social media pages. It was turning into a bad,
and a depressing, habit.

It had started out innocently enough—once a year on
their birthdays. Then slowly it had gone to once a month
to once a week to, well, daily. She'd simply been curious
in the beginning. Then those small insights into their perfect family had become an addiction.

She'd never actually met them, but she'd seen them once.
Fourteen-year-old Finn had been playing basketball with a
bunch of his friends the day she'd walked up the tree-lined
driveway to their colonial mansion. While twelve-year-
old Brooke played Barbies under a big oak tree with her
friends. Vivi had been seventeen at the time.

Her father had already been dead six months by then.
Her grandmother, doubling up on pain meds for the
cancer ravaging her body, had unwittingly given Vivi
enough information to track down her birth mother.
Vivi'd taken a bus to Greenwich, then hitchhiked to
Round Hill. Ten minutes after knocking on the door and
being shown in by a maid, Vivi went home the same way.

Her mother had stood in the doorway, making sure she didn't interact with Finn and Brooke. Afraid her oldest child would bring her perfect world down around her diamond-studded ears.

She could have; bigamy was a felony. But she wouldn't do that to Finn, who'd watched her walk away with a concerned look in his eyes, or Brooke, who'd waved goodbye with a sweet smile on her angelic face. They weren't like Vivi. They were innocent, protected. They wouldn't be able to handle the stigma of their high-society mother going to jail. Neither would their mother. Which was probably why two minutes into their conversation, Claire Donovan had pulled out her checkbook. Vivi had been tempted to take the bribe. Fifty thousand dollars was a lot of money. But even back then she had her pride.

As the years passed, the pain of her mother's rejection had faded. In some ways, Vivi had come to understand why her mother had abandoned her. She'd been a mistake. The result of too much to drink on prom night. The prom queen and the bad boy had been forced to marry. It wasn't long before her father ended up in jail, her mother working at a high-end resort on the other side of town to make ends meet. When Vivi was two, a man rode up in a white Cadillac and whisked her mother away to his castle in Connecticut. He had no idea his pretty bride-to-be was married with a child of her own.

Vivi rubbed her temple. She wasn't busy enough if she was dwelling on this crap now, letting it get under her skin. She needed to do something, she thought, as she got out of bed, pulling on panties and a T-shirt. She padded to the kitchen and plugged in the coffeemaker. What she needed was a job. Her best friends were wealthy; Vivi was not. She had a nest egg, but it was a hummingbird-sized nest egg. It wouldn't take long to deplete.

Chance was right. She should get her butt back to New York ASAP. But her knees got weak just thinking of leaving Maddie, Skye, and the kids with everything going on. They needed her, and so did Chance. Between the Drugstore Bandits, Natalee, his mother-in-law, Earl, and this thing with the Callahans, he had too much on his plate. If he didn't stay focused, he'd end up in the hospital alongside Ray. She couldn't let that happen. Somehow she had to get him to share the load.

All she had to do was find a way to stay in town and earn a paycheck. She scowled at the intermittent drizzle of coffee splashing into the pot. It was as sparse as her job prospects. She didn't have a choice. She had to call Meredith and get her job back. After their last conversation, sucking up would be required. Vivi hated sucking up about as much as she hated writing her Dear Vivi column. At the rate the coffee drip-dropped into the pot, it would be hours before she managed a full cup. She wasn't about to call Meredith without at least two cups under her belt.

As Vivi walked to the bedroom to get dressed, someone knocked on the apartment door. Probably her best friends coming to do some sucking up of their own. If they had coffee with them, Vivi decided she'd forgive them for not bailing her out yesterday. She opened the door and stuck out her hand.

Nell shook it. "Good morning to you, too. You better get a move on or we'll be late." The older woman gave Vivi an up-and-down look.

Vivi glanced at her T-shirt, tugging on the hem to

cover her black thong. "Late? Late for…" She trailed off when Nell and her two friends walked past her.

Evelyn Tate, a tiny woman who'd spent way too much time in the sun, gave Vivi a crinkled smile.

"We'll wait for you in the living room while you get dressed," said Stella Wright, who looked like an older version of Yvonne De Carlo in *The Munsters*.

"Hold it, why am I getting dressed?" Vivi called to their retreating backs. "Dammit," she muttered when they didn't respond, and went to shut the door.

Maddie shouldered her way inside, dragging Connor's stroller in with her.

"Okay, did I miss the memo? What's…" Vivi began, pushing the door closed.

"Hold it, I'm coming," Skye called out. "Just give the brake a kick, Betty Jean."

Once Maddie no longer blocked the entrance, Vivi peered around the door to see Skye and her stepmother, Betty Jean, with her mile-high blonde hair, carrying Evie's pink stroller up the stairs.

At the sound of Betty Jean huffing and puffing, Vivi said, "Why don't you leave the stroller outside and carry Evie? It would be a lot easier, don't you think? That thing looks like it weighs two hundred pounds, and Evie's what…eight?"

Skye, with one foot on the top step and one below, looked over her shoulder. "Honestly, you're as bad as Liz. Evie's not underweight. She has a delicate bone structure. She's twelve pounds, a perfectly normal weight for a five-month-old. If you don't believe me, ask—"

Vivi held up a hand. "Relax, I believe you." She forgot how sensitive her best friend could be. When Skye first discovered she was pregnant, there were people who voiced their doubts about her parenting abilities— namely Grandma and Daddy-To-Be. In a way, Vivi understood their initial concerns. Skye was free-spirited and unconventional.

But she was an awesome mother, just like Maddie, who wheeled Connor in his stroller toward the living room. "Umm, aren't you going to take him out?"

Maddie rocked the stroller. "No, he's a little cranky this morning."

"Okay, then, leave him in there." Vivi turned back to Skye and Betty Jean, who'd reached the landing. "I don't think there's room for both strollers. Maybe you should—"

Evie screwed up her sweet face and wailed when Betty Jean went to take her out of the stroller.

"Best to leave her in it. She's teething," Skye said, bouncing the stroller up and down.

Vivi was relieved Evie's tears were due to her teeth and not to seeing her. "So, does someone—"

Grace opened the exterior door. Her son, Jack Junior, held her hand. The little boy with his curly dark hair was adorable, but he was a wild child. "Sorry I'm late. Did you tell her?" Grace asked Skye, who made a zip-it motion with her finger.

What the…Oh, good God, not again. Casting a nervous glance from little Jack to Evie, Vivi said, "You guys don't expect me to take care of the kids, do you? Because they don't like me very much." If this was what the next couple of weeks in Christmas were going to be like, writing her advice column didn't sound like such a bad gig. From New York.

"Ah, no." Skye booked it inside with her cooing step-mama following behind.

"Skye, what—"

"No, of course not," Grace interrupted Vivi, as she lifted her son into her arms and climbed the stairs. "But I'm sure you're wrong and the kids love you. Right, little Jack, can you say hi to Vivi?"

"No way," he said, burying his face in his mother's neck.

Vivi sighed, following them to the living room. "Told you. Now, would someone like to tell me what's going on?"

Nell stuck her head out of the kitchen. "Get dressed. Appointment with the bank manager is at eleven. We don't have a lot of time. Coffeemaker's on the fritz. Who wants tea?"

"Wait . . . why would I want to see the—"

Skye, sitting on a chair while moving the stroller back and forth, cast Vivi an anxious glance. "You haven't had a coffee yet?"

"No, and I'm beginning to feel like I'm going to need one. Would someone—" She bowed her head at the knock on the door.

Skye, Maddie, and Grace shared a silent exchange. "I'll get it, and I'll grab you a cup of coffee from the bakery, Vivi." Grace stood, went to hand her son to Vivi, then handed him to Betty Jean instead.

"Make sure you double up on the chocolate sprinkles," Skye suggested.

"And the sugar," Maddie added, as Grace headed for the door.

Fingers pressed to her temples, Vivi looked at Mrs. Tate. "Evelyn, do you want to tell me what this is all about?"

"Get dressed," Nell yelled from the kitchen.

"Nell has a plan, dear. It's a very good one."

Nell's plans were never good. They always ended in disaster. At least for Vivi they did. She couldn't believe her best friends were going along with a Nell plan. Chance's words on the plane came back to her. He was right. Maddie and Skye had gone to the dark side. She could tell by the looks in their eyes. "No. Whatever it is. No."

"Hey," Hailey said, coming up beside Vivi and slapping her on the back. "Welcome to the Christmas Business Association. Good to have you on board. Me and Holly thought we could do a weekly beauty column. Maybe something like Hot Looks from Christmas's Resident Hotties. What do you think? Catchy, right?"

Vivi stared at her with her mouth open.

"Yeah, I know, great idea, isn't it?" Hailey said, clearly misconstruing the whole mouth-hanging-open thing.

Vivi closed her mouth, then opened it again when she realized what was going on. "You should be talking to Skye. She knows more about blogs than I do. Skye." She angled her head at Hailey.

Maddie sighed. "Vivi, if you just hear us out—"

"A blog? No, I'm talking about a column in your newspaper."

"Sorry, but I think the *Spectator* is full-up in the columns department."

"*Spectator*? It's the *Christmas Chronicle*. And how can it be full-up, you just took over today."

"She won't be taking over if you keep yapping. She's not even dressed," Nell said, coming into the living room with a teapot. Stella Wright followed with a tray loaded down with cups, a pitcher of cream, and a bowl of sugar.

Vivi drew her incredulous gaze to her best friends. "I don't have the money to buy a paper."

"It's a steal of a deal," Nell said. "The bank foreclosed last week. There's some guy looking to buy the building. He wants to open a tittie bar."

Betty Jean covered little Jack's ears. "What's his mama going to think when he starts saying that word, Nell? And don't you worry about the financing, sugar. I've got more money than God." She looked up at the ceiling to say "Thank you, Jesus," then returned her blue-shadowed eyes to Vivi. "My little honey bun wants you here in Christmas, and what my little honey bun wants, she gets." She patted Skye's foot.

With the way Betty Jean spoiled Skye, it was amazing she hadn't turned into a demanding diva. But this was one wish Skye's stepmama wouldn't be able to fulfill. While the idea of owning a newspaper set off a tiny thrill inside her, the fact the newspaper was in a small town currently lacking in skyscrapers, Bagel Bagel, and Roasters Coffee and overflowing with wild animals, a dog named Princess, and interfering older women extinguished the buzz of excitement within seconds of it flaring to life. "Thanks, Betty Jean, but I can't take your money."

Maddie looked up from digging in Connor's stroller. She popped the pacifier into his mouth. "You can take mine and Skye's. We'll be your silent partners."

Vivi leaned against the white-plaster pillar. "Come on, Maddie. I know you guys want me to move here, but small-town newspapers are a dying breed. I'll never turn a profit." And Maddie, the Queen of Finance, didn't invest in anything that didn't make money.

"Yes, you will. I crunched the numbers last night."

She grabbed her purse from under Connor's stroller and pulled out a file. "Here it is in black and white. Content's still king, but advertising is key. And you have several people in this room ready to sign on."

Betty Jean nodded. "Envirochicks will buy a weekly two-page spread and so will Au Naturel." Betty Jean and Skye's Envirochicks clothing line was set to give Lululemon a run for their activewear dollar. And Betty Jean's organic makeup line was number one on the Home Shopping Network. Any newspaper, big or small, would kill for their advertising dollars.

Tiny sparks of excitement buzzed through Vivi. "You know I love you guys, but I love New York, too. I have a gr...good life there. I don't know—"

"Last I heard, Chance McBride didn't live in New York. And you two were looking pretty cozy at the diner yesterday." Hailey smirked.

Skye and Maddie stared at Vivi. "You were at the diner with Chance?"

"It was nothing. He was trying to make up for throwing me in jail." She gave Hailey a thanks-a-lot look. "And last I heard, Chance didn't live in Christmas, either." She realized what she'd said and quickly amended. "Not that it would make any difference to me if he did."

"It does to his family," Stella said. "That boy belongs in Christmas."

Vivi narrowed her eyes at Nell, who waggled her eyebrows at her. "Get dressed, girlie. We have a newspaper to save."

"Sorry." Grace ran into the room with the coffee, handing the cup to Vivi. "What did I miss?"

"Tittie bar." Little Jack grinned.

\* \* \*

Chance stood behind Lauren with his hands on her shoulders. "Dad?"

His father moved the penlight from side to side in front of Ray's open right eye, then his left. He straightened. "He's tracking the light. It's a good sign, Lauren," Paul said with a smile.

She relaxed in the chair by the bed, her hand holding Ray's through the bars. "But why doesn't he just wake up?"

"It's not like in the movies, honey. It will take some time. His vitals are stable. We're going to move him from the ICU." His father walked around the bed and patted Lauren's arm. "Why don't you go down and grab a bite to eat?"

"I'm good. Chance brought me dinner."

"Okay, but you have to take care of yourself, Lauren. Ray's going to need you healthy when he wakes up."

Chance rubbed her shoulder. "I'll come by after I finish my shift."

"How long before he comes out of it?" he asked his father once they were in the hall.

"Your guess is as good as mine. Tomorrow, a couple days, a week."

"I hope it's sooner than later." For both Lauren and Ray's sake. And, admittedly, Chance was frustrated with the lack of progress on the case.

"He may not be able to tell you anything when he wakes up, son."

Chance nodded. He knew that. As they walked to the elevators, he cast his father a sidelong glance. Normally clean-shaven, he sported at least three days of growth on his face. "You look like shit. You might want to take your own advice and take care of yourself."

His father rubbed his jaw. "Long day, that's all."

"Go home and take it easy. Watch the game."

"Not the same without Liz." He stabbed the down button. "In two days we would have been married. Now she's got Stevens living in her house. He asked her to marry him, you know. A few months ago."

"Yeah, I heard—"

His father stepped into the elevator, talking over Chance. "And she has the nerve to accuse me of sneaking around with Karen behind her back."

"Dad, in her defense, you did have lipstick..."

Chance leaned against the elevator wall, crossing his booted feet at the ankles when his father continued talking as if he hadn't said anything. "Two minutes, all I asked for was two minutes to explain to her that it was my ninety-year-old patient who left the lipstick on me and not Karen. But oh, no, I'm not even entitled to that. She stormed off. Probably ran to Stevens and told him all about it."

"So, do the same."

"Run to Stevens and tell him what?"

"Jesus, Dad, where's your game? No, take Karen out for a drink." Karen was young and beautiful, and more importantly, his dad didn't want to marry her. It was the perfect solution. "And for God's sake, clean yourself up. You don't want Liz to think you're pining after her, do you?"

His father brightened a bit. "You think it would work?"

"Yeah," Chance said as the elevator came to a stop.

"Okay, son, I'll give Karen a call. Maybe we'll stop by

the Penalty Box. Too bad you're on duty. You could join the party."

Sometimes he forgot how old his father was. Chance and his brothers should have helped him brush up on his dating skills before letting him back out there. "I wouldn't call you and Karen on a date a party, Dad."

His father snorted, following him out of the elevator. "I'm talking about the party for Vivi."

He stopped midstride and turned, ignoring the heavy weight in his gut at the thought she was leaving. After last night, there was a part of him that didn't want her to go. But it was for the best. "If I get a chance, I'll stop by and say good-bye."

"Good-bye? She's not going anywhere. She just bought the *Chronicle*." His father cast him a hopeful glance. "She's moving to Christmas for good."

*          *          *

While Chance checked out possible sightings of a '76 black Mustang over the last few hours, he'd tried to reach his aunt and Vivi. He'd struck out on all counts. At least his aunt and Vivi's noncommunication was easy enough to check on. He stopped in at the station before heading to the Penalty Box. As soon as he walked into the bar, he understood the reason for their lack of response. It was doubtful they'd hear the ping of the message above the noise. The party was in full swing.

He nodded to Sawyer as he passed the bar and headed to where Vivi, wearing a jean jacket and white V-neck T-shirt, sat alone at a table, nursing a drink. Looked like her entire party had abandoned her to hit the dance floor. His aunt and her pals were leading at least thirty people in an exuberant rendition of the Village People's "YMCA." His brother and Ethan glared at him through their upraised arms as they danced along with their wives. He couldn't figure out the attitude until he spotted his father and Karen near the jukebox. Chance shrugged. His dad looked a hell of a lot happier than he had a few hours ago.

"Hey, Slick." He pulled out the chair beside her. "How come you're not out there celebrating with your friends?"

She lowered the frothy white drink from her mouth. "You heard."

He grinned, wiping the milk mustache from her upper lip with his finger. "Yeah, I heard." He tasted the drink off his finger and made a face. "You should stick to beer. Drink too much of these, and you'll be hungover for a week."

"That's the plan. A few more Lois Lanes, and I'll wake up to discover this is all a bad dream."

"Lois Lanes?"

"Yeah." She lifted the drink and scowled at the frosted glass. "Sawyer named it after me. He should've called it The Idiot." She leaned into Chance, resting her head on his shoulder. "What the hell was I thinking?"

He tipped her chin to look into her eyes. "You're already drunk, aren't you?"

"Possibly." She closed one eye and then the other. "Probably. You're supposed to be my friend. Why didn't you stop me?"

He held back a smile. She was a cute drunk. "I'll stop you now, how's that?" He moved the drink out of her reach, calling to Brandi, who was serving another table, to bring Vivi some water when she had a minute.

"I didn't mean stop me from drinking. I meant stopping me from buying the damn newspaper." She groaned, burying her face in his neck.

He smoothed his hand down her long, glossy hair, trying not to react to her warm breath on his skin. "You could have said no, honey."

Her head snapped up. Thanks to his quick reflexes, he'd moved his in time to avoid a broken jaw. "I did." She held up both hands, wiggling her fingers. "Ten times. But none of them would take no for an answer. They talked right over me. Have you ever tried to win a war of words with Nell, or for that matter, Maddie and Skye? For every reason I gave them not to buy the paper, they gave me three why I should. And theirs sounded better than mine." Her expression grew serious, her anxious violet eyes searching his face. "Do you think it's a stupid idea? Do you think I can make it work?"

For all her confidence and hard-ass attitude, Vivi Westfield had no idea how incredible she really was. He blamed her mother for that. Which is probably why, even though the last thing he wanted was her running the newspaper in Christmas while he investigated the Drugstore Bandits, he couldn't use her fears against her. He lifted his hand, tucking her hair behind her ear. "I think it's a great idea, Slick. If anyone can make a go of the paper, it's you."

# Chapter Eighteen

Vivi finished her early-morning run with an all-out sprint alongside the boardwalk. Pushing herself to the edge of her endurance, her lungs burned. She slowed to a jog as she reached the path to the park and checked her watch—five miles in forty-five minutes. Not a personal best, but she'd take it. Running outdoors was definitely more punishing than the indoor track at the gym. There were perks though, like the sun shining on her face, the light breeze off the mountains cooling her skin, and the peaceful gurgle of the stream she ran beside. Yes, even a city girl like her could admit the scenery was spectacular. Since she hadn't run into any bears or wolves, she might be convinced to start every day this way.

She walked to the weeping willow on the edge of the path, placing her right palm on the tree. Bending her left knee, she wrapped her hand around her foot and pulled it toward her bottom.

"You're doing it wrong. Line up your knees and straighten your back," a familiar deep male voice directed.

She glanced to her right. And to think she'd congratulated herself on not coming across any wild animals this morning. The uniformed man stalking toward her reminded her of a lion—all predatory male. "Good morning to you, too."

"It would have been if I hadn't read your first edition of the *Chronicle*." Chance came to stand behind her, placing his big hand over hers. He moved her leg down and over an inch.

She suppressed a shiver at the feel of him at her back, at his warm sandalwood scent wafting past her nose. His comment should have been enough to suppress the unwanted reaction. She was proud of her first edition. It's why she'd gone for a run. It had been her way of celebrating the new direction her life had taken. The past week had been crazy busy, but a good busy. She felt more fulfilled and challenged than she had in years. She'd wanted to get the paper out as soon as possible. And she'd done it with help from her friends, and Nell and her friends.

So she wasn't exactly happy to hear Chance's unflattering remark, but before she had the opportunity to ask him what his problem was, he said, "What were you thinking running the story about the Drugstore Bandits? I told you about the computers off the record, Vivi."

She knew he did. She'd gone to the station two days ago to let him know she was running the story. He'd been working as hard as her and had finally caught a break. All the burglaries had one thing in common—a large delivery of prescription drugs the day of the break-in. Since the pharmacies were spread over three counties, the odds were against an inside job.

Chance had worked the angle that they'd hacked into the pharmacy's computer system the same way they'd hacked into the security systems and hit pay dirt. Whoever was behind the Drugstore Bandits had scary good computer skills. But so did Chance's youngest brother Easton, who was now consulting on the case. If he could find an IP address, they'd be one step closer to putting the Drugstore Bandits behind bars.

She twisted from the waist. "I don't know what you're talking about. I...McBride," she huffed when he turned her around.

"Stretch. You alluded to it, Vivi. So if you were involved with the robberies and didn't want to get caught, what would you do?"

"All I said was new evidence had come to light and a break in the case was imminent."

He ignored her, moving closer, crowding her against the tree. "I'll tell you what you'd do, what they'll do. They'll want to know what you know, Vivi, and they'll figure out a way to find out. You put yourself on their radar."

She lowered her leg to face him. "In your overprotective, suspicious mind, I'm on everyone's radar, McBride. I can handle myself. I'll be careful." If he got this bent out of shape over the Bandit story, which was nothing in her mind, it was a good thing she hadn't told him Darwin Callahan had e-mailed her. Callahan Senior had let her know he'd discovered who she was. He wasn't happy, but she wouldn't exactly call the wording in his e-mail a threat. Besides, she didn't want another lecture or I-told-you-so from Mr. Hypervigilant.

"Careful? You don't know what the word means. You're a hothead. It wasn't enough that you waved a red flag at the Drugstore Bandits, you called Earl Skully out in your op-ed piece."

"The car he sold me wouldn't have passed a safety test. It nearly blew up with me in it."

"You paid five hundred dollars for the car. What did you expect?"

She lifted her chin. "If a business in town rips off a customer and puts them in danger, which Earl did, I'm going to make sure people know about it. I consider it a community service."

"Community service…is that what you call your Around the Town column? Because let me tell you, Slick, your cutesy names aren't fooling—"

"Wait, Around the Town? I have no idea what you're talking about."

"Give me a break. It's on page fifteen, right below your Dear Vivi column." He took the rolled newspaper out of his back pocket and handed it to her. "Now, thanks to you, everyone knows Gil Sands is having an affair with Lisa Flowers, including Gil's wife." He stabbed the page.

And there it was in black and white. She shook her head. "I don't understand. I didn't…" She briefly closed her eyes on a groan, then poked him in the chest. "This is your aunt's doing, McBride. I never should have let her work with me." She knew it was a bad idea right from the get-go, but she'd been slightly overwhelmed the first couple of days and had welcomed Nell, Evelyn, and Stella's help.

Help? Ha! They were probably going to get her run out of town with their little addition. Actually, that was the least of her worries. She'd have to call Ethan and find out the legal ramifications of her using "Dear Vivi." She wasn't sure if the *Spectator* held the rights to the moniker. It's why she'd told Nell she couldn't run a Dear Vivi column until she'd spoken to Ethan. But Nell had wanted to start the paper off with a bang. Oh, it had started off with a bang, all right.

"I swear to God, I'm going to wring her neck," Vivi said, slapping the newspaper against her thigh as she headed down the path at a jog.

Chance caught her by the hand and hauled her to a stop. "Slow down. Don't go off half-cocked."

"This was supposed to be a great day for me, McBride. I was happy, really happy, for the first time in a long time. I felt like maybe this was what I was meant to do all along. Like Skye's silly platitude 'everything for a reason' actually held some merit. And now, thanks to you and your aunt, it's ruined."

His expression softened. "I'm sorry, Slick. I didn't mean to ruin your day. I'm worried about you, that's all."

"Maybe you should be worrying about your aunt instead. Because when I get ahold of—"

"Okay, how about you knock off the threats. I don't want to have to throw you in jail on your special day." He dipped his head, looking her in the eyes. "Let me make it up to you. I'll take you to the diner for a burger. I'm off at six. We can celebrate."

That was sweet, and she didn't want him to be sweet. She was gearing up for a good, long rant, and he'd stolen her thunder. She sighed. "Thank you. I appreciate the offer, but I have a meeting tonight." She'd rather go to bed.

At the thought, an image of her and Chance naked and sweaty in rumpled sheets popped into her head. Sheesh, her brain mustn't have gotten the memo that they were friends now—and not *that* kind of friends. Now her body was on the same page as her brain because her neglected lady parts warmed with anticipation. *Sorry to disappoint you girls, not going to happen.* It was better this way: no drama, no angst.

"I don't mind eating late," he said.

"I've seen the agenda. The meeting will probably go until midnight."

"I'll take you out tomorrow, then." He tapped a finger on her nose. "Behave yourself. No more poking your stick in the hornets' nest, okay?"

"I'll look after my stick, you look after yours." She rolled her eyes when his lips quirked at the corner. "You've got a dirty mind."

He laughed, putting up his hands as he walked backward. "Didn't say a thing. Catch you later, Slick," he said, all nice and friendly.

Nice and friendly would be fine if he didn't look so damn good walking to his truck parked on Main Street. She needed a shower, a cold one.

\*    \*    \*

Vivi locked the door to the *Chronicle*. She could use another cold shower, and this one had nothing to do with the Chance effect. She needed to wake the hell up. Her day had been brutal. Nell, Stella, and Evelyn had made themselves scarce, leaving Vivi to deal with Gil, his wife, Gil's mistress, and Earl Skully. If this was a sign of things to come, Vivi needed to up her liability insurance.

"Guess I'm too late," Zach Callahan said as he sauntered toward her with an aw-shucks smile.

*What now?* was Vivi's first reaction. Instead, she said, "Hey, Zach. Too late for what?"

He inclined his head at the pale yellow wood front of the *Chronicle*. "I thought you might be hiring. I worked at the high school newspaper. I'm good—"

"I wish I could, Zach, but I really don't have the funds in my budget to hire anyone."

"I've got my own truck. I can do deliveries."

"Sorry, buddy. Seniors are doing the deliveries for free." Which went in the Reason to Keep Nell column. Vivi took in the disheartened expression on Zach's face as he kicked a stone off the sidewalk with the toe of his black high-tops and had a flash of insight. "This doesn't have anything to do with Chance asking what you do for a living, does it?"

He shrugged. "He made me feel like a loser. I want him to know I can take care of Nat."

Vivi felt a twinge of sympathy for the kid and patted his shoulder. "It's not you, Zach." Well, it kind of was, or at least it was who he was related to. But there was nothing Zach could do about his family, and he obviously felt bad enough. "Chance would be the same with anyone Natalee dated. It's a big-brother thing. He's just trying to protect her."

"She doesn't need protection from me, and she doesn't need him looking out for her," he said, his voice low and rough.

He lost some of her initial sympathy with the tough-guy attitude. "Doesn't matter what you think. That's the way it is. Look, I've got a meeting. I'll keep you in mind if something comes up."

"Thanks. Appreciate it."

"No problem." She went to walk away, then remembered the list she'd made for Natalee. Vivi turned to find Zach's intent gaze on her. Weird. He smoothed away whatever she thought she'd seen on his face. "I almost forgot." She dug in her messenger bag and pulled out a pad of paper, ripping off the top sheet. "Chance mentioned Natalee was looking into colleges. He said she wanted to major in English. I found a couple of schools she might be interested in. Would you mind giving her this?"

He took the paper and scanned the list. "You're wasting your time. She won't go."

The way he said it made Vivi think he wouldn't let her go. She was afraid Chance might have Zach's number after all. "Doesn't hurt to try."

"Whatever. I won't tell her this is from you." He held Vivi's gaze. "She doesn't like you, you know. She doesn't want you and Chance together." There was a warning note in his voice.

"Chance and I aren't together, so she doesn't have anything to worry about."

"Good. I mean, that's good for you. She can be..." He shrugged, leaving the implied threat hanging in the air. "Better let you go to your meeting."

"Yeah. Take care." She walked away, feeling his eyes on her back.

"You take care, too, Vivi."

Something in his voice made her turn around. This time she held his gaze, making sure he got the message. "Always do, Zach. I'm real good at taking care of myself." If the little jerk was trying to scare her, he'd have to do better than that.

*From the pot into the fire*, she thought as she walked

into the conference room at the town hall. Zach had nothing on Nell McBride. Vivi dropped her messenger bag onto the table and took the seat across from Nell, Evelyn, and Stella. She stabbed a finger at the three of them. "You're all fired."

Nell, looking sheepish, doodled on the pad of paper in front her and grumbled, "You can't fire us. We're volunteers."

Evelyn Tate nudged Nell, then said to Vivi, "We're sorry, dear. We didn't mean to cause you trouble."

"Like we told Chance, it wasn't our fault, but we should have told you what Nell did. So I suppose we're guilty by omission. Sorry, Vivi. We'd like to keep working at the paper. And we've come up with some ideas to make it up to you," Stella said with a tentative smile.

Well, good. It's about time someone took the old meddler to task. She ignored the warm and fuzzies at the thought that Chance had done so on her behalf. That's what friends do, she reminded herself.

Nell sighed. "All right. Maybe I took it too far."

"Ya think?" Skye said, pulling out the chair beside Vivi to sit down. "Ethan has spent most of the day talking to the lawyers at the *Spectator* because of what you pulled, Nell." She patted Vivi's hand. "He said not to worry. You're good on all counts. He'll explain everything to you tomorrow." She fanned herself. "He's really hot when he speaks legalese, so prepare yourself."

"I'll try not to faint," Vivi said dryly, then tilted her head to study Skye. "Sounds like everything's good on the home front."

"Better than good. Richard and Claudia are leaving tomorrow." She gave Vivi a fist bump.

"About time," Nell said. "Maybe now we can get the wedding back on track. Liz…"

Maddie cleared her throat, widening her eyes and nudging her head at the door as Liz and Cat walked in.

"Which wedding would that be, Nell? Surely not mine and a certain doctor who can't keep his zipper—"

"Mom," Cat muttered, pulling out a chair for Liz. "Behave or I'm taking you home."

"Yes, mother-in-law dearest, behave. We don't want your blood pressure going up," Skye said, taking obvious delight in teasing Liz. Last year, Skye had been on the receiving end of those same exact words.

Liz arched a brow. "You are lucky I love you, dearest daughter-in-law."

"Who wouldn't love my honey bun?" Betty Jean said, coming up behind Skye to put her arms around her chest, rocking her from side to side.

"All right, lovefest is over. Time to get to work." Maddie tapped the gavel on the table. "Meeting's called to order," she said as Grace, Hailey, and the rest of the business owners quickly took their seats. "Before we get started, I'd like to welcome our newest member to the Christmas Business Association, Vivi Westfield." Maddie motioned for her to stand.

Vivi gave a self-conscious shake of her head.

"Come on now, stand up and be recognized. You did good, girlie. Circulation is already up one hundred percent." Nell buffed her nails on her *Chronicle* T-shirt.

Everyone clapped when Vivi reluctantly got to her feet. Circulation was up, a fact that had Vivi dancing around the office this afternoon when she'd hit the magic number.

"And you saved the building from being turned into a tittie bar," Nell finished to resounding groans.

Vivi wasn't big on speeches, but she owed several people her thanks. "As all of you well know, without some arm-twisting, I wouldn't have bought the *Chronicle*. I also wouldn't have had the money to do so without my best friends and business partners, Maddie McBride and Skye O'Connor. So thank you, all of you." She caught Nell's expectant look. "Especially, Nell, Evelyn, and Stella for everything they've done. Even if they nearly got me sued."

"You should thank Chance, too. If he hadn't told me to keep you busy, I wouldn't have come up with the idea."

"What do you mean he told you to—"

Maddie banged the gavel. "Order. Meeting's called to order. We don't want to be here all night, do we?"

Three hours later, Vivi was beginning to think they would be. And from her copious notes, she wouldn't be sleeping for the next year. She had pages upon pages of events and promotions to cover: the building of Santa's Village, Christmas in July, year-round letters to Santa, her Dear Vivi column, Around the Town...

"I think we've just about covered..." Maddie began.

"No, wait. We've saved the best for last. Tell them, Nell," Evelyn urged her friend.

"Christmas Cuties." Nell made a ta-da motion with her hands.

"Huh, like animals and kids?" Vivi asked.

"No, we're going to get the best-looking men in Christmas to pose naked with a Santa hat placed strategically over their junk. We'll feature one Hot Bod a week."

Vivi shot Nell a narrowed-eyed look. Before they'd

known who he was, Skye and Maddie referred to Chance as Hot Bod after getting a load of him half-naked via Skype. He was hot, but there was no way she'd put him in her paper for other women to ogle.

So if that's who Nell was thinking of, Vivi'd soon set her straight. "Exactly who were you planning to ask to pose, Nell? Not that I'm approving the idea, but—"

Nell smirked. "My nephew Paul, of course."

Before Liz or anyone else had a chance to react, Hot Bod himself strode into the conference room. Chance's sharp gaze scanned the room until it landed on Vivi. She didn't like the way his grass-green eyes went from relieved to wary. "What is it?" she asked.

"Someone broke into the *Chronicle*. They trashed the place."

# Chapter Nineteen

Chance held the door open, keeping a close eye on Vivi as she took in the damage to the *Chronicle*. The desks were tossed, computers smashed, filing cabinets and shelves overturned with books and papers strewn from one end of the space to the other. She'd been happy here, happier than she'd been in a long time. Hearing her say that in the park had just about slayed him. He'd give anything to take away the defeated look he now saw on her face.

"Careful," he warned when she stepped inside, "there's glass everywhere." Whoever had broken in had come through the side window in the alley. Someone had heard the noise and called it in. By the time Jill had gotten there, the damage had been done, the perp nowhere in sight.

"Okay," Vivi said, her voice flat.

He heard the shocked gasps and angry muttering from

behind him. Madison, Skye, and the rest of the council had arrived. His aunt, who'd been on her cell phone, shoved it in the pocket of her jeans and went to push past him.

He held her back. "Nell, you can't go in until we process the scene. Vivi, honey, don't touch anything. Have a look around and tell me if anything's missing."

She pushed her palms up her face, leaving them on the top of her head. "How will I know? Everything's..." She tipped her head back, staring at the ceiling.

"No one move," he ordered the women. Papers and glass crunched underfoot as he walked to Vivi. He took her in his arms. "I know it looks bad, but once they've dusted for prints, we'll have the place cleaned up in no time."

She wouldn't meet his eyes, holding herself stiff in his arms, biting on her full bottom lip. He ducked his head to look in her eyes. She turned away and said in a throaty whisper, "Don't."

He lowered his mouth to her ear. "You can cry, you know."

"I'm not going to cry," she scoffed, but her glassy eyes told another story. "I'm just...mad. Who would do..." She released a brittle laugh. "Stupid question, right?"

Before he could answer her, Cat approached. "If you're okay with it, Chance, I'll help Jill out. Knock on a few doors. See if anyone heard or saw anything."

"Appreciate it."

"No problem." She rested a hand on Vivi's shoulder as she scanned the room with a cop's eyes. Raising a brow, she lifted her gaze to his. "Personal."

Yeah, he'd thought the same thing. This was overkill,

not a simple break and enter. Damn shame Cat was no longer on the force. She was a good cop. "Looks like."

"Hang in there, Vivi. We'll find whoever did this. I'll be back to give you a hand with the cleanup."

"Thanks," Vivi said, looking up at him as Cat skirted the debris and headed out. "Who do you think did this?"

"We'll talk about it in a minute. Right now I need you to check your computer."

"All right, but I doubt it's salvageable." She eased out of his arms and walked toward the overturned desk on the right.

"You have anything on there about the Drugstore Bandits?" He glanced at the women milling around on the sidewalk and lowered his voice. "Anything about the leads we were following, the ones not in the paper?"

"The computers are outdated. I haven't uploaded the files yet. I have them on my laptop." Her eyes narrowed. "You think the Drugstore Bandits are behind this?"

"Yeah, I do. You made them nervous, Slick." And that made him nervous. Made him wonder how he'd keep her safe. He had some ideas about how he'd do that but doubted she'd agree. He had to give it a shot anyway. "You're staying with me until things calm down."

"No, I'm not. I told you before, McBride, I can take care of myself." She crouched beside her desk, her hand on the computer. "You and Cat think this is personal. So that rules out the Drugstore Bandits, doesn't..." She looked up at him. "If the Callahans were involved, it would be personal, wouldn't it?"

"Yeah, it would." He turned at the sound of his brother's voice. Gage spoke to Madison, then walked toward them—followed by a specially trained civilian crime scene investigator Gage contracted on the infrequent times he needed one. Chance had used him, too. The man acknowledged him with a nod and got to work.

"You okay?" Gage asked Vivi.

"Been better," she said, coming to her feet. She nodded at the computer. "They took the hard drive."

He waited for his brother's reaction to the news.

"We'll check on Earl's, Gil's, his wife's, and Lisa Flowers's whereabouts at the time of the break-in."

As he'd suspected he would, Gage left out the people who should be at the top of his list. "What about the Callahans?"

His brother bowed his head, gave it a slight shake, then looked at Chance. "Let it go. They're not—"

"Wouldn't hurt to ask, would it?" Vivi said, avoiding looking at Chance while speaking directly to his brother. "I got an e-mail from Darwin Callahan earlier this week. Not exactly a threatening one, but he implied if I did or said anything that might negatively impact his parole hearing next month, he had people on the outside who'd take care of me for him."

"Enlighten me, will you? What part of that did you not perceive to be a threat? And why the hell didn't you tell me as soon as you received it?" Chance motioned to her messenger bag. "Let me see the e-mail."

"I don't have my laptop with me. My battery died. I left it at the apartment." Once again, she avoided eye contact.

Oh, come on. She couldn't be holding something else back. But his gut said otherwise. "Who else, who else threatened you today?"

"It was nothing."

"Vivi, you let me and Chance decide if it was nothing, okay? What happened?"

"Zach stopped by asking for a job. You made him feel like a loser the other night, and for whatever reason, he figured working here would show you he was serious about providing for Natalee."

He met his brother's gaze over her head. Good, he wasn't the only one who thought that sounded like a load of crap. One more person to add to the growing list of suspects. Vivi continued, "Anyway, I'd made a list of colleges for Natalee to check out and asked him to give it to her. He, ah, he implied that Natalee hated me. Basically warned me to watch my back."

Vivi Westfield never failed to surprise him. But he supposed he shouldn't be. Taking care of people, looking out for them, was her thing. Even if it was a young woman who didn't like her. "He's yanking your chain. Nat's a sweet kid. She'd never hurt anyone." He'd have a talk with her though. Make sure she knew she had no reason to be jealous of Vivi. No one would take Kate's place in his heart.

"We'll be about an hour here. Why don't you check out Callahan's e-mail with Vivi...Hang on a minute." His brother answered his cell. While he listened to whoever was on the other end, a muscle ticked in his jaw as his gaze moved from Chance to Vivi. "Okay, got it. Thanks, Jill." He disconnected. "Black Mustang was spotted parked in the lane beside the bakery about forty minutes ago."

\*       \*       \*

Chance stood over Vivi. "Pack a bag. You're staying with me."

She sat on the couch with her knees pulled to her chest, struggling to hold it together. She bowed her head in order to keep her panic from his all-seeing eyes. The apartment hadn't been trashed like the *Chronicle*, but they'd stolen her laptop. They now had access to Chance's theories about the Drugstore Bandits. And even more devastating, at least to her, they had access to her entire life—to her every thought, every dream, every stupid regret and mistake. Things she didn't want anyone to know. She felt violated, exposed.

Maddie and Skye sat on either side of her. "Please, Vivi, stay with Chance," Skye pleaded.

They expected her to argue. She wasn't going to. She wanted to stay with him. For the first time in a long time, she was scared. The fears she'd battled after Jimmy "the Knife" Moriarty broke into her apartment in New York came back to taunt her. Seeing what Jimmy, a known murderer and rapist, had done to her personal belongings, what he'd threatened to do to her, had left a mark. She'd gotten her revenge, even though it cost her her job and nearly her life. But it hadn't been enough to keep the nightly panic attacks at bay. Three months, it had taken three months before she'd slept through the night. These guys didn't scare her as much as Jimmy, but that same sense of helplessness had returned.

Chance crouched in front of her, lifting her chin with his fingers. "If I have to carry you out of here, you're coming home with me. Now either you pack your bag or I do it for you."

"I can pack my own bag. I just needed a minute to think." She doubted he bought the excuse, but she had to say something. She didn't want him, Maddie, or Skye knowing the break-ins had gotten to her. She hated weakness, especially in herself. "Everything was on my laptop: banking, contact info, everything."

He nodded, stood up, and took his cell from his pocket. "I'll call Easton. He should be able to remotely wipe your hard drive."

"Really? That'd be great. Thanks." She felt better at the thought they wouldn't be able to access her personal files. "You'll need my password." She caught the uncomfortable look that came over his face and threw up her hands. "I don't believe you. You already have my password, don't you?"

"Oh, oh," Skye murmured, then got up to answer the door. Chance had made everyone but Skye and Maddie wait outside.

"Don't get worked up. I didn't use it. I—"

She believed him, but getting worked up would keep her tears at bay. So she went with it. "As if I believe that. And don't think I've forgotten that it's because of you that Nell steamrolled me into buying the *Chronicle*."

"You can't put the entire blame on Nell, Vivi. Me and Skye did some steamrolling of our own," Maddie said.

"You're right, you did." Vivi stood up. "And I don't know why I let all of you twist my arm. This was the absolute worst decision of my life." She glared at Chance, who looked at her with an amused expression on his face, working her into full-out rant mode. It felt good. The tears were gone now. "No, wait, I stand corrected. Getting involved with *you* was the worst decision of my life."

He reached for her, lifting her off her feet so they were nose to nose. "You're full of it. But if that's what you've got to tell yourself to make you feel better, honey, go for it." And then he kissed her. Right on the mouth. It wasn't a friend's kiss. It wasn't even a friends-with-benefits kiss. It felt like a you-drive-me-crazy-but-I-love-you-anyway kiss.

Which was probably the reason why, when he set her back on her feet, she stared at him with her mouth hanging open. He'd completely burst her rant bubble.

"Finally," Nell said from behind her. "Took you long enough. Looks like we're going to have a wedding in Christmas after all."

Chance took Vivi by the shoulders, steering her past Nell and the group of women now gathered in the living room. "I'll deal with her. You pack your bag."

As she walked toward the bedroom, Vivi realized what kind of kiss it was. The same one he'd given her on the plane. He knew—he knew she was scared. Knew what her angry rant had been about. She supposed the knowledge should have her rethinking her plan to stay with him, but it didn't. The way he'd effortlessly lifted her off her feet, his big hands wrapped around her arms, and his mouth, that amazing mouth, on hers had done more to quiet her fears than her temper tantrum.

"Whoa, that was some kiss. I thought you two were just friends now," Maddie said, following Vivi into the bedroom.

"Yeah, that was so not a friendly kiss," Skye said, parking her butt on the end of the bed.

"Yes it was." She caught Skye and Maddie's shared grins. "And not the benefits kind."

Vivi packed up her toiletries in the bathroom then walked to the dresser, pulling a couple pairs of underwear from the drawer and two T-shirts. She turned to put them in her messenger bag only to discover her best friends had her suitcase opened in the middle of the bed. Within minutes, they'd packed everything she'd brought with her to Christmas.

She sat on the bed, crossing her arms. "What do you two think you're doing?"

Skye shrugged. "Better to be prepared."

Maddie tugged on the zipper and looked at her. "Okay, can we be honest? Or more to the point, you be honest. I know you, Vivi Westfield, and I know you are still very much in love with Chance McBride. Don't try and deny it," she said when Vivi went to do just that.

"Maddie's right, Vivi. And that man out there loves you whether he'll admit it or not. You didn't see him watching you when he brought you to the *Chronicle*. We did. All you two need is some one-on-one time to make him realize it. Staying with him will give you that and more."

\*       \*       \*

Vivi didn't get an opportunity to argue with her friends. Chance had come to get her, hustling her out of the apartment and into his truck. If she'd been able to convince them there was nothing more than a friendship between her and Chance, maybe she would have been able to squash that small flutter of hope taking flight inside her. For the entire drive, he'd been watching her with the same expression she imagined Skye had seen at the *Chronicle*. The look that had her best friends convinced that he was in love with her. It had to be because those soft sidelong glances, the way his gaze roamed her face every so often, had resurrected the butterflies in her stomach. Those romantic feelings seemed to be coming back to life, too.

"You're quiet. You okay?" he asked, reaching out to tuck her hair behind her ear.

Her stupid heart did a happy dance. "I'm good. Just thinking about everything I have to do tomorrow."

"Nell's got the seniors of Christmas on speed dial. They're going in to clean up as soon as Gage gives them the okay."

"It's almost eleven. I can't let them do that." She pulled her cell phone from her jeans pocket.

He closed his hand over hers. "Let her do it. She's worried they broke in because of her column. It'll make her feel better. Besides, she says half of them don't sleep anyway."

"You and I both know the break-in had nothing to do with Nell's Around the Town column. If anything, it did exactly what she said it would do. We had a huge uptick in new subscriptions."

Chance snorted. "Great, there'll be no stopping her now."

"Please don't say that. I'm going to have a hard enough time getting to sleep without worrying about what she'll get up to next." Her Christmas Cuties idea came to mind.

"Don't worry. Once I take care of you, you'll have no problem going to sleep."

"Ah, we talked about this, remember? No benefits." She could really use some benefits right now, but no matter what Skye and Maddie thought—no matter what Vivi thought she saw in his eyes—that would be opening herself up to a boatload of pain.

"You gotta do something about that dirty mind of yours, Slick. We're going for a swim, and then I'll finish you off with a rubdown."

She must have a dirty mind because her brain got stuck

on "rubdown" and "finish you off." She had firsthand experience with a Chance McBride rubdown, and unless she wanted to have a big O in front of him, which she didn't, his talented fingers were getting nowhere near her. She decided his first suggestion was safer. "I didn't see a pool. Is it on the other side of the cabin?"

"City girl," he scoffed. "We're swimming in the lake."

"Funny, for a minute there I thought you were serious."

He laughed. "I am. It'll be good for you."

"Are you crazy? It's probably ten degrees, and dark, real dark. We wouldn't be able to see the snakes and fish and stuff." She shuddered, thinking of the weeds wrapping around her legs. "Anyway, I don't have a bathing suit."

"Temperature will be a little fresh, but it'll be good for you. And it's dark. You don't need a suit."

"I'm not skinny-dipping with you, McBride," she said as they pulled off the main road. She was surprised they were almost at the cabin. Surprised because Chance hadn't reacted to driving past the scene of Kate's accident. He hadn't gotten that tense look on his face. Was it possible he was slowly coming to terms with Kate's death? She squashed the thought. She wasn't going to let Maddie and Skye's crazy ideas take hold in her head.

Chance's jaw tightened as he pressed the garage door opener. "Looks like you got a reprieve, Slick. No skinny-dipping tonight. We've got company."

She followed his gaze to the white four-by-four parked alongside the front walkway.

# Chapter Twenty

Chance strangled the steering wheel as he pulled into the garage. He didn't need to deal with Nat and Callahan right now. He wanted to take care of Vivi. To wipe away the fear he'd seen in her eyes. As he'd hoped, the kiss he'd given her at the apartment had distracted her, gotten her out of her head at least for a short while. Hadn't done a whole hell of a lot for him, other than make him want to get her naked and in his bed. Too bad she was holding firm to the friends-without-benefits thing, because they could both do with some benefits tonight. In his experience, there was nothing like hot, sweaty monkey sex to alleviate stress. And he was carrying around a shitload of it tonight. Their one good lead was blown.

Easton hadn't been able to remotely wipe Vivi's hard drive. Whoever was behind the Drugstore Bandits knew what they were doing. They'd blocked all of his brother's attempts to get into the computer—not an easy feat.

So as far as Operation Takedown was concerned, they

were back to square one. He didn't blame Vivi. No reason for her to think the information wasn't safe on her laptop. And once he'd dealt with whatever had brought Nat and Callahan to his place, he had to break the news to her. She'd feel violated all over again, and there wasn't a damn thing he could do about it. And violated is what he was feeling right now with a Callahan making himself at home in his place, in his and Kate's home. The thought had him seeing red, and he slammed the door of the truck, heading for the stairs. Only to be stopped cold by a feminine shriek. He whirled around . . . no sign of Vivi.

He backtracked. "Slick, what . . ." He trailed off as he rounded the truck. She was on her knees with her arms over her head. He went to her, crouching beside her. "Honey, what's . . ."

She looked at him, a combination of anger and fear in her pretty eyes. "Bats. You have bats. And do not tell me I'm imagining it and you didn't see them because they whooshed past my head. This close, McBride"—she pinched her thumb and forefinger together, waving them in his face—"to getting caught in my hair."

He'd been so deep in his head, he supposed it was possible he hadn't noticed. It wouldn't be the first time there were bats in the garage. Wouldn't be the last. But that wasn't the answer his little city slicker needed to hear. Her night had been rough enough. He smoothed his hand down her hair. "It was just a mama and daddy bird protecting their nest. Come on." He stood, helping her to her feet.

With a hand on her head, she cast a nervous glance to the ceiling. "Okay, but I could have sworn they were bats."

"Nah, just a couple of birds." He fought back a smile at the look of relief on her face.

Her eyes narrowed. "Liar." She stabbed a finger in his chest. "Do not humor me. They were bats."

He wrapped his hand around hers, lifting it to his lips. He kissed her palm. "Maybe. But they're as afraid of you as you are of them." He laced his fingers through hers, leading her up the stairs.

"Tell that to the people in Louisiana who were attacked by vampire bats and died, McBride." She tugged her hand from his. "I need my suitcase."

"You read too much. I'll get your suitcase later. Right now I want to find out why the hell Nat brought Callahan to my place."

She hooked her finger in his belt loop, stopping him from opening the door. "Calm down. I get that you don't like the kid, but maybe you'd get more out of him if you played nice. Don't mention him asking me for a—" At the sound of Princess barking from behind the closed door, she groaned. "Bats and now Cujo." She tugged on his belt loop. "Bend down."

"Slick, she's not going to bite you." He gave his head an amused shake when she ignored him and climbed onto his back.

"Tell that to someone whose butt cheek she hasn't sunk her teeth into." She wrapped her arms around his neck, her legs around his waist, and wiggled her army-green flip-flop. "I like my toes."

He chuckled. "Sure you don't want to slide around to the front? You used to like…Hey." He rubbed his head where she yanked on his hair at the same time Nat opened the door. His sister-in-law's eyes flitted over the two of them.

He wanted to tell her it wasn't what it looked like. But it was. And it was time he was honest with himself. He cared about Vivi. Today had shown him how much. He wanted her in his life. He didn't know exactly what a relationship between them would look like or how it would play out, but he owed it to both of them to give it a try. A nervous tension built in his chest. He might be getting ahead of himself. After how he'd treated her, she might not want a relationship with him.

Obviously catching the unhappy look in Nat's eyes, Vivi began to slide off him. He moved his hands under her ass, lifting her back in place. "Stay where you are. Down, Princess," he ordered the dog yapping at his feet. "Nat, put her in her pen."

She picked up the dog. "I, uh, heard about the break-in and thought you'd be in town most of the night. They're calling for a storm." She nuzzled the dog to her chest. Princess ignored her, growling at Vivi instead while Nat continued, "She's afraid of the thunder. I was going to take her home with me."

Explained why she was here, but not why she'd brought Callahan along. "That's fine, Nat, but next time give me a heads-up." He followed her inside, his muscles tensing as he caught sight of Callahan in his La-Z-Boy with his feet up, watching *Live Free or Die Hard*.

"Relax," Vivi whispered in his ear.

The kid lifted his eyes from the screen. "Hope you don't mind me making myself at home."

"Forget relaxing," Vivi murmured as she slid off his back. "Go wipe the smirk off the little bastard's face."

He'd been tempted to do just that before she opened her mouth. Now all he could do was smile. "Settle down, Slick." He nudged her toward the couch before asking Callahan, "Where were you between eight and ten tonight?"

"Hey, no way. You can't pin the break-ins on me." He jerked the chair into an upright position and vaulted to his feet. "I was with Nat all night. Ask her."

"Is that true?" he asked his sister-in-law as she returned to the living room. Vivi didn't take her eyes off Callahan. No doubt trying to get a read on him.

Looking from Chance to her boyfriend, Nat nodded.

"Come on, Nat. We don't need this bullshit," the kid said.

"What time did you guys get here?" Vivi asked in a nonconfrontational tone.

Nat opened her mouth, closing it when Callahan said, "'Bout two hours ago."

Vivi's eyes were on the TV. She winced when Willis took a hit, then returned her attention to Callahan. "Sorry, can't get enough of that guy. I can understand how time got away from you. You probably got into the movie, right?"

Callahan relaxed. Stupid kid, he didn't know that in some ways Vivi was more dangerous than Chance. "Yeah," Callahan said with an easy nod.

She gave the kid a flat smile. "Zach, you're only twenty minutes into the movie. Why did you lie?"

At the flash of temper in Callahan's eyes, Chance moved toward him. "Don't even think about it."

The kid backed into the chair. "This is bullshit, man. You've always had it in for my family. You're...Screw it. I was protecting Nat. I knew after what I said to Vivi earlier, she'd try to pin the break-in on her. But it wasn't either of us."

Nat paled, turning panicked eyes on Chance. "I didn't do anything. I wouldn't do something like that, Chance. You know me. I was at home with Mom. You can call her. She'll tell you."

"You just lied to me, Nat. Not sure how well I know you anymore."

Her face crumpled. She wrapped her arms around her stomach and rocked, tears rolling down her cheeks. "I know. I'm sorry. I didn't want—"

Callahan interrupted her. "You don't need to worry about me hurting her, McBride. You're real good at doing that all by yourself." The kid moved to Nat's side, putting an arm around her shoulders. "Come on. Let's go."

"You know, Zach, for a smart kid, you can be pretty stupid." Vivi got up from the couch and walked to the kitchen, opening the cabinet under the sink. She came back with a paper towel and handed it to Nat. "Natalee knows Chance loves her, so stop trying to drive a wedge between them. Because when push comes to shove, she'll pick him over you. Family always wins. So maybe you should stop trying to push his buttons. All he asked for was the truth, from both of you."

"He pushes mine every time he sees me. He doesn't want Nat with me. And he makes me nervous. Anything goes wrong, I know he's going to come looking for me. That's why we lied. Why Nat lied. She's trying to protect me, too. Right, Nat?"

Vivi's "family always wins" comment bothered Chance. He wondered if she was thinking of him or her deadbeat mother. He didn't like to think he'd made her feel that she didn't matter enough, that she wasn't good enough. But he couldn't deal with that right now. He'd been watching Nat the entire time Vivi talked and had seen the fear in her eyes. It's possible he'd put the emotion there, made them nervous enough to lie, but his gut said there was more going on. And it wasn't something good. He needed to get

Nat on her own. And he had to talk to his mother-in-law. He'd been putting it off.

Nat swiped at her eyes and nodded.

Chance walked to Vivi's side, briefly skimmed his fingers over hers to convey how much he appreciated what she'd done. And he supposed to let Nat know that he did. "For now, I'll buy your scared excuse. But this is the last time. Either of you lies again, and you'll be talking to me at the station. Now get out of here."

"It wasn't an excuse. We…" Vivi crossed her arms. Callahan shot her a nervous glance. "Um, yeah, thanks for believing us, man…" Vivi sighed. "Mr. McBride, sir. We'll be going now." He took Nat by the hand.

Nat glanced at Callahan from under her lashes, then looked up at Chance. "I'm really sorry. I…I keep disappointing you." A tear trickled down her cheek. "Please don't be mad at me."

He brought his hand to her face, wiping the moisture away with his thumb. "No more lies, kiddo." He kissed the top of her head. "Go straight home. It's late." He walked them to the door, watching until the lights from the four-by-four faded from view.

"You're worried about her," Vivi said, coming to stand beside him.

"Yeah, I am. You think I'm overreacting?" He moved her hair over her shoulder, looking down at her gorgeous face illuminated by the moonlight.

"No, I don't think you are." She didn't look at him, staring straight ahead with her brow furrowed. He didn't know if she was thinking about her response, avoiding his gaze, or searching for an animal. He smiled—probably the latter. "Don't worry, I'll protect you from the wild beasts."

"I wasn't... Wait a minute, did you see something out there, too?"

He was about to brush her off, but instead went and got his flashlight from the hall closet. After the break-ins and with the Drugstore Bandits on the loose, better to err on the side of caution. "No, but doesn't hurt to check it out. I'll get your suitcase while I'm out there."

Her eyes widened. "You're going out in the woods in the middle of the night... by yourself?"

"You wanna come with me?"

"Are you out of your ever-loving mind? Take Princess."

He laughed, drawing his gun from the back of his jeans. "Your concern for my safety is overwhelming, honey. I won't be long."

\*     \*     \*

Vivi had called out to Chance every five minutes. The last time she'd yelled through the half-open door, she'd heard the exasperation in his voice when he said he was fine and decided to track the glow of his flashlight from the guest bedroom instead. She yawned, caught her head bobbing, and opened the window. Since she couldn't see him, she stretched out on the bed and listened to him moving around out there.

She woke up to a violent crash. The bedroom was black as pitch. Oh, God, she'd fallen asleep. She heard Princess howling in the room beside her and scrambled from the bed. "Chance!" Vivi took off in a panic and ran into a wall.

The wall grunted. "Jesus, Slick, I'm right here. What's wrong?" His arm went around her.

She sagged against his warm, bare chest. "I fell asleep, and then I heard a crash. I thought... I thought." She lightly smacked his shoulder. "Why didn't you wake me up? I was worried about you."

He leaned back with her in his arms, patted the wall, then the room lit up.

She blinked her eyes. When they finally adjusted to the bright light, he was looking down at her with an amused expression on his beard-stubbled face. "You were so worried, you fell asleep?" He hooked his finger in her T-shirt. "I tried to wake you up."

She stepped away from him, pulling her T-shirt from her chest to look down. Along with her jeans, her bra and panties were gone, too. "You undressed me?"

"Yeah, and you know those sexy sounds you make when you're awake? You make them in your sleep, too."

Her cheeks warmed. He grinned. "Don't worry, Slick. I didn't look. We're friends without benefits, remember?"

Only too well. She wished she'd never made that stupid rule in the first place. And from the heated look in his eyes, she thought he might be thinking the same. No, like the glowing orbs earlier, she was probably imagining things. Which reminded her. "Did you find anything?"

"Yeah, and we'll talk about it in the morning. You're beat." He put his hands on her shoulders and turned her around. "Get back in bed."

"Come on, I won't go to sleep until I know—"

"It's three in the morning. And I'm beat." He lifted the covers. She crawled underneath them with a frustrated sigh. He looked down at her, his lips lifting at the corner. "All right, there were tire tracks to the right of the property off the main road. Might be nothing, but I took a few pictures."

She pushed herself up on her elbows. "Could you tell if—"

He placed a palm on her chest, gently pushing her down. "No. Sleep," he said and walked to the door, flipping off the light.

The room lit up as a thunderous crash shook the cabin. Princess howled and Vivi screamed. The light came on. "It's just a storm, Slick. Nothing to be—" His gaze roamed her face, and he bowed his head. He flipped off the light. "I'll be right back."

She opened her mouth to tell him she was fine, then closed it when lightning once again lit up the room and thunder boomed in the distance. Normally, an electrical storm didn't make her nervous. But after the break-in and out here in the middle of nowhere, it did. She'd probably lose her "independent woman" card, but she didn't care. She'd get it back tomorrow.

"Stop whining," Chance muttered as he walked into the room.

"I'm not whining."

"I wasn't talking to you. I was talking to Princess."

Vivi sat up, trying to make him out. "McBride, do not bring her in this room."

"Relax, she's in her cage."

She heard a thud, then the bed dipped and Chance crawled in beside her. His big body brushed against hers. She fought the urge to wrap herself around all that hard, warm muscle and cleared her throat. "Maybe we should, you know, put some pillows between us."

"Why? You'd just crawl over them to get to me." He patted her thigh. "Don't worry, Slick. I know you can't help yourself. You're a cuddler."

"I am not a cuddler."

# Chapter Twenty-One

Vivi heard the low growl and opened one eye. *Not again*, she thought, remembering the morning she'd woken up in Chance's bed only to have her hopes and dreams crushed. But this was different. She wasn't in his and Kate's bed, and she and Chance hadn't made love. And that low growl wasn't coming from the floor, it was coming from the bed.

She slowly turned her head and came nose to nose with Cujo. "Chance!" Vivi threw the covers over her head, burrowing deep beneath them.

"Calm down, Slick. I'll take her out."

If she wasn't hiding from Cujo, she might have appreciated the amusement she heard in Chance's rough, sleepladen voice. An entirely different tone than the one she'd woken up to that morning two weeks before. Whoa baby, he was either really happy to see her or he'd slept with a gun tucked in his pajama pants. She carefully moved her hand in hopes he wouldn't notice.

He patted her head as he moved from the bed. "Don't worry, friends don't get a hard-on for friends. It's a morning thing."

She shoved the covers from her head. "I'm not twelve, McBride. I know that *that*—" she waved her hand at his tented navy sleep pants—"has nothing to do with me."

"Wouldn't go that far," he said, looking much too tempting standing with his hair all messy and Cujo snuggled up to his sun-bronzed chest. "Just didn't want you to think I'd take advantage of our friendship." He winked, then walking to the door said, "But honey, it would make it easier to think only friendly thoughts if you wore your panties next time we slept together."

"You're the one who took them off me," she called to his retreating back.

"Careful, you keep talking like that and I'll have a hard time hanging on to my PG thoughts." He popped his head back in the room. "I'm getting a visual right now of you throwing your leg over mine and..." He snapped his fingers. "See, just like that, straight to NC-17."

She covered her burning cheeks and muttered, "You really are a superjerk." Too bad along with being a superjerk, he was also superhot, which was making her hot.

"Oh, and, honey, don't worry about that little scratch on your hand."

She turned her hands over to inspect them, her eyes widening at the long, puffy red line on her left one. She pointed to the scratch. "Little, you call this little? This is not..." Then she realized there was only one way Cujo had been able to attack her. "I don't believe you! You had her in bed with us the entire night."

"She was crying, Slick. She's afraid of thunder, and

you were asleep. I knew she wouldn't bite you. Not when I'm—" She held up her hand as evidence. He rubbed his chin. "Okay, I don't like blaming the victim, but, honey, you're a little possessive. You put your arm around my chest and pushed Princess away. She was trying to save herself from falling off the bed."

"I'm not possessive."

He made a face and nodded. "You kinda are. You don't like to share. But don't worry, there's enough of me to go around."

She groaned, turning on her stomach to bury her head under the pillow. "You're a pain in the ass, McBride, and so is your dog."

"Don't take offense, Princess. She's cranky in the morning. She'll be fine once she has a cup of coffee," she heard him say as he walked down the hall.

She lifted the pillow and yelled, "Not if you're making it, she won't!" At the sound of his deep, sexy laugh she muttered, "You're a riot, McBride," and leaned across the bed, reaching for her phone on the nightstand. It wasn't there. She did a visual search of the room, then got out of bed. Going down on her hands and knees, she lifted the bed skirt, spotting her phone on the other side. Realizing the target she made, she got to her feet and dove across the bed, reaching for her cell. She picked it up and... "McBride, your dog ate my phone!"

No response. He was probably outside while the dog did her business, which meant it was time for Vivi to do hers. She walked to her suitcase, unzipped it, and pulled out her clothes for the day, grabbing her toothbrush as well.

She'd just stepped into the shower when she realized

she'd forgotten her shampoo. Chance's hair-and-body wash wasn't going to cut it. Her hair needed some major conditioning this morning, but she couldn't resist a quick sniff—lavender and sandalwood. No wonder he smelled so good. She returned the bottle to the side of the shower and grabbed a towel.

Wrapping the length of fluffy white cotton around herself, she peeked out the bathroom door. All clear. No sign of Cujo. She sprinted to the bedroom and dug around the suitcase for her shampoo and conditioner. Her phone jangled on the bed. Huh. She thought Cujo had destroyed it.

She checked caller ID, but small holes perforated the plastic, and she couldn't read the screen. She pressed a finger to her temple when Nell McBride's voice came over the line.

"Hey, boss. We're back in business. Place is all cleaned up. Anything you want me and the girls to work on?"

Thinking of Nell and the girls working on anything made Vivi nervous, but more than that, she was grateful. She sat on the edge of the bed, finding herself a little emotional. She cleared the lump from her throat. "That's great, Nell. Thank you. I, uh, I really appreciate you doing that for me. I shouldn't have left you to do the cleanup on your own."

"Pish, everyone pitched in. Took us no time at all. Christmas isn't like the big city. We take care of our own in this town, girlie. You'll get used to it. Oh, and another thing, we can take Gil, his wife, and Lisa Flowers off the suspect list. Me and the girls snooped around a bit, and they're alibied up the wazoo. Ted and Fred are checking out Earl."

Her earlier nerves returned. "Umm, Nell, I'm not sure how—"

Chance stuck his head in the room. "Coffee's ready, Slick. Princess is in her pen."

She nodded, then realized where he was headed. "Wait, McBride, you can't—" She bowed her head at the sound of the bathroom door shutting.

"What can't I do?"

"No, not you, Nell—your nephew."

A sly chuckle came over the line. "You two having fun?"

"No, no fun. We're not having fun. We're just friends."

"Sure you are. See you in a few, boss. Paul bailed on us, so me and the girls will go over our candidates for Christmas Cuties. But don't worry, we can hold down the fort if you and my nephew want to continue having *fun*. Buh-bye."

Had she really been thinking there might be something to be said for small-town living? Maybe a small town without Nell McBride.

Vivi disconnected and tossed her phone. Grabbing the shampoo and conditioner, she headed for the bathroom. She knocked on the door. "I need to have my shower first. My hair takes longer to dry than yours."

"I'll be out in five."

"Oh, come on. I was in there first. McBride." She lifted her hand to bang on the door and nearly nailed Chance's foam-covered jaw instead.

Standing in front of her wearing the matching towel to hers around his waist, he raised a brow and held up a razor. "Five minutes, Slick. Go get a coffee." His tone implied she needed one.

"You're doing this on purpose just to drive me crazy." The look he gave her said she was already there. She threw up her hands and pivoted, heading for the bedroom. "This isn't going to work. I'm not staying here. I'm moving back to my place."

"You're not going anywhere." Grabbing her arm, he turned her to face him. "Have you forgotten what the *Chronicle* looked like? Ray's in the hospital because of these guys. They're not fooling around."

A nervous tremor caused goose bumps to break out over her arms at the reminder. But his high-handed manner ticked her off. She lifted her chin. "I can take care of myself."

His chest expanded on a noisy breath, and his eyes narrowed. "No, you can't."

"Excuse me? Who do you—"

Before she knew what he was doing, he spun her around, hooking an arm around her neck and one around her waist. Her arms locked at her sides. "Now's your chance, Slick. Show me how . . . Jesus," he said when she stomped on his foot. He wrapped his leg around hers.

"This doesn't prove anything. They're not like you. You're trained—" The bands of steel tightened so she couldn't move. But she wasn't about to let him think she was helpless. She bent her head, then threw it back. He moved his.

She groaned, positive she'd given herself whiplash.

"Ouch, that's gotta hurt, honey. Ready to concede?"

She heard the cocky amusement in his voice and her temper spiked. She opened her mouth and lowered her head.

He laughed, dropping his arm before she could sink

her teeth into it. "You fight like a girl," he said as he spun her around and threw her on the bed. One bounce and he was on top of her, smothering her with his lethally hard body.

She looked into his smiling eyes, trying to ignore the feel of all that warm muscle bearing down upon her. "That wasn't fair." She wriggled to get out from under him. Her lady parts got the wrong message and began to cheer.

"Careful, honey. You're going to lose the towel." He rubbed his foam-covered jaw over her chest.

Her breath caught in her throat at the erotic feel. She bit her bottom lip to contain a needy moan, but a breathy sigh escaped.

He lifted his head, his grass-green eyes serious. "I don't want to be friends anymore."

She knew what he wanted, but she couldn't do it. A benefits-only relationship with Chance would ruin her. She blinked against the sudden burn of tears—desperate to contain them. "Why not? "Her voice came out sad and lost. As one-sided as their relationship was, she didn't want to lose him completely.

His hand moved up her thigh and under the towel. "It's not enough. I want more." He lowered his mouth to hers. His lips were soft but firm, demanding. She tried not to respond but was helpless against the drugging sensation of his kiss. Time seemed to stand still as he seduced her with his mouth. Then he brushed his lips lightly over hers, a soft graze, before feathering kisses to her jaw to her cheek to her ear. "When you're not with me, all I do is think about you."

Everything inside her froze. She was afraid he didn't

say what she thought he did. That his kiss had messed with her hearing along with her heart.

"I can't fight it anymore. I want to see where this goes. I'm done walking away."

"I can't breathe," she choked out, her lungs paralyzed with emotion. Oh, God, she didn't want to cry and ruin the moment. A moment she'd all but given up on.

He searched her face, offering her a tentative smile. "Sorry." He removed his hand from her waist to lever himself up on his elbows. "Better?"

She shook her head. "No. More, I want more."

He closed his eyes, lowering his forehead to hers. "I don't know if I can. For now, this is all I've got to offer."

"That's not what I meant." She threaded her fingers through his hair, drawing his mouth closer. "It's enough, Chance. For now, it's enough." It was more than she'd expected.

"Thank, Christ. You scared the hell out of me, Slick. I don't want to lose you."

An uneasy feeling stole some of her happiness. "Because you need me to distract you from thinking about Kate and the baby?"

She tensed when he didn't respond. There was an emotion in his eyes she couldn't read. She shouldn't have mentioned Kate and the baby, not now. "No." He framed her face with his hands. "Don't do that, okay? Don't compare what I had with Kate with what I have with you."

*Because you will never be able to compete with the love he lost.* She winced as the thought came into her head. She didn't want it there.

As if he could read her mind, he said, "Since Kate died, I've been with other women. You are the only one, the only one, who I ever wanted to try again with, Vivi. Before you, I existed. You've made we want more."

"I...I'm glad." She'd been about to tell him she loved him, but held back in case he'd feel pressured to say the same. She didn't want him to tell her he loved her because he thought that's what she expected, what she needed to hear.

"Time, okay? Just give me a little more time."

"You using your X-ray vision to read my mind now, Superman?" she said in an attempt to take away the tension lines bracketing his mouth. This was a man who'd locked away his grief for five years. It was a miracle he'd come this far in only two weeks.

"Don't need X-ray vision, honey. It's written all over your beautiful face." His voice was low and subdued. She hadn't meant to make him feel guilty or sad.

"Okay, what am I thinking about now?" As a way to distract him, she rolled her hips.

"No one will ever accuse you of being subtle, Slick," he said with a laugh, then lowered his mouth. "You are the most incredible, infuriating, passionate, smart, moody, hotheaded, gorgeous woman I have ever met. And in case I haven't made myself clear enough, you're mine."

"That's a lot of adjectives, McBride, but since the positive ones beat out the negatives, I'll let you get away with it. And you're right, I am yours. Just as much as you're mine."

He angled his head. "You done now?" She nodded. "Good," he rolled onto his back, taking her with him. He moved his hand to her thigh. "Please tell me benefits are included in this package."

"Lots and lots of benefits," she said, removing her towel as she lowered her mouth to his.

"I'm loving this relationship already," he said against her lips.

\*     \*     \*

Chance rested his hand at the small of Vivi's back while opening the door to the *Chronicle* with the other. "Okay, thanks, time to go now." She made a shooing motion with her hand.

He looked down at her. "You weren't this anxious to get rid of me thirty minutes ago."

"Yes, but I'm at work now, and your aunt and her friends are watching us. So…" She nodded at the door.

"Hey, ladies." He greeted the three older women as he surveyed the space. "Great job. Didn't they do an amazing job, honey?" He slung an arm over her shoulders.

"Fantastic," she said through clenched teeth, catching Nell's cagey smile. This was exactly what Vivi had been afraid of. She knew he'd give them away. She nudged him when he twirled her hair around his finger. "No PDA, McBride, remember?"

"This," he said, lifting his finger, the one her hair was wrapped around, "is not PDA. This is." Before she could stop him, he kissed her full on the mouth in front of his wedding-obsessed aunt.

She glared at him when he lifted his head. He responded by tweaking the side of her nose with his finger. "You're cute when you're pissed."

"You won't think I'm so cute when I rescind the benefits portion of your package."

He laughed, patting her on the butt as he headed for the door. She shouldn't be surprised he didn't take her threat seriously. She'd have to be less effusive with her praise next time they made love. Maybe smother those stupid moans, too.

"Bye, honey. Take care of my girl, ladies," he said as he walked out the door.

Vivi tossed her messenger bag on her desk and sat down. "Not a word," she warned the three older women without looking up.

She heard sniffling and glanced to her right. The three of them were crying, passing around tissues. Vivi groaned and buried her face in her hands.

"What happened? Did someone die?" Cat asked, holding two coffees as she hip-checked the door open.

"No, this girl, this wonderful girl here, worked a miracle." Nell waved her soggy tissue at Vivi. "I never would've believed it...I mean, I thought she could, but to see the way he looked at her. Our boy's come back to us."

Cat handed a coffee to Vivi. "Is she talking about Chance?"

Vivi ignored the question. "I think I love you," she said, putting the cup to her lips. "You don't know how badly I needed this."

"Of course I'm talking about Chance. Who else would I be talking about?" Nell rolled her chair over to Vivi's desk. "If we get on it right away, I'm sure we can hire the caterer we had booked for Paul and Liz's wedding. How does the Fourth of July sound?"

Vivi choked on her coffee and waved off Nell, who went to pound her back.

"I love weddings." Evelyn pressed her hands to her chest, releasing a dreamy sigh.

"No, no wedding. We're not close to being there yet." If they ever were. He hadn't even told her he loved her. Vivi was about to call Chance and let him deal with his aunt. It was his fault they were even having this conversation. But the thought it would scare him off held her back.

Nell patted her hand. She must have seen the panic on Vivi's face. "We'll talk about it a week from now."

"I..." She trailed off as Chance's dad opened the door and gave her one of his you-walk-on-water looks.

"You," he beamed, pointing his finger at her, "are a miracle worker." And in case she didn't understand just how happy he was, he walked over and lifted her out of her chair, pulling her into a hug.

And that pretty much summed up the rest of Vivi's day. Maddie, Skye, Betty Jean, and what felt like the entire town of Christmas had dropped by to share how happy they were. But instead of sharing in their joy, with each person she found a little of her happiness slipping away. Their expectations fueled her insecurities.

At three in the afternoon, she decided she'd had about all that she could take. Maddie had conveniently dropped off a laptop and given her the use of her car for the next few days. "Ladies, I'm going to take off and work from home."

"You can't fool us, dear," Evelyn said. "You're going to make Chance a special dinner to celebrate, aren't you?"

She had planned on stopping at the grocery store, but there was nothing special about nachos and beer. Other than that she and Chance enjoyed both. Taking the easy way out, she smiled and nodded.

By the time she pushed her junk-laden cart to the checkout, the pounding in her head had lessened. The cashier with the blue hair beamed at her. Good God, not again.

"I heard all about you and Chance McBride, and I have to tell you, I'm tickled. Just tickled. No one deserves to be happy more than him. Tragic, just tragic what happened to dear, sweet Katie."

Vivi pressed two fingers to her temple, bringing the woman's name tag into focus. "Thanks, Patty. Now if you could maybe hurry it along, I'd appreciate it. We wouldn't want the ice cream to melt." She faked a smile.

Patty's steel-wool brows drew together. Vivi didn't need to be a mind reader. She was far from the dear, sweet type. But whatever Patty thought of Vivi, it didn't stop the older woman from regaling her with stories from Kate and Chance's prom king and queen days.

The woman stopped mid-story, looking over Vivi's shoulder with a nervous expression on her face. As long as she stopped talking, someone could be holding up the place for all Vivi cared.

"Oh, Mary, I'm so sorry. I didn't see you there."

Vivi raised her gaze to the ceiling. Really? Who had she ticked off up there?

"Don't give it another thought, Patty. It's always nice to hear someone talk about Katie." A gentle hand touched Vivi's arm.

She turned to look into the eyes of an older version of Kate McBride. The woman had once been as beautiful as her daughter, but time and grief had taken a toll. Her skin was sallow, her hair a dull blonde. She wore what looked to be a blue housedress, a pair of blue ballet slippers on her feet. Petite and fine-boned, she was the type of woman who brought out your protective instincts.

She smiled at Vivi. "It's so nice to finally meet you. I'd been hoping I would."

Vivi covered the woman's hand with her own and lightly squeezed. "Thank you. It's nice to meet you, too." Also nerve-wracking.

Chance's mother-in-law gave her a concerned look. "Are you all right?"

She wiped the beads of perspiration from her forehead. "I'm good. Just a little warm." She smiled and fanned herself.

Patty stood, taking everything in. The woman would probably be on the phone as soon as they had one foot out the door. Mary glanced from Vivi to the cashier. "Patty." She nodded at Vivi's groceries.

The cashier took the hint, and within minutes, Vivi was checked out. "Thanks, Patty." Vivi picked up her three bags and was about to say good-bye to Mary, but didn't feel right leaving without saying more than a few words to Chance's mother-in-law. She waited for her, transferring her own bags to one hand to pick up Mary's bags with the other.

The older woman smiled. "I'm stronger than I look, you know."

"I thought you might have some questions for me, and they were better asked in private," Vivi said as she pushed open the glass door with her shoulder.

"You're a no-nonsense woman. I like that. It would appeal to Chance, too, I think. How is my son-in-law? He's been avoiding me." She plucked at the top button of her housedress. "He's probably angry with me for bailing out Earl."

"He's been busy with the drugstore burglaries and Ray. I'm sure once things settle down, he'll come for a visit." Vivi looked around the parking lot. "Where's your car?"

"Oh, I walked." Mary held out her hands. "Here, I'll take those and let you get on with your day."

"No, I was just going…" She felt uncomfortable referring to the cabin as home. "Can I give you a lift?"

Mary inclined her head. "You don't mind?"

"Not at all." She led the older woman to the car and put the groceries in the backseat. Mary settled in the passenger side and gave her directions.

Pulling onto Main Street, she cast Mary a sidelong glance. "If you don't mind me asking, why did you bail out Earl?"

"He's my brother. I had so much. It didn't feel right not to help him out." She shifted in the seat. "He's not a bad man, Vivi. Just a troubled one. But the men he was involved with, they were bad. I wouldn't be able to live with myself if something happened to him. You tell Chance I won't give Earl another cent of the money he's given me. And I haven't touched the money for Natalee. It's in a college fund just like Chance wanted."

"But I…Does Natalee know that?"

Her eyes clouded. "She does now. I thought I'd told her, but she says I didn't." She looked down at her clasped hands. "After Katie died…I wasn't much of a mother to Natalee."

A wave of sympathy for both mother and daughter overcame her, and she rubbed Mary's shoulder. "I'm sure she understands."

"No, I don't think she does. I'm trying now though. And with Chance home, it will be better. She adores him, you know. Adored both of them. She spent more time with Chance and Katie than she did with me. I hope he can convince her to go to school. She's a bright girl with so much potential. But after Katie died, she lost interest in everything. Except Zach. She had him at least."

Ignoring a stab of guilt for what she was about to do, Vivi said, "They seem really close. Do you like him?"

"He's a good boy. Very protective of Natalee. Doesn't let her out of his sight."

And that's what Vivi was worried about. Too many women confused jealousy and overprotectiveness with love, and before they knew it, they were in a dangerous situation.

"She told me about last night. I tried to explain to her why Chance would react like he did. I think I made it worse."

"You mean because he blames Jake Callahan for the accident? You don't, do you?" Vivi asked.

She shook her head. "No, but I understand why Chance did. I can't tell you the sleep I've lost trying to understand why Katie went out in that blizzard." Mary looked up and pointed to a white bungalow sitting on a well-manicured lawn. "That's my house."

When Vivi pulled into the driveway, Mary asked, "Would you like to come in for a cup of tea?"

"Sure. Go ahead. I'll bring in your groceries." Vivi did her best to cover her reaction when she walked into the house behind Mary. It was a shrine to Kate McBride. Her sympathy for Natalee grew. She couldn't imagine what it was like to have your dead sister filling up every available space with no room left for you. The only pictures of Natalee were ones with Kate and Chance. Forty minutes later, sitting with Mary at the kitchen table, Vivi decided she should have dropped the groceries and run. It was like Mary had kept her memories bottled up until she met her.

"He spoiled my baby rotten. She'd just smile when I told her how lucky she was. She knew it though. Couldn't help but know, the way he doted on her. Treated her like a china doll." She glanced at the cup gripped in Vivi's white-knuckled hands. "Listen to me carrying on and you already finished your tea. I'll get you another cup." She pushed back from the table.

"Thanks, Mary, but I probably should get going. I have to lock up the *Chronicle*," she lied, not wanting to hurt the woman's feelings.

"You sure you can't have just one more cup?"

Vivi tried to ignore the soft, pleading look in Mary's eyes but couldn't do it. "Okay, one more."

"Oh, good. It's been so long since I've had company." She smiled at Vivi over her shoulder, then went to refill her cup. She gasped, the delicate piece of china slipping through her fingers onto the floor.

Vivi pushed back her chair. "Mary, what—"

The older woman whirled around, her face pale. "It's Earl." Her eyes widened when the front door opened. "Hide." She motioned to the table.

Vivi half laughed. "I'm not hiding, Mary."

"You don't understand. He hates the McBrides, and he's lost business because of your article in the paper. Please, Vivi, please hide, he has a terrible temper."

Earl Skully just went to the top of Vivi's suspect list. "It's okay, Mary. Come and sit down. I promise, it'll be all right."

\*     \*     \*

Vivi glanced in the rearview mirror. Chance had followed her to the cabin in his truck. His expression hadn't changed since he'd arrived at Mary's—he was livid. Vivi didn't know why he was mad at her. She hadn't done anything wrong. Earl was the one who'd been unreasonable. He'd tried to bodily throw her out of the house. All Vivi had done was protect herself. She'd done a good job of it, too. She caught sight of her eye in the mirror and made a face. She should have ducked when Earl threw his first punch, but he would have hit Mary instead. If Mary hadn't called the sheriff, given another five minutes, Vivi would have worn Earl out. The man was overweight and out of shape. And still on the top of her suspect list.

She pulled beside the front walkway. Chance drove past her without a glance and parked in the garage. She didn't get out of the car. If he was going to be a jerk, she'd stay at the apartment. She looked up to see him standing at the garage door, staring at her with that scary look on his face and a large wrapped box in his hand. She flipped him off. Maybe that wasn't the most mature thing to do, or the smartest, because now he looked even angrier and stalked to her car.

He shifted the box in his arms to open the driver's-side door. "Out."

"No, not until you apologize. I told you what happened. It wasn't my fault."

"Never is. You don't think things through and consider the consequences. You shouldn't have been at Mary's."

"Why? She's lonely. I was being nice, Chance. To your mother-in-law. I sat there and listened..." She shook her head, swallowing the lump in her throat. "Never mind."

"Don't make me tell you again. Get out of the car."

The fight fizzled out of her, and she did what he said. She followed him inside and walked straight to the bedroom. From behind her, she heard him blow out a frustrated breath. She lay down on the bed, curling onto her side. A few minutes later, the mattress dipped, and she opened her eyes.

He set the box between them, reaching out to gently trace her bruised eye with the tip of his finger. "What am I going to do with you?"

*Love me.* "Get me an Advil and some raw meat."

His mouth quirked. "I think we'll go with an ice pack instead." He nudged the box toward her. "Open it."

"You bought me something? Like a present?"

"Don't act so surprised." He crossed his arms and angled his head. "I don't know why I'm giving it to you. Not after what you pulled."

She ignored him, her sole focus on unwrapping the box. Before she could stop them, hot tears rolled down her cheeks.

"Hey, why are you crying?" He took the box from her and set it on the floor, then drew her into his arms. "I'm sorry. Swear to God, I'll never get mad at you again. Please, honey, stop crying. You're killing me."

She buried her face in his neck and sobbed. "You bought me an espresso machine."

# Chapter Twenty-Two

Chance turned the truck onto Main Street. "You want me to stop at the bakery and get you another coffee?"

"I'm good, thanks." She lifted the thermal Lois Lane cup he'd bought to go with her coffee machine. If anyone had witnessed her emotional reaction two days earlier, they would have thought he'd given her a diamond ring. Her tears had nearly done him in. He'd never seen her cry before and hoped never to see her do so again. Which meant he had to dial back his temper and his need to protect her, at the same time keeping her away from his mother-in-law. Other than defending her run-in with Earl, she'd been evasive about her time with Mary. But whether Vivi copped to it or not, that visit was part of the reason for the tears. It didn't take a shrink to know what had happened. He knew what seeing the shrine to Kate, a pictorial montage of their life together, had done to him. So he could imagine how seeing it would make Vivi feel.

And his overreaction to the situation with Earl was due in part to Chance being on emotional overload at the time.

She looked up from the computer opened on her lap. "There's time to stop if you want one. I'm early."

"I'll get one at the station." He grimaced at the bruise on her face. The color matched her beautiful eyes. "You should be at home resting."

She laughed. "For a black eye? I'm not a wuss, you know. This is nothing. You should have seen..." She rubbed her forehead.

"Go on, finish what you were going to say."

"I bet Earl looks worse than me."

No doubt he did, but that was not what she was going to say. The woman was a magnet for trouble. Mostly of her own making. "Remind me to teach you how to block a punch."

Her eyes lit with interest. "Really? You'll teach me to fight?"

*Jesus.* "No, I'm not teaching you to fight. I'll teach you how to protect yourself."

"You're no fun."

"That's not what you said earlier this morning."

"I was in coffee heaven at the time." She gave him one of her rare, radiant smiles. "I love my present, you know."

"I got that, honey." She was giving him the sweet, and like every time she did, his chest got tight. He pulled in front of the *Chronicle*.

She groaned when he shut off the engine. "No, no way. You can't come in."

"I'm just going to check on things, and then I'll leave."

"No PDA, and this time I mean it, McBride. It's unprofessional and winds up Nell, Stella, and Evelyn." She shuddered.

"You know, Slick, most women like when their man shows them some affection in public."

"When are you going to realize I'm not most women?"

"You're a legend in your own mind."

She snorted. "Says the guy who calls himself Superman."

He slid his hand under her long, thick hair, giving her neck a light squeeze. "I need a little something to get me through my day." He tapped his lips. "Come on, it's not PDA when no one can see us."

She rolled her eyes, then leaned in and kissed his cheek. He turned his head so her lips ended up right where he wanted them. Then he kissed her. A deep kiss with tongue and heat.

Someone knocked on the passenger-side window. He lifted his eyes to see his aunt and her friends staring in at them. He couldn't help it; he laughed.

"It's them, isn't it?" Vivi said against his mouth.

He lowered the window. "We'll be right there, Aunt Nell. Vivi had something in her eye."

Vivi gave him a you're-so-dead look as she pushed away from him. "He was—"

Nell's eyes widened when she got a full-on view of Vivi. "Whooee, hope Earl looks worse than you, girlie. That's some shiner." She turned her attention to Chance. "Heard your brother's not happy with you right now, so you mind your p's and q's, you hear. Already warned Jake we didn't want any trouble."

"Callahan's here…at the *Chronicle*?" Chance was already halfway out the door before his aunt answered. He didn't care that his brother had busted his chops over him punching Earl, he'd have done the same if it were Madison. And if Gage thought he could stop him from having it out with Callahan, he'd better think again. The guy had some nerve showing up here. "You"—he pointed at Vivi—"stay where you are."

"Like hell I am." She jumped out of the truck and raced to the door, barring his entrance.

He should have known she wouldn't listen to him. Kate would have meekly done as he asked. There were times, like now, when he missed being with a woman who didn't question him at every turn. Unlike the woman who currently had her back against the door, arms spread wide. He picked her up and moved her out of the way. "This is between me and him. Keep out of it."

"This is my place of business. I'm the boss, not you. You want to come in, you'll do as I say."

He couldn't help but smile at her attitude, which surprised him, since his blood was boiling at the sight of Callahan leaning against a desk with his arms crossed. Chance turned to her. "Looks like I already am in, Slick."

She scooted past him, fast-walking to her desk. "Sit," she ordered Callahan, who gave her a disconcerted look. One Chance imagined he himself had worn when dealing with Vivi. She wheeled her chair from behind her desk and motioned to him. "Sit."

"Slick, I'm not…" She moved behind him, bumping the chair into the back of his legs. Callahan snorted. But he didn't remain amused for long because Nell did the same to him.

Chance gave up. Taking a seat, he released a frustrated sigh when Vivi pushed him behind her desk. Nell pushed Callahan in front of it.

Vivi's narrowed gaze moved from him to Callahan. "Ladies, I need some pictures of Santa's Village for the next issue." After rifling through her desk drawer, she pulled out a camera.

"We'll go later." The three older women, who had ringside seats, leaned forward in their chairs.

"Nell." Chance nodded at the door. She sighed and got up to take the camera from Vivi, her friends following her out the door.

Vivi waited until they disappeared from view. "All right, here's how it's going to go." She placed her hands on Chance's shoulders. "No yelling, no fighting, no messing up my place. You first, Jake. Why are you here?"

"You know why I'm here. You have questions, you come to me. Don't send two cops into *my* place of business to snoop around. Did you really think I wouldn't make them just because they're hot?"

"I have no idea what you're talking about, Callahan. I didn't—"

"Wasn't talking to you, McBride. I was talking to her." He pointed at Vivi.

Chance looked over his shoulder. "What did you do?"

She made a face. "I may have suggested to Cat and Jill that they pay a visit to the Garage. What? They're single and like a good time now and again. No law against that, is there?"

"They weren't there to have a good time. They were trying to connect me and my brother to the break-ins. With the number of people you pissed off, I'd think you'd have a long enough suspect list without including us." His steel-gray gaze moved from Vivi to Chance. "But I'll always be your prime suspect, won't I, McBride?"

"You have an alibi between eight and ten on Friday night?" Chance asked.

Jake pulled out a piece of paper from the breast pocket of his short-sleeve work shirt, tossing it on the desk. "Mike and I were at a meeting in Denver with suppliers. Numbers and names are on there."

"What about Zach?"

Callahan jumped up, his chair flying backward with the force of the movement. He slammed his palms on the desk. "Leave Zach out of it. He has nothing to do with your vendetta against me. He's suffered enough because of what you put our family through."

Vivi's fingers pressed into Chance's shoulders. "Sit down, Jake. I think it's about time you and Chance cleared the air. This thing between the two of you has gone on long enough, don't you think?"

"Stay out of it, Slick."

"She's right." Callahan held his gaze. "I had nothing to do with your wife's accident. I shot off my mouth because you'd backed me into a corner, McBride. When you put the old man away eight years ago, I had to come home and take care of my family. I was twenty years old and didn't have a clue how to keep the garage afloat while taking care of my brothers and trying to live down Darwin's reputation. My old man deserved what he got. We didn't. And just when I started to see daylight, you decide, because of him, I was running meth. Every time I turned around, there you were, breathing down my neck. You pointing the finger at me scared off half my business." Jake sat down. Resting his elbows on his knees, he scrubbed his hands over his face.

The muscles in Chance's neck and shoulders tightened. He was beginning to think he'd been wrong about Jake. "A confidential informant gave me your name."

"Let me guess, Earl Skully was your CI." He gave his head a brief, angry shake. "The guy should have been serving time with the old man. He was in on it. He gave you my name because he wanted my business. He'd say anything to get it."

He was right about Earl. The only reason he wasn't doing time was because he'd rolled on Darwin Callahan. Chance hadn't wanted to give him the deal, but it hadn't been his call to make. "Any reason to think your father and Earl are teaming up again?" For the last six months, Earl had been visiting Darwin in prison.

"Old man's a lot of things, but he's not stupid. He knows who fingered him." His eyes narrowed. "You think there's some connection between them and the"—he made air quotes—"Drugstore Bandits?"

"Your father said something to Vivi that set off her radar." He smiled at her. She'd been rubbing his shoulders the entire time in what he imagined was an attempt to keep him calm. "She's got good radar."

Jake rolled a shoulder. "I haven't seen the old man since you put him away. So I can't say what he is or isn't involved with, but if he is, he might use Earl as his outside man."

"But he knows Earl turned him in," Vivi said.

Chance nodded. "Sure he does, but Earl's a coward, and Darwin knows some not-so-nice people. He could be setting Earl up to take the fall or threatening him, getting him to do his dirty work."

"Yeah, sounds like something the old man would do. Not that I feel sorry for Skully." Jake cracked the knuckles in his right hand. "The old man's going to drag us down again."

"Chance won't let that happen, will you?"

"No, I won't." Chance held Jake's gaze. "If your father's involved, I'll do whatever I can to protect you and your brothers from the fallout. I owe you, Jake." He stood up and extended his hand. "I know it doesn't make up for what I did, but I'm sorry."

Jake got up and shook his hand. "I was young and had a smart mouth, said some things I shouldn't have. I know where your head was at that night. We lost our mother. If I thought someone was involved in her death, I would have done the same."

"No excuse for what I did, but I appreciate you saying so."

"Jake, it's obvious you don't have a relationship with your father, but Zach does, so..." Vivi began.

Jake's gaze shot to Vivi. "No, he doesn't. We cut off all communication with the old man years ago."

Chance hated to break it to Jake, but he needed to know. "Unless someone's forging your brother's signature, Zach's been visiting your father once a week for the last five years."

Jake looked like he'd been sucker punched. He put his hand behind him, reaching for the chair, and slowly sat down. "I don't believe this. Why would he do that? He knows how we feel about the old man."

"He was young. No matter what you think of Darwin, he's his father. Maybe Zach was willing to overlook things you weren't," Vivi suggested. She would know. She'd visited her father in prison, bailed him out, and helped him get on his feet.

Zach scrubbed his hands over his face. "I watched the kid like a hawk. How could he...He's too smart for his own good. I should have forced him to go to college."

"It's not too late. I could, ah, look into schools for him, if you'd like. What was his area of interest?"

Chance knew what Vivi was up to. For Jake and Mike's sake, he hoped she hadn't nailed it. But she did.

"Computer science. And I appreciate the offer, Vivi, but unless the school's around here, he won't go." He cast Chance an uneasy look. "Guess by now you know he's with Natalee."

"Yeah, I do." He kept his expression neutral. "How do you feel about their relationship?"

"Too damn young. No offense to Natalee, but they're too locked into each other. It's not healthy." With a sheepish grin, he said, "But what do I know? I've never had a relationship that lasted more than a few weeks." He glanced at his watch and came to his feet. "I better get out of here. I'd appreciate it if you keep me in the loop."

"If you hear anything or your father tries to contact you, let me know." Chance took his wallet from his back pocket and handed him his card.

"I'll keep my eyes and ears open. But the old man won't contact me. He knows better."

As soon as Jake headed out the door, Vivi nudged Chance out of the way and sat down at her desk. She pulled out a pad of paper. "It's always about the money, right?"

He rested his hip on her desk, watching her as she wrote Earl's and Zach's names. "Pretty much, jealousy and revenge a close second and third."

"So let's think about this. For all intents and purposes, Darwin Callahan will be a free man in a month. He'll need money, and Jake and Mike aren't going to help him out. But then we have Zach, who obviously has, and wants to maintain, a relationship with his father. Darwin Callahan is smart; he's charming and a con. He'd know how to play on Zach's sympathies. And he'd teach him the ropes."

Like her father had taught her, but Vivi had a strong moral compass and strength of character that Zach possibly lacked.

"All true, but it's circumstantial." He rubbed his chin. "And I'm liking Earl for this."

She looked up from her notes, studying him as she tapped her pen on the pad of paper. "Be careful, Chance. Don't let your guilt over how you treated Jake make you back off Zach."

He opened his legs and pulled her between them, burying his face in her neck. He inhaled her soft vanilla scent. She was right. "You think it's Zach, don't you?"

She nodded, playing with the hair at the nape of his neck. "Yeah, I do, and I wish I didn't. Jake is going to have a tough time if it's Zach."

"No doubt. He gave up a career in NASCAR to raise him, you know. Bets were on that, in a year or two, he'd be at the top."

She leaned back. "How do you feel now that you know Jake had nothing to do with Kate's accident? Did it help?"

He eased her out of his arms. She thought it was good for him to talk about Kate and the accident, but he disagreed. And he knew what she was really asking. Did knowing Jake wasn't involved ease his own guilt? "No. You didn't know her, Vivi. She wouldn't drive in a blizzard. She wasn't like you. She was cautious. She wouldn't do something stupid."

She blinked. "Oh, okay." Flipping her hair over her

shoulder, she lowered herself into the chair. "I better get back to work."

He'd seen the hurt in her violet eyes before she'd looked away. He crouched beside her. "Hey." He lifted her chin. "You know what I mean, Slick."

"Yeah, hard not to." She moved her messenger bag and a bunch of glossy brochures fell onto the floor.

He reached down to pick them up. They were advertisements for wedding dresses and caterers. He slowly raised his eyes. "Vivi, honey, I told you—"

She opened her computer. "Don't worry, McBride. They're not mine."

# Chapter Twenty-Three

Vivi sat at the island eating a bagel while rereading her comment on the computer screen. Cujo, sitting on the floor by the stool, growled. She raised her brow at the Yorkie, reminding the dog of their deal. Cujo's head went down. Then she stretched out on the hardwood floor and gave a couple of yips. "Good doggie," Vivi said, breaking off a chunk of her bagel. She tossed the piece to Cujo at the same time the door off the garage opened.

Vivi closed her sister's Facebook page and brought up the *Chronicle*'s before swiveling to face Chance. "You were gone early." Her voice came out kind of whiney, and she covered an inward groan with a smile. What the heck was wrong with her? She was getting as bad as the women who wrote to her. Then again, she shouldn't be so hard on herself. He'd been gone before she'd woken up, and being woken up by Chance McBride was pretty spectacular.

He ambled toward her with a lazy grin on his face,

which was pretty spectacular, too. "Happy to see you two getting along, but you have to come up with a new strategy, Slick. You're gonna make her fat."

Focused as he was on Cujo, he obviously didn't pick up on Vivi's whiney voice. "The way she tears around the cabin, I don't think you have to worry about her not fitting into her tutu." She didn't mention that, thanks to her, Cujo had probably lost a pound the night before last. Who knew death by chocolate was possible. Vivi'd since Googled what she could and couldn't feed the dog. She had no intention of messing with what worked. Her toes and butt were quite happy she and Cujo had reached a detente.

Chance patted the dog dancing at his feet, then lowered his head to kiss Vivi. "I missed you, too," he said against her lips. She didn't bother protesting; she was too busy indulging in one of her favorite pastimes.

He broke the connection, leaving her breathless and frustrated. She scowled at the reason for the loss of Chance's talented mouth on hers. Cujo yipped, scratching at her master's jean-clad leg. He picked up the dog, rubbing her belly. "Did you take her out this morning?"

"Of course, I did. We went for a long walk." She took a bite of her bagel. Good thing talking wasn't in the dog's repertoire of tricks or Vivi would be busted. She'd sat on the front step with Cujo on a shortened leash while the dog did her business.

"Sure you did," Chance said with a knowing grin and headed for the patio doors. He returned a couple minutes later without Cujo, leaving her, Vivi presumed, in the dog run.

Something she hadn't done this morning, for good

reason. "You do realize bald eagles can eat dogs the size of Cujo, right? They swoop—"

"Honey, you don't have to worry about her. There's mesh at the top of the run."

"I wasn't worried. I just thought it was something you should know." At the twitch of his very fine lips, she changed the subject. "So, where were you this morning?"

He grabbed a coffee mug off the shelf. "Dropped by the hospital to see Ray while I waited for the hardware store to open. I want to replace the shingles on the roof before we head to Dad's."

The storm two weeks ago had damaged the roof. Vivi couldn't help but hope Chance's repair job would last all day and they could avoid the Father's Day barbeque at Paul's. Nell would be there. Chance's aunt had hijacked the latest issue of the *Chronicle*. Instead of being devoted to advertising the Christmas in July celebration as Vivi had planned, summer weddings took center stage. When Vivi confronted her about it, Nell said it was part of her plan to get Paul and Liz back on track. But she'd had a look on her face that made Vivi nervous. And when Vivi overheard the three older women talking about the next book in Nell's series about Christmas, she got really nervous. The book's title was *Wedding Bells in Christmas*. She returned her attention to Chance, who'd practically broken out in a cold sweat when he got a look at the issue.

"Ray remember anything?" Chance's former deputy had finally come out of his coma ten days ago. Once his injuries healed, he would be fine with some rehabilitation.

"Nothing. Last thing he remembers is spotting the Mustang."

She heard the frustration in his voice. Earl and Zach

were the task force's prime suspects, but so far they didn't have enough evidence to bring them in for questioning. They didn't want to send them to ground, either. Since there had been no further break-ins or sightings of the black Mustang, Vivi thought that may have happened already. It's why she'd suggested they draw the Drugstore Bandits out with a sizable delivery of narcotics to a pharmacy in nearby Eagle Creek. "Did you mention to Gage what we talked about yesterday?"

"Yeah, we're going to give it a shot. Easton's setting up the fake delivery for two days from now. They probably won't bite, but it's better than sitting around twiddling our thumbs." Chance filled his mug and came around the island, lifting his chin at the screen. "What are you working on?"

"Your aunt kicked me off as an administrator on the *Chronicle*'s page. I'm trying to figure out how to get back on." Nell had moved her search for Christmas Cutie candidates to social media without, of course, Vivi's consent. So far one candidate had posted his picture. Vivi was surprised Facebook hadn't put them in time-out.

"Jesus." Chance rubbed his eyes as if trying to clear the image of the naked—other than a Santa hat covering his crotch—sixty-something-year-old man. "You shouldn't have let her set up the page." Handing Vivi his mug, he nudged her aside. As he leaned in front of her, she took a sip of his coffee and admired the way his back stretched his white T-shirt. He tapped away at the keys for a couple of minutes, then straightened. "You're good to go."

"You're my hero."

"You're easy to impress." His gaze flicked over the piles of paper scattered across the island, and he gave his head a slight shake. "You're taking over the damn kitchen, woman. It's time we cleared you out a space to work at home."

That's just one more thing she liked about Chance. He never got on her case for bringing work home. The other night, he'd helped her clear out a backlog of Dear Vivi letters. She'd never enjoyed writing her responses as much. It had been fun getting a male perspective. Chance had been horrified when she told him she was renaming the column Dear Vivi and Chance in deference to his input. She imagined he was worried about his alpha-man card being revoked.

But right now, the thought uppermost in her mind was that he wanted to make a place for her here. She warned herself not to read too much into the suggestion. It wasn't as if he were asking her to move in with him. Once the Drugstore Bandits had been put behind bars, she'd be back to living above the bakery. She pressed a finger to her temple. Dammit, she'd totally forgotten Grace had the place rented in two weeks' time. She made a mental note to start looking for somewhere to live tomorrow.

Chance watched her, his brow furrowed. "You can't tell me you like working at the island."

"I don't mind. I think it bugs you more than it bugs me. But I can set up..." She was about to suggest the Aspen log trestle table in the dining room when an idea came to her. It wasn't out of the blue, really. Ever since her visit with Chance's mother-in-law, she'd been thinking about the third bedroom filled with Kate's and the baby's things. In her opinion, it was as unhealthy as Mary's shrine to Kate. For Chance to be able to move on, he needed to deal with the room.

She took a moment to prepare herself in case he reacted badly to her suggestion, then continued, "In the extra bedroom, if that works for you. That way I can leave everything out, and I won't have to hear you complaining about my mess." She kept her tone light and teasing. If she didn't know him so well, she may have missed the flash of pain in his green eyes. Her stomach clenched. She didn't want to hurt him. But she knew in her heart this was something he had to do. And while she may not have made the suggestion for selfish reasons, he needed to be able to move on for their relationship to work.

She didn't realize she'd been holding her breath until he nodded, and the pressure in her chest released on a silent exhale.

"Yeah, okay, but you'll have to clear some stuff out. It's pretty cramped in there," Chance said as he held her gaze, letting her know that he saw through her. He would, wouldn't he? This man with the all-seeing eyes knew her. Maybe even better than Vivi knew herself. Which, admittedly, scared her at times. Because it meant she couldn't hide from him. But neither could he hide from her.

"I can do that," she said quietly.

He nodded again, this time slowly, then he leaned across her. "And while you're taking care of my shit, Slick, you might want to take care of your own." He brought up her sister's Facebook page, turning his head to look into her eyes. "You're veering into creepy stalker territory, honey. Don't you think it's time you reached out to them? They're adults now. Your mother isn't around to stop them from having a relationship with you anymore. Give them a chance to get to know you."

Her face warmed. He must have seen her lowering the

page when he walked into the house. Leave it to her to get involved with a guy nothing got past. "You're one to talk about creepy stalkers, *Superman*."

"I was looking out for you, not stalking you. There's a difference. What you're..." He looked back at the screen, then began to laugh. "Lois Lane?"

"Don't read..." She bowed her head.

"Telling your sister her fiancé has the eyes of a serial killer and attaching a picture of Ted Bundy might not be the best way to start off your relationship. She's more likely to block you."

Vivi nudged him out of the way. He moved behind her, resting his hands on her shoulders. "All right, now you look at this guy and tell me there's not something off about him."

Chance put his hand over hers on the mouse and clicked through Brooke's pictures. "Looks like he's full of himself, loves her old man's money more than he loves her, and"— he scrolled through some of his comments—"sounds like a controlling asshat." Vivi's comment disappeared. Chance grimaced. "Sorry, honey. Looks like she shut you down."

Vivi shrugged as if losing her only link to her sister didn't bother her. Maybe she had taken it too far. But the guy did look like Ted Bundy, and worse, he couched snide remarks about Brooke's career as a joke. Vivi worried that because of Claire's death from a stroke six months ago, her sister wasn't thinking clearly. It wasn't Vivi's business. She should stay out of it.

"I'll set you up with a new account, and you can be friends again. We'll call you Superwoman."

Since Vivi was pretending it wasn't a big deal, she

should probably tell him not to bother. Then she remembered how well he knew her, and said, "Thanks." She'd check her brother's page when Chance wasn't around. With the ISIS conflict in Iraq, Finn shouldn't be taking the *Time* assignment.

Chance tapped his cheek with his finger, and she kissed his stubbled jaw. "That'll do for now. You can show me how grateful you are when we get back from Dad's."

\*        \*        \*

Three hours later, Vivi surveyed the spare bedroom. She was exhausted. Emotionally done in. She didn't know who had begun the task of boxing Kate's and the baby's things, but she knew why they'd stopped. She picked up the last of the stuffed animals—a pink teddy bear—to put it in the green garbage bag.

"I bought that for the baby," a soft feminine voice said from behind her.

Vivi screamed, throwing the stuffed animal. The teddy bear said, "I love you," as it sailed through the air. Her heart beating double time in her chest, Vivi stole a glance over her shoulder. "You nearly gave me a heart attack," she said as Natalee walked into the bedroom. Vivi lay on the white carpet, placing her arms over her eyes in hopes Natalee didn't notice her damp eyelashes.

The hammering on the roof stopped. "Slick, you okay?" Chance's voice came through the open window.

"Good, I'm good," she yelled back. "I thought I saw a mouse."

She thought she heard him mutter, "Fearless, my ass."

"Sorry I scared you. I should have called out or something," Natalee said, walking to the cradle Princess was trying to get out of. As she picked up the dog, Natalee looked around the room. "Nell left this for me to do before Chance came home. I thought I could, but... Sorry." She lifted a shoulder, her cheeks stained pink.

"Nothing to apologize for. It's not easy, Natalee. I get it." Vivi sat up. "Maddie told me there's a shelter for abused women and their children, so I thought... I don't know, do you think that your sister would have liked her and the baby's things to go there?"

Natalee gave Vivi a small smile, the first true smile she'd had from her. "She'd like that. Katie used to volunteer there. She was a social worker, you know. But after they got engaged, Chance made her quit working. She volunteered instead. It's not like they needed the money."

Nervous flutters danced in Vivi's stomach. She didn't know what she was worrying about. Chance's reaction to the latest issue of the *Chronicle* left no doubt in her mind he was no longer the marrying kind. "I'm sure she was a wonderful social worker."

Natalee nodded. "Everyone loved her. But she became too emotionally involved with her clients. It's why Chance made her quit. She was too tenderhearted. She got burnt out."

Well, that wasn't a problem Vivi would ever have to worry about.

Natalee let Princess down and picked up the teddy bear. "Do you mind if I keep this?"

"No, gosh, no, keep anything you want. You can go through the bags, too. But I, uh, did put a few things aside for you." Vivi got up from the floor and walked to the two piles on the dresser. She'd made one for Chance, too.

"You did?" Natalee said, walking to Vivi's side with Cujo trotting behind her.

Vivi kept a wary eye on the dog. "I know your mom has lots of pictures, but there's some really nice ones of you and Kate." She pointed to the jewelry box. "I kept a couple of pieces for Chance, but I thought you might like the rest. And..." Vivi spoke past the tightness in her throat, inwardly cursing the emotion's stranglehold grip, "This is Kate's wedding dress." She smoothed her hand over the box. "I think you should keep it."

She briefly closed her eyes at the sound of Natalee's choked sob, then put an arm around the younger woman's narrow shoulders. "I'm sorry. I didn't mean to upset you. I don't think the pain ever goes away, Natalee, but it should get easier."

"It won't. It can't. It was..." She turned into Vivi's arms and cried.

"A horrible accident. A horrible tragedy for all of you." Vivi rubbed Natalee's back. "I didn't know Kate, but I'm sure she would want you to be happy. To remember all the good times you had." Vivi leaned back to wipe the tears from Natalee's cheeks. "I've seen the pictures. You had a great relationship with your sister. Not everyone's so lucky."

Natalee rubbed her eyes and stepped back. "You don't have a good relationship with your sister?"

Vivi gave a startled jerk. There was no reason for Natalee to know she had a sister unless she or Zach had been involved in the break-in and had seen Vivi's computer. No, she was overreacting. It had been a generic question. "I don't have a sister. But I do have my best friends. And if God forbid anything happened to one of them, I can tell you what they'd do if they thought I wasn't moving on with my life."

Natalee gave her a watery smile. "Kick your butt."

Vivi laughed. "Maddie would kick my butt. Skye, she'd probably do some weird cleansing thing." Her throat ached as she thought of the one thing she had left to do. She walked to the cradle. Cujo growled. She shot the dog a look. Cujo obediently hit the floor. "Good doggie," Vivi said, then took a hunk of beef jerky out of her pocket and tossed it to the dog.

"Umm, Vivi, what did you give her?"

"Just some of this." She held up the beef jerky, then shot a panicked glance at the dog. "Don't tell me she can die from this, too? I fed her chocolate the other night. But I'm sure the website said this was okay."

Natalee pressed her lips together as though trying not to laugh. She knelt down and pulled the hunk of beef jerky from Cujo's mouth. "It is, but you're supposed to give her only a tiny bit."

"Oh, well, that's good. But that"—she pointed at Natalee's fingers—"is really gross. You're covered in gunk."

She shrugged and wiped her hand on her jeans. "I don't mind."

"Obviously," Vivi said with a shudder as she went to stand beside the cradle. "I didn't want to give this away. It looks handmade." There were pictures of a glowing Kate knitting by the fire, and Vivi had kept the pink-knitted baby clothes, too. "Do you know…"

Natalee's lightheartedness of a few moments ago disappeared. "Chance made it."

A beautiful cradle made by a beautiful man for his

beautiful wife and their baby-to-be. She couldn't give it away. Maybe someday Chance would have another child. Vivi squashed the thought. No, there would be no child or wife for Chance. A girlfriend, yes. But he wouldn't put his heart at risk again. And there was a part of Vivi that didn't blame him.

"Okay, we'll keep the cradle." But at least for now, she thought it might be best kept out of sight. "I'll put it in the attic." She thought about the mice. "Or I'll hold the ladder and you can."

"I'll take care of it." Chance's voice came through the open window.

All she could see through the screen was the side of his sweat-slicked bare chest and muscled arm. As far as she could tell, he seemed okay. "Great," she said, then turned to Natalee. "Do you want a soda or something?"

Once again Chance's voice drifted through the open window. "Nat, hide those cookies from her. There'll be nothing left for me if she gets at them."

"Cookies? Those caramel-filled chocolate ones your mom served at tea?"

"Yeah, they're Chance's favorite, too. She felt bad about Uncle Earl punching you. So do I. I wish I'd been there. I can usually calm him down."

Vivi picked up three framed photos. "Your mom has nothing to feel bad about, and neither do you." Natalee followed her to the master bedroom. "Does Earl lose his temper a lot with your mom?" Vivi set the photo of Kate knitting on top of the pine dresser, placing the one from their wedding beside it.

"Only when he's drinking. I know what you're thinking, Vivi." Natalee drew her gaze from the photos, "but he'd never hurt her. And my mom, even when, well, even when she wasn't herself, wouldn't put up with that."

"Glad to hear it. There's never an excuse for abuse—not a bad temper, not alcohol or jealousy." She added the last part as an afterthought. Casting a sidelong glance at Natalee as they walked from Chance's bedroom, she watched for a reaction. She didn't get one. But she did when she placed the framed photo of Chance, Kate, and Natalee on the fireplace mantel. Someone had taken the shot from the water. The three of them were on the dock, Natalee bent over laughing as Chance tossed Kate into the water.

There was nothing left of that vivacious, happy young girl in the photo. And Vivi thought it was a shame her sister's death had stolen Natalee's light. The tears rolling down Kate's sister's cheeks tugged at Vivi's heartstrings, and she found herself wanting to help Natalee as much as she did Chance. "I think you should come work for me at the *Chronicle*." And while she may have made the suggestion as a means of distracting Natalee, it didn't escape her that having the younger woman around would make it easier for Vivi to get a better read on Natalee's relationship with Zach while discovering how deeply involved he was with his father.

She swiped at her cheeks. "Why are you doing this?"

"I could use some help at the paper. I think it'd be good for you. I've found the best way to deal with grief is to do something you love, and your mom and Chance said you used to love to write."

"I do, but that's not what I meant. I thought you'd want to get rid of any reminders of Kate, but you put up pictures of her and visit with my mom, and you don't mind me coming around."

"Of course I don't mind you coming around. Chance loves you, Natalee, and he will always love your sister. I don't want him to forget her and what they had. I just want you both to realize your lives didn't end when Kate died. You can love again, be happy again. It won't be the same, but that doesn't mean it can't be just as good." She'd said too much, revealed too much of her hopes for her future with Chance. She slung her arm over Natalee's shoulders. "Come on, let's go eat some cookies before Chance gets in here."

Natalee gave her a winsome smile. "I think I'll take you up on your offer. I'd like to work at the *Chronicle*."

"Great. You can help me figure out how Nell and her friends keep hijacking the paper." Vivi pulled out a stool for Natalee and snagged two cookies from the china plate.

"I'm sorry I wasn't very nice to you when we first met. You make Chance happy, and that makes it..." She focused on the cookie in her hand. "All I ever wanted is for Chance to be happy. You must be getting excited about the wedding."

"Uh, what wedding are you talking about?"

"Yours and Chance's. Nell just put up a contest on the *Chronicle*'s Facebook page for followers to pick your wedding cake. The Superman one is pretty cute."

And just when Vivi didn't think her day could get much worse, she heard Chance's muttered curse from behind her.

# Chapter Twenty-Four

Chance sat sprawled in a rustic wooden chair drinking a beer with his brother in the backyard of their childhood home.

Gage glanced to where Nat tossed a ball with Annie while Lily pushed a pink-tutu-wearing Princess around the grass in a doll carriage. "I was surprised to see Nat," his brother said.

"Vivi invited her to come along. Didn't think Dad would mind."

"Of course he doesn't." His brother's gaze went to where Vivi, wearing a black bikini top and denim shorts, sat on a blanket with Madison and Connor under a tree. "Couldn't help but notice your girl was giving you the cold shoulder. What did you do now?"

Overreacted. He couldn't help it. He'd had what he thought might be a panic attack when he heard Nat congratulate Vivi on their upcoming nuptials. His brain had shut down. Too bad his mouth didn't do the same. And now she wasn't talking to him. That surprised him and worried him. Vivi wasn't the silent type. If she was pissed at someone, they heard about it. "I went off on her about all the wedding crap in the paper and on Facebook."

"Why would you...Okay, I get it. But you have to know it's Nell's doing, not Vivi's. Our aunt has you two pegged for book number four, I guarantee it."

That choking feeling from earlier returned. "She better find herself another couple. It's not happening."

His brother clinked his bottle to his. "Welcome to the club, big brother. That's what we all said."

"Yeah, well, she can't bulldoze me. I'm going to have a chat with our dear, old aunt and set her straight."

Gage chuckled into his beer bottle. "Good luck with that. Speak of the devil, here she comes." His brother nodded at the sliding glass doors, spewing his beer when Nell walked out wearing a white T-shirt with Superman and Lois Lane hanging from two pink wedding bells.

"I'm going to kill her," Chance muttered, putting down his beer bottle.

"Looks like you'll have to get in line." Gage grinned, watching Vivi stride across the lawn.

Chance shot out of the chair. His aunt didn't swim, and the pool was in pushing vicinity. He made it in time to insert himself between Vivi and Nell. "Relax, Slick. I'll take care of it."

"Really? You're telling *me* to relax? Aren't you the same man who lost it when you thought I was planning our wedding behind your back? Guess you didn't get a good look at her T-shirt. Maybe you should turn around." And there it was again, only instead of seeing the hurt in her expressive violet eyes, he heard a hint of the emotion in her husky voice.

"I saw it, Slick. Let's go—"

"Calm your nerves. I know you'll never get married again, Chance. So does Vivi. She's one of those feminist gals anyway. She probably wouldn't marry you if you wanted her to." Nell glanced at the patio doors and dropped her voice to a conspiratorial whisper. "I want Paul and Liz to think I'm focused on you two so they won't be prepared for my next move."

Vivi snorted, but Chance thought Nell might be telling the truth. It was something his aunt's diabolical little mind would come up with.

"Just give me a couple more days," Nell continued. "Liz will be pea green with envy when she sees next week's issue. Sophia ordered some wedding dresses for you, Vivi, just—"

Vivi lunged for his aunt. Chance grabbed her around the waist, ducked a shoulder into her middle, and got her in a fireman's hold. "McBride, put me down," she yelled as he headed for the patio doors.

"Chance, you skipped a step. You have to marry the girl before you carry her across the threshold," his aunt chortled.

"Nell, do not even think about taking my…" Chance saw the camera flash in the glass door, wincing when Vivi cursed out loud.

"Honey, little kid's ears," he reminded her as he stepped into the kitchen.

"I don't care. She's—"

"Got a good one, Vivi. We'll just Photoshop your bikini top a bit. Your girls were peeking out."

Vivi groaned against his back, then slapped him when he started to laugh. "It's not funny, McBride. I'm going to—"

"Vivi, what's wrong? Did you hurt yourself, honey?" his father asked as he walked into the kitchen.

"No, but I'm going to hurt your aunt, and if your son doesn't put me down, I'm going to hurt him, too."

His father cast him a worried look. "Maybe you should put her down, son."

Chance turned his head and said under his breath, "Remember your girls. We don't want my dad to have a heart attack." She stiffened, then wiggled around, her fingers brushing against his back as he imagined her rearranging her bikini top. "Don't worry about her, Dad." Chance walked through the living room to the bedrooms. "A mild case of heatstroke. She'll feel better once she lies down for a minute."

"Put on the fan, and I'll get her some water," his father called after him.

"I've got it under control." He closed the door to his old bedroom, locking it to keep his worrywart of a father out. He shouldn't have joked about the heatstroke. Dr. Paul would be hovering over Vivi for the rest of the day.

"Put me down."

His hands at her waist, he made sure her slide down the front of him was slow, luxuriating in the feel of her warm, vanilla-scented body. He realized his mistake when she pinned him with a killer glare. If he didn't make it up to her fast, he'd better make that memory last because Vivi Westfield was in kick-ass mode.

Her lush lips set in a flat line, she sidestepped him and headed for the door.

"Honey, come on. Don't go. We need to talk." He grabbed her hand.

"Don't *honey* me. I heard all I want to hear from you." She went to unlock the door.

"I wouldn't if I were you. My dad thinks you have heatstroke. He won't leave you alone." He moved behind her, flattening his open palm on the door above her head.

"What? Did you inherit a manipulative gene from your aunt or something? You people are crazy." She pressed her forehead to the door.

"Crazy about you," he said, moving her hair over her shoulder to kiss the back of her neck.

She shivered. "That's not fair."

"The kiss or me telling you I'm crazy about you?" He placed his hands on her narrow waist, stroking her flat stomach with his fingers while continuing to kiss her neck.

"Both."

He brought his mouth to her ear, nuzzling his jaw in her hair. "I don't play fair. I'm sorry I was an ass. I didn't mean to hurt you."

"You didn't."

He nipped her earlobe. "I did so." Taking a step back, he turned her to face him. He wanted to look into her beautiful eyes when he told her what he'd been fighting, what he'd been running away from since she'd come into his life all those long months ago. He opened his mouth to tell her, but he couldn't. He wanted to, but physically, he couldn't. It felt like someone had their foot on his throat. "I don't want to lose you." The pressure eased. "I am crazy about you. Don't give me the silent treatment again, okay? It freaks me the hell out. If you're pissed at me, tell me. If I hurt your feelings, yell at me."

She lost the angry look in her eyes and brought her hand to his face. "You won't lose me. I love you. Even when you're being a superjerk." She reached up on her toes and kissed him.

\*     \*     \*

Chance followed Vivi to the picnic table. "How did we get stuck at the kids' table?" he said for her ears alone.

She glanced to where the adults sat in a semicircle near the pool. "If I had to take a guess, they don't want you anywhere near Paul and Liz. They're actually talking and making goo-goo eyes at each other." He heard the amusement in her voice.

"Nah, they haven't said more than two words to each other." He ignored her goo-goo-eyes comment because he'd seen a couple of those and thought they might be worse than them talking. "You're the reason we're at the kids' table. They're afraid to let you near Nell with a knife in your hand."

"You're hilarious." He nearly bumped into her when she stopped in her tracks. "Hey, wait a minute. Evie and Connor don't count as kids yet. What are they doing at our table?"

He nudged her. "Get moving, our burgers are getting cold."

Connor and Evie were strapped into baby seats on the middle of the picnic table. Vivi slid onto the bench opposite Nat, Lily, and Annie while Chance took the seat beside her.

"Hey, guys, how's..." Vivi began, and Evie's lip quivered. Connor squinched up his face like he had gas. Vivi put her head on the table and groaned. "They hate me."

Lily reached over and patted Vivi's head. "They don't hate you. I think it's your voice."

"What's wrong with my voice?"

Annie and Nat tried not to laugh while Lily explained her theory, which Chance was interested to hear. "Most ladies talk like this when they talk to babies." Lily raised her voice to a feminine, high-pitched tone. "But you talk like this," she said, deepening her voice.

"I do not sound like a man," Vivi said in an offended tone of voice. Evie started to cry, and Connor whimpered. Vivi eyed her burger, pinching off a small piece.

*Jesus.* Chance covered her hand with his. "You can't bribe them with food like you do Princess," he said, struggling not to laugh.

"Why not? They have teeth."

Lily sighed. "Auntie, they're babies." She leaned over and got a bottle, handing it to Vivi.

She eyed the bottle and the baby, then tried to get Evie to open her mouth. "Good baby, drink your bottle." She mimicked Lily's voice.

Annie's and Nat's eyes bugged out, and they shoved their burgers in their mouths in an effort, he figured, to keep from howling with laughter. Chance rocked Connor's seat to keep the baby from crying, and also in hopes that Vivi wouldn't realize it was him and his silent laughter shaking the bench.

"Here, I'll show you how," Lily said when Evie's face got red, and she looked ready to let loose.

"That's it." Vivi picked up her plate. "I'm going to take my creepy-man-voice out of here and eat with the adults."

With a hand on her arm, Chance stopped her from sliding off the bench. He leaned in to whisper in her ear. "You don't have a creepy-man-voice. You could make a fortune as a sex-phone operator. I could listen to you talk all day." It was true. When she'd opened her mouth the day he met her, he'd been a goner.

She patted his face. "Thanks, but I'm still going to sit with the adults."

"It's not her voice," Annie said, once Vivi left. "Evie and Connor know they make her nervous."

Chance thought his niece might have a point. Twenty minutes later, he could commiserate with Vivi. But it wasn't nerves that had his stomach roiling. It was the memories. His father, who'd been talking to Ethan and Gage, happened to look over at the same time Lily handed Evie to Chance. His dad got out of his chair and walked over. Chance saw the worry on his father's face. He remembered, too.

Today marked the first Father's Day Chance had spent with his dad since the one when Kate shared her news. He could see her, glowing with a secret smile on her sweet face. She'd handed him and his dad the small wrapped packages. They'd opened them to find pink baby booties with pink, foil-wrapped chocolate cigars.

Evie looked up at him with a gummy smile and patted his face. With her blonde hair and butterscotch eyes, he imagined his Emma would have looked like her. And that's when it hit him, how long it had actually been. Emma would be coming close to her fifth birthday.

"Here, son. Let me take her."

He held his father's gaze. "I'm good, Dad." And for once, it wasn't a lie.

"Uh, you might be, but I don't think Vivi is. Honey,

stop jumping around and she'll calm down," his father called out.

Chance turned to see Vivi running on the spot, hands in the air clutching a cookie and a bottle of water, while Princess barked and nipped at her bare feet. Vivi gave a panicked yelp and eyed the chocolate cookie.

"Slick, don't you dare give her that cookie…"

She didn't. Instead, she poured her bottled water on Princess's head.

*Tough, my ass.* The woman was afraid of flying, babies, dogs, and pretty much anything with four legs. But she wasn't afraid to tell Chance she loved him.

\*      \*      \*

Wrapped in a towel, Vivi blew Princess dry. If she'd known dumping water on the dog's head would turn her into the obedient, mild-mannered animal sitting docilely in the bathroom sink, Vivi would've done it the first day they met. Guess all she had to do was show Princess who was boss. She turned off the blow dryer and ran her fingers through Princess's newly shorn coat. "That's better, now you can see."

Vivi had stepped out of the shower to find Princess waiting for her. She'd thought the dog was eyeing her toes, then realized she wouldn't be able to see them with all that hair in her eyes. Feeling bad for dumping water on her, Vivi had decided, with no small amount of trepidation, to make it up to Princess by snipping her overlong bangs. When that went well, Vivi got a little scissor happy. The first thing to go was the stupid topknot—no more bows for Princess. And that led to a few more snips to even her out. Well, that's what Vivi told herself anyway.

It's possible she was just killing time in hopes Chance had gone for his swim and would leave her alone.

Yes, it was hot, and she'd smelled like beef jerky and wet dog as he had so sweetly pointed out. But swimming in the dark water? She'd settled on a shower instead. Not even Chance's teasing attempts had been enough to get her to cave. She wasn't a chicken. Swimming this late at night with only...

An ice-cold finger tracked down her spine. She was an idiot. What had she been thinking letting him swim at night alone? She calmed herself with the thought this was not just any man, this was Chance McBride with his warrior's body and a mind trained for danger. Still, it wouldn't hurt to check on him. She picked up Princess, who gave a couple of happy yips and licked Vivi...right on the lips. She lifted the dog to look her in the eyes, which she was surprised to find weren't serial-killer eyes after all. They were soft and sweet.

"We're friends now, but not that kind, so no more licking." Princess whined. Vivi sighed and turned her cheek. "Okay, get it out of your system." Once Princess had delivered a sandpapery kiss to her cheek, Vivi patted her and headed for the living room.

As she reached the floor-to-ceiling window, her hand went to her throat, her heart pitter-patting in her chest. Damn the man. Candles glowed along either side of the dock. It was romantic and beautiful, and so unfair. She had no choice but to join him now. A full moon shimmered a path across the lake. She searched the water at the front of the dock for some sign of him.

"Looking for me?"

She jumped at the sound of his voice from behind her.

"You nearly gave me a heart attack." She thought she might have squeezed the life out of Princess, too. Looking over her shoulder, she watched as Chance prowled toward her wearing only a pair of low-riding khaki shorts, all of his sun-bronzed muscles on full, mouthwatering display.

"Sorry," he murmured when he reached her, touching his lips to her shoulder, running one of the cold, wet beer bottles he held down her arm.

"You're forgiven." She angled her head so he could continue trailing those hot, branding kisses up her neck, groaning her frustration when he stopped inches shy of the sensitive place beneath her ear. She loved when he kissed her there, and he knew it.

"Come with me down to the dock, and I'll kiss you there"—he gave her a teasing lick—"all night."

As if she could refuse after the effort he'd put in. She tipped her head back to rest it on his shoulder. "Yes, I'll come with you down to the dock. You don't play fair, McBride. You're as sneaky as your aunt."

He grinned, then his eyes widened. "What the hell happened to Princess?"

"Um, I gave her a haircut," she said, a nervous, questioning tone in her voice. Maybe she'd overstepped. It was his...Kate's dog, not hers. "How would you like to wear a fur coat in the summer? She was hot."

"Settle down, Slick. I'm not mad. She looks like a puppy again. You like your haircut, don't you, Princess?" He leaned over Vivi's shoulder, rubbing his head against the dog. "And I think you like Vivi, too."

"She just needed to know who's boss," Vivi said, unable to keep the smug tone from her voice.

Chance shot her a worried glance, touching the beer

bottle to his head. "Don't even think about it. You are not coming near me with a pair of scissors. I like my hair just the way it is."

She put Princess down, turning into Chance's arms. "I do, too," she said, running her fingers through his thick dark blond hair.

"You don't have to cut my hair. You've got me wrapped around your little finger, Slick."

"Sometimes you say the sweetest things, McBride." And did them, too.

His mouth curved, and he handed her the beer bottles, sweeping her into his arms. "I should have recorded that," he said, as he opened the patio door. Princess whined as he closed it behind him. "Not this time. I don't want to share my girl tonight."

"Twice within seconds, McBride? You better be careful or it'll become a habit."

He smiled down at her, his even, white teeth flashing. "Get used to it."

She was, and she smothered the voice in her head that warned her to be careful. It was too late for the warning. "I can walk, you know."

"Safer this way. I don't want you to step on anything that'll send you back to the house."

She stiffened. "Like what?"

"Relax, I've got you. I'll never let anything hurt you." With the full moon and swath of stars lighting up the night sky, she saw the almost imperceptible tightening of his strong, masculine features. Her wounded warrior still had a ways to go.

She forced a lightness to her voice as he carefully set her feet on the plaid blanket he'd thoughtfully laid out on the dock. "Don't worry. If I can handle Princess, I can handle anything. I'm not going anywhere, McBride. Well, not until you put the Drugstore Bandits behind bars at least. The apartment's rented the end of June so…" she began, handing him a bottle. With a firm grip on her towel, she lowered herself onto the blanket.

"You're not going anywhere, period," he said as he sat beside her. "I thought we'd already settled this, Slick." His hand wrapped around the neck of the bottle, he moved it between them. "You and me, we're together now."

"We are, but I wasn't sure if that meant you wanted me to—" She bowed her head when he gave his a frustrated shake, set his beer bottle on the dock, and got to his feet.

He held out his hand. "Come on."

"No, I want to talk about this."

"We will, once I have you naked and in my arms."

She smiled and patted the blanket. "We can do that right here."

He kept his eyes on her as he undid his shorts and stripped them off. "In the water. Now." Without waiting for her response, which she was having trouble forming due to the delectable view he provided, he turned around, giving her a brief look at his muscled back, tight backside, and powerful legs before diving into the water.

He reappeared moments later, looking like he belonged on a movie set or in a magazine as he smoothed his hair back from his gorgeous face with his hands. "Come to me."

There was something beneath the command in his deep voice that had her rising to her feet. Her eyes locked to his as she walked to the edge of the dock. The dancing moonlight shimmered across the water, illuminating his serious, almost pained expression. For some reason this was important to him. Maybe he needed to know she trusted him to take care of her, to protect her.

She looked into the dark depths. Oh God, she really didn't want to get in the water. But from day one this man had pushed her out of her comfort zone. Why did she expect him to change now? Taking a deep breath, she loosened her towel, letting it drop to her feet.

"Jesus, God," Chance said, his voice gruff, his eyes drinking her in.

He'd seen every inch of her body, kissed and caressed it, too, but the way he looked at her now felt strangely more intimate. She lifted her hands, about to cover herself, but dropped them to her sides when he said, "Don't ever hide yourself from me. You are the most beautiful woman I have ever seen, Vivi Westfield. I..." He had that pained look on his face again, then he smiled and held up his hands. "I'll catch you."

Vivi didn't let herself think, she just closed her eyes and jumped, panicking when the water closed over her head. She sank deeper into the murky depths until strong hands clamped on either side of her waist, drawing her against a hard, familiar body. Breaking through the surface, she spurted water. Chance had that look on his face again as he stared into her eyes.

She wound her arms around his neck, kicking her feet even though she knew she was safe in his arms. The cool, silky water lapped against her body, gently rocking them together. He moved his hands from her waist, smoothing her hair from her face. His Adam's apple bobbed in his throat as he swallowed and grimaced, then said harshly, "I love you."

She bit the inside of her lip. She knew he did. She'd known when he told her he was crazy about her earlier today. His eyes narrowed when she didn't immediately respond. She smiled. "Could you tell me again? Only this time without looking like someone has a gun pointed at your head."

"I just told you I love you, woman. You're supposed to be happy, maybe even cry a little."

"You didn't cry when I told you I loved you." He tipped his head back and looked up at the stars. Thinking she'd teased him enough, she kissed his neck. "I love you, Chance McBride. I loved you when you were James Harris, and I loved you when you were Superman. And I'm happy you love me, too."

"You're lucky I love you, because you came this close to being picked up and thrown." He jerked his thumb behind him, indicating where she would've ended up. Then he looked into her eyes. "James Harris loved you, too, and so did Superman. Only they didn't know it then."

"It's okay. Men are a little slower on the uptake." She rubbed against him, wrapping her legs around his waist. "Maybe now that we got the mushy stuff out of the way, we can get to the good stuff."

"I didn't stand a chance against you," he said, cradling the back of her head in the palm of his hand as he lowered his mouth to hers, swallowing her panicked yelp as he stopped kicking and they sank beneath the water.

# Chapter Twenty-Five

I know you're excited," Vivi said to Princess, who pounced as soon as she opened the mudroom door. "Don't pee. I'll take you out in a sec." Vivi deposited the groceries on the counter. She'd decided to make Chance a nice dinner and snuck out an hour early from work. He'd had a crappy day. Make that a crappy couple of days. As he'd suspected, the Drugstore Bandits hadn't taken the bait and yesterday's sting operation had been a bust. A lot of man-hours and money wasted. It's why they pulled Earl and Zach in for questioning this morning.

Neither Chance nor Gage had wanted to bring them in, but the DEA and FBI agents overrode their argument that they'd tip their hands. Chance had stopped by the *Chronicle* after they'd questioned Zach. He didn't get anything out of Zach, but Jake had given him a black eye. To say Jake was an unhappy man was an understatement. He was livid Chance broke his word. Jake didn't realize how hard he'd fought not to. Vivi suspected Chance might also be on his sister-in-law's bad side. Natalee hadn't shown up for work today, nor had she taken any of Vivi's calls.

As thunder rumbled across the lake, Vivi grabbed Princess's leash off the kitchen counter. The incoming storm was another reason she'd rushed home. Although she wouldn't admit it to anyone, she'd been worried about her former nemesis. Once Princess had done her business, Vivi changed into a pair of black silk sleep pants and a lacy black tank top. She hoped Chance appreciated her effort. She'd rather be wearing a sloppy sweatshirt with her go-to jean shorts.

She covered up with an apron. Smiling as she thought of Chance's reaction if she met him at the door wearing only the white apron and a red pair of do-me shoes. She filed the idea away for another time. She had work to do. Grace had told Vivi anyone could make her spaghetti and meatballs, but that was Grace. By the time Vivi rolled the last of the meatballs, an hour had passed. She'd been right. Grace lied. This was not an easy-peasy recipe. But the sauce bubbling on the back burner smelled amazing. Vivi gave in to Princess's whining and tossed her a small piece of leftover ground beef, making sure there was no garlic or onion in the meat before she did. Then she set about creating a romantic atmosphere with candles and flowers.

As she surveyed the dining room table, she decided she'd earn some serious Brownie points from McBride. But as the minutes ticked by on the clock over the mantel, the points he'd accumulated over the last several days diminished. *Pathetic. He tells you he loves you, and you turn into a clingy woman.* She turned down the sauce, then curled up on the couch with Princess. And as the rain beat down on the copper roof, she wondered what advice she'd give a woman whose man was now an hour late. She smiled and picked up the phone. Some sexy-talk time should do the trick. If he did have to work late, all he'd be thinking about was getting home to her. If he didn't, her sex-phone-operator voice that he professed to love so much would guarantee he thought twice about intentionally being late again.

He answered on the first ring. She mentally returned one of his Brownie points. "Hey, honey, sorry I didn't call." Two points for the apology. "Last-minute change of plans. On the off chance we're wrong about Earl and Zach and the real guys can't resist the bait, DEA authorized a second stakeout in Eagle Creek."

She returned all of his points. "So does that mean you're stuck sitting in your car all night with nothing to do?"

"Yeah, I'm here until at least midnight. Do you have a cold?"

She rolled her eyes and cleared her throat. "No, but maybe I'm coming down with one because I'm very, very hot."

"Give Dad a call. He'll come over and check you out."

Okay, she must not be doing this right. How could he not catch on? She tried again. "I don't think that's a good idea. I'm wearing only an apron and red high heels." She smiled, waiting for his reaction. She'd put some serious sexy vibes into her voice.

He laughed. "An apron? You don't cook, and you don't wear high heels. Get some clothes on and call him."

Vivi looked at Princess. "He's an idiot."

"Did you say something, honey?"

All right, time to go for broke. She closed her eyes, imagining Chance was here with her. She opened them. That was just embarrassing. She mentally rehearsed what to say before lowering her voice. "Yes, I did, lover. I'm a very bad girl. And I'm going to be really, really bad when you come home." And then she told him what she was going to do to him. She covered her face with her hand. She probably should be covering poor Princess's ears. What kind of a dog mother was she?

She heard choking and what sounded like muffled laughter. "Jesus, baby, you gotta stop right now. I'm on—"

She really sucked at this if he was laughing. She'd give it one last shot. "Turned on, I know. So am I, baby." She was so not horny. This phone-sex thing was overrated. "My nipples..."

"Gage, I swear to God, if you don't—"

Her eyes went wide. She stared at phone. "Oh, God," she moaned and disconnected. She'd just had one-sided phone sex while Gage listened. Her best friend's husband. Her boyfriend's brother. What was he thinking? The phone rang. She let it go to voice mail. When it rang the fourth time, she picked up. She'd gone from freaking-the-hell embarrassed to ticked-the-hell off. "I hate you."

"No, you don't. You love me. I'm sorry, honey. I tried to tell you—"

"Am I on speaker now?"

"No, and I'm standing outside in the middle of nowhere in the rain. No one can hear you but me. Tell me again what you're going to do to me when I get home. I—"

"Are you freaking kidding me? You're cut off, McBride. Maybe if you had taken me off speaker ten minutes ago, I—"

"I tried, the goddamn thing was stuck. But I covered Gage's ears. He hardly heard anything. Just that bit about what you're going to do with your—"

"Really? You don't think I'm embarrassed enough without you repeating what I said?" She covered her face. Princess walked up her chest to lick her hand.

"You have nothing to be embarrassed about. That was the hottest thing I have ever heard."

"It was stupid. I suck at phone sex."

"You're amazing at phone sex. But seriously, honey, all you have to do is say my name to make me hard."

Well, that was somewhat gratifying. Until she thought about what Gage had overheard. "You better make sure your brother doesn't breathe a word of this. I won't be able to look at Maddie without wondering if…"

"What do you think he's doing right now? He's on the phone trying to get your best friend to—"

"T-M-freaking-I."

"God, I love you. And you've just ensured that every minute I'm sitting in that car I'm going to be thinking of you in nothing but an apron and red do-me shoes."

Wow, it actually worked. "Maybe I like you again."

He laughed, then his voice went deep and sexy, and he told her what he was going to do to her when he came home. "I love you again," she said breathlessly when he finished.

"You never stopped." She heard the smile in his voice and smiled back. "Honey, I've gotta go. Have a nap. You're going to need lots of energy when I come home."

*Maybe a nap isn't such a bad idea after all*, she thought when she disconnected. Phone sex must have the same effect as the real deal because she did indeed fall asleep. Waking up to a flash of lightning over the water and her phone ringing, she squinted at the clock above the fireplace. It was ten o'clock. Maybe Chance was coming home early. She picked up. "Hey, are you—"

A computer-enhanced voice came over the line. "I have information about Kate McBride's death. If you want it, meet me at the gas station on Old Mill Road in twenty minutes. Come alone."

She couldn't tell if the voice was male or female, young or old. "Who is this? What information do you—" The line went dead.

Vivi sat up and debated whether to call Chance. He was on a stakeout until midnight. If she didn't act now... She'd dealt with informants in the past and had never run into any trouble. Well, maybe once or twice. But she wasn't nervous. She knew the gas station. It was on the road into Christmas. It wasn't isolated, and it was well lit. She'd be fine. If she was nervous about anything, it was the information they had. Was it something that would turn Chance's world upside down? If someone had intentionally set out to harm Kate, it would. It was that thought that decided it for Vivi. She'd handle this on her own.

Princess shivered when a clap of thunder rattled the windows. "Okay, pal, we're going for a ride."

Vivi didn't bother changing. She turned off the sauce, then threw on a raincoat and stepped into her rubber boots, gathering Princess in her arms. She slung her messenger bag over her shoulder, checking to be sure her camera and voice recorder were inside. Shoving her cell phone in her pocket, she headed out the door. Once inside the car, she jacked up the heat. Princess whined, crawling onto her lap.

Maybe if the weather wasn't as bad, she'd let Princess

stay in her lap, but not tonight. Vivi ran back in the house and grabbed a throw pillow and blanket from the couch, glancing at the clock as she did. She was cutting it close. She got back in the car, tucked the dog snugly into the front passenger seat, and backed out of the garage.

Turning the wipers to high, she leaned forward to peer through the teeming rain. Thunder rumbled and lightning cracked in the woods to her left. If she wasn't confident in her driving abilities, she might have thought twice about going out on a night like this. But she was a good driver. Her father had trained her well. As she drove down the dark, windy road, she couldn't help but wonder what had made Kate go out in a blizzard. It was a question she imagined Chance had asked himself a million times. Maybe Vivi would finally be able to put the matter to rest for him. At the end of the cabin road, she turned right. Just that slight deviation from Kate's path the night she died made Vivi feel better.

Until a cold sensation trickled down her spine. She pushed thoughts of Kate from her mind. She needed to concentrate. Glancing at the time on the radio, Vivi lightly pressed on the gas. Two beams of light flashed through the passenger-side window as a car pulled out of a lane and onto the road behind her. Bright lights filled her car. Idiots. They had their high beams on and were riding her ass. She eased off the gas, motioning for them to pass. They sped up. She had no choice but to do the same. She leaned on the horn to get their attention. They kept coming, and coming. They slammed into her, her head whipping back. She hit the shoulder, wheels spinning on the gravel. She swore as she fought to regain control of the car.

Princess whimpered. She didn't dare reach out to comfort her. "It's okay, Princess. Everything will be all right."

They came at her again. Screw the rain, she had no choice. She hit the gas. Lightning lit up the sky and that's when she saw the make of the car. It was a black Mustang. She couldn't take her hands off the wheel to call Chance. They were five minutes out of Christmas. All she had to do was hang on until then. As if the driver of the Mustang had read her mind, he revved his engine and came at her. Lightning crackled across the sky at the same time the car smashed into her. She saw the driver. A shocked cry escaped from her mouth. They'd been wrong. So very wrong. Betrayal and anger swamped Vivi, and for one small second, she lost her focus. And that's all it took.

\*       \*       \*

Chance peeled back the bun on his burger. "Give me your pickle," he said to his brother.

"I'm not giving you my pickle."

"Vivi gives me her pickle."

His brother laughed. "From what I heard tonight, she gives you a lot more than her pickle." Gage grinned. "That was hot. Her voice—"

"Seriously? Shut up or I'll shove your burger down your throat."

Gage snorted, then sobered, shifting in the passenger seat. "You love her, don't you?"

"Yeah, I do. I'm crazy about her." It felt good to finally admit it to someone other than Vivi. There were times he wanted to shout it from the rooftops. To let the whole world, at least the small town, know that she was his. He wanted to get home to her instead of sitting in the car watching the minutes tick by. Nothing was happening. The stakeout was a bust.

"Sounds like she feels the same. Did you tell her you love her?"

"Of course, I did." He smiled, remembering. Jesus, he shouldn't be thinking about that night, he was frustrated enough.

"Well look at you. I'm impressed. Given how long it took you, she must have been pretty emotional."

"Vivi, emotional?" He told his brother what she'd said.

Once he finished laughing, Gage wiped his eyes. "Geezus, you're screwed. You've met your match, big brother."

He knew he had. She was perfect for him, but as it had the past few days, the thought made him feel disloyal to Kate. He knew it shouldn't, but there it was. It's why there'd been no shouting from the rooftops.

"Don't," his brother said. "You have no reason to feel guilty. It's been five years." He should have known he couldn't put anything past Gage. His brother continued, "Kate was perfect for the man you once were. Vivi is perfect for the man you are now."

"You're right, and I'd like to get home to my perfect woman. So what do you say we call it a night? Nothing's going—"

A call coming over the radio interrupted him. "All units respond to a single-vehicle accident on Mountain Road. Emergency crews have been dispatched."

They heard Jill respond that she was en route. ETA three minutes.

Every muscle in his body tensed. Gage put his hand on his shoulder. "Do not even go there. Vivi's at home waiting for you. Call her."

He grabbed his phone, trying to hide his panic from his brother. Please, God, not again, he prayed. If anything... She didn't pick up. He tried five times before he raised his frantic gaze to his brother.

Gage's fingers tightened on his shoulder, and he pulled out his own phone. "Hey, honey, have you heard from Vivi?" His brother nodded, and Chance held his breath. *Please, fucking God, please.* "Yeah, no, everything's okay. I'll see you soon."

"She hasn't heard from her, has she?" He couldn't believe he managed to get the words past the painful lump growing with each passing second in his throat. He couldn't breathe.

"Hang in there. I'll call Jill." His brother's cell rang before he could make the call. It was Jill. Gage averted his eyes as he listened to his deputy, the muscle ticking in his jaw. "Right. Okay. Yeah. We're on our way." With each word his brother clipped out, Chance felt his heart break into pieces until there was nothing left. The light that had filled him when Vivi walked into his life went out.

He heard his brother yelling at him from a distance. Gage shook him. "Listen to me. You are not going to lose her. Do you hear me? Dammit, Chance. Look at me."

He slowly lifted his eyes. Tears rolled down Gage's face. He pulled Chance against him. "Stay with me. It's going to be all right. She's alive. They got her out. Dad's on his way to the hospital. Jill's in the ambulance with her. She's not alone. She's tough, Chance. She's a fighter. Hang on to that."

Chance didn't know how he'd gotten in the passenger seat, how long it had taken them to get to the hospital, or who his brother had been talking to on the way. Nothing mattered. Not his brother telling him she'd be all right, that she was tough. He'd been here before. He should have known he'd be here again. But he had known, hadn't he? That's why he'd left her the first time. Why he'd fought so hard against loving her.

The hospital doors swooshed open. The bright lights and antiseptic smell slapped at him. "Yeah, he needs a doctor," he heard his brother say.

*What the fuck was he talking about?*

"You busted your hand. And watch your mouth."

Shit, he didn't think he'd said that out loud. "I don't need a doctor." He made it to the waiting room and sat down, staring unseeing at the white wall. He knew they were all there. Family and friends. They'd been here before.

"Chance."

"Not now, honey," Gage said to his wife and led her away.

Jill came into the room and walked to Gage's side. They talked, glancing his way. He stood up. A firm hand pushed him down onto the chair. Trainer crouched in front of him. "Focus on me, Chance. You're in shock." He pressed a cup in Chance's hand. "Drink this. Your dad's with Vivi. She's in X-ray. She's stable. She has a concussion. As far as we can tell, her injuries are minor." Chance raised his gaze when the doc paused. Trainer looked away, then looked back at him. "You've been given a second chance. A gift. I know what you're feeling right now, I do, but don't shut down. Don't go so deep inside yourself, you won't be able to find your way back. Talk to the EMTs and Jill. Vivi shouldn't have walked away from the accident, Chance. Someone was watching over her."

"He's right, Chance," Jill said quietly. "I didn't think..." She blew out a breath, shook her head. "It's a miracle."

He needed to know why she'd been out there. "Did she say anything? Did she tell you what happened?"

Jill glanced at Gage, and he gave her a tight nod. "She said something about a lead on a story and that she'd lost control of the car. Princess is okay. She wouldn't leave Vivi's side."

Chance put the cup on the chair beside him and got to his feet. "Take care of her," he said to Trainer and walked away.

# Chapter Twenty-Six

Every muscle in Vivi's body ached, but none of those aches compared to the one in her heart. Chance had left her again. He'd walked away without a word, without a note in his bold handwriting. No matter what Maddie and Skye tried to make her believe, he wasn't coming back to her or Christmas. He was gone for good. She imagined it was the reason his brother could barely look at her. She didn't know why Gage insisted he be the one to take her home from the hospital. Home, the cabin wasn't her home anymore. Nowhere would ever feel like home again.

She cast Gage a sidelong glance from where she sat in the passenger seat. His handsome profile hard and unyielding. She wished Maddie had come along. Gage had refused to let her, and Vivi knew why. It was only a matter of time before he questioned her about the accident. He'd tried at the hospital earlier this morning. Maddie and Skye had made him stop. He'd picked up on

Vivi's lie. Like his brother, there wasn't much that got past Gage McBride.

But until she discovered why Natalee had driven her off the road, Vivi would keep her own counsel. She felt as if, in some way, she owed it to Kate and Mary to find out the truth. Because while Natalee was without a doubt the person behind the wheel, Vivi couldn't shake the feeling someone had forced her to do what she did. She'd played the moment over and over again in her mind. Each time she did, the image of Natalee became clearer. Her wild, terrified eyes, her mouth opened as if she screamed "No." Or was Vivi imagining the look of terror on Natalee's face because she didn't want to believe the young woman she'd come to like, and thought liked her, could do something so horrific.

"Tell me again what story you got the lead on?"

"We've gone over this already, Gage. I know I shouldn't have gone out that late at night in a storm. I'm the one who was in the accident. So as bad as you're trying to make me feel, it wasn't intentional. I didn't drive off the road on purpose." She was lucky she hadn't died. Everyone said so. She was also lucky that the car had not survived, otherwise Gage would have immediately seen through her lie. The car had exploded as they wheeled her into the ambulance.

"You didn't see him. You weren't with him when the call came over the radio." Gage's knuckles whitened around the steering wheel, a muscle pulsating in his jaw. "You survived, Vivi. But he died. He died last night."

She bowed her head, her throat tightening as she tried to hold back her tears. She'd overheard Matt talking to Paul in her room. They hadn't known she was awake. And Gage didn't know that hearing the state Chance was in just about killed her. She would do anything to make it up to him, but he wouldn't let her. He wouldn't take her calls. It wasn't fair. She hadn't gone looking for trouble. Trouble had come looking for her. Hot tears burned tracks down her face, falling onto Princess, who was curled up on her lap. Vivi moved her head so her hair fell forward, hiding her face from Gage. Princess looked up, then came to her on furry paws. Placing them on Vivi's chest, she licked the moisture from her cheeks. And that's when Vivi lost it, holding the only link she had left to Chance close to her chest. At least Princess loved her.

"Aw hell, honey." Gage moved her hair over her shoulder. "I didn't mean to make you cry. Come on now, you'll hurt your ribs. Five years ago we lost him, Vivi. And because of you, we got him back. He loves—"

"No, he doesn't. If he did, he couldn't walk away. I needed him. I needed him, and he left me," she sobbed. "I would never leave him. I would do anything I had to to protect him. All I wanted to do was protect him."

"Vivi, what do you mean all you wanted to do was to protect him? Protect him from what?"

That's what happened when she got emotional; she revealed too much. "Nothing, Gage. I didn't mean anything by it. I'm just tired and sore and heartbroken. Chance doesn't hold a license on heartache, you know."

"I know, honey." He turned onto the road to the cabin. "I don't think it's a good idea, you staying on your own. We'll pick up your things, and I'll take you home with me."

"I want to be here if he comes back." She caught the distressed look on Gage's face before he could hide it from her. Chance wasn't coming home. "You're right, I shouldn't be here. I just want to be alone for a little while. I've got some things to do. If you don't mind picking me up tonight, I'd appreciate it."

Vivi held a hopeful breath as Gage opened the garage door. Of course his truck wasn't there. Only a man who loved her would stick around to see if she was all right. To hold her hand while she was in the hospital. To bring her home the next day. Those thoughts fanned the small spark of anger that lay beneath her heartache, fueling the flame until slowly it burned away some of the pain.

Gage got out of the Suburban. "Let me just check around first, okay?"

She nodded. With Natalee on the loose, she'd feel safer if he did. *See that, McBride. I'm not stupid. I don't go looking for trouble.* Her eyes filled, blurring her vision. *Damn you, Chance, why did you leave me?* She scrubbed at her eyes. He left her for the same reason her mother did. He didn't love her enough.

Gage unlocked the door and walked inside. Vivi got out of the truck, letting Princess down to do her business. Much to the nurses' chagrin, Paul had let the dog stay with Vivi at the hospital. "It's just you and me now," she said to Princess, unable to keep a small warble from her voice. She'd have to find an apartment that allowed animals.

Gage appeared at the mudroom door, eyeing her carefully. "Are you sure you don't want me to stick around?"

"No, I'm good." She picked up Princess and made her way up the stairs.

He stepped back to let her pass. "Vivi, I know it may not feel like it right now, but Chance loves you."

"If he did, he'd be here." Princess struggled to get out of her arms, and she let her down.

As though Gage realized nothing he said would change her mind, he confirmed a time to pick her up and left. She locked the door behind him, then walked through to the living room and kitchen, scanning the space. She knew what she was doing and hated that she'd become so needy and emotional. She'd just been run off the road, and here she was, desperately searching for some sign that he'd been here, that he'd be back. That was not going to get her the answers she needed.

At the sound of Princess barking down the hall, she tensed. She was being ridiculous. Gage had done a walk-through. Then again, it had been a quick one. She pulled her phone from the back pocket of the jeans Skye had delivered this morning along with a white Envirochicks sweatshirt to replace her torn and bloodied clothes.

"Come here, Princess," Vivi called out, grabbing a rolling pin as she walked past the island. She followed the sound of Princess's anxious yips to the third bedroom. Muffled feminine sobbing came from within the room, and Vivi's lungs seized. She didn't know if she felt better that the sound was more human than otherworldly. "Who's there?" she said, picking up Princess and hugging her to her chest.

"It's me." The closet door slid open. Natalee sat huddled in the corner. She lifted her pale, blotchy face, rocking in place as tears trickled from her puffy, bloodshot eyes. "I'm sorry. I'm so sorry. I didn't want to do it. He... he made me do it."

Vivi crouched down. There was a part of her that wanted to reach out and comfort Natalee, but she held back. Although Kate's sister's words jibed with what Vivi had thought she'd seen, she reverted back to the more familiar and comforting habit of trusting no one. "Who made you do it?"

"Zach. He had a gun. I didn't want to hurt you, Vivi. Honest. Please, please believe me." Her eyes were pleading.

Her answer wasn't unexpected, but Vivi needed to understand Zach's motivation before she believed Natalee. It didn't make sense to her. At least not yet. "Why me? Why not Chance?"

"Because you were easier to get to than Chance. And Zach…he thought you were trying to break us up. I told him you weren't. I promised I wouldn't leave him if he'd leave you alone. But he freaked out after Chance brought him in for questioning. He was afraid they'd find out he was behind the break-ins. If you…if you died, Chance would go away again and leave him and his family alone. Zach hates Chance, Vivi. He wanted to make him pay for what he's done to his family. He wanted to make him suffer."

Zach Callahan was a twisted little bastard. And as twisted as he was, his plan would have made sense in his mind. But what didn't make sense was why Natalee hadn't left the guy a long time ago. Abuse? Maybe. But right now Vivi had something more pressing to worry about "Where's Zach? Does he know you're here?"

Natalee's eyes went wide and panicked. "No. He's at his house, I think. When he dropped me off at home after…" She held Vivi's gaze. "I didn't want you to die. But he was screaming at me and waving the gun around and every time I backed off, he'd put his foot over mine on the gas."

"Why involve you? Why didn't he just do it himself?"

"Because he wanted something else to hold over my head," she whispered.

"What do you mean, something else?" Whatever fine thread Natalee had been holding on to snapped at Vivi's question. She let go of Princess, who went immediately to the sobbing, broken young woman. Vivi did the same, taking her hand. "It's okay. Everything's going to be okay now."

"No, no it won't. It won't ever be okay. I did it. I killed my sister," she screamed through huge gulping sobs.

Vivi stared at the hysterical young woman who collapsed in her arms, unable to process Natalee's shocking admission. She had to be mistaken. She gently moved Natalee into a sitting position. "Talk to me, sweetie. Tell me why you think you're responsible for Kate's accident."

It took several halting tries before Natalee was able to tell Vivi what happened that long-ago night. She'd been at a party and had too much to drink. Shy, and more interested in her grades, Natalee didn't have many friends. She didn't need them; she had her sister and Chance. But all that changed at sixteen when she developed a crush on a boy from school. There was always a boy.

She wanted to fit in and be popular, catch his notice. She got more than she bargained for. Three boys had lured her into a bedroom. Natalee managed to get away and ran crying from the house. She walked almost a mile to get to the strip mall in the snowstorm and called her sister from the pay phone. Kate wanted to send Chance, but Natalee was embarrassed, and she'd been drinking underage. She didn't want her overprotective brother-in-law making trouble for the boys. She made Kate promise not to tell him. Forty minutes later, Zach Callahan pulled up in his four-by-four. Natalee had seen him around school. He was a nerd like her, and he seemed nice. She accepted a ride home. She was freezing, and her sister hadn't come to get her. She'd tried calling, but Kate didn't pick up. Zach brought Natalee home. He was with her when the deputies arrived at their door.

Vivi rocked her in her arms. She now understood the hold Zach had on Natalee for all these years, but it ended today. "It wasn't your fault, sweetie. It was just a horrible accident."

"Don't tell him. Don't tell Chance. He'll hate me. He'll never forgive me."

"Yes, he will. He loves you. And Natalee, he needs to know." So he'd stop blaming himself. But that's not something she'd say to Natalee. Vivi wouldn't be the one to tell him though. He'd shut her down again. Gage or his younger brother Easton would be able to reach him. "You have to tell your mother, too."

"No, I can't." She buried her face in her hands. "She'll hate me. Everyone will hate me."

"No, they won't. I know it won't be easy, but once this is out in the open, maybe you'll finally be able to stop hating yourself." She took Natalee's face between her hands. "You told me, and I don't hate you."

Natalee searched her face. "You don't?"

"No, I don't." She got up and helped Natalee to her feet. "We have lots to talk about, but now's not the time. I'm going to call Gage. Until Zach is behind bars, neither of us is safe." Vivi tried punching in Gage's number, but the phone didn't work. She briefly closed her eyes. She should've checked it before sending Gage on his way. "Do you have your phone with you?"

She shook her head. "I left it at home. I think Zach put a tracking device on it. He always seems to know where I am." Her eyes went wide. "My car."

This wasn't good. "I didn't see your car," she said, once again trying her phone.

A tinge of color pinked Natalee's cheeks. "I, uh, pulled it off the road into the trees."

Vivi remembered the night of the break-in when Chance found the tire tracks in the woods. "You've parked there before, haven't you?"

She nodded, her flush deepening. "I'm sorry. I just..."

"Not now. We have to get out of here." Vivi bent down to pick up Princess. The dog growled, surprising her. Her surprise turned to fear when Princess took off barking from the bedroom.

"Nat, I know you're here," Zach yelled. "Get out... Get away from me, you stupid mutt, or I'll shoot you."

\*       \*       \*

Chance came awake at the sound of someone approaching. He squinted against the morning sun to see his father with a bouquet of daisies in his hand. Chance rubbed his face and sat up. He hadn't meant to fall asleep, especially not here, lying in the grass beside his wife's grave.

His father lowered himself to the ground. "I thought you'd be gone by now."

So did he. From the hospital, he'd gone home and packed his duffle bag with every intention of leaving town. But slowly the realization that Vivi was alive drew him from the dark place he'd buried himself in. Or maybe it had been the anger he'd felt upon discovering a story had taken her from the safety of the cabin into the driving rain. Until that moment, he'd been dead inside.

"She's leaving the hospital this morning. Your brother's driving her home."

"To the cabin?" Everywhere he looked, she'd been there. The sauce she'd made on the back burner, the apron lying beside the couch, the dining room table laid out with candles and flowers. Her clothes on the floor of the bedroom where she'd walked out of them like she always did. Her vanilla-scented shampoo and the soap they'd shared in the shower after they'd made love that morning. He heard her laugh, saw her rare, radiant smile. A smile that wasn't so rare anymore.

The images of her had been as tough to escape as the woman. And he fought them as hard as he'd fought admitting that he loved her. It's why he'd come to Kate and Emma's grave. To remind himself of what loss felt like—only it had the opposite effect. He'd spent the night sitting in the rain talking to his dead wife. Telling her everything he hadn't had a chance to. Telling her about Vivi.

He drew his attention back to his father. Paul nodded, staring out over the rows of gravestones before turning to Chance with a sad look in his eyes. "It should be you driving her home, not your brother. You should have been with her at the hospital." His dad looked at the daisies in his hand. "Your mother and I raised you better than this. I know what hearing that call did to you. And how you felt when you thought you'd lost Vivi, too. I wouldn't wish what you went through on my worst enemy. But to walk away from her like you did? I'm disappointed in you, son. And that's not something I ever thought I'd say to you."

"Dad, I—"

"Don't interrupt me. I have more to say, and I'm damned well going to say it." Chance drew back in surprise at the change that had come over his mild-mannered father. "It's a lucky man who finds true love once in this life. Do you know how blessed you are to have found it twice? To have found a woman like Vivi? A woman who loves you as much as she does? A woman who, no matter how much you deny it, you love, too. I won't let you run away again because you're scared. So you just get that thought out of your head. We'll deal with this as a family. We'll get you some help. None of us knows how long we have, son. We have to—"

"Dad, do you think we could wrap this up? I'd like to pick up my girl from the hospital."

His father blinked, then grinned, slapping him on the shoulder. "Well, why didn't you say so?"

"I tried." Chance groaned as he came to his feet. Every muscle in his body ached. And his hand hurt like a son of a bitch. He reached out his good hand to help his father to his feet. "Dad, I'm sorry I was an ass about you marrying Liz. I thought I was protecting you, but I ended up messing things up for you instead. I want you to be happy. And I think Liz makes you happy. I can talk to her if you'd like."

"It wasn't entirely your fault, son. You may not have noticed, but I tend to overreact when anyone I care about gets hurt or sick. It drives Liz crazy."

"You don't say?"

"You're not funny." He eyed Chance's hand. "You need to get that looked at. And this"—he pointed to himself—"is me trying not to overreact, because that hand looks god-awful. So humor your old man and have it taken care of when you pick up Vivi."

"Yes, Dad."

"I love you." His dad hugged him, then handed him half his bouquet. "Kate always loved daisies."

"Yeah, she did," he said, looking at the flowers in his hand.

"She'd want you to be happy, son."

"I know she would, Dad." He did. And if he could convince Vivi to forgive him for screwing up again, he'd be a very happy man. He crouched by the grave to trace Kate's and Emma's names with his finger. "Good-bye, my golden girls. I'll always love you." He laid the flowers at the base of the white marble and walked away.

\*   \*   \*

Chance had missed Vivi by a couple of minutes, but his dad refused to let him leave before he had his hand looked at. Because, of course, his father had followed him to the hospital. Chance had tried to phone Vivi, but every one of his calls went straight to voice mail. His brother had finally returned the messages he'd left on his phone ten minutes ago. He'd just dropped Vivi at the cabin and tore a strip off Chance for hurting her. Which was why Chance paid a quick visit to Naughty and Nice, the ladies' high-end clothing store on Main Street, to buy a pair of red high heels and three boxes of chocolates from Sophia's sister-in-law Autumn, the owner of Sugar and Spice next door.

Tossing the bags in the front seat of his truck, Chance got in the driver's seat. His cell rang. He frowned at the caller ID. Jake Callahan was the last person Chance expected to hear from. "Hey, Jake, what—"

"It's him, McBride. You were right. He's behind the Drugstore Bandits. He's the goddamn ringleader." Jake sounded like he was close to losing it.

"Calm down. Start from the beginning. Are we talking about your dad or—"

"No, dammit. My baby brother." Chance heard another angry male voice in the background. "Mike and I got to talking last night. We wanted to clear Zach, so we searched his room and computer. It's all there. We found Vivi's laptop, too. And McBride, he had a couple of guns under his bed. We took them."

"Where is he now?"

"We don't know. We were out all night looking for him. He's not taking our calls. It looks like he came home, but there's no sign of him now."

"All right, stay out of his room. I'll put out an APB on Zach. Don't either you or Mike confront him if he comes home."

"He wouldn't—"

"You don't know that. I'll keep you informed. And Jake, I'm sorry. I really had hoped it wasn't Zach."

As soon as he disconnected from Jake, he called Gage. They'd meet up at the Callahans' once Chance picked up Vivi. Until Zach was in custody, he wasn't letting her out of his sight. After almost losing her, it would take more than Zach being behind bars to ease the need to keep her close. He suspected that was what was behind the nagging feeling in his gut, the one that had him breaking every speed limit to get home to her. And then he turned onto the cabin road and saw Callahan's white four-by-four parked outside the garage.

Chance quickly shut down his emotions before they incapacitated him. The only way to deal with the situation was to treat it as a job. He was real good at his job. And Vivi was smart. If anyone could handle Callahan until Chance took him out, it was her. He unlocked the glove compartment and retrieved his gun, weighing it in his left hand. Even broken, he'd shoot better with his right. He got out of the truck and walked to a tree, slamming the cast against it. Biting back a grunt of pain, he peeled the plaster off his hand and moved in.

Going in low and fast, he put his back to the wall and called his brother. "He's at the cabin. Come in quiet." He disconnected, pulling himself up to look into the second bedroom window. All clear. He eased it open.

"Shut up, you don't know what you're talking about," he heard Callahan say from the direction of the living room. At times like this, Chance wished he wasn't as big. It took some maneuvering to get through the window. He winced as he hit the floor with more noise than he intended.

"What was that?"

Chance took cover behind the door.

"Stop waving your gun around. A bird probably hit the window behind you. It happens all the time." He sagged with relief against the wall. Vivi was alive, and she sounded calm and in control. He'd never underestimate her again. She'd given him the information he needed without alerting Callahan. There was no doubt in Chance's mind that she knew someone had entered the house.

"Vivi's right, Zach. You don't have to do this. Your dad forced you to rob the drugstores. And Ray's okay and so is Vivi."

"You're forgetting, Nat. You ran her off the road, not me."

"You were holding a gun to her head, Zach. I'd say that negates her culpability, wouldn't you?"

*Slick, you've got some explaining to do*, he thought as he made his way down the hall with his back against the wall.

"I'm not turning myself in. We're leaving, Nat. Ow,

shit, she bit me. Call off that bitch if you don't want me to shoot her."

"She's just trying to protect Natalee. Go to your bed, Princess. Shoo, get going. That's a good girl."

Chance heard the clicking of Princess's nails as she raced toward him. He wished Vivi thought as much about her own safety as she did everyone else's. He picked Princess up, and she frantically licked his face. With a quick glance to his left, he moved to his bedroom and shut her in her cage. It was a smart move on Vivi's part. It was safer for everyone if the dog was locked away.

"No, I'm not going with you. Don't touch me!" Nat screamed.

"Natalee, look at me. It's better if you go with him. Zach loves you. He won't let anyone hurt you. He's right, you know. They won't believe that you're innocent."

"But..."

"It'll be okay. You go to the bathroom and freshen up. I'll pack you a bag. If you don't trust us, Zach, you can come along."

Chance ducked into his bedroom, praying that Callahan took the bait.

"Do you think I'm stupid? Of course I'm coming with you."

Chance smiled. Nat walked down the hall with Vivi following close behind her. Vivi cast a sidelong glance to the left. Chance made sure she saw him and winked. He stuck his gun in the waistband of his jeans. She'd know what to do.

She didn't disappoint. A foot in front of the bathroom, she grabbed Nat. Hurling them both into the bedroom, she slammed the door.

"You better open..." Zach began before Chance came up behind him and hooked one arm around his neck, pivoting him away from the door at the same time he smashed the kid's right hand against the wall. Zach screamed and dropped the gun. Chance kicked the kid's feet from under him, laying him out on the floor facedown. "Don't move, and keep your mouth shut." Jerking Zach's arms behind his back, Chance cuffed him, then texted Gage.

"Chance?"

Moving to the door, he opened it, drinking in the sight of Vivi before gently drawing her into his arms. He held her for a long moment, allowing the thought that she was alive and safe and in his arms to sink in. He turned at the sound of the front door opening. "Back here, Gage."

His brother, followed by Jill and the FBI and DEA agents, walked down the hall. The agents hauled a sobbing Zach to his feet. "Good job, Deputy," they said to Chance as Jill read Callahan his rights.

"Thanks, I had a good partner." He smiled down at Vivi, then looked at his brother as the others led Zach away. "Can you give us a minute?"

"Sure." Gage rubbed the back of his neck.

He narrowed his eyes at his brother. "What did you do?"

"It's a small town, you know how it works. Word got out, and I let everyone know you guys were all right. But I think they want to see for themselves. I figure you've got fifteen minutes tops before they all land on your doorstep." He leaned in and kissed the top of Vivi's head. "Glad you're all right, honey."

She gave him a tired smile. "Thanks."

Gage glanced at Natalee sitting on the end of the bed

with her head bowed, arms wrapped around her waist. "She okay?"

"I think so. I'll check on her in a minute."

As Gage walked away, Vivi dropped her head on Chance's chest. "I didn't think you were coming back."

"I told you I wouldn't walk away again." She tipped her head back. "I lost my way, but it's the last time that will ever happen. You're not getting rid of me, Slick." He smoothed his hands down her arms, searching for some sign of injury. "He didn't hurt you, did he?"

"No, I'm okay."

He looked over her head. "What about Nat?"

She glanced over her shoulder, then turned back to him. "She has something important to tell you. When she does, don't..." She searched his face and rested her palm against his cheek. "You'll handle it the right way."

"This have anything to do with you withholding information about your *accident*?"

She grimaced. "I had a good reason. I wasn't being a hothead or—"

He pressed a finger to her lips. "I'm sure you did. You can tell me all about it later." Then he lowered his head. "I love you."

She pressed her soft lips to his. As brief as that tender touch was, she told him everything he needed to know. She forgave him. As though to confirm it, she said, "I love you, too. Now go talk to Natalee."

\*    \*    \*

Chance lay beside Vivi on the blanket, staring up at the stars. It was the perfect ending to what had been an emotional roller coaster of a day. After five years of believing he'd been responsible for his wife's death, Nat had removed the burden of guilt in five minutes. In time, with some help from him, Vivi, and Mary, he hoped they could relieve Nat of hers. It wouldn't be easy. No one knew that better than Chance. But it was time to let Kate and Emma rest in peace.

Vivi, her head on his chest, murmured, "I didn't think they were ever going to leave."

"They may have got that when you opened the door and told them not to let it hit them on the ass."

"I did not say that."

"Not in so many words, but the intent was there." He stroked her hair, unable to hold back a yawn. "Don't worry about it. I'm glad you did."

She lifted her head. "You're beat."

"Yeah, I am. And so are you. I saw you nodding off when Nell, Stella, and Evelyn cornered you on the couch."

"I know you did. I couldn't make a move without you tracking me or following me. You're as bad as Princess."

"You have to cut me some slack, honey. It's going to take me some time to get…"

She leaned up and kissed him. "It's all right. I know you're going to be hypervigilant for a while."

"Might have to get used to a little more PDA, too."

"You know you're going to be able to play the sympathy card for only so long, right?"

"Jesus, you are such a hard-ass."

"You love my hard ass."

He patted her butt. "Yes I do. And I love your smart mouth, so maybe you can lay one on me right now."

"Lay one on you?"

"Yeah." He tapped his fingers to his lips. "Right here."

"I don't know. I think we should change it up a bit." She smiled then lowered her mouth to his chest, nipped her way down, soothing each love bite with a lick and a kiss.

He tunneled his fingers in her hair. Jesus, wrong hand. He couldn't contain his groan of pain. Vivi's head jerked up. Then she moaned and rubbed her neck. "This sucks," she said, lying back down beside him. She carefully lifted his hand to her mouth. "And first thing in the morning, we're going to the hospital to get a new cast put on. I thought your dad was going to have a heart attack when he saw your hand."

"Yeah, it was quite the performance. Hey, did you see him and Liz out on the dock together? They seemed to be getting along pretty good."

"Yes, well done, Grasshopper. Your aunt trained you well."

"You caught that, did you?"

"Oh, lover, when are you going to learn that nothing gets by me?"

"Lover?" He turned his head to look at her. "I think you just came up with a solution to our problem."

"We're going to have phone sex?"

"More like talk dirty." He got comfortable. "Okay, start talking, honey."

# Chapter Twenty-Seven

*Three months later*

Vivi threw open the door to Paul's house and rushed inside, her red high heel catching in the area rug. She grabbed the door in time to save herself from falling on her face.

"Careful, honey," Chance's dad called out from where he stood in front of the fireplace in his black tux. His blue eyes crinkled at the corners. "Little anxious to see my son, are you?"

"No, I…All right, I may be a tad anxious," she said with a self-conscious smile. Chance had been out of town on a job for two weeks. It had been the longest they'd been apart since they'd moved in together. And she'd hated every minute of it, though she wouldn't admit it to anyone, least of all Chance. She didn't want him to give up a job he loved because she missed him like crazy. His flight home had been delayed, and with the wedding scheduled for two this afternoon, he had to head straight to his dad's.

The sound of male laughter to her right had her taking an anxious step in that direction, but catching a glimpse of the framed photo in Paul's hand, she crossed the living room to his side instead. "You okay?" she asked, looking at a wedding photo of Paul and Anna with their best friends, Liz and Deacon.

"I'm good, honey." He placed the photo back on the mantel, skimming his finger over Anna's smiling face. "Time goes by so fast. It's hard to believe we were married almost forty years ago." He turned to Vivi with a half smile. "And here I am getting married again."

She straightened his bow tie. "Yes, and you look as handsome as you did then. Liz is a lucky woman."

"I'm the lucky one."

Vivi released a sigh of relief. She'd been worried he was getting cold feet and she'd have to stage an intervention. "You both are." Reaching up, she kissed his cheek. "Happy wedding day."

"Thanks, honey." He placed his hands on her shoulders and dipped his head to look in her eyes. "My son is a very lucky man. Lucky to have found you. And one day in the not-too-distant future, I expect him to make an honest woman out of you."

Good God, she couldn't deal with this right now. She'd put the latest debacle with Nell out of her head, and it had to stay out of it or she'd strangle the older woman and ruin the wedding. Which is probably why her laugh sounded forced rather than amused. "I don't mind being a dishonest woman. We're both happy to keep things the way they are."

It was true. She'd come to terms with the fact that Chance would never marry her. He loved her, and that was good enough for Vivi. Okay, so there might be a small part of her, extremely small—infinitesimal, really—that might have been holding on to some faint hope that a few years from now he'd change his mind. Otherwise, Nell hijacking yesterday's issue of the *Chronicle* and including a fake Dear Vivi letter from Superman asking Lois Lane to marry him wouldn't have set her off the way it did. She didn't even want to think what Chance would have thought or done had he seen it.

But he wouldn't. No one would. Because Vivi had caught his wedding-obsessed aunt's latest attempt at manipulating them before the paper had gone out and now had a trunk full of undelivered newspapers. As a precaution, she'd shut down the paper's Twitter and Facebook pages.

"I'm not sure I believe you, but I'll let it go. For now." He smiled, then nudged his head in the direction of the bedroom. "Go say hello to him. And tell them to hurry up or we'll be late."

Which wouldn't be good because Liz would think Paul had gotten cold feet. Again. Over the last couple of months, they'd driven everyone crazy going back and forth about the wedding. Nell had taken matters into her own hands three weeks ago, arranging for Chance and Ethan to drop their respective parents off at an isolated cabin on Blue Mountain and drive away. As much as Vivi didn't want to give the old meddler credit, she had to. Nell's plan had worked. With Liz and Paul anyway. But it was not going to work with Vivi and Chance.

Her stomach twisted in an anxious, angry knot and Vivi shoved Nell and the Dear Vivi letter out of her head, following the sound of male voices to Paul's bedroom. She stood outside the door and smoothed down her short black dress with red leather piping. Hefting a red leather bag onto her shoulder, she knocked.

"Hope you're decent, boys, because I'm coming in." She opened the door and pressed a hand to her chest at the jaw-dropping sight that greeted her. Three stunningly handsome men in various states of undress. They were lucky their aunt hadn't walked in on them or they would have found themselves on the front page of the *Chronicle*. Or at the very least as the Christmas Cutie feature of the week.

Chance, who'd been standing at the window on the phone, turned. Those grass-green eyes of his smiled at her before taking a slow and very thorough tour of her body, the smile in his eyes making it to his firm lips when he reached her shoes. Her eyes took their own tour. He looked good enough to eat standing there in an unbuttoned white dress shirt, the top button of his black pants open and riding low on his hips. She was about to run across the room and throw herself into his arms when he held up two fingers.

All right, that wasn't exactly the reunion she'd been hoping for. He turned back to the window, tunneling his fingers through his hair. "Give me a break. My plane just landed four hours ago. I'm not going out on another job this soon. Find someone else."

She briefly closed her eyes at the thought of Chance leaving again. It took some effort to force a smile on her face for his brothers. But when she turned to them, Gage and Easton were focused on Chance. They didn't look any happier than she felt. In fact, they looked more than a little concerned.

"What's going on?" she asked Easton. If anyone would know, it would be Chance's baby brother. He'd recently accepted an offer to work for the same security company as Chance. Only Easton, as a computer specialist, could work from anywhere. Rumor had it he was moving home. His father wasn't the only one happy about the prospect. So were the single women in Christmas. Easton McBride was as jaw-droppingly gorgeous as his brothers.

He glanced at Gage before turning eyes the same brilliant blue as his father's on Vivi. Easton limped toward her. He'd been badly wounded in a mortar attack six months ago. He'd been lucky to have survived, let alone keep his leg.

Placing his hands on her shoulders, he looked over her head at Chance, whose voice had grown quieter. "If they manage to strong-arm him into taking the assignment, talk him out of it, Vivi."

She searched his face, her chest tightening at what she saw there. "It's dangerous?"

"It's a fuc ... It's a suicide mission."

"Can't they get someone else? He just got back."

"They want him. He's the best they've got."

"Easton's right, Vivi," Gage said, his eyes on Chance. "You're the only one he'll listen to. If you tell him not to go, he won't."

"I can't do that. He loves his job. I can't..." Noting she'd lost Gage's and Easton's attention, she trailed off. Both men were making a show of buttoning their shirts.

Arms went around her waist, and Chance lowered his face to the side of hers, drawing her back to his chest. "But he loves you more."

She tipped her head, resting it on his shoulder to look into his eyes. "And I love you and want you safe, but I don't want you to—"

He smiled against her lips. "Shut up and kiss me." He lifted his hand to wave off his brothers. At least she thought that was what he did. She was too busy doing what he asked her to to notice or care. Greedy for the feel of his mouth on hers, for his tongue tangling with hers and the promise of what was to come, she turned in his arms without breaking their connection. Sliding her hands up his warm, hard chest, she ignored their audience's snorts of laughter.

"All right, you... Oh." She heard the smile in Paul's voice. "Sorry to break it up, you two, but if we're not out of here in five minutes, we'll be late."

When Chance lifted his mouth from hers, it took everything she had to hold back a disappointed groan. He smiled down at her, and it finally hit her that she'd just kissed the hell out of him in front of his family. Heat climbed her cheeks as she planted her forehead in his bare chest.

"Give us a minute," Chance said, stroking her hair. She felt the silent laughter rumbling through his chest and pinched him. Of course he'd think it was funny. "E, what the hell is that on your neck?" he asked his brother.

"Let me have a look at that, son," his father said, a note of concern in his voice.

"Dad, I'm fine. It's..." Easton sighed.

Gage laughed. "Stop fussing with him, Dad. It's a

hickey. He and Cat got reacquainted last night at the rehearsal party, didn't you, little brother?"

Vivi's curiosity won out over her embarrassment, and she lifted her head to glance at a red-faced Easton. Cat had been acting weird at the rehearsal party, and she wondered if Easton was the reason why. Vivi'd had only a brief conversation with Cat before the dinner, leaving immediately afterward because she didn't trust herself around Nell.

"Uh, son, did Cat have long hair or short at the time you were . . . getting reacquainted?"

"Cat has short hair, Dad. I . . ." His eyes narrowed at his father. "Do not tell me they did that switch thing they used to do as kids?" Paul grimaced. "I don't freaking believe this."

"Chloe got herself in a little situation, so she thought it would be best if she and Cat traded places for the weekend."

"What did she do now?" Easton muttered, then held up his hand. "Don't tell me. I don't want to know."

"I do," Chance said.

"Me too," said Gage.

So did Vivi, but at that exact same moment, she felt something on Chance's chest that drew her attention. She moved his shirt and, at the sight of the new ink on his chest, squeezed her eyes shut. Beneath "Never Forget Kate and Emma" was "Always Remember Vivi." A sob bubbled up inside her, and she swallowed convulsively in an attempt to contain the sound. She couldn't cry. She'd just indulged in major PDA in front of his family, she would not cry in front of them, too. And then it happened, and there was nothing she could do to stop them—big fat, sloppy tears rolled down her cheeks. She rested her forehead against Chance's chest in hopes he wouldn't...

"Hey, honey, what's wrong?" He leaned back, tipping her chin up with his fingers. His worried gaze searched her face.

She shook her head, swiping at her eyes. "Nothing." The word came out garbled.

"She's probably upset about you taking the job," Easton said, moving to her side to rest a comforting hand on her shoulder.

"He's not taking the job," Gage said, rubbing her back.

"What job are your brothers talking about, Chance?" Paul came to stand beside her, stroking her hair as he looked at his son.

"Relax, Dad. I'm not taking the assignment. I think it's about time I went out on my own." He dipped his head. "Does that make you feel better, honey?"

"Um-hm." She nodded, still trying to get her emotions under control.

"About time," Gage said, and Easton and his father enthusiastically agreed. Vivi would too if she could stop her damn sniffling. She didn't know what was wrong with her. Maybe it was because she was so glad to finally have Chance home, and thanks to Nell, she'd had such a nerve-wracking day yesterday.

"Ethan would be interested in hiring you to do investigative work, you know," Gage added.

When Paul and Easton began suggesting other opportunities, Chance cut them off. "Okay, guys, thanks. Now if you don't mind, I'd like a few minutes alone with my girl. We'll meet you at the ranch."

Paul, Easton, and Gage each kissed her on the head, then gathered up their jackets from the bed and left. "The wedding's at two, so—" Paul began.

"Two minutes," Chance said, looking down at her when his dad shut the door. "Are you going to tell me what the tears are all about?"

"This." She trailed her fingers over the tattoo, blinking as fresh tears welled in her eyes. "You burned me into your heart, too."

"You were always there, Vivi."

"Do not say stuff like that or you'll have me blubbering like an idiot." She covered her face with her hand. "What am I talking about? I am blubbering. I was blubbering. In front of your family. And I was making out with you, too. What are they going to think of me?"

"That I'm a lucky man." He removed her hand from her face. "They love you, Slick. They consider you part of the family." He ducked his head. "You sure there's nothing wrong? Everything okay with the paper?"

"Why? What—"

His gaze roamed her face. He seemed confused and maybe a little bit worried. No surprise, since she totally overreacted. "This week's issue didn't go out, Vivi. I was just wondering—"

"How did you know that?"

"Ah, is there something we need to talk about? You seem tense."

She was so going to kill Nell. "No, there was a problem with the printer, and I couldn't get the issue out on time. It sucks because Natalee did such a great job with her story. But it's okay, I'll run it next week." Forcing a smile, she began doing up his buttons. "Can't waste time talking about that now. You have to get ready. We don't want to be the reason the wedding is delayed."

\*     \*     \*

Vivi watched Chance and his brother head down the path to where the ceremony was being held. She didn't know if she was happy Easton had decided to hitch a ride with them to the ranch or not. Yes, it had saved any further discussion about the reason the paper didn't go out, but there was something going on with Chance. He seemed quiet. Distracted, even. And every so often she'd catch him watching her with a look of concern. What did she expect after her performance?

Then again, it probably had nothing to do with her. He'd just quit a job that he loved. Though he hardly seemed upset about it. Ten minutes into the ride to the ranch, Chance and his brother had decided to go into the security business together. They'd keep it small and in Colorado. Which Vivi was all for. So maybe his mood did have something to do with her.

"Chance." She started across the lawn after him, cursing the high heels as they sank into the grass.

He said something to his brother, then turned. His mouth twitched at her ungainly approach, and he walked toward her, meeting her halfway. "I know you'd probably rather be wearing flip-flops, Slick, but promise me you'll keep those shoes on." He tucked her hair behind her ear. "Did I tell you how crazy beautiful you look today?"

And that was another thing, he hadn't. She gave him a half smile and shook her head. "No, but thank you. You look crazy beautiful, too." She took the lapels of his tux in her hands and reached up to kiss the underside of his jaw.

"I'm sorry I was an idiot earlier. I love your tattoo, and I love you. I missed you."

He covered her hands with his. "Is that all you wanted to tell me?"

"Yes, I... Why? Are you upset about something?"

"No, of course not." He kissed her forehead. "I missed you, too, honey. I better go."

And he did, and Vivi didn't miss the fact he hadn't told her *he* loved *her*. *Don't be an idiot*, she berated herself as she made her way into the house, *he doesn't have to say it every time you do.*

She walked through the living room, backtracking at the sight of the gorgeous, long-haired brunette in the pumpkin-orange dress sprawled in a wing-back chair. "Cat?"

"How did you know it's me?"

"Your sister doesn't sit as elegantly as you do, and she doesn't pinch the bridge of her nose when she's ticked off."

Cat nodded. "You're good. No one else seems to be able to tell the difference." She rose to her feet.

"So I heard. Chloe made out with Easton last night, and he thought it was you."

Cat made a face. "I know. Chloe thought he knew it was her." She itched her head, the wig moving when she did. "Why do I let her talk me into this crap? Now every time I look at the wedding photos, this is what I'm going to see." She scratched her head again. "I should have made her cut her hair."

"Or you could have just said no."

"Right. You forget who pays my salary."

Vivi leaned against the back of the couch. "What's going on?"

Cat sighed. "Remember when I was home for the wedding in May and stayed for a couple of weeks?" Vivi nodded. "Well, my gullible sister fell for a guy who forgot to tell her he was married. Since she's a complete Anglophile and he's a Brit, it probably wouldn't have mattered to Chloe that he was. But it mattered to his wife, who caught them in flagrante delicto. And Lady Whatever threatened to kill Chloe, so"—Cat lifted her hands—"here I am."

"You don't really think she's in danger, do you?"

"No, but try—"

"All right, let's get the show on the road," Chloe said as she strode toward them wearing a short-haired wig and a short pumpkin-orange dress. She winked at her sister. "Sounded just like you, didn't I?"

"Shoot me now," Cat muttered.

Vivi fought back a smile. Chloe was a better actress than she'd given her credit for. They were joined in the living room by Maddie, Skye, Lily with Evie in her arms, and Annie with Connor in hers. Maddie and Skye wiped at their eyes. "What's wrong?" Vivi asked.

"Ethan and Liz just had a moment," Skye said with a watery smile.

"Oh, and I missed it." Chloe pressed her hands to her chest. "Come on, Kit Kat, let's have a moment with Mommsy, too."

"This should be an interesting day," Maddie said once the two women were out of earshot. "I take it you heard what happened last night after you left?" When Vivi nodded, Maddie asked, "Are you feeling better?"

"Yeah, why..." Oh, right, she'd said she had a headache. "Yes, much better, thanks."

Maddie's and Skye's eyes narrowed at her.

Thankfully, before they could question her further, Annie said, "I have to get out there," and moved to hand Connor, who wore an adorable black tux, to Vivi.

"Wait." Vivi held up a hand and fished an animal cracker from the box in her bag. "Okay, you can give him to me now." Annie grinned and put Connor in Vivi's arms. She handed him the cookie, and he gave her a drooly smile.

Evie grunted, holding her arms out to Vivi and making grabby motions with her hands. Vivi dug a couple more animal crackers from her purse.

"Vivi, do not feed them throughout the entire ceremony," Maddie warned when Lily transferred Evie to Vivi's other arm.

"Of course I won't. Okay, babies," she said, handing Evie her cookie and getting a wet kiss on the cheek in exchange, "wave bye to your mommies." The kids did as she said, and she started for the door. "Ah, hang on. Lily, can you help me with my shoes?" She didn't want to trip while carrying Connor and Evie. Lily took off her shoes and stuffed them in Vivi's purse.

Matt Trainer, looking handsome in his black tux, opened the door for her. He smiled. "I think you forgot something." He nodded toward her feet.

"Safer this way," she said, looking to where the McBride men stood by a gazebo decorated in autumn leaves with black urns filled with orange and yellow flowers on either side.

Matt rested his hand on the small of her back. "I'll take you to your seat." He chuckled when Connor tried to shove a cookie in his mouth. "Thanks, buddy," Matt said, "but I'm good."

Black iron pots filled with tall grass and fall flowers sat on either side of the aisle. The wooden chairs were already filled with guests. As Matt guided Vivi onto the burlap runner decorated with orange and yellow rose petals, everyone turned in their seats.

Fred leaned into the aisle. "People are wondering where their papers are," the older man stage-whispered.

Of course everyone heard him, and that started a chorus of, "I didn't get mine. Me either. Are they coming today?"

Vivi forced a smile. "Problem with the printer. You'll get it next week. Promise." She walked faster, but they kept calling after her.

"But our sale's this week," someone yelled.

"Are you okay, Vivi? You're flushed," Matt said.

"Good. I'm good." She furtively wiped her sweaty brow on Connor's head.

"Thanks, Matt. I'll take it from here," Chance said, sliding an arm around her waist.

"What are you doing? Get up there with your dad and brothers."

"No, not until you tell me what's going on with you." He guided her toward a seat in the front row. The one right beside his aunt Nell. Vivi dug in her heels. "No, I can't sit there."

"Slick, sit. You look like you're going to—"

"What the Sam Hill is wrong with you, girlie? You're all sweaty and flushed."

"I'm warning you, Nell. Don't talk to me. This is all your fault."

"My fault? How is it—"

"I know what…" She leaned in and whispered so Chance wouldn't hear her. "I know it was you who wrote the Dear Vivi letter. And it's not going to work, so just stop it, okay?"

Chance took Connor and Evie from her, handing them off to Gage and Easton, then he returned to crouch in front of her. "Vivi, look at me."

"No, you don't understand." She shot a quick glance over her shoulder and groaned. "Chance, everyone's looking at us. Get back up there with your dad and brothers. The wedding's about to start," she said, waving to where Annie stood at the microphone with strains of Train's "Marry Me" playing in the background.

He took both her hands in his. "It wasn't Aunt Nell, honey. It was me. I wrote you the letter."

"No, you couldn't have. You don't want to get married. And Superman asked Lois Lane to marry her in the letter."

Nell jumped to her feet. "Stop the wedding! Stop the music!"

"Nell, what are you doing? I thought you wanted me and Liz to get married," Paul said.

At the same time Vivi was dying of embarrassment, Chance was going down on one knee.

Her head jerked up, her heart hammering in her chest. "It really was you. You want to marry me?"

"Yeah, I do."

"Praise the Lord. Hallelujah."

"Aunt Nell," Chance muttered as he reached into his pocket and took out a black velvet box. He shifted to look back at his father. "You okay with me doing this now?"

Paul beamed. "I couldn't ask for a better wedding present, son."

"Oh, God, Chance, I've ruined everything."

He smiled at her. "The only way you could ruin it, Slick, is if you say no."

"No, I mean yes . . . yes!" She launched herself into his arms.

\*     \*     \*

Under the tent, Vivi swayed in Chance's arms to John Legend's "All of Me." Her arms looped around his neck, she lifted her hand to admire her platinum, diamond, and sapphire engagement ring sparkling under the fairy lights. It was perfect, just like the man who held her in his arms.

He smiled down at her. "You like it?"

"No, I love it. Almost as much as I loved your proposal. It was beautiful and romantic. Everyone thought so." And they'd all had the opportunity to read his proposal because Nell and her friends had snuck out to Vivi's SUV during the dinner and unloaded the newspapers. Since Vivi had felt bad about hijacking the paper, she didn't mind. She'd wanted everyone to read Natalee's article. She was a fabulous writer, and the message of how harmful keeping secrets can be was an important one.

While editing the article, Vivi realized she had her own secret to deal with and had finally worked up the courage to contact Brooke and Finn. She didn't know if they'd ever have a real sibling relationship, but at least they were communicating. And of course she'd wanted everyone to read Superman's letter to Lois Lane.

"You don't think your dad and Liz minded us stealing some of their thunder, do you?"

"Are you kidding? Look at them. They're oblivious to anyone but each other."

He was right. The couple were in the middle of the dance

floor, staring into each other's eyes. They looked beautiful and happy. And so did everyone else. Beside them, Maddie danced with Gage, Lily with her baby brother, Annie with Evie, and Skye with Ethan, and Lauren sat on Ray's lap as he moved his wheelchair to the music.

And in that moment, Vivi realized she'd found everything she'd always dreamed of and never truly believed she'd ever have in the small town of Christmas. She supposed that shouldn't come as a surprise after what she'd uncovered while researching Christmas's history. There was a reason dreams came true in the small town. And if she didn't think she'd ignite another feud between the Danes, O'Connors, and McBrides, she'd write a series of articles for the *Chronicle*.

She had no doubt those articles would bring her the journalistic attention she'd always craved. But the need for recognition in her chosen career didn't drive her like it used to. No, for the first time she could remember, Vivi Westfield was happy with her life just the way it was. And she had her husband-to-be to thank for that.

"What are you thinking about?"

She smiled up at him. "You. Thank you for making me a very happy woman today. I love you."

"It's dangerous to give me the sweet in the middle of the dance floor, Slick. You know that, don't you?"

"You love the sweet."

"I do, and I love you," he said, lowering his mouth to hers.

When several people laughingly shouted, "Get a room!" Chance broke the kiss. "Let's go home."

"I think your dad and Liz have the same idea," she said as Paul walked off the dance floor with his wife in tow.

"Time to toss the bouquet, folks," Paul announced, turning Liz's back to the crowd. The dance floor cleared, then filled with the single women from town.

Chance pulled out a chair at the friends and family table. Sitting down, he drew Vivi onto his lap. "My bet's on Aunt Nell to catch the bouquet."

"Sophia," Skye said, and Vivi agreed, clinking their wine glasses together.

"Lily," Maddie said.

"Well, it sure as hell won't be Cat," Ethan said, pointing to where his sister stood to the back of the crowd with her arms crossed. Chloe jumped up and down in front of her, waving her arms.

Liz tossed the bouquet. The mass of yellow and orange roses tied with champagne satin sailed over everyone's heads...and hit Cat square in the chest. Since Cat didn't make a move to grab the bouquet, her sister did.

They all laughed, and then Gage groaned. "Aunt Nell's got that look in her eyes again."

Vivi turned to see Nell standing to the side of the dance floor with her head cocked, studying Cat with a familiar expression on her face. As if Nell sensed their attention, she grinned in their direction and wiggled five fingers.

Easton, who'd hung out at the bar most of the night, joined them. Frowning at his aunt, he pulled out a chair. "Why's Aunt Nell grinning like a loon and waving at you guys?"

"She's not waving, little brother. She's just set her sights on her victim for the next book in her series," Gage said, and looked at Chance and Vivi. "Let's hope there's not as much excitement in that book as yours."

"If the ending turns out as happy as ours, I hope there is."

Maddie laughed. "Says the woman who didn't believe in happy ever after."

"Because there was only one man who could give me mine"—she cupped Chance's face in her hand—"and I didn't think he'd be willing to take a chance on me."

"There you go giving me the sweet again." He turned his face to kiss her palm, then raised his grass-green eyes to hers. "You may not have been my first love, but you are my last." He stood with her in his arms. "Let's go home, Lois."

Cat O'Connor is no actress, but she finds herself filling in for her identical twin sister—soap opera star Chloe O'Connor. Then Cat finds herself falling in love with her sister's aristocratic British boyfriend…

Is it the role of a lifetime?

Please see the next page for

a preview of

*Snowbound at Christmas.*

# Chapter One

Sprawled in a white club chair in her sister's bubblegum-pink dressing room, Cat O'Connor added up the numbers of the job-satisfaction quiz she'd just taken. It wasn't like she needed a quiz to tell her that she was dissatisfied, but she didn't have anything else to occupy her time. Whoever thought the entertainment industry was exciting had never been on the set of a daytime soap opera from seven in the morning until seven at night. Mind. Crushingly. Boring.

Okay, so sitting in an unmarked car on a stakeout had been kind of boring, too. But at least there'd been the potential for excitement. Nothing beat the thrill of taking some lowlife off the street. Of taking... She briefly closed her eyes. She couldn't go there. Couldn't think of the hell the FBI had put her through and what she'd been forced to give up.

Refocusing on the magazine, she read the level that

corresponded to her score. "Danger Zone! You are burned out. Leave your job immediately before you destroy your mental and physical well-being."

Cat tossed the magazine onto the table. It was true. She couldn't put it off any longer. Working for Chloe was sucking the life out of her. She felt like she was fifty instead of thirty-one. She pinched her stomach through the *I Love Tessa Hart* T-shirt that Chloe insisted Cat wear to work and jiggled the quarter inch of fat between her fingers. Her identical twin wasn't driving Cat to drink— she was driving her to eat donuts. Cat had consumed more donuts in the year that she'd worked for Chloe than in her five years with the Denver PD.

She stood up and bounced on the balls of her feet, shaking out her hands. She'd do it today. As soon as Chloe returned from blocking out her scene, Cat would tell her. She'd been protecting Chloe since they came out of the womb five minutes apart. Something her sister would no doubt deny, but it was true. Pudgy, with an overbite and a lazy eye, her nose always buried in a book, her head in the clouds, Chloe had needed Cat's protection from grade school through high school. She didn't need it now.

Cat tensed when the door opened and Chloe swept into the dressing room wearing a ruffled peach dress and matching high heels, her long, wavy dark hair flowing down her back. Sinking gracefully onto the chair Cat had just vacated, Chloe brought the back of her hand to her brow with a dramatic sigh.

Cat opened her mouth to say *I quit* at the same time her sister said, "Kit Kat, I need my pills. Get me my pills, please."

What she needed was a swift kick in the derriere. But

instead of acting on the thought, Cat retrieved the prescription bottle from her sister's makeup table. Calm Chloe was easier to deal with than Dramatic Chloe. Unbeknownst to her sister, they were sugar pills. Their sister-in-law Skye had come up with the idea as a way to deal with Chloe's panic attacks. Or as Cat privately referred to them, her Scarlett O'Hara act. Most of the time they worked.

Cat opened the bottle and shook two pills into her sister's waiting palm. Chloe raised a perfectly plucked brow. "I need something to wash them down. Did you get my tea?"

Oh, she got her tea, all right. She'd scoured the streets of LA looking for her Anglophile sister's special British brew. Thanks to gridlock traffic, it took Cat three hours to get back to the studio in Burbank this morning. Stifling a sarcastic retort, Cat poured the freshly steeped tea, timed as always to be ready for Chloe's return, into the Royal Doulton teacup.

Her pinky raised oh-so-daintily in the air, Chloe took a sip, then pulled a face. "Kit Kat, this is not the brand I asked for."

Silently counting to ten as she retrieved the yellow box from the shelf, Cat held it up. "*This* is what you told me to buy."

And this was why she had to quit. Not only was she bored, Chloe was driving her insane. At times, Cat wanted to strangle her. She wouldn't, of course, but their relationship had suffered. Cat loved her sister, but lately she didn't like her very much.

"Well, it's not the one I want." Chloe pursed her peach-glossed lips, then waved her hand. "Don't worry about it.

I have an hour until I have to be on set. You have time to get me the right—"

"I'm not going to buy you more tea." Cat rubbed her sweaty palms on her jeans. It was now or never. "Chloe, I have something important to talk to you about."

"Me too." Chloe cast her a sidelong glance, then popped the pills in her mouth. She took a sip of tea.

"I'm quitting."

Chloe choked, motioning for Cat to pat her back. Cat sighed and leaned over, doing as her sister directed. Chloe's rapid blinking caused her bottom and top false eyelashes to stick together. While tugging her lid from her eyeball, she squinted at Cat. "You're quitting? But you love working for me."

It wasn't an act. Chloe saw what she wanted to see. And the genuine confusion on her sister's face only added to Cat's guilt. Which Chloe erased with the next words out of her mouth. "Is it because I get all the attention?" She gave Cat a commiserating smile. "I understand how difficult it is to feel invisible, you know. But where else would you make the kind of money I'm paying you for doing, well, nothing?"

There was so much Cat could say to that, but it wouldn't do her any good. Better to leave with their relationship somewhat intact. "Since I don't do *anything*, you shouldn't need two weeks' notice." She headed for the door before her sister inserted her foot in her mouth again, and Cat said something she'd regret.

"You're leaving now?" Chloe asked, a hint of panic in her voice.

"I thought I'd go home and start packing. Book my flight. Don't worry, I'll be back in time to pick you up."

Just one more of her duties. Cat was Chloe's chauffeur as well her bodyguard, manager, and gopher. A smile played on her lips. Not anymore she wasn't. Warm, giddy relief flooded her body. She'd bask in the freedom for a few days before facing the reality of finding a job.

Chloe flapped both hands in front of her face. "Kit Kat, I don't think the pills worked. I feel faint."

Cat walked over and shoved her sister's head between her legs. "Just breathe. Not like that," she said when Chloe started braying like a donkey. Dammit, she was not letting her suck her back in. Chloe was a hypochondriac. There was nothing wrong with her. Cat removed her hand from her sister's head and crossed to the makeup table, opening a drawer to take out a brown paper bag. As soon as Chloe put it over her mouth and nose, her breathing evened out.

Lowering the bag, Chloe lifted pleading green eyes. "Kit Kat, I know you have much more important things to take care of, but"—she swallowed convulsively, rubbing her chest—"I have a physical scene this afternoon. And after my spell, I worry about my heart. I'd hate to think how guilty you'd feel if I dropped dead when you so easily could take my place."

As Cat opened her mouth to say no, Chloe continued. "I don't like to bring it up, but..." She brought it up all the time. Her sister was a delicate flower with the mind of a Venus flytrap. "If you hadn't been so greedy in the womb and sucked up all the oxygen, I wouldn't have been born with a hole in my heart. So the least you can do is this one small favor for me."

Chloe wasn't exaggerating. Much. She had been born with a hole in her heart and spent the first month of her life in a NIC unit. Up until the age of four, she'd been in and out of the hospital before the hole closed on its own. When they were growing up, their parents had overprotected Chloe, treating her like an invalid. In Cat's opinion, that had been more damaging than the hole had ever been.

She supposed she shouldn't cast stones. Like her parents, Cat enabled her sister, too. And while intellectually she knew she was making matters worse, emotionally, she couldn't seem to help herself. Which was the reason why, an hour later, she awkwardly lowered herself into the stylist chair wearing a tight black pencil skirt and black bustier.

"Wipe the smirk off your face, Ty," Cat said, adjusting the satin top.

"*Moi*, smirk? I think not, my darling pussy." Ty, in his uniform of skinny black pants and tight T-shirt, grinned at her in the mirror. "If you're going to keep doing this, you should consider extensions." He tugged on Cat's wig, and it slipped to the side. In her senior year of high school, Cat lopped off her long locks after another episode of trading places with her sister had gone horribly wrong.

Tutting, Ty reached across her for the bobby pins.

The hairstylist was one of her favorite people on the set of *As the Sun Sets*. She'd miss him when she left. But he was about the only thing she'd miss. She didn't like Hollywood. Or Hollyweird, as she thought of it. "This is the last time."

"That's what you said two weeks ago."

"I quit, Ty. Today is my last day on the set. I'm heading home on Monday." She winced when he jabbed her scalp with a bobby pin.

"I nearly lost my lunch." He patted her head. "Don't scare me like that ever again."

"I'm serious. I'm leaving."

Pressing his palms together, he rested his chin on the tips of his manicured fingers and looked at her mournfully through large, square, red-framed glasses. She sighed. She loved him, but he was as much a drama queen as her sister. "I'm going to miss you, too. But I'll see you in a couple of weeks when you come to Christmas."

When Chloe heard the production team was looking for a location in the mountains to film their holiday segments, she'd suggested their hometown, putting them in contact with Madison McBride, the town's mayor, who offered free room and board to sweeten the pot. It didn't take much sweetening after the production team got a look at Christmas.

Nestled in a valley at the foot of the Rocky Mountains, the small town was a nature lover's dream. Cat was proud of her hometown with its friendly people and old-world charm. But it was the recently completed Santa's Village that had sealed the deal.

Ty swept the back of his hand dramatically across his cheek. "Who is going to vet my dates and make sure I'm safe? And who is going to let me cry on their shoulder when I get my heart broken?" He wrapped his arms around her neck, meeting her eyes in the mirror. "Pussy, you can't leave me."

One of the crew walked by with George, the classically handsome man who played Chloe's on-screen husband, Byron Hart. "Chloe, remember?" Cat whispered. No one could know she was taking her sister's place. Cat wasn't a member of the Screen Actors Guild.

He straightened, fluffing her hair. "You're leaving because your sister is such a biatch, aren't you?"

"No, it's time for me…" The set manager called

Chloe's name. "We'll go out this weekend. I'll bring Chloe along. If you give her a chance, I think you two could be friends."

He flipped up his hand. "Just because I'm a fairy doesn't mean I have a magic wand that will turn your sister into you."

Cat rolled her eyes and turned to walk away.

"Hang on." Ty grabbed her arm and shoved two more bobby pins in her hair. "Be careful. Brunhilda attacks you in this scene, and after your sister pushed for the change that cut down her on-air time, she won't hold back," he said, referring to the redheaded actress Molly. She'd tried out for the part of Tessa Hart and ended up with the lesser role of Tessa's backstabbing sister Paula.

Cat thanked him for the warning and headed for the set. Walking without tripping in the mile-high shoes was one thing; walking with the elegant grace of her sister, another. Ten minutes at the most, Cat reminded herself, and she'd be out of here for good. The thought lightened her step as she walked onto what served as the foyer of the Hart mansion.

She smothered a gasp when her heel shot out from under her on the polished black-and-white marble, clamping a hand on her head to keep her wig in place. Once she regained her balance, she made a show of checking her shoe.

"Tessa darling, are you all right?" The silver-haired Byron called down from the top of the ornate wooden staircase.

Cat frowned. *Tessa darling*? Then shrugged. What did she know? Maybe he liked to get into character before taping. She acknowledged his concern with a small wave and took her mark, mentally going over the scene she'd practiced with Chloe earlier.

All she had to do was keep Molly from pulling off her wig. Piece of cake. Cat had a black belt and had aced her defensive tactics training. But when the bell chimed and she opened the mansion's door to the redhead, Cat had an aw-hell moment. She'd never fought in heels on a slippery floor. She contemplated kicking them off when Molly launched herself at her, which wasn't in the script, at least not yet. Ducking, Cat raised her arm to block the woman's red talons. Molly kept coming, pushing Cat totally off her mark. Why today of all days did the woman decide to improvise? They were supposed to have their come-to-Jesus moment at the front door, not in the middle of the foyer.

*Lines*, Cat reminded herself. *Just say Chloe's lines.* "Paula, what's wrong? What..." She trailed off, following the direction of the redhead's gaze to where the large crystal chandelier swayed drunkenly over her head.

Grabbing Molly by the arms, Cat spun them out of the way. A gust of air brushed against her back as the chandelier crashed to the marble floor.

Shouts went up from the cast and crew as they converged on them. The director in his yellow Hawaiian shirt pushed past the crowd of people. "Chloe, are you all right?"

"I'm good," she assured him.

"So am I, Phil," Molly said, glaring at Cat before storming off the set.

The director's gaze followed the other actress before he returned his attention to Cat. "Quick thinking, Chloe. Well done." He patted her back then moved from her side, waving over the set and crew managers. "Would someone like to explain to me what the hell happened here?"

That's what Cat wanted to know. Glass crunched underfoot as she went to crouch beside the chandelier and examine the brushed silver chain links. The wire had been cut. Cat looked up at the ceiling. Her plan to leave her sister's employ was now on hold.

\*     \*     \*

Special Agent Grayson Alexander couldn't remember the last time he'd taken a vacation. To his way of thinking, the bad guys didn't take a holiday, so why should he? But his last case had changed his mind. He was skirting the edge of burn-out. It was the only explanation he could come up with for his epic screwup. He'd put not only the operation on the line, but his life.

Valeria Ramos had played him, and he hadn't discovered it until it was almost too late. A gorgeous brunette with a killer bod, she'd passed herself off as a victim when in truth she was the head of the drug cartel. The memory of how badly his instincts had failed him grated. They'd never failed him in the past. Forget that he was damn good at his job, for a guy who'd grown up around actresses, he should've been able to make Valeria from day one. So, yeah, he needed a couple of weeks off to decompress and get his head back in the game.

He propped his bag and skis by the door of his Beachwood Canyon home, anxious to get out of the smog-filled city. The mountains were calling his name. He'd get his thrills and chills on the Black Diamond slopes instead of on the job. Whatever tension remained at the end of the day, he'd burn off with a ski bunny or two or three.

It wasn't as if he had someone to come home to. He'd learned the hard way that his job wasn't conducive to long-term relationships. Or maybe it was just him.

As he opened the panel to activate the alarm, his cell rang. He thought about not answering until he saw who it was.

"Mr. Alexander, Linda Hanson from Shady Palms. Your grandmother has gone missing again."

And he knew exactly where she'd turn up. He should've moved. He angled his security cam at the street. Sure enough, a yellow cab was pulling into his driveway. "She's here, Ms. Hanson. I'll have her back to the home within the hour." If he had to tie her up to get her there. He wondered what her story would be this time. Last month, she was sure the nurses were drugging her.

The woman on the other end of the line cleared her throat. "Mr. Alexander, I'm afraid that won't be possible. The previous administrator was more willing than I am to look the other way. Dame Alexander is a disruptive influence. You'll have to find another facility—"

Yeah, right. Shady Palms was just one of many retirement homes his great-grandmother had terrorized in the past five years. And he should know, since the duty of taking care of GG fell on him. Not on his cousins or his father or his aunt and uncle—him. In a voice infused with as much charm and warmth as he could manage given his frustration, he said, "Linda, we'll discuss this when I get there. I'm sure we can come to—"

"No we won't, Mr. Alexander. All your charm and good looks will be wasted on me. I'm too old to be swayed by a handsome face."

He was wondering if his badge and an imaginary

infraction might do the trick when a five-foot-nothing, immaculately groomed, older woman with a white angora cat tucked under her arm scowled up at the security camera.

"Grayson, I know you're there. Let me in," Dame Estelle Alexander commanded in an upper-crust British accent, lifting her cane to knock on the door.

"Linda, I'll..." He blew out a noisy breath. She'd hung up on him. At the insistent rapping, he jerked open the door before Estelle bashed it in. "GG, you promised you weren't going to run away again."

She batted him out of the way with her cane and sniffed. "I didn't run away, I escaped. They're trying to kill me."

He wouldn't be surprised if some of the staff at Shady Palms wanted to kill her. He'd felt the same on occasion, as he imagined her last four husbands did. His great-grandmother was a drama queen and a royal pain in the ass.

"Don't keep the young man waiting, Grayson." She lifted her haughty chin at the sixty-something man standing at the door with...four suitcases at his feet. Gray briefly closed his eyes before digging his wallet from the back pocket of his jeans. The man gave him a commiserating smile and handed him the cat's pink princess bed.

"Thanks," Gray muttered, tucking the bed under his arm as he hauled the luggage into the house. Piling the bags by the door, he turned to break the news to his grandmother. "GG, I'm heading out of town, so you'll have to stay with..." He cursed under his breath and strode to his bedroom. "Do not put that cat on my bed." Of course she did exactly as she pleased and put the long-haired animal on his black comforter. "GG, you know I'm allergic to—"

"It's all in your head." She waved a dismissive bejeweled hand, then turned to open his drawers. "Where's my luggage?"

"I'll get it," he muttered and closed the door. Leaning against the wood-paneled wall, he took his cell from the pocket of his leather jacket and called his cousin India. He'd had it. Someone other than him was taking care of GG. He needed this vacation. And it was about time one of them stepped up to the plate. His call to India went straight to voice mail—with a message that said she was in London. At the beep, he said, "Indy, how many times do I have to tell you not to let everyone know you're out of the country? It's not safe. Call me as soon as you get this." He paused; his cousin never returned messages. "GG is dying."

He called his aunt and uncle and got their voice mail with a message informing him they were on safari in Africa. Of course they were. He left them the same message he left their daughter. He didn't even bother calling his father. He'd get no help from that end. The only time Gray heard from the Eighth Earl of Waverly was when he needed cash.

He called Indy's brother Jamie, relieved when an actual voice came over the line. "Hey, Jamie. I need—"

"Hey, Gray, my man. I was just picking up the phone to call you. I've got a job for you."

He never should've told Jamie he was taking a few weeks off. His cousin provided security for the rich and famous. "No. I'm leaving for Bear Valley in twenty minutes, and GG's here. You have to come and get her."

"She run away from Heaven's Gate again?"

She'd been in Heaven's Gate two years ago. "Yeah, and

you're up. I tried to get your sister and parents, but they're out of town."

"I'd like to help you out, but Lacy and GG don't get along."

"Who's Lacy? Never mind, just come and get your grandmother."

"Seriously, bro, I can't leave her with Lacy, and I'm heading out of town on a job. Which is why I need your help. I just got a call from the producers of *As the Sun Sets*. They're worried about the safety of their star Chloe O'Connor, and I've agreed to provide security and find out who's behind the attempts on her life. They want—"

Gray disconnected, thumbing through his contact list as he walked to the front door. There had to be a distant cousin on here somewhere. His cousin called again. Gray didn't answer.

Jamie texted. *I'm calling my marker. You owe me.*

As much as Gray hated to admit it, he did owe him. Jamie had heard a rumor about Valeria Ramos's previous relationship with one of his former clients and passed it on to Gray. The information had changed the focus of his investigation and saved his life. He walked to the bar in the corner of his living room, poured himself a scotch, and called his cousin. "All right, I'll do it. But as soon as I wrap up the case, you're taking GG off my hands."

Once his cousin agreed, reluctantly of course, he gave Gray a brief rundown on the cast and crew. Gray relaxed for the first time since GG pulled into his driveway. He'd wrap the case up in a couple of days at most, and GG would no longer be his problem. He already had his primary suspect: Chloe's sister and the beneficiary of her will. Cat O'Connor.

# Fall in Love with Forever Romance

**PASSIONATELY YOURS**
**by Cara Elliott**

*Secret passions are wont to lead a lady into trouble...* The third rebellious Sloane sister gets her chance at true love in the next Hellions of High Street Regency romance from bestselling author Cara Elliott.

**THIEF OF SHADOWS**
**by Elizabeth Hoyt**

Only $5.00 for a limited time! A masked avenger dressed in a harlequin's motley protects the innocents of St. Giles at night. When a rescue mission leaves him wounded, the kind soul who comes to his rescue is the one woman he'd never have expected...

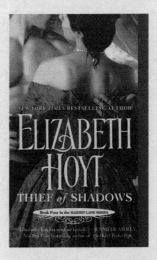

# Fall in Love with Forever Romance

### RESCUING THE BAD BOY
### by Jessica Lemmon

Donovan Pate is coming back to Evergreen Cove a changed man...well, except for the fact that he still can't seem to keep his eyes—or hands—off the mind-blowingly gorgeous Sofie Martin. Sofie swore she was over bad boy Donovan Pate. But when he rolls back into town as gorgeous as ever and still making her traitorous heart skip a beat, she knows history is seriously in danger of repeating itself.

### NO BETTER MAN
### by Sara Richardson

In the *New York Times* bestselling tradition of Kristan Higgins and Jill Shalvis comes the first book in Sara Richardson's contemporary romance Heart of the Rockies series set in breathtaking Aspen, Colorado.

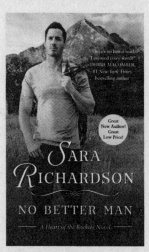

# *Fall in Love with Forever Romance*

### WEDDING BELLS IN CHRISTMAS
by Debbie Mason

Former lovers Vivian and Chance are back in Christmas, Colorado, for a wedding. To survive the week and the town's meddling matchmakers, they decide to play the part of an adoring couple—an irresistible charade that may give them a second chance at the real thing...

### CHERRY LANE
by Rochelle Alers

When attorney Devon Gilmore finds herself with a surprise baby on the way, she knows she needs to begin a new life. Devon needs a place to settle down—a place like Cavanaugh Island, where the pace is slow, the weather is fine, and the men are even finer. But will David Sullivan, the most eligible bachelor in town, be ready for an instant family?

## Fall in Love with Forever Romance

**SANCTUARY COVE**
by Rochelle Alers

Only $5.00 for a limited time! Still reeling from her husband's untimely death, Deborah Robinson returns to her grandmother's ancestral home on Cavanaugh Island. As friendship with gorgeous Dr. Asa Monroe blossoms into romance, Deborah and Asa discover they may have a second chance at love.

**ANGELS LANDING**
by Rochelle Alers

Only $5.00 for a limited time! When Kara Newell shockingly inherits a large estate on an island off the South Carolina coast, the charming town of Angels Landing awaits her...along with ex-marine Jeffrey Hamilton. As Kara and Jeffrey confront the town gossips together, they'll learn to forgive their pasts in order to find a future filled with happiness.